MARROW

TRISHA WOLFE

BRYNNE WEAVER

CONTENT WARNING

Please be advised that Marrow is a dark romance with potentially troubling scenes and themes that some readers might find triggering.

Potentially triggering content:

- Graphic physical violence, torture, and murder
- Decaying and dismembered bodies
- Explicit language
- Death of a sick or injured wild animal
- Parental death; loss of close family members
- Parental neglect and physical abuse
- Chronic illness of a loved one
- Untreated PTSD, including flashbacks
- Medical procedures and bodily trauma / hospital settings
- One sex scene between FMC and another man BEFORE the FMC and MMC are interact with one another on page (no cheating)
- Explicit, detailed sexual content. The sexual activity is

consensual, though some consensual non-consensual (CNC) activities are depicted. It includes some kinks and behaviors that some readers might find triggering, including breath play, temperature play, impact play, somnophilia, and rough sex.

Please contact Brynne Weaver or Trisha Wolfe if you have any questions.

MARROW PLAYLIST

If you're reading a digital copy of Marrow, the full playlist can also be downloaded at Apple Music and Spotify. It's also posted on Brynne's socials in her Linktree!

Apple

Spotify

Chapter 1 - Celestial Fire
Paper Love - Allie X
I'm not a woman, I'm a god - Halsey
Do You? - TroyBoi

Chapter 2 - Follow
Dreamers - K.Flay
Better Off - Elijah Woods x Jamie Fine

Chapter 3 - What Three Words
Living Hell - Bella Poarch
Devil I Know - Allie X

Chapter 4 - Core
Paranoid - Lauv
Stonecold - machineheart
Invisible - Lovelife

Chapter 5 - Flick, Snap
This Town - ELIA EX
Anything You Want - HYDDE & MOONZz

Chapter 6 - Compact Tissue
Afterlife - XYLØ

Not So Bad In LA - Allie X

Chapter 7 - Captive
Rattle the Cage - ELIA EX
Honey and Milk - Andrew Belle
Evergreen - A Silent Film

Chapter 8 - Paint It Red
I Don't Even Care About You - MISSIO
Angel - Massive Attack

Chapter 9 - Shattered
America - XYLØ
Drowning - DWNTWN

Chapter 10 - Cold Kiss
Gimme - Banks
Save Yourself (feat. Gloria Kim) - Vanic

Chapter 11 - Winters
NFWMB - Hozier
Dark - Luke Sital-Singh
True Love Is Violent - Allie X

Chapter 12 - Twenty-Fifth Floor
Throw a Fit - Tinashe
Shimmy (feat. Blackillac) - MISSIO
Genghis Khan - Miike Snow

Chapter 13 - Strike Of The Wheel
Riverside - Agnes Obel
Hurt Nobody - Andrew Belle

Ana - Say Lou Lou

Chapter 14 - Cartilage
If I Hated You - Fletcher
Second Nature - Stalking Gia

Chapter 15 - Blue
Turn the Corner - Neil Pollard & Louise Dowd
Girl Of My Dreams - FLETCHER
Glow - RHODES

Chapter 16 - Elskede
Down Low - Alex Winston
Back In My Body - Maggie Rogers
Hard for a Man - Say Lou Lou

Chapter 17 - Inertia
Hypnotic - Zella Day
Okay - Chase Atlantic
2 On (feat. ScHoolboy Q) - Tinashe

Chapter 18 - Abyss
Losing Our Control - The Naked And Famous
Look to the Dawn - Yoe Mase
Heaven Sent - Mr. Little Jeans

Chapter 19 - Luminous
Arcade (feat. FLETCHER) - Duncan Laurence
Oh Woman Oh Man - London Grammar
Losing Hand - A Silent Film

Chapter 20 - Arrows

Anastasia - A Silent Film
The Enemy - Andrew Belle
Half a Man - Dean Lewis

Chapter 21 - Vessels
All We Didn't Say - Louise Dowd & Toni Halliday
Love Me Wrong - Allie X & Troye Sivan
Gemini Feed - BANKS

Chapter 22 - Fallen
My Heart Has Teeth (feat. Skylar Grey) - deadmau5
I Wanna Fight and You Know It - MISSIO
The Inversion - Joywave

Chapter 23 - Marrow
Fuel to Fire - Agnes Obel
Bottom of the Deep Blue Sea - MISSIO

Chapter 24 - Oath
Where Snowbirds Have Flown - A Silent Film
Quietly Yours - Birdy

Epilogue - Thaw
Down - Andrew Belle
Breathless - Caroline Polachek
When You Were Mine (feat. Tegan & Sara) - Night Terrors of 1927

To anyone who dreamt of someone who would burn the world for them, who loved the villain, who rooted for the dark souls in their fairy tales...
We hope Jack and Kyrie ignite your beautiful black hearts.

"Every fairy tale had a bloody lining. Every one had teeth and claws."
— Alice Hoffman

"I would die for her. I would kill for her. Either way, what bliss."
— Gomez, The Addams Family

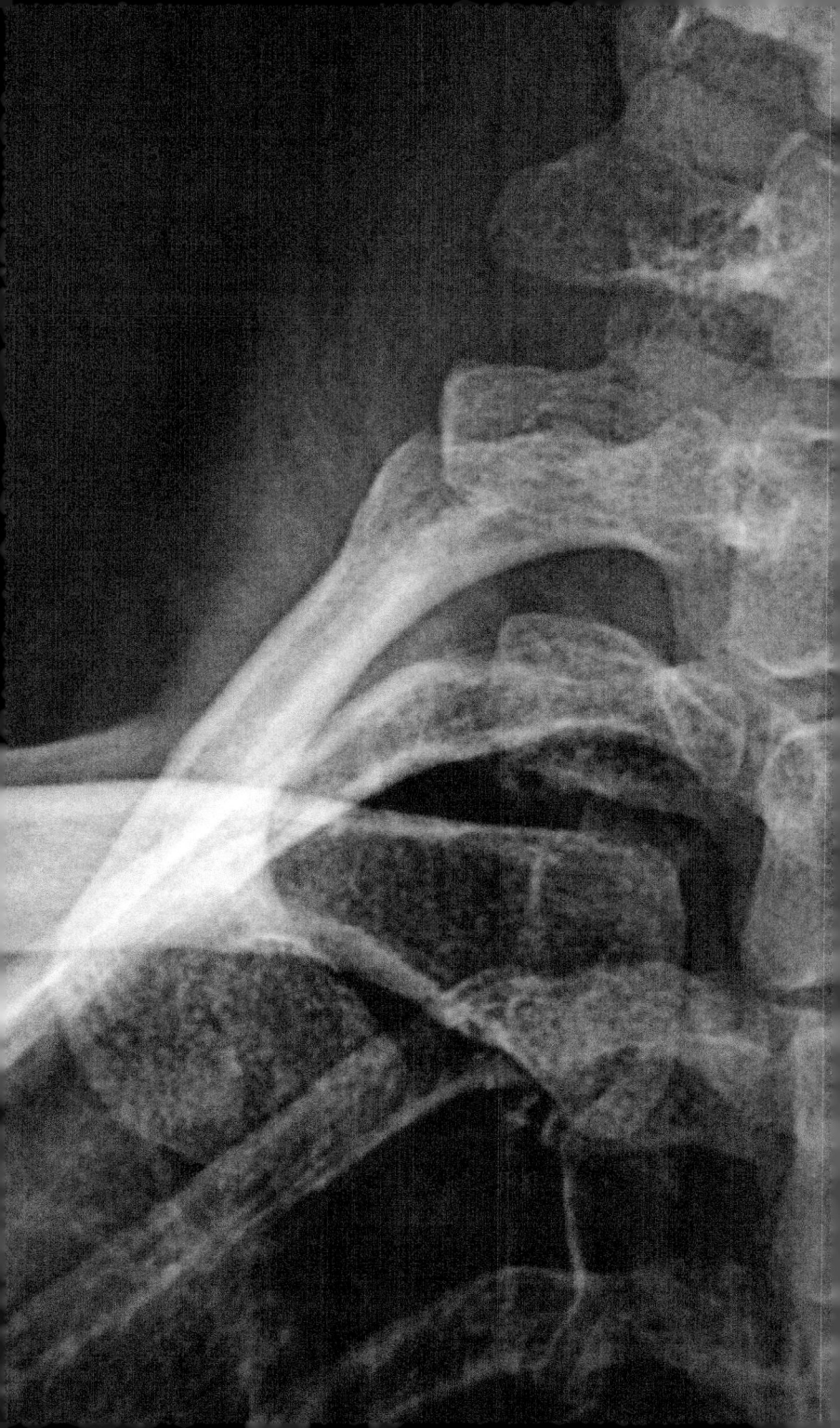

ONE
CELESTIAL FIRE
KYRIE

By the time we're standing at the gates of damnation, Jack Sorensen will beg me to throw him to the Devil. I will paint our path to Hell with his blood. With his dreams. His aspirations. His failures, each one rendered by my hand. I will leave a trail of his destruction behind us that will shine for all eternity. And I will enjoy every fucking second of his torturous journey...

Just as soon as my acceptance speech for the Allistair Brentwood Philanthropy Awards is over.

I scan the crowd. Dr. Sorensen's absence will become a thin scar over my memory of this day, cut with the precision of a scalpel, just like he intended. Nevertheless, my smile is undimmed. I clap with enthusiasm for the other winners. When Joy Lin brings over champagne, we clink glasses and toast one another. I'm just as effervescent as the bubbles clinging to the flute. But when they slide down my throat, they burst in the heat of my rage.

"Is Jack backstage? I haven't seen him all night. Is he actually here?" Joy asks, her eyes darting across the room of black ties and bleached smiles before her gaze lands on mine, heavy with scrutiny. I smooth my hand over the chestnut waves cascading over my shoulder as I give her a nonplussed shrug.

"No big deal if he's not. I'm sure Dr. Cannon will present," I reply, only allowing myself to grind my teeth when Joy looks away with a grimace.

Of course he's not fucking here.

Sure enough, as the host sets up the award for Philanthropy in Education, it's Dr. Cannon's name he announces to give the introductory speech, not Dr. Sorensen.

No, not Dr. Sorensen.

Jack Sorensen, whose research wouldn't be funded without my efforts to raise over two million dollars for his field school. Whose students have been awarded scholarships from the fund I created. Whose accolades have been stacked on the foundation that I built. Without me, Jack Sorensen would be just another brilliant academic whose work shines like a distant star in the sky, pretty but underwhelming, always battling to be freed from the black blanket of mediocrity. Because of me, Jack Sorensen shines like the harvest moon.

I am the sun whose light reflects on his cold, remote mask.

And I am the celestial fire that will destroy him.

"...and since joining the West Paine University faculty three years ago, Dr. Roth has dedicated her free time to enhancing the W. M. Bass Forensic College Field Research School, enabling the university to acquire nearly fifty acres in field research space with our newly-opened specialized laboratory facilities on-site," Dr. Cannon says as images of students working in the pristine lab appear on the screen backdrop, stealing my attention from spiraling thoughts of murder by match and gasoline. "She has played a critical role in the body donation program, has been instrumental in creating a world-class academic conference that draws the best forensic professionals to West Paine University annually, and founded a scholarship program that supports the education of three deserving graduate students each year." Dr. Cannon finds me beneath the spotlights illuminating the stage and smiles with genuine warmth. "I am honored to present Dr. Roth with the Brentwood Award for Philanthropy in Education."

The crowd claps and I rise from my seat next to Joy. My smile widens, words of congratulations guiding my way to the stage. I gather the floor-length skirt of my gown as I ascend the steps and stride to the podium to shake Dr. Cannon's hand. His sweaty, hot palm grips mine and I hold the etched glass award by its mahogany base as the event photographer takes our picture. When Dr. Cannon finally lets go and steps back, I look across the room.

My attention snags on a tall figure in the shadows close to the doors. He leans against the wall with a drink in hand, perfectly at ease in the absence of the light.

Jack Fucking Sorensen.

I force my gaze away and smile across the audience. "Thank you so much, Dr. Cannon, for the wonderful introduction. And to the Brentwood Foundation, I deeply appreciate the opportunity to not only accept this award, but also to shamelessly plug our university's exceptional forensics program. I see you over there, Mrs. Spencer. Don't think I'm not coming by your table before the night is done," I joke, and the crowd laughs as the ancient woman waves, stacks of diamonds glittering on her fingers. "But in all seriousness, I owe my gratitude to generous donors like Mrs. Spencer. Since I joined West Paine University, I had a vision of what we could become: one of the top forensics research facilities in the country. Your support has allowed us to achieve and maintain that status. Our students are the best of the next generation of forensic scientists and crime scene investigators, and they are learning and honing their skills in a world-class academic environment. Our faculty is leading the field in forensic research, contributing to significant advancements in forensic archaeology, entomology, and botany. These achievements would not be possible without our donors. I'm humbled by this recognition and would like to thank my colleagues who are instrumental in our ongoing success."

I proceed to list off every name I have memorized. Hugh Cannon. Joy Lin. Amal, Christine, Luke. Madeleine Gauthier, even though she's as useful as tits on a rock. Brad Thompson, even though he's often dim and sometimes a douche. Mike Mitchner, the head custodian of the labs, even he gets a shout-out.

The one name I do not speak is Jack Sorensen.

He was going to be at the top of my list. The name that draws so much attention to our academic program. The head lecturer of our Forensic Anthropology department, whose research in human decomposition has put us on the map.

I leave him out.

I find Jack in the shadows, imagining every detail of his face, his cold gray eyes veiled by darkness. I hold his figure with a charming smile. "Now that I've named literally everyone but my dog and my second cousin twice removed, I just wanted to say a final thank you," I say as the audience laughs. My eyes stay latched to the phantom at the door as I raise the award, then I slide my gaze to a table in the middle of the front row. "To the Brentwood family, who continue

Allistair's legacy of generosity and commitment to others with such a lovely event. I'm honored. Thank you."

The audience claps. Photos flash. I smile. I wave. I descend the steps to more words of congratulations and stride back to my table.

Joy passes me a champagne flute but holds on to the stem. "You forgot someone," she says.

I pry the chilled glass from her fingers. "I'm not sure what you mean, Joy. Cheers." I clink my flute to hers and turn away to the sound of her sigh.

"Congratulations, Kyrie," Dr. Cannon says as he sits to my right and picks up my award to examine the lettering etched on the glass. "Another accolade to add to your impressive collection. Will you be using this one as a bookend or a paperweight?"

"Neither. I'll polish it daily and I might even keep it at the very center of my desk." ...*Where it will surely irritate Jack every time he's forced to walk past my office.*

"I hope my introduction was sufficient. I do apologize about Jack, it must have been a pressing conflict to keep him tied up."

"The introduction was lovely, Hugh. Thank you," I say with a pat on his weathered hand as I paste on a saccharine smile. "Actually, I believe I saw Dr. Sorensen arrive while I was on stage. Do you think he'd have time to speak with Mrs. Spencer? She's about due for her annual donation and you know how much she loves speaking with him."

Dr. Cannon's onyx gaze flows across the room as he hunts his quarry until I gesture toward the doors where Jack's presence still lingers, a malevolent specter haunting the shadows.

"Ah yes," he says as he pushes his chair back and stands,

the ice cubes clinking against the glass as they slosh in his whisky. "Excellent idea, Dr. Roth. Have a lovely evening."

I follow Dr. Cannon's hunched shoulders as he weaves through tables and guests, but really it's Jack's form my gaze latches on to. We both know he can't escape our boss now that he's been spotted, and it's common knowledge that he despises sweet-talking the old woman out of her cash.

A malicious smile blooms across my lips. I know he can see it. I feel the cold kiss of his eyes on my skin.

"Hey, Kyrie. Great speech. Congrats," a voice says, replacing the empty space of Hugh's absence. Brad's hand drops on my bare shoulder as he takes the seat to my right. "Love the dress, by the way. I bet Donald Whitmore was ready to throw bags of money onto the stage."

I barely resist an eye roll as Brad winks. "Thank you, Bradley. Having a good night so far?" I tip my head toward the glass of beer he takes a long draft from before I notice the look in his eyes as he follows movement across the room. It looks almost like suspicion, or concern. Maybe even a touch of fear.

I follow his line of sight, straight to Jack Sorensen.

Jack drifts behind Dr. Cannon on a winding path through the tables toward Mrs. Spencer. He doesn't just walk, he stalks, like a panther hunting in long grass, his movement fluid but powerful, purposeful. Lethally beautiful, with his short dark hair and strong jaw and fluid grace beneath a sharp black suit. I shift my attention back to our table before he looks in our direction, and despite everything, it still nearly hurts to look away.

"Yeah," Brad finally says with a brittle smile. He doesn't sound convincing at all. When my interest in his reaction registers, he tries a little harder. "Yeah, what about you? Having fun?"

My eyes slide to Jack, his back turned as he and Dr. Cannon stop at Mrs. Spencer's table. "You know me, Brad," I reply as I savor every moment of tension creeping through Jack's shoulders. "If I'm not having fun, I'm making it." I knock back the rest of my glass and rise.

I become sucked into the swell of the evening, waves of conversation and glasses of champagne coursing through my veins. It cleanses me just a little, debriding a festering wound, leaving raw edges behind. But something else remains. A tiny thorn. A barb that burrows beneath skin, making its presence known every time it's prodded....every time I catch sight of Brad.

That same look of trepidation from earlier seems to linger in his eyes. His fingers fidget around his glass. He struggles to converse with ease when usually it's a mission to shut him up. Brad loves this kind of event. His easy smile and rugged professor looks make up for his academic mediocrity and his occasionally douchey comment. He's often on the prowl for someone to fuck, and when I'm bored I sometimes oblige. But tonight he's just...off.

"Everything okay, Brad?" I ask, my voice quiet enough that only he will hear. His eyes dart from where they're caught on something across the room, but I'm able to follow the trajectory of his interest. I know he was just looking at Mrs. Spencer's table where Jack still lingers, his back facing us.

"Yeah," Brad replies. He pauses on a breath as though he wants to say more, but he raises his glass to his lips instead and takes a long sip.

"Are you sure something's not bothering you?"

"I..." he trails off, draining the rest of his beer as his gaze flicks again toward Mrs. Spencer's table. He glances at his watch.

He's going to run.

It's like blood on a trail. Like a deer crashing through the woods, trying to evade a wolf. Something is there. And I need to know what it is.

"I think I've had enough of this gala. Want to get out of here?" I ask, dropping a hand onto Brad's knee beneath the table. His eyes widen and for the first time tonight, it feels like his attention is truly on me when he gives a slight nod. "I'll go first and order an Uber. Give me ten and meet me outside."

I flash Brad a bright smile and stand, saying a few good-byes as I make my way to the exit. When I glance toward Mrs. Spencer's table, Jack is gone.

Outside, the early November night is cool and clear, my breath fogging beneath the lamplight as I wait on the curb, my thin jacket draped over my shoulders. Brad doesn't linger inside, fortunately, and joins me after ten minutes, opening the door of the Uber for me before heading to the other side of the vehicle. In twenty minutes, we're pulling up to Brad's home, a 1920s bungalow only a few blocks from my house.

I waste no time in going after what I want.

"What's bothering you, Bradley?" I ask as I pull away from a kiss to gently push him down onto his bed, undoing the zipper of his dress pants and shimmying them and his briefs over his hips. I grasp his erection and he groans as I slide my grip down the shaft. "You seem distracted tonight."

Brad hisses as I rake my fingernails over his balls. "I'm sorry," he says, his voice lost in a moan as I bend to lick the head of his cock, sucking it into my mouth. I swirl my tongue across the crown, my eyes never leaving his face as he tilts his head back. "Jesus, Kyrie."

I take more of him into my mouth as the tension of the

evening melts from his muscles. He eases into the pleasure of my touch, and I lavish him with licks and deep strokes and caresses. Brad's breathing becomes ragged, his pulse pounding beneath my fingertips as I rest them on his inner thighs. When he seems centered on me I release him from my mouth, pumping his slick shaft as I reach for a condom in his nightstand.

"Better now, baby?" I ask when the condom is on and I lower myself onto his cock, grinding my hips for friction on my clit as Brad moans. "Tell me what's bothering you. Let me take it away."

I trail paths across Brad's chest with my nails and pick up a rhythm of strokes, building my pleasure, scraping at a need that won't be fully released. Brad's palms find my breasts, calloused caresses roaming my flesh.

"The Bass Fields," Brad says through gritted teeth as I reward him with deeper thrusts, spreading my legs wider. "Mason found discrepancies."

My heart kicks into another gear and I fight to keep my rhythm undisrupted. "Mason? The master's student?"

I hear Brad's movement against the duvet as he nods in the dark. "First it was a body a few months ago. Donation records didn't match with a body in that location. Mason couldn't find the hyoid bone, though everything else was intact."

A gentle laugh escapes my lips. I lean down to place a kiss to Brad's neck. "You know that's not definitive proof of anything, Bradley," I whisper against his ear. "One of the other grad students might have messed up the records, or Madeleine might have entered the data incorrectly when she logged the locations. You know what she can be like."

Brad's hands roam my back. "That's what I said."

Something lingers in his words, hovering in the air

between us. I push myself up and search the shadows of his face. "But?"

"A few days ago, Mason documented the pink teeth phenomenon on a male body. But he knew the man. Mason hadn't told anyone, in case we prevented him from working on the body. It's the last analysis he needs for his thesis. It was his uncle's friend. He died in surgery."

Surgery would definitely not result in asphyxiation, which would have caused the pink discoloration on the stems of the body's teeth. And I do know a certain person who enjoys a good strangulation. *Oh how naughty, Dr. Sorensen.*

"The hyoid?"

"Intact."

I hum a thoughtful purr, a thousand scenarios tumbling through my head. A familiar need churns low in my belly and I grind harder on Brad's cock, pleasure unraveling with every thrust. I coo words of praise and sing Brad's name until I come, and he drives his hips beneath me as he claims his own release. It's over too quickly to feel anything more than a fading swirl of endorphins, and my heart rate already slows to a nearly normal rhythm by the time I'm climbing off Brad to rest at his side.

"Jack signed-off on both donations," Brad whispers as he traces pensive patterns onto my arm. "He placed both bodies in the field. We need to look into the details, see if something is amiss with the donation records. Maybe take the most recent remains to the medical examiner and verify the identity against dental records."

"Agreed," I reply, nodding against his chest. "We need to be careful. If Jack is up to something, we don't want to spook him or put Mason into a difficult position." I push away from Brad before he can draw his arms tight around me, then I back away from the bed. "I just need the restroom, want anything while I'm up?"

"I'm good, babe."

I turn before I cringe into the shadows, padding away into the dark, heading to the bathroom before continuing to the kitchen. I'm familiar enough with Brad's place to make us a couple of drinks, taking the whisky on ice back with me to the bedroom. We don't speak more about the discrepancies in the records, and I make sure to divert to other topics as we sip our drinks. But my mind roams back to the campus. To the grounds of the Bass Research Fields. To Jack Sorensen.

I stare up at the ceiling as Brad falls asleep. The mild sedative I dropped into his whisky keeps his breathing slow and even. When he starts to snore I rise, my movement silent as I rifle through his closet to retrieve a pair of his sweats, a hoodie, and his slippers. I give him one last check before I jog down the hall, changing in his laundry room. I leave out the back door and escape into the night, heading for my house, my smile sheathed by shadow.

Sometimes, the universe gives you exactly what you need. And I'm not the kind of girl to just take what it has to offer.

I'm the one to seize it.

TWO
FOLLOW

JACK

Muffled sounds of the gala fade into the scenic backdrop of the Brentwood building behind a thick veil of crisp, fall air. I pull in a satisfying lungful to cleanse the muggy feel of crowded bodies pressed too closely together and stalk toward the edge of the steps, just in time to watch a white Corolla pull away from the curb.

Annoyance gathers beneath my ribs in a tight spasm. Enough of an irritation to make my bones itch.

I don't like the loss of control.

I had one objective in mind for tonight, and it didn't involve stalking Dr. Roth.

In fact, she's managed to upset more than a few of my plans this evening.

With the reminder, I remove my phone from my blazer inseam to note the time. Right now, I should be seated inside Black Rock Distillery, the bar favored by college students. Colby Cameron is there, like he is every Thursday. He has a routine for his study sessions.

I never miss a study session.

Phone clenched tight in my gloved hand, I move toward

the parking lot, torn between sticking to my routine and trailing my colleagues.

Precaution has to come first.

Especially when one of those colleagues is the outgoing, outspoken Dr. Roth.

She has a serious problem keeping quiet.

The woman is like a frenzied ball of energy; she never settles long enough for me to pin her down.

The first time I encountered the strange, annoying creature, I had the overwhelming urge to strangle her and trap her constant prattle of words in her slender throat. Then stuff her in a freezer just to see her in a calm state.

I'll admit, I'm curious enough to wonder what her animated features would look like suspended, motionless, her thick lashes resting stationary over her high cheekbones. Her plump, berry lips drained of color.

One reason I throttled the urge was because I don't shit where I eat.

As crude as the cliché is, it's a nonnegotiable rule that has kept me safely hidden my whole life.

Another reason is, like the distinct perfume she wears that announces her presence before she enters a room, Dr. Kyrie Roth's magnetic personality draws all attention on her.

When one requires the shadows to maneuver, one should be grateful for the sunshine that provides them. No matter how irritated your eyes become while staring at the bright, bothersome light.

The onslaught of torturous thoughts further wastes my time as I reach my Beamer and slip behind the wheel. I remove my black gloves and crank the engine. The A/C vent blasts my face with arctic air. I don't change the temperature settings.

The stretch of busy roads leading away from downtown narrow into suburban streets as I tail the white car at a distance. My jaw sets as I realize where my two co-workers are heading.

Dr. Bradley Thompson's house.

Before the car ahead brakes, I veer off onto the shoulder and park behind a wall of manicured shrubbery. I kill the engine and watch as they both exit the car and make their way up the walkway to the front door of Brad's modest home.

All hope they were simply sharing a ride is defeated, and I push back in my seat to settle in and wait. An intimate relationship between Dr. Thompson and Dr. Roth doesn't bode well. People have this irritating tendency to share details and secrets when sex is involved.

An unwanted image of Kyrie sneaks across my vision, and I reach for my leather satchel on the floormat and remove the spiral bound notebook. I flip to my most recent sketch.

My fingers reverently trace the contrasting play of light and shadows along the anatomy of the leg. I use a hard graphite pencil to capture and define the muscle structure, then a softer pencil to outline the bones. This technique is more delicate as, where light cannot penetrate the body, there will be darker tones.

Then there is only the open view to what lay beneath the flesh and veins and sinew.

I imagine the detail on the femur pectineal line is smooth and fine, no indentations due to his youthful age. Depicting the flesh flayed away from the bone is like tearing open wrapping paper to discover what's inside. One of my favorite parts is to compare the accuracy of my rendering to the actual bones.

But as it's not yet time to unwrap Colby, I close the notebook and glance at my Rolex, gauging the time Brad and Kyrie have spent inside. I have to handle a nosy colleague first.

An intrusive thought of sweaty, overheated skin slipping together fills my head. I can almost smell the stench of sex drifting from Brad's house, and my nostrils flare in revulsion at the thought of them together.

After two hours of watching the front door, Dr. Roth still hasn't emerged. The stale air inside the car presses against my skin like a moist towel, humid and suffocating. I remove my clammy palms from the steering wheel and open the door, welcoming the hit of fresh air.

The lights inside the house blinked out a while ago. I take my chances that Brad doesn't have much stamina and they're now asleep. Carelessly, the front door has been left unlocked. I slip my gloves on and let myself in, doing a quick sweep around the living space.

I made sure there are no cameras or an alarm system the first time I searched Brad's home. For all his arising paranoia, I figured he'd at least get a dog. His bedroom is off to the right of the narrow hallway. I creep along the hardwood toward the cracked door and nudge it farther open.

Brad is asleep on the left side of the bed nearest the door. Dr. Roth is missing. My hackles raise and I dart a look around the darkened space, using the sliver of moonlight from the slatted blinds to search the corners, listening for any movement from the ensuite bathroom.

The stillness of the house settles my nerves, and I enter the room and stare down at Brad.

The single white sheet is rumpled around his stomach. A blue foil has been discarded on the bedside table, along with two glasses of alcohol.

A trace of her perfume still lingers—bitter notes of angelica flower and sweet vanilla. The collision of scents loiter in the stagnant air, combusting within my chest.

Fists balled, I watch the rise and fall of Brad's pale chest, curbing the impulse to smother him with his sweaty pillow.

As far as Brad goes, he's useless in my department. No great loss would come from him simply slipping away in his sleep. But lucky for him, there is nothing interesting about his bone structure. My time spent on him is merely out of necessity, so I'll be quick about it.

I glance at the condom wrapper again and a tight knot forms at the base of my spine. If not for the name I need that only he can provide, I might just break my rule and take a giant shit right in my territory, then smear Brad's face in it.

The imagery leaves an unpleasant aftertaste in my mouth, and I decide to leave. My original plan was to get Brad wasted at the gala, drugging him if need be, to retrieve the information. Then have him removed from West Paine permanently, making the disposal of *my problem* less of a burden due to proximity.

I still have time.

As I move through the house, I note the back door, realizing Dr. Roth must have left out that way. Curiosity directs my steps past the laundry room, where I see discarded clothes piled on the floor. I lift the garment with my gloved hand, recognizing the gown Kyrie wore at the event tonight.

Her scent envelops me, and my hand clenches around the shimmery material.

I've never been one to pretend to fathom human nature —but everything about Dr. Roth is infuriatingly confusing to me. I've even imagined strapping her to a table and dissecting her on more than a few occasions.

I place the gown back in the same spot before I leave the house.

My drive to the university takes a little over twenty minutes. I use my keycard to gain entry to the research labs, where I'll be logged with a timestamp. I first seat myself behind my workstation and open a community file with my last saved draft, giving myself a reason to be here at this hour. I made sure Dr. Cannon heard me twice tonight when I stated how my research project on locating burial sites needed completion by this week, reiterating how impatient I was to leave the gala.

As I push away from the desk and head toward Brad's office, I sweep aside all thoughts of Dr. Roth vanishing into the night without a gown, and focus on plundering through Brad's notes.

He's so damn helpful, keeping the body logs so well organized. He can't remember to return my proton magnetometer, but he can micromanage his underling grad student to crosscheck the donation records for accuracy.

Which uncovered the hyoid of a recent donation missing from the body.

Such an obvious oversight had to be a mistake.

I'm cautious. I have a system in place. The record was flagged and then cleared. It should've ended there. But I saw it in Brad's eyes when he first mentioned it to me, the twist of confusion followed by the spark of fear.

Because Dr. Jack Sorensen doesn't make a mistake.

I've memorized this look. It's the expression I normally crave. It's what sets my ice-cold blood aflame and ramps my dormant heart rate when I stare into my victims' eyes as they take their last breath.

So in the fraction of a second where it coasted across Brad's features as a micro expression, I recognized his dread.

He knew.

And he was scared of me.

Which means it's only a matter of time before he finds the rest of the pieces to puzzle together why I've been so dedicated to my body decomposition research for the past six years at the university.

By design, I don't stay in one place for more than a few years. However, when West Paine incorporated nearly fifty acres for the university's body farm program, making it the third largest in the country, it became difficult to find a better, more ideal location.

Finding nothing of relevance to the record in Brad's journals, I look at the locked drawer to my right. Before I'm tempted to break the lock, I back away from the desk, then shut my computer down.

There's still time.

I won't be brought down by someone as unremarkable as *Brad.*

A crescent moon hangs in the black night to guide my way toward the body farm. Walking the fifteen acres of wooded terrain helps clear my thoughts. I pass the different zones of the farm, where bodies have been left to decompose in a number of environments and settings.

Over the past six years here, I've never made a mistake.

I've never been questioned.

Routine and discipline have been my key factors to operating below radar. I recall the day my routine was interrupted for the first time, and the bubbly, tinkling laugh which followed.

It would be asinine to blame Dr. Roth for this...upset.

It's not as if she has purposely set out to destroy me. However, the fact remains that, until she arrived at my university, I had *never* allowed for a mistake.

The distinctive sound of metal shuffling earth drifts to my ears, and I halt walking.

I strain to listen as a soft groan echos against the thinly spaced pines. I move in the direction of the noise, soon catching sight of a trail marking the muddy earth. Deep footprints line the side of the long stretch of track leading to the stream embankment.

My steps falter and I draw to a stop before the clearing when I see the reason for the disturbance.

Dr. Kyrie Roth drops a shovel into the riverbank, releasing a groan as she drives a booted foot onto the step, then heaves a scoop of silt. She pauses a moment to drag in a breath, and I stop breathing on reflex.

When she resumes digging, I expel a slow breath and pan the area, my gaze falling on a large expedition pack.

I should leave. Right now. But my instinct to reverse my steps is thwarted by the extreme, clawing curiosity infecting me at watching her dig up the earth. Her dark hair pulled up into some messy style, diamond earrings glinting in the moonlight, makeup still in place—yet she's covered in mud.

Is this why she left her gown at Brad's? So she could sneak off and—

What the actual hell is she doing?

Her heavy breaths plume the air around her in puffs of silver fog, and my chest tightens at the alluring sight. God, I almost smile, the sensation so fucking foreign a morsel of unease burrows in deep. It wouldn't be difficult to seize this opportunity. Impulsive, yes—but oh, so damn tempting.

I could have that shovel in my hand in a matter of

seconds. In the next five minutes, Dr. Roth could be buried in the very hole she's digging.

Rather, with panged regret, I decide to satisfy my curiosity instead.

I sink my hand into my pocket and clutch the object there before I bring it out and flip the silver top open. I strike the flint wheel of the lighter, and a thin ribbon of flame dances against the dark night.

Kyrie stops shoveling at the sound.

THREE

WHAT THREE WORDS

KYRIE

"S eems I'm late for another party this evening."

I still the motion of my shovel and smile into the dark.

"Though I'm sure chronic lateness is one of your many character flaws, Dr. Sorensen, you're actually right on schedule." I glance at him over my shoulder, his lethal frame illuminated by moonlight and a thread of flame as he stands on the rise of the creek's sharp bank behind me. A snap kills the fire as he closes the lid of the lighter and pockets it. "In fact," I say as I return to shoveling the thick silt, the water flooding my efforts, "you've been here the whole time."

Intrigue thickens the silence between us.

I wait for Jack to ask me what I mean, but he doesn't. There's only a near-silent rustle of leaves behind me and I know he's closing the distance to where I'm working.

"*Split sobered barons*, Jack," I say without turning around.

The movement behind me stops.

Silence.

"What?"

"*Split sobered barons.*"

More silence.

I straighten and raise my shovel to point downstream, globs of silt splashing into the dark water. "*Unleashing disappeared toast.*" I shift to point to the fields beyond the far bank, the tall grasses consumed by night. "My favorite, *missing credited koala.* What Three Words, Jack."

I glance over my shoulder. He's much closer than I anticipated, already on the narrow floodplain just a few feet away, his shoulders tight with tension in the dim light. He looks at the black expedition backpack lying beyond me before meeting my eyes with calculating menace. Confusion and curiosity are the only things that have stopped him from creeping closer.

"Is this a puzzle?" he asks.

I beam a smile at him in reply. I was expecting he'd give me an arrogant, derisive smirk and ask me if I've lost my shit, but he hasn't. He's playing along, trying to figure this out.

"It's one piece, Jack. Sure." I drive the sharp end of the shovel into the silt and lean on the handle, my boots squelching, the creek water trickling around the rubber encasing my ankles. "I guess you've never heard of What Three Words?"

Jack doesn't answer. *This won't do.*

I heave a heavy sigh and roll my eyes. "Come on, don't crap out on me now."

"No," Jack replies, his voice deep and stern.

I reward him with a bright grin which does nothing to dim the moonlit malice glittering in his eyes. "It's a geocoding system. Every three meter section of the globe is assigned its own unique, three-word code. This," I say, sweeping my hand toward my feet, "is *split sobered barons.*"

Jack's head tilts. His eyes narrow.

I work my hand free of my glove and retrieve my burner phone from my pocket, entering the passcode to open the home screen and bring up the app. I press the dot of my current location and face the screen toward him. "See? Right here. *Split sobered barons. Unleashing disappeared toast* is the location of the body you disposed of back in March. *Missing credited koala* is where the man Mason thought he knew was buried in Field Three. There are the others too, all saved away right up here, thanks to Mason's fastidious data entry skills," I say, tapping my temple with my free hand as I lock the screen and pocket the phone.

The space between us seems to crackle like static. The air is still and cold. Silver fog escapes my parted lips in the starlight but I can't see Jack's exhalations. Maybe he's holding his breath or maybe he's born of the night and the cold. Either could be true.

We hold one another in a locked stare until I smile and pull my glove back on, twinkling my fingers toward him as I do. "And before you slither any closer, you should know that if anything happens to me, *anything*, you will be the first person they come for. Every location. Every body. Every photograph. Every little scrap of evidence I've secured. It will all go straight to the FBI. My well-being is truly in your very best interests."

I can almost hear Jack's muscles tensing, his sinew scraping. Bone bracing. I'm sure he's ready to throw caution into the creek and attack. But he doesn't. He stays planted in a sliver of moonlight, his eyes holding mine as though fused.

"Who's in the bag, Kyrie?" Jack asks, his voice a threat wrapped in velvet.

I resist the urge to clap my hands and squeak, driving

the shovel into the silt instead. I've loosened a deep and wide enough area now that I can move to the next step in the process, so I lumber out of the suctioning mud and head to the backpack.

"You know, Jack, this is probably the most interaction we've had all month and I have to tell you, I'm having a great time, for once," I say as I release the first clip from the top of the bag with unnecessary slowness, keeping my eyes on Dr. Sorensen as I do. Even though I've both piqued his curiosity and threatened him with his most feared consequences, I don't trust the fucker. Not one bit.

"*Who is in the bag*," he repeats. There might be a tiny twinge of desperation hidden in the depths of his words.

"Are you worried I took someone important to you?" I pout as my fingers stall on the second clasp.

"Kyrie—"

"You have no sense of fun, Jack," I lament with a dramatic shake of my head. I release the clip and the draw-string holding the top of the bag closed, peeling back layers of plastic. The twist of hair rustles against my gloves and my fingers clutch around it, and then I tug, withdrawing the severed head. A lifeless face and half-lidded, glassy eyes swivel between us. "Mason Dumont."

To his credit, Jack does a pretty good job pretending he's not surprised. But he is. And he's pissed, too. I hear it in the way his leather gloves creak as his hands fold into tight fists.

"You killed Mason Dumont," he says slowly, not a question, but a confirmation.

"No. *You* killed Mason Dumont." I walk back to the water and lower Mason's head into the silt, those gelatinous blue eyes staring at the stars. I raise one foot to squish against his face and push his head deep into the mud. "Your boots are a bit large for me. I had to wear, like, six pairs of socks and they're still too big."

Jack's eyes dart down to his waders before he pins me with a feral glare. I smile and flutter back the edges of the jacket I stole from his lab two years ago to rest my fists on my hips, revealing a weighted vest and belt.

"You've gotta be what...one hundred and ninety pounds? That was my guess," I say as I walk back to the bag and pull out Mason's disarticulated arms, shreds of his torn shirt fluttering as I give Jack a little wave with both of the limp hands as I take them back to the creek and drop them in the silt. "Don't worry, I made sure to strut here all 'Important Serial Killer Man' style so that the diligent detectives of Westview will know it was you if you decide to do anything stupid. *I'm so important I can't say fucking* thank you *to the one person who's given me everything I could ever want, like research money and facilities and this big-ass farm for dead bodies galore. No, no, no. Now watch out, forest creatures, Important Serial Killer man coming through.*"

"Jesus fucking Christ, Kyrie," he hisses. "This is all because I didn't kiss your ass in gratitude?"

I don't answer as I head back to the bag with long strides and grab a severed thigh, tossing it into the water with a splash. When I pull the other free of the bag, I give the dark and empty interior of the backpack a thoughtful frown. "You seem to have forgotten some important pieces, Jack," I say as I rise. For the first time since the gala, my glare is just as lethal as his.

There's a long silence as I take the last severed hunk of flesh to its watery grave, blood tapping across the damp grass as I go. When I drop it in, I walk atop the limbs, working them deeper into the silt, knowing the tread of Jack's boots will leave marks in the cooling flesh. "*Pigeage,*

Jack. I've always wanted to try that in Les Pastras. Stomping some grapes in Provence in August? Please. Sign me the fuck up. I need a holiday after trying to provide for your ungrateful ass for the last three years."

"So, that's really what this is all about. When I didn't fall at your feet like everyone else, you decided to frame me." Jack pauses as though he expects me to reply. When I don't, he lets out a dark and mirthless chuckle. "*Die Rache einer Frau kennt keine Grenzen.* I didn't think you were quite that much of a cliché, Dr. Roth."

"I guess I break all your expectations then, don't I, Dr. Sorensen?" I reply with a bright smile.

With Mason's limbs pushed down into the silt, I grab the shovel and start dismantling the pile of dirt I've set aside to cover them over. Jack observes me, calculating, weighing, maybe butting his big brain against every wall in the maze I'm creating between us. But he doesn't move. He doesn't come closer. Not even when I tip a little in the awkward waders and have to right myself by plunging the shovel down into the bodily remains with a surprised squeak. When I turn around, he's right where I left him, and I know my confidence in his obedience unnerves him just as much as anything else he's seen or heard tonight.

When I'm done, I use the shovel as a cane to slurp my way out of the thick, heavy mud, then I toss it next to the bag.

"What do you want?" Jack asks.

I could close my eyes and bask in the honeyed need that drips in my chest when I imagine a thousand possibilities of how I could answer. The richness of his voice wraps around me. The smoothness of his every word has a sharp and hidden edge, one I want to run my finger across, to see if it will really make me bleed.

We stand and regard one another, the creek trickling behind me. A barred owl calls far in the distance. The windless night carries the sound.

I draw closer to Jack, my eyes never leaving his, though I sense him tensing in the periphery. I stop when I'm close enough to touch him, letting my hands slip into my jacket pockets in a show of trust. In the dim light, I see him raise a dark brow, a soundless question. *What do you want?* he soundlessly repeats.

"I want you to tell me about the first time we met," I say.

There's a flicker of movement in Jack's brows, a stutter in the cadence of his blink. He glances away to the dark water and back again, his full lips set in a straight line. If there was more light, I'd be able to see the changes in those gray eyes that pick up the colors of his surroundings like camouflage.

He looks away again, his expression smoothed out once more but distant. "Angélique Noire perfume. That's the first thing I remember."

"I didn't take you for a perfume guy," I say with a smile.

Jack glances at me before returning his gaze to the creek. "I turned and you were at the door to the old lab with Dr. Cannon. You wore a deep purple dress. Your hair was up. Your perfume carried into the room."

My smile fades as Jack's eyes find mine and don't let go. I nod for him to continue and he takes a step closer. I let him.

"You came into the room with your hand extended. Dr. Cannon introduced you as Dr. Roth, but I already knew who you were," Jack says. My heart thuds faster in my chest. A long neglected hope stirs beneath my sternum, and I tip my head to the side in a question. "He'd sent a departmental message with your photo that morning. But it didn't look like you, not when you were standing before me with a smile that could consume every sin."

My heart detours as though it's been stitched to a pendulum. I want to step back from Jack, but I don't.

"I'd asked if your first name was pronounced *keer-ee-yay*, like the prayer, Kyrie eleison. I didn't think your smile could get brighter, but when I said that, it did. '*Keer-ee* is fine,' you replied. 'My parents wanted me to have Christ's name, but it never really fit'. I suppose that makes a lot more sense now."

I try not to nod, but a faint bob of my head escapes my control. Something thickens in my throat. I remember that moment of our meeting so clearly that it's like watching it through a polished crystal ball. For a fleeting breath of time, it had felt like everything fit together, like our first conversation was exactly as I'd hoped for. A recognition of likeness. A connection with someone like me. The way Jack tells this story, it feels like that connection was real, like it existed for him too.

But that's a lie.

Jack is just trying to bridge the gulf between us now in the hope that I'll have mercy on him. Everything that came after the conversation he's just described has buried that possibility beneath the thick sediment of time.

And he knows it. That's why Jack is silent now.

His eyes glint in the moonlight as they take in the curves and angles of my face, dropping to my lips. They linger there before resting on my neck for a moment that seems too calculating to be intimate, too cold to be anything but cruel. And cruel is exactly what he was from that pivotal moment onward. Questioning my experience, my merit, my worthiness at every turn. No matter how hard I worked or how much my efforts benefited him, he was always there with those steel gray eyes to watch for a mistake and then slice me down.

"It's quite a pretty story the way you tell it," I say, my voice barely more than a whisper. I take a step closer and his gaze slides back to mine. His face is a perfect balance of silver light and deep shadows, so hauntingly, achingly beautiful. But he is a beast. He's feral beneath this angelic façade.

And he still can't seem to accept that he's not the only apex predator here.

"The only problem is, Jack...you're wrong," I say, striking out with the last word.

I hit Jack's chest with a Taser. He lets out a strangled, gritty groan and drops to the dirt. His body convulses in distress as I uncap a syringe with my other hand. When I kill the shock of the device, I drive the needle into his jugular and deliver the pre-filled dose of midazolam to the delicious sound of his protesting moan.

I pull Jack into the recovery position and watch for just a moment as his breathing deepens. His eyes don't leave mine, not even as their sharpness dims and dulls beneath the pull of the sedative.

I've been waiting for this moment, this look between us when Jack realizes he's gotten me wrong all this time. I've wanted it since the time he berated me for the notorious CRYO freezer incident in the lab, when he accused me of destroying his tissue samples through sheer ineptitude. It was the first time I truly accepted that I might have to put my little beast down.

Who's inept now, you fucker.

Just before he falls unconscious, I lean in close. I press a gentle kiss to his cheek. And then I bring my lips to his ear, giving him a gift he might not remember when he wakes.

"You're wrong, Jack," I repeat in a whisper, a wraith to follow him into a dreamless sleep. "That wasn't the first time we met."

When I pull away, he's unconscious.

I rise to stand over my sleeping nemesis, and then I leave him in the dark...

...right where he's always been.

FOUR
CORE
JACK

A crisp, gauzy layer of fresh snow collects on top of my body. My breathing has shallowed, my lungs no longer feel the sharp bite of winter. My arms and legs have gone numb, my skin frozen and nerves dulled, unable to send pain signals to my brain.

I lay here in the freezing night as a continual hush falls over the woods with thick snowflakes.

Fatigue settles deep in my bones with the frozen ground, dragging me beneath consciousness. It's tempting to let go, to just keep falling under. I've never felt more at peace then I am now, wrapped in a blanket of ice, sheltered from the world of misery.

The sound of snow crunching beneath heavy footfalls splits the empty silence, and I stop breathing altogether.

The steps encroach closer until I feel the snow shift against my cheek.

"Where are you, you little shit."

The raspy voice slurs each word. I smell nothing but the cold, yet the memory of his putrid breath fans my face.

I hear the distinct clink of his Zippo. Then the strike.

On reflex, I strive to curl my numb fingers around the solid object buried under the snow.

"When I find you—"

It's the last muffled words that touch my ears before time warps.

Distorted images flicker in freeze-frames as I claw to the surface. A slash of bright-red streaks a canopy of white. Vacant eyes absorb the black night as the flash of steel glints...before the images begin to fade into the recesses of my mind.

As consciousness grips me, I know the second my eyes part open I've been drugged.

I feel the sedative swimming in my bloodstream as fuzzy confusion stuffs my head. My temples pulse as my vision adjusts to make out the moonlit tree branches above. I bring my hand to my neck, feeling the tender patch of skin where Kyrie sank the needle.

The bruising ache in my chest snags my attention.

She fucking tased me.

But if she wanted me dead, I'd be buried in the riverbank.

I roll over and push myself up, my eyes further clearing to take in my gray-washed surroundings.

"Dammit." I still have my phone, and I bring it out to check the time. I've been knocked out for maybe two hours. Diazepam, or possibly midazolam. A fast-acting sedative that also leaves the system pretty quickly.

"That wasn't the first time we met."

The bitter tone of her voice is a taunt against my throbbing headache.

I glance around for the body, the dismembered one Kyrie removed from a bag and tossed around the creek. The stream travels in a slow current, the embankment deserted.

This woman doesn't want me dead—but she does want something.

Directly in front of me, the shovel is stabbed into the silty earth.

Right now, it's clear she wants me to dig.

THE SCENT of Kona coffee drifts through the department as I stand over the stainless steel table in the lab. For the first time, I'm tempted to pour a cup, in dire need of stimulation that not even my newest prospect can provide.

Before me are the cleaned remains of a recent donation. Three large monitors are arranged along the back wall, my desk directly beneath. One monitor projects the decomp data I've collected for the research grant, a field trip I've spent the past year devotedly, methodically working toward.

All of which has drastically stalled as last night plays on a menacing loop inside my head.

While I spent the remaining hours of the early morning digging up and collecting the severed body parts of a grad student, I thought back to every interaction I've had with Dr. Roth over the past three years. Which, I have no doubt, was her very intention.

By the time I had Mason Dumont relocated in a fresh burial site, I realized Kyrie never actually intended for me to be caught with a mutilated body, regardless of the evidence she planted at the scene.

She only left half of the body in the creek.

The other half she took with her.

Her threat was clear; if I go after her, if I try to silence her permanently, she has a contingency in place to expose me. A little melodramatic—if not fitting—after witnessing her in action.

Treading on the side of caution has always been my first rule.

Kyrie gets to live. For now.

If for no other reason than she's piqued my curiosity with a number of things she brought to light. I've never been confronted with a challenge I couldn't conquer, and eliminate.

And Dr. Kyrie Roth has presented an enticing challenge.

As the morning sun slips through the slatted blinds of the lab, I refocus my attention on the partial skeletal remains, comprising of a skull, vertebrae, and sternum. There are eighty axial bones in the core unit. But there is one bone in particular I'm fascinated by, that which I've devoted the better part of my research career to.

With a gloved hand, I select the hyoid. Positioned beneath the mandible, the horseshoe-shaped bone is unique as it's the only bone presented on the skeleton that is not connected to any others. Suspended, it's held in place by the attached ligaments and muscles.

To say I have an affinity with this free-floating, solo bone is obvious; there is no structure or support needed by the framework in order to exist.

When identifying remains, anthropologists and forensic experts by default look to the skull and pubic bones to determine age, race, and sex. However, in the event such bones are not present or compromised, the hyoid can reveal all of the above and more. One just needs to be skilled in the finer nuances of the bone.

My research on hyoid fusion and bone density for

forensic purposes will revolutionize the remains identification process.

The dark irony of my extracurricular passions and professional interests hasn't escaped me.

Dr. Cannon passes the lab doorway, then steps back to peek his head inside. "Morning, Jack." He glances at the clock, the dark-brown skin around his eyes creased in confusion. "You're here early. I figured everyone would sleep in after the gala last night."

My smile is a thin line. "I came in early for the donation." *I never left.*

Luckily I keep several changes of clothes in my office, and though I don't recommend it, the campus showers are convenient when you need to wash the stench of sweat and death off you.

"Good deal," he says, nodding and glancing around again as if struggling to make conversation. "Thank you again for your courteousness to Mrs. Spencer. I know charming donors isn't your favorite thing, but she's been one of our biggest—"

"Not a problem," I say, returning my focus to the cleaned bones on the table. I pick up the Boley gauge as a hint to end the conversation. Hugh Cannon doesn't have to fill the silence.

"All right, then. Have a great day, Jack."

I flick my gaze upward as he heads down the hallway and lower the tool. I've already measured the teeth, and I've already read the data displayed on the monitor. I don't want to be distracted when Dr. Roth arrives, which is why I place the hyoid aside for later inspection.

The fact Kyrie's tantrum is costing me valuable research time proves what I've thought since day one: she's not deserving of her position.

She's obviously observant, and intelligent enough to have picked up on my activities. After following her last night, I would've been inclined to believe she simply seduced Brad to learn of his theories about me.

But the sight of her holding a severed arm stomps that simple logic into the silty ground.

She's a killer.

A coldblooded predator.

She spotted me before I recognized her—and this is what has my grip tightening around the gauge handle. I forcefully set the tool aside, then flatten my palms to the table. The cool press of steel bleeds through the latex to douse the small lick of flame.

I relied on my preconceived notions, and that was my fatal flaw.

Always confirm your conclusions.

What could've happened to a girl like Kyrie to turn her into a killer? Women serial killers are a rare breed, rarer even than duos.

She has shown no clear sign of being a psychopath, so she wasn't likely born this way. Some inciting incident in her life had to trigger this transmutation.

Unearthing this key piece about her is going to be the one puzzle piece I need to use against her to get her out of my life.

Typically, for killers discovered hunting on the same turf, one of them decides to leave for fear of discovery. Two top predators cannot occupy one hunting ground.

As a wildlife biologist, Kyrie understands this better than anyone.

Our own biological makeup rejects a pack mentality. If one or the other refuses to surrender territory, the only option left is elimination.

Survival by any means necessary.

I'm not sure when she discovered me, but she has since chosen to stay.

This is *her* one fatal flaw.

She thinks she's smarter than me, and can manipulate me the way she manipulates everyone else around her. She has no idea what she's up against.

She handed me a clue when she said we'd met before.

Whatever Kyrie wants from me, it starts there, figuring out that moment in time.

For the next half hour, I watch a handful of students trickle into the department. At the sight of Kyrie, a bubble of excitement fizzes up, and I mentally tamp down the annoying sensation. On reflex, I touch my pocket, seeking the object always there, only to find it missing once again.

Jaw clenched, I needlessly begin remeasuring the discolored incisors as my peripheral tracks her movements. She's wearing a black pencil skirt and champagne blouse. Her russet hair is swept up into a stylish updo, makeup in place, looking well-rested and like she didn't just spend the night burying a body.

She's carrying her award—the one I was supposed to present her with last night. She smiles brightly and accepts congratulatory praise from a number of colleagues before she places the trophy on a shelf along her office wall.

When she finally notices the bouquet of flowers on her desk, her eyes immediately dart to Brad's office across the hallway.

No. They're not from flaccid lover boy.

She admires the rare Himalayan blue poppies while searching for a card, then her beaming smile falls when she catches sight of the ribbon tied around the stems.

Her gaze locks with mine.

It's impossible to describe the burst of adrenaline that zips through my veins. By design, I'm careful to keep my personal life separate from work, at least when in the confines of the lab space. It makes for a string of monotonous days until I'm able to achieve that rush again, but I can't deny this is fucking close.

Her gaze narrows on me, and I refrain from letting my lips curl into a satisfied smile.

I watch as she delicately unravels the ribbon, spools it into a tight ball, and slips the material into her skirt pocket.

I remove the disposable gloves and toss them into the hazardous waste basket on my way toward her office. I stop at the doorway and lean against the frame.

"Sleep well, Jack?" Kyrie asks, triggering a reactive ache on the bruised flesh of my chest from the Taser.

"Like I was tased and drugged with midazolam," I say, meeting her baiting remark.

She bats her thick eyelashes at me.

"I think this is the first time I've ever been inside your office." I take in the accolades on the bookshelf, the framed pictures. I don't know if they're of family or friends, but they look staged. Like she could have edited the photos that came with the frames to Photoshop herself into them.

She expertly slides a smile into place, her full pink lips drawing my notice. "Technically, Jack, you're not inside my office."

I accept the challenge and boldly step inside, sensing the charge ripple the air of the small room as we each try to dominate the space.

"Your mother?" I ask, nodding in the direction of a grainy photo central on the shelf.

The slightest flicker of unease passes over her face, a little purse of her lips, before she schools her features into a pleasant veneer. "You're not here for small talk," she says. "You hate small talk. Or, really, any talk."

I let my mouth tip into a slanted smirk. She likes to brag about how well she knows me, has studied me. I could come right out and ask her what our very first encounter was—but I have no doubt that would only serve to further enflame her. She's been patiently working alongside me for three years; she's not giving me the answer so easily now.

"Do you like your gift?" I ask, lowering my gaze to the pale-blue flowers.

"Delighted. They're beautiful."

"They're a rare species," I say, moving an inch closer to her desk. "I grow them myself, along with a few other special breeds."

"Stimulating," she deadpans. Then she tilts her head as she studies the petals of the flowers more closely. The variations in the color range from vibrant to soft pale-blue. Not an easy feat, I might add, as I've had to breed the poppies for three years to get the desired color.

When her gaze flicks up to meet mine, I see the hues there in her irises, that array of the darkest blue near the center fanning out to the palest shades of gray-blue near the dark ring.

Kyrie pushes the bouquet aside. "Did you like *my* gift?" She cocks her hip and pats her pocket, insinuating the strip of material I tore from the torso after I dug it up.

Technically, I dug up *half* a body.

I slip my hand down my cashmere necktie, gaining composure over the flare of anger her ridicule incites. I palm the edge of the desk, lowering my face to become eye level with her.

"Your present felt incomplete, Dr. Roth. Where is the rest of it?" I demand.

This brightens her smile to the full, overbearing wattage. "Wouldn't you like to know."

The image of my hands around her throat rises up so fiercely, I have to push away from the desk surface to remove her from my reach. I close the glass door, shutting out the distractions and sealing us inside.

"This isn't a game, Kyrie," I say, my tone dropping to a lethal decibel as I face her. "You're behaving like a child, throwing a tantrum because I don't recall our first encounter together?"

Her mouth pinches into a forced pout. "*Aww*. I bet you don't treat your other one-night stands so dismissively."

I nod slowly. I know I didn't fuck this woman and then ignore her. That's not how I operate.

As I walk closer, I sink my hands into my pockets so I'm not tempted to strangle her.

"You're not a jilted lover, Kyrie, but you are sloppy," I say, earning a derisive scowl from her. From our past inter-actions, I know she doesn't like my reprimands. "You let your emotions govern your actions. You acted on impulse, like a damn amateur, when you murdered that grad student. Right here at the university where you work."

Once the words are unleashed, I can't take them back. They detonate the air between us like an imploding star, and there's no stopping either of us from being sucked into the void.

"There are consequences," I say, keeping my voice low.

With the gala taking place last night, like Cannon suggested, a few people might lay out today. One student not showing up won't trigger much notice. But after two days, the questions will start. The calls. Friends wondering where they are. Family calling the university.

"You're a funny guy, Jack." She walks around her desk and parks her hip on the edge, crossing her arms. "No one really gets how comical you are. But I do. Because, either you just have really dry humor, or you're a fucking hypocrite." She turns her gaze on the lab and my work station across the hall before directing a scathing look at me. "Missing. Credited. Koala."

The geocoded location of one of my victims. This one buried deep in the decomp site. It's what she was prattling on about last night, the locations of the bodies I've disposed of around the body farm.

I remain quiet, letting the tension thicken between us.

Like I knew she would, she's the first to talk; she can't stand for even a moment's silence. "How come you think I did it?" she asks.

My brow furrows. "Do I need to paint the picture of you waving a severed hand at me?"

She shrugs dismissively. "I just mean, that's not what the evidence says. Matter of fact, between the both of us, I believe I'm the only one with an alibi for last night." She tilts her head to look around me and wiggles her fingers in a flirtatious wave to Brad.

My jaw clenches.

"So..." she drawls. "There *are* consequences. For you, Jack." Her lips tip into a smug little smile.

She's enjoying this.

Whatever this woman's endgame is, it's definitely to make me suffer.

I could stop this now. It would be simple enough to follow her home tonight. Wait until she's asleep in her bed. Drop my hand over her mouth and subdue her. I wouldn't need a sedative. Or a Taser. I could have Dr. Roth tied up in my personal cold room in less than twenty-four hours, where I could torture the answers from her, then get rid of the annoying problem.

Life would resume as normal.

I could even pin it on Brad. Get rid of two of my problems at the same time.

But the longer I stare at Dr. Kyrie Roth, caught in the knowing gleam banked behind her pale-blue eyes, the more curious I become.

While it's true curiosity killed the stupid cat, it's also the cornerstone of research facilities and breakthrough discoveries.

I err on the side of caution, always. If she's aggressive enough to kill one meddling grad student, she might be aggressively dedicated enough to keep her secrets. Or just crazy—crazy has a tendency to make things difficult.

The truth is, I need more information. I need time to dig into her background and excavate answers. I never execute a plan before I have all the details aligned and everything in place. So far, we've been playing by her rules. I'm at her mercy.

It's time to flip the game board.

And if all else fails, there's always plan B.

Her polished bones would look good displayed on my trophy mantel.

"What do you want?" I ask her outright.

She licks her lips enticingly. "I honestly don't think you've earned that answer from me yet, Jack. Why don't you try groveling?"

A grin sneaks onto my face. I take one step forward to bring us closer. "How about a counter offer."

She arches a sculpted eyebrow. "I'm listening."

"I can tell you what *I* want," I say, letting my gaze drag over her body in deliberate pursuit. If I'm not mistaken, her reaction proves I affect her; the dip along the slender column of her throat; the tiny shiver that racks her body. "I want you the hell out of my department. Out of my university. My town. Territory."

She recovers quickly, all flirtatious façade dissolving beneath her severe expression. "Not going to happen. I've worked hard to be—"

"You were a favor hire," I cut her off. "I saw the referral from your professor to Dr. Cannon. I admit, you worked the social ladder-climbing circuit really, really hard, but you didn't earn it on your own accord, with the required experience at this level."

With less work experience than all the other applicants combined, I still don't understand how Hugh hired such a green wildlife biologist. All I know is nothing has been the same since Dr. Kyrie Roth stepped foot inside my university.

If looks could flay, my skin would be a pile of ribbon around my feet. Satisfaction swells in my veins.

"I had no idea how utterly misogynistic you are, Dr. Sorensen."

"Call it what you want, but merit goes farther than referrals with me." I shrug, letting her believe this is why I never gave her the praise she so obviously and desperately wanted from me. "Maybe if you had first put in the years of needed experience, we'd have had a completely different professional relationship, Dr. Roth. Instead, you invaded my territory with lacking skills, and issued a challenge."

Her eyes narrow. "We're no longer talking about career paths, are we?"

"I take affronts to *both* very seriously."

The truth is—as petty as it sounds—I was here first. If

she wants to get primitive about it, I marked my territory long before her cute ass pranced into West Paine.

I've only ever encountered one other predator stalking my territory. Ten years ago, that particular rivalry ended with him dead, his body incinerated—bones and all—and me vacating my hunting ground.

Yet I'm the apex predator that came out on top.

History has a precedence here.

Kyrie bites the corner of her lip, then: "You have no idea how full of shit you are," she says, her tone taking on a severe edge.

"I'm not too impressed with opinions, either," I say, and before she can retort, "There can only be one, Kyrie."

My use of her first name surprises her, and she huffs a sardonic laugh. "Two men enter. One man leaves." Her eyebrow wings up again in challenge. "Not very politically correct. Perhaps we should update the rules of Thunderdome to a more gender neutral wording."

I slide my tongue over the smooth surface of my teeth, then toss a glance at Brad through the glass wall as a dark thought presses against my resolve. I had another plan for eliminating the Brad dilemma, but maybe he could still serve a purpose.

Someone needs to suffer. Might as well be him.

Plus, I really dislike that fucker.

"Dr. Bradley Thompson is a problem for us," I say.

"Is he?" Kyrie shakes her head as she walks around her desk. She picks up a manila folder and flips through the pages, feigning interest. "I don't really find Brad a problem, Jack. Maybe you should try sucking his cock. He likes that. He might even back out of the competition with you for the research trip to Madrid."

"You really are that naïve as to what you've done."

This gains her full attention. She sets the folder down.

"When Brad finds out the student who discovered the discrepancy has gone missing—"

"He's going to point a finger at you," she fires back.

"And then I'm going to play this for the police." I reach into my blazer inseam and produce my phone. I hold it between us and hit the Play button on the screen.

"So, that's really what this is all about. When I didn't fall at your feet like everyone else, you decided to frame me."

Then her voice fills the office: *"I guess I break all your expectations then, don't I, Dr. Sorensen?"*

I hit Stop on the recording. "There's quite a bit more of your very informative monologue. You do like to talk, Kyrie." I gift her a smug smile. "If I go down... Well, you know the rest."

"God. So obvious," she says.

"Yet effective." I pocket my phone, and her smile stretches, like she has another secret just waiting to spill past her lips.

"All right, Jack," she finally concedes. "Body Farm Thunderdome has commenced." She spreads her arms wide. "What's the objective?"

My gaze slides to the office across the hallway, where Dr. Brad Thompson is doing a poor job of covertly watching us with a look of distress on his pale face.

"Brad has to go," I say.

"That's too easy."

As much as I want to eviscerate him and leave his entrails and organs to be pecked over by birds, killing Brad right now isn't wise. "Brad needs to leave," I clarify. "Of his own volition. He either has to be so afraid, or so annoyed—" I glare at her, implying this is her expertise "—with his position here, that he voluntarily transfers out, forgetting all about the discrepancy."

Kyrie doesn't agree right away, which I almost respect. She considers it for a moment before saying, "And whoever gets Brad to leave wins, I assume. The loser taking his long walk of shame right off campus grounds."

"Or *her* walk... But yes, that's the idea. At which time, I'll erase my phone recording, and you'll tell me where the other half of the remains are located."

Her lips twist into a sly smile as she extends her hand. "Fine. You have a deal, Jack. Let the best *person* win."

A hesitant beat stretches between us where I stare at her hand, absorbing the fine framework of her metacarpals and slender phalanges. My eyes track upward along her radius, and when I take her hand in mine, my breath reflexively stills as I rest my fingers along her delicate wrist bones.

I shake her hand once in agreement, and as she goes to pull away, I draw her forward. "You have something of mine," I whisper next to her ear.

Her breath shallows, revealing the slightest tremble of her body, before she says, "I have no idea what you're talking about."

After another heavy beat, I release her hand and back away. I keep my gaze trained on her until I'm at the door, then I give her my back.

I hear the distinctive *flick* of my lighter. Stalled in the doorway, I glance back to see Kyrie strike the flint wheel. A tiny flame springs to life, the reflection dances in her eyes.

Kyrie flips the cap closed to douse the flame. Then she plucks a blue flower from the bouquet and snaps the long stem, placing the flower behind her ear with a wink. "Game on, Jack."

FIVE

FLICK, SNAP

F*lick, snap. Flick, snap.*

I press my teeth into my bottom lip and try to crush the grin that begs to ignite on my face. I fail to keep it at bay. I re-read Hugh's message for the third time this morning, excitement and nerves zipping through my fingers as I fidget with the lighter in my grip.

> TO: FORENSICFACULTYMAILBOX@WEST-
>   PAINE.COM
> FROM: HUGH CANNON
>   [HCANNON@WESTPAINE.COM]
> SUBJECT: URGENT: DEPARTMENTAL
>   MEETING
> ALL,
> I WILL SEND OUT A CALENDAR HOLD
>   MOMENTARILY FOR A MANDATORY
>   DEPARTMENTAL MEETING AT 10 A.M. -
>   PLEASE CANCEL ANY CONFLICTING
>   MEETINGS OR CLASSES THAT YOU HAVE
>   AT THIS TIME. ALL FIELD CLASSES,

BODY DONATIONS, OR RECOVERY PLANS
ARE CANCELED UNTIL FURTHER NOTICE.
    Best,
    Hugh

I open and close the stainless-steel lid with metronomic precision until the calendar reminder chimes a fifteen minute warning for the meeting.

Flick, snap. Flick, snap.

My grin takes on a wicked edge.

I pick up my office phone and dial Madeleine's extension. She answers on the second ring.

"Bonjour, ma belle," she says and I roll my eyes. She's about as French as a stale baguette from the QwikFill gas station on 2nd Ave. Madeleine was born in fucking Milwaukee, for Christsakes. But I plaster that smile back on my face. *They can hear your sunshine through the phone*, my mom once said when I'd gone with her to 'bring your kid to work day', dutifully writing down her pearls of wisdom as I watched her navigate her daily routine as Ashgrove's top real estate agent. *Smiles sell, baby!*

"Hey Madeleine," I chime. "Are you coming to the meeting?"

"Of course," she replies, an edge of mystery deepening her voice. "Any idea what it's about?"

I've got a viable theory. "No. None at all. Hey, quick favor if you have a sec?"

"Sure, what's up?"

"Can you swing by Jack's office to grab Hugh's copy of *Statistics and Probability in Forensic Anthropology*? I passed Hugh in the hall earlier and he asked if I had it, but the last I saw it was in Jack's office," I say, obviously leaving out the part where I took the textbook from Jack's shelf while he was in class. "Since you're just down the hall—"

"It's no problem, of course," Madeleine interjects. The mystery is gone from her voice, replaced with bright and lyrical notes of anticipation. "I'll go right now. See you at the meeting."

She barely manages to say goodbye before disconnecting the call in her haste.

Flick, snap.

I rise from my chair with a long stretch toward the ceiling, warming the muscles in my back that are still tight from my recent clandestine activities. With a deep, cleansing sigh, I grab the book from my desk drawer and pocket the lighter, then stride toward the conference room down the hall.

The windows of the long room face the Bass Research Fields, the overcast afternoon light reflecting on the polished oval table. Leather swivel chairs that still smell new are tucked neatly around it, the glass whiteboard at the end of the room streak-free and gleaming. I'm the first of the faculty to arrive and I head to a side table where carafes of fresh coffee and tea and a tray of pastries have just been laid out, pouring a cup of black coffee as I try to force myself not to calculate how much of my hard-earned funding is diverted to Hugh's frivolous meeting expenses.

"Cannon always comes through with the strawberry danishes," Brad says as stops next to me, brushing my hip with his fingers on his way to reach for the pastry tray, unraveling the plastic wrap to withdraw a sticky danish.

One thousand, one hundred and fifty-two dollars and thirty-four cents annually, my inner voice proclaims.

Christ.

"Yeah," I say, gripping the lighter in my pocket. "Maybe

he could try not ordering in from O'Toole's for a change. Shit adds up," I grumble. Brad only chuckles around the flaky pastry already stuffing his maw.

"But the strawberry danishes," he pleads around another bite that consumes more than half the pastry.

I roll my eyes but say nothing in reply, turning with my coffee in hand as the sound of voices pulls my attention to the door. Hugh enters next with Joy following close behind, then a moment later Madeleine with a toss of a grateful smile in my direction. Dr. Sorensen is on her heels, his irritation roiling beneath the smooth veneer of his slate gray eyes and pressed black shirt and perfectly tailored pants. His gaze hooks on mine before darting to the book in my hand. When our eyes meet once more, his narrow.

"Dr. Cannon, I found your textbook," I say with my most charming smile as I approach our weathered boss with the book extended. "Dr. Sorensen must have left it in the staff room. I found it on top of the microwave."

Dr. Cannon thanks me while grumbling about his mortal enemy: The Microwave. He swears the innocuous appliance shocked him two months ago when he was heating his cup-a-soup, a feat which has yet to be repeated. General consensus among the department is that he microwaved the metal spoon.

I give Jack a sickly sweet smile. His glacial glare turns lethal.

I've decided that he's much more fun as my nemesis than the friend who refuses to thaw.

I move back just enough from the table for the other faculty members entering the room to file in line for drinks and pastries, the nervous energy crackling within the conversations that flood the space. I say a few words of small talk to those coworkers passing in line and sip my coffee as

Jack draws ever nearer. The temperature of the room seems to plummet the closer he comes and yet my skin grows hotter. A lick of heat crawls from my chest, roaming up my neck, latching on to my pulse, skirting over my jaw to creep into the flesh of my cheeks. The first time Jack's eyes leave mine, it's to watch my throat bob as I swallow.

"Dr. Sorensen," I say as he draws to a halt before me. As usual, I don't think he's going to respond.

I withdraw my hand from my pocket.

Flick, snap.

Jack's eyes narrow to thin slits. His jaw tics. The scent of vetiver rises between us.

"Good morning, Dr. Roth."

Flick, snap.

"You should have a pastry," I whisper as I lean a little closer, that earthy, woodsy scent of vetiver flooding my nostrils. "You're being such a good boy. What's the point of clicker training without a reward?"

With a final snap, I slip the lighter back into the safety of my pocket, my saccharine smile following Jack as he stops next to my shoulder. His eyes scour my face, carving a path through the color still warming my cheeks, dipping down to my lips before they come to rest on the column of my throat. "I'm not very food motivated," he says, his voice so quiet among the chatter of our colleagues that only I can hear him.

I snort a derisive huff of a laugh. "Is this your weak attempt at seduction, Jack?"

He leans a fraction closer, his arm mere millimeters from my shoulder. "If I wanted to seduce you, I'd have you on your knees right now in the cold room with that treacherous little mouth of yours wrapped around my cock, begging me for more," he whispers.

For a heartbeat, everything in the room disappears.

Everything except Jack.

All that remains is his cool gaze trapped on my neck, my pulse answering with a surge of blood in my jugular, drumming like Morse code. A cruel smile tips up one corner of Jack's lips as his shoulder lifts with a disinterested shrug. "Perhaps your throat is just better suited to other carnal pleasures."

Jack steps away from me, sidling up to the table to pour his coffee.

An ember twists in my chest like it's burning through wood. I should want to take my drink and pour it down the front of his pants. But I don't. An entirely different kind of scenario plays out in my head, one where we're in the cold storage room, where my knees are numbed by the frost on the floor, where my nipples are painfully tight against my bra. One where I own Jack Sorensen's pleasure, no matter how tightly he grips my hair or how hard he fucks my mouth. One where he bows to me, even though I'm the one on their knees.

I take a long sip of my scalding coffee to burn that imagery right out of my mind.

He's a dick. *He's a dick he's a dick he's a dick.* You like dicks but not that kind. So bust out your arsenal and get the fucker back.

"Brad," I call above the chatter of coworkers. Jack's presence at the table behind me is as biting and cold as the aura of a glacier. Brad looks up from his favorite spot at the conference table, his second danish suspended at his open mouth. "I hear congratulations are in order."

Brad's eyebrows raise in question. I don't have to turn around to feel the icy kiss of Jack's gaze land on my skin.

"Your proposal for the joint field research trip on the

effects of groundwater recharge on the distribution of skeletal remains for the ICFS grant...? It was accepted, didn't you know?"

Of course he didn't know. *I know*, because my friend Dr. Hargrave is on the review committee and she told me yesterday. I may have also persuaded her to not accept Jack's much superior proposal on burial depth and decomposition rates.

Words of congratulations flow around the room and Brad looks genuinely delighted by the news. He catches my eye for just a moment and I smile, but it's only Jack who seems to notice the devious glint in my eye when he stops at my side.

"No trip to Madrid for me this year, I assume," he whispers.

When I turn my smile toward him, it's fucking dazzling. "I guess not. Suck my sweet pussy lips, Jack."

I walk away and take my place at the table just as Hugh calls the department to have a seat. Jack sits across from me, his expression unreadable. If he's anxious about what's coming, he gives nothing away.

"Thank you all for meeting on such short notice," Hugh says as he takes a seat at the head of the table. The ever-present bags under his eyes seem a little puffier, their shadows a little deeper. His brows furrow as he casts his gaze around the table. "We have a serious issue to discuss this morning. One of our master's students, Mason, has been reported missing."

Murmurs and gasps rise around the table, my own among them, with Brad's voice loudest of all. I catch his gaze and mimic his expression. Wide eyes. Open mouth. Touch of fear. I take it one step further and put my hand over my heart. I don't dare look at Jack, whose presence looms across the table with the gravitational pull of a small planet.

"When was Mason last seen?" Brad asks.

"Thursday afternoon," Hugh replies. "He's been working part-time at Louie's and didn't show for his lunch shift on the weekend. When he didn't appear for his shift last night either and no one could reach him, he was reported missing. A public announcement is going out now." A heavy sigh passes from Hugh's lips. He leans forward, lacing his fingers, his gaze passing over the room of whispers and worry. "A missing persons search will commence here at the Bass Fields, among other potential locations where Mason frequents. There will be no field research until further notice. I've spoken to the police department, and search parties will be arriving any moment. I've offered the use of Lecture Hall B as a location for their base of operations."

"The other students, what should we be telling them?" Joy asks, her eyes glassy beneath the unforgiving lights.

"If they have any information about Mason's where-abouts, anything, they should alert the police immediately. Two counselors will also be here shortly for mental health support for students and staff."

Questions and murmurs volley through the room, discussion turning to how to best look after the other students when it becomes clear that Hugh can't or won't make further comments on the nature of Mason's disappear-ance. The weight of Jack's gaze beckons me like witchcraft, summoning me to meet his eyes, but I don't submit. The more I avoid looking at him, the heavier his presence looms, and I relish every delicious moment of his tension. But I'm not the only one aware of his polar aura across the table. Brad darts scrutinous glances in Jack's direction until some sugar-induced frenetic energy spurs him out of his chair and he starts pacing by the windows. I think he's about to put a voice to all his suspicions about the discrepancies in the body donation program and Jack's potential involvement when there's a knock at the door.

"Come in," Hugh calls, weariness already creeping into his voice with the stress of this meeting.

The door opens.

My past comes crashing into my present as Eric Hayes enters the room.

And I finally meet Jack's eyes.

SIX

COMPACT TISSUE

The conference room plummets a noticeable few degrees cooler in temperature as the man wearing a cheap suit and gun harness enters, and Kyrie's wide gaze locks with mine.

I've never witnessed her purposely avoid another person before. She's always the first to seek notice, a beaming smile sent to disarm and bait before that person realizes they've been ensnared.

Curiosity crawls along my senses, and I give my attention to the man holding up an FBI shield.

"I'm Special Agent Eric Hayes with the Violent Crime division," he says. Placing his badge back into the inseam of his ill-fitting blazer, he pans the room with a shrewd gaze. "I appreciate your director giving me this time to address the matter at hand."

Brad has stopped pacing and now directs an anxious look toward the agent. "Violent crime? Has there been an update about Mason?"

It's Hugh who addresses the outburst. "No, I'm sorry, Dr. Thompson. Nothing yet."

"Don't be alarmed, folks," Hayes follows up promptly. "My branch has been notified in response to another closely related matter. I'm just here to ask some questions."

Despite his attempt to downplay the FBI's involvement, no one here is convinced. Hands wring on the table. Eyes blink rapidly. Nervous twitching and shuffling of positions adds a thick layer of unease beneath the already tense silence. As if every single person here has some sinister secret to hide. Police and government officials have a tendency to make even a saint question their morals.

I sneak a glimpse at Kyrie directly across from me at the table. Her gaze is now aimed at the pale wood, a curtain of her dark brown hair draped over the side of her face. My eyebrows furrow in question, but she avoids me just the same.

I naturally don't feel so at ease in the presence of law enforcement. But I'm not the one who has half a mutilated body buried somewhere. Which makes me question if the remains have already been uncovered.

Why else would the FBI show up now?

I try harder to catch Kyrie's gaze, and notice I'm not the only one vying for her attention. The agent walks behind her, stops to look down briefly before he removes a notepad from his jacket pocket. Very old-school, hardboiled fashion. It almost makes me smirk.

After Hugh gives a brief commentary on our HR rights and asks for a collective agreeance to answer questions for the agency, Agent Hayes targets Brad. "Dr. Thompson, is it?"

Brad's defenses visibly erect. His shoulders tense. "That's correct."

"How long did Mason Dumont intern in your department, Dr. Thompson?" the agent asks.

"Nine months, I believe," Brad says, then shakes his head. "I'd have to check the records, of course, but I think that's close. He was a very thorough research analyst. Mason worked primarily with the Bass Fields' body farm program. Five days is a long time for him to be missing with no word, right?"

Brad sends a guarded glance my way, then blinks and shifts his stare. His thoughts might as well be written on the projection screen, he's that transparent. Agitation worms into my cool demeanor and I seek Kyrie's gaze again. All Brad needs is the slightest nudge by this agent, and he'll implicate me in Mason's disappearance. He's already nervously giving away too much.

Law enforcement etiquette 101: never answer a question not asked.

After jotting down a note, Agent Hayes says, "We haven't drawn any conclusions yet, Dr. Thompson. Did Mr. Dumont ever report any strange findings or inconsistencies in the body farm records to you?"

My heart knocks a beat faster against my chest wall. I refrain from looking at the agent, giving away no noticeable reaction, but internally, my blood is roaring.

Finally, Kyrie makes eye contact with me, both of us seemingly coming to the same conclusion at once.

Not only did Mason bring the body discrepancy to Brad, he shared his worries with an outside source.

The fucking FBI.

Mason is the only one who could have involved them. No one other than Brad—who spooks at his own shadow— knew of the victim with a missing hyoid buried in the research fields.

There's no other way the FBI could be aware of Mason's discovery. He had to have contacted them himself.

As Brad does his best to articulate a coherent response to Agent Hayes, explaining how an oversight with a donated body or records could be incorrectly documented by the interns—all while stealing nervous glances my way— I decide Brad was definitely not the one to report it. He's far more frightened of me than the FBI.

I gauge Kyrie's behavior, questioning if she knew of Mason's actions.

No. That would be recklessly stupid. Far too careless even for her impulsive nature.

Killing Mason after he knowingly contacted the feds would be sure to bring the authorities to our doorstep. Something neither of us would want.

"Thank you for your more than helpful input, Dr. Thompson," Agent Hayes says. "I may need to contact you again should I need further insight on the body farm records."

My gaze darts to Hugh, the word *warrant* burning like a branding iron at the back of my throat as I hold it back.

Agent Hayes lines me in his sights. He's not tall. Five-nine, maybe. He's roughly mid-fifties and has a pouchy gut from sitting at a desk versus being in the field. His thinning hair is cropped close to his scalp, hinting to some military background. He wants others to see him as being in charge, having the answers, domineering, but he tries too hard to appear intimidating when the lines bracketing his mouth reveal how much shit he takes from his superiors daily.

The agent checks his notepad before addressing me. "Dr. Sorensen," his eyes find mine, "you have a very impressive career."

"Thank you."

The corner of his mouth tics. "Do you recall the last time Mr. Dumont was seen in your department?"

I raise my eyebrows and push back in my chair, releasing a terse breath as I pretend to think. "I don't."

The agent waits for me to say more. When I offer nothing further, he nods and pushes forward. "According to the logs Dr. Cannon provided, Mr. Dumont was working on a..." He checks his notes again. "A donation in your department."

"That seems right," I say.

"But you don't recall speaking with him, or seeing him—"

"Dr. Sorensen isn't big on communicating or even noticing that others work in his department."

There's a shared round of snickers to break some of the tension. It's Kyrie who suddenly speaks up to come to my aid. I hold her gaze across the table, and she gives me the faintest smile.

"Dr. Roth," the agent says, and moves across the room in order to look at her directly. "It is Dr. Kyrie Roth, correct?"

She licks her lips and frowns at the agent. "Yes, that's my name. How can I help you, Agent Hayes?"

Kyrie's ability to mask her expression and blend into any environment is, admittedly, impressive. I should have realized this trait beforehand. So many tiny tells are coming to light as I study her today, and I realize how she even masked herself from me.

It wasn't hard; my ego did most of the work for her.

Hayes regards her with a curious mix of apprehension and concern, like a father sorely disappointed in their child, but who still wants to shelter them. Could be a side effect of his misogyny; men in his position with his authority often overcorrect this attribute. Or he could have a daughter of his own, which would explain the flash of familiarity I glimpse in the agent's squinted gaze when he asks her his next question.

"How long have you been employed at the university, Dr. Roth?"

She clasps her hands together on the table surface. "Three amazing years."

The agent doesn't take any notes. "You've done a lot of amazing things here during your time, as I understand. Expanding the Bass Fields research program, for one. That's kind of like your baby, isn't it?"

She only hesitates a beat, then her practiced smile forms. "I just won an award the other night, but I couldn't have done any of it without the tireless and dedicated help of my colleagues."

Hayes nods. "There are no accolades being given today, Dr. Roth. Just the facts."

His derisive remark burrows under her protective armor, and she smiles wider. "Of course."

"And in your three years here, have you noticed any of the inconsistencies Dr. Thompson was referring to?"

With a tilt of her head, Kyrie says, "Oh, sure." She keeps her voice steady, pleasant but with a subtle hint of concern for the missing member of our team. "I mean, not to throw anyone under the bus, we have the best grad students in the country in our program, but they're still in school, still learning. Crunching late hours for tests. It's human to make mistakes."

His smile is forced, but he logs a note. "Were you aware of any strife between Mason Dumont and anyone else in the program?"

She blinks, shakes her head. "I don't believe so, no."

"What about the bar the students frequent..." He flips a

page in his notepad. "Black Rock Distillery. Did you ever hear Mason talking about going there?"

"I'm sorry, no," she says simply.

From here, it's a game of ping-pong between them. Gleaning nothing helpful from Kyrie, the agent moves on, traveling around the room and collecting additional information on the missing Mr. Dumont. Mason was well-liked. Not the top of his class, but exceptional enough to be praised by his professors. Nothing alarming is uncovered about him, other than the fact none of his professors, friends, or family have heard from him in nearly five days.

I watch students shuffle by the conference room, curiously peeking over with red-rimmed eyes, their concern for a friend or fellow student evident in their distressed performance. The professional staff within this room are concerned with deadlines and how the case might delay or disrupt their work. They're putting on a good front to display concern, but really, we're all exceedingly egotistical by nature. You don't get to the top of the ladder by carving out space in your thoughts to care for one lone grad student.

That's why the hunting in the Tri-City college towns is so good.

And why I didn't notice the rising reports of missing male students and men. I'm guilty of the same bloated ego of my colleagues, which kept me from recognizing another hunter in my midst.

That vanity will cost me.

As the meeting comes to a close, Hugh allows the agent to pass out his personal contact on cards to the team. Kyrie is the first to slip out of the room.

I bypass Agent Hayes, living up to my dismissive reputation, and trail Kyrie through the warren of glass offices. As she turns down a hallway, I coast up beside her and clasp her bicep, steering her into the cold room.

"Jack, what the hell?"

I swing the door closed, trapping us inside with the steel modular lockers bricked along the walls. There are rows of storage for biological reagents and chemicals that, along with the bodies, need to be stored at a chilling thirty-nine degrees Fahrenheit.

The immediate drop in my body temperature cools my overheated blood. It affects Kyrie too, as I notice how she rubs her forearm, her eyes blazing despite the chilled enclosure. My gaze drifts to her hardened nipples peaked against her thin white blouse.

"Did you want something, Jack?" Her demanding tone bites into my erratic thoughts. "Like, say, to tell me the date of your resignation and to congratulate me on winning? Or are you here to make good on your threat to have me on my knees." One perfect eyebrow arches. "I honestly didn't suspect you as being one to fraternize in the workplace."

And like that, all cool composure cracks. Impatience stirs in my veins, and I back her against the steel body lockers, caging her in like a feral animal.

"That might be the only way to shut you up," I say, the visual of stuffing my studded cock down her throat more than tempting to get that desired effect now.

A swallow drags along the delicate column of her throat. "Then why—?"

"The FBI didn't show up here because of one student reported missing," I say, my voice cast low between us. "They're here because of a *pattern* of men going missing."

Agent Hayes didn't list any names, but he didn't have to. He hedged around the college bar, implying Mason was a possible victim connected to a rash of disappearances—

ones that could be directly connected to the body farm program.

Her wide eyes soften a fraction, disarming. "*One* agent," she says. "Not the whole FBI or a task force. Hardly a reason to be meeting all clandestine in the body cooler." Before I can remark, she adds, "That agent didn't say anything about a pattern. You're paranoid."

"And you're careless." I bite into my bottom lip, my hands balled at my sides, restraining myself from the urge to clean up my own careless mess.

I take a purposeful step back, putting enough distance between us to shield myself from her body heat. Kyrie has the innate ability to look on the positive side, but even she should be more concerned about a fed snooping around.

My gaze narrows on her as I say, "You think sending Brad to Madrid on my grant field trip makes you the winner and solves our problem. That trip is three weeks away. We need Brad gone *now*."

Her body trembles from the cold, her teeth chattering a little as she sucks in a breath. Against my will, my cock jerks at the sight. The titanium studs rub abrasively against my briefs and make it damn hard not to reach down to adjust myself.

"You're right," she says, surprising me. "Brad's not real good at keeping his cool like some." She flashes amused eyes up at me. "It's a huge inconvenience—"

"That you killed a student in our department, bringing the feds to our door? Yeah, it is." I push in another inch closer to her. "Did you know your victim had contacted the feds?" I demand.

I study her pursed features; she's pretty even when indignant. "Do you honestly, really think so fucking little of me?"

My nostrils flare, the scent of her perfume invading my senses. "That's not an answer."

She huffs a soundless laugh. "No, Jack. I did not know Mason had already contacted the feds before I injected him with *SUX* and chopped up his body. Next time, I'll make sure to be extra thorough when killing someone to cover your ass. Satisfied?"

The crude visual she paints allows me to imagine in graphic, arousing detail how she subdued and killed her victim. I blink hard to clear the mental imagery as I dissect her admission beneath the sarcasm.

Kyrie discovered Mason had planned to go around Brad and send the FBI information that could implicate me—or possibly her. I can't be sure whose ass she's actually looking out for, seeing as she more than wants me to suffer.

I glance away as she tucks a wayward strand of hair behind her ear. "As for Brad, I had a plan for him," I say. "I was handling him."

"At a glacial-fucking-pace," she snaps. "By the time you would have 'handled him'"—she makes air quotes, quickly wrapping her arms around her quivering body—"Mason would've led Brad to three more discrepancies. He had a file, Jack. I erased the hard drive on his laptop. He was going to give Brad that information after the gala." She cocks a neat eyebrow. "So, you're welcome."

I release a hard breath through my nose, then drive my hand through my hair. I should have left West Paine three years ago. The reasons I didn't pale in comparison to the shitstorm brewing now.

"I said, *you're welcome*," she stresses.

"Don't pretend any part of Thursday night was for me," I say, the unwanted memory of her entering Brad's front door raiding my thoughts. "You have your own selfish motivation."

As my gaze tracks Kyrie pressed to the lockers, I fight the illogical voice whispering that my reasons for staying were merely excuses. We are all selfish creatures in the end. Some destructive part of me craved to be near this woman, despite all sound logic. I knew it then, her light to my dark, her brimming kinetic energy animating my lifeless corpse.

This rivalry between us started long before now.

Challenging Dr. Roth became almost as satisfying as feeling my victims take their last breath.

My gaze settles on the pale tint of her trembling mouth, the blood drained from her plump lips. No part of me wants to make her warm. I'm gripped with the sudden and dangerous urge to tear the flimsy buttons of her blouse open to see the gooseflesh covering her skin.

I should leave.

Tonight.

The wise choice is to pack my belongings and head out of town. I've had my next destination in place for a while. All I have to do is walk away and not look back.

"So what do you suppose we do?" The question leaves my mouth, shocking the both of us.

"I'll handle Brad," she says, voice shaky. "Without evidence or proof of any discrepancies, I can calm him down just fine without having to go to extreme measures."

Right now, I finish the statement for her.

Brad might be malleable for the time being, but his expiration date expired the moment he invaded my territory.

I silently agree with a firm nod. "And the body?"

She releases a breath, her lips quivering, as she flattens her palms to the steel and pushes herself forward. I don't move back.

"I don't see why we should cancel all our fun…" She boldly pinches my tie between her fingers. "Besides, you still have that pesky recording of me. Are you willing to delete it, Jack? Give up your leverage?" She twists my tie around her palm, the heated friction of her hand grazing my chest. "A girl has to look out for herself in this world."

A blaze whips down my spine, igniting my actions before I realize I've made a move. I have Kyrie's throat in my clutch, my palm pressed to her trachea, fingers anchored to the side of her neck. I look down into her sweet face and drink in the flicker of fear before she's able to mask it.

"You're not a girl," I say, my tone bordering on lethal. "You're an irritating inconvenience that is begging to have her ass reddened."

Her pupils dilate. "And don't you just hate how much that excites you."

My cock jumps in response, the temptation to crush her windpipe a fierce need coiled around my shrinking restraint. I choke up on her throat as she swallows, and the feel of her hyoid enticingly presses against the web of my hand.

I bring her face inches from mine. "Give me one fucking reason why I shouldn't smother you and put your limp body in one of these lockers."

Struggling to breathe, she removes her hand from my chest and sinks her fingers into her skirt pocket. Placing the silver object within my periphery, she strikes the lighter.

I relax my grip, and she says, "Because you have no idea what else I have on you, Jack. Now be a good boy and remove your hand."

I keep her in my grasp, some dark demand refusing to release her just yet.

Freeing her throat one finger at a time, I slowly withdraw. It's like forcing apart two opposite poles of a magnet.

She touches her neck, her dainty fingers inspecting for injury.

"I know how to strangle without causing damage," I say. "If I want to hurt you, I will."

"Okay, Jack. New objective." Lifting her chin, she squares her shoulders. "I say we up the stakes of the rivalry. Brad will be gone soon enough, and I agree we can call a draw there. But this special agent? He really does have to go."

"And how do you suggest either of us accomplish that, petal?"

Her eyebrows hike at the pet name. "Honestly, you have no sense of fun, Jack." She steps close. "Use your imagination." Then she moves around me.

"Where are you going?"

"As much as I enjoy freezing to death with you in the cold room, I think we might want to leave. Separately. Soon. You know, so as not to cause suspicion." She smiles and bats her thick eyelashes. "Unless you want our colleagues to think we're having an affair."

At my severe silence, she exhales heavily and says, "For appearance's sake, I'm going to join the search party."

I nod. "Good idea."

"So thrilled to gain your approval."

As she reaches for the door, I circle my fingers around her wrist. "Get rid of the ribbon from the flowers," I tell her. "Dispose of the body."

She holds my gaze. "Stay here for another few minutes before you leave," she says, directing her own order. "Your cold-hearted self can take it."

A fleeting image of being buried beneath a bank of cold

white dust covers my vision, momentarily stalling me, and Kyrie pulls out of my grasp. The memory fades as quickly as Kyrie slips through the door.

I'm left in the cold room with more questions than when I entered, and a hard cock. A flare of anger bites into my resolve to remain behaved. The urge to stalk and hunt my prey pulses in my veins, but with a fed lurking around town, there will be no satisfaction tonight.

I'll have to get my rocks off another way.

SEVEN
CAPTIVE
KYRIE

"You should be happy," I say as I drag a chair to the security glass, its legs grating against the concrete floor with a piercing whine. I lower myself onto the clinical steel, bracing my forearms against my knees. "Jack was set to kill you in a matter of days. He'd probably slice you open, maybe even take some of your bones. If you meet all his discerning criteria, he might even do it while you're *still alive*." My eyes widen with theatrical flair. I even add a spooky *'oooh'*, twinkling my gloved fingers toward my captive.

The man on the other side of the glass sputters and sobs.

I sigh and rest my chin on my folded fingers as I regard my sniveling captive with a gentle smile. He's handsome without being hot, athletic without being strong. Like a substandard tennis player. Maybe a golf wannabe. His big brown eyes shine with tears and I have a sudden urge to lick his cheek, to taste the fear on his skin.

"What I like about you, however, is that you fit my criteria too," I say. "Not that it would have mattered if you didn't tick all the boxes on my shitbag list. Right now, Jack is enough of a shitbag for both of you."

"Let me go, please. *Please*. I promise I won't tell anyone." My captive presses his hands to the glass, his expression a delicious mixture of sorrow and terror. "I won't go to the police. I'll go somewhere else, whatever you want. I'll leave town. I'll make myself disappear."

I give him a pout and a furrowed brow. "Trust me. You're safer where you are." The unspoken *'for now'* lingers at the edges of my widening grin as I lean back in my chair and study the man behind the glass. "Colby Cameron. Frat boy pussy slayer extraordinaire. The Candyman, isn't that what your loser friends call you?"

"No, I don't—"

"*Shut the fuck up*," I snarl, erupting from my chair to smack the glass with both palms. "I know all about you. I know all about your kind. I've been studying your species for a decade."

I tamp down my menacing, feral glare, closing my eyes as I draw my dark waves over my shoulder in a soothing stroke. I tug gently on a thick strand as a steady exhale slips through my lips. When I open my eyes, my saccharine mask is back in place.

Smiles sell, baby!

"Did your friends know how you really got so many girls into your bed? It wasn't just your all-American charm, was it. It wasn't that cute face of yours. It was the little something extra you'd slip into their drinks. A sweet drop of sedation from the Candyman." I swipe my latex-covered finger across the glass and turn away. "I think your friends knew what you did. Why else would they give you such a fucking stupid nickname."

I walk away from the glass cage, heading past the stainless steel gurney in the center of the room, past the photos and notes taped to the concrete walls, past the table of implements chilled by the air from the whirling vent in the ceiling. I stop at the chest freezer and run my touch across the pitted white surface as it hums beneath my fingertips. "Like I said," I whisper to the secrets in the cold box. "I know your kind. I have *survived* your kind."

A blast of icy air caresses my hands as I open the lid of the freezer. Goosebumps stipple my skin and I think of Jack. Once upon a time, for a pivotal moment, his presence brought a blessed kiss of cold across my skin, a balm for the pain that burned like a flame in my chest. I thought if I could find him, if I could be near him, that it would always be that way. I believed that Jack was the only one who could numb this suffering. If I could create an environment where we could both thrive, then maybe I wouldn't be so alone anymore. But that was just a naïve dream. In reality, little by little, he's only made it worse. He's stoked my rage into an inferno that simmers beneath a fragile shell, the lick of its molten heat too close to the surface for me to contain any longer.

There's only one thing left for me to do now.

Make. Jack. Suffer.

I reach into the freezer and pull out Mason's lower leg, keeping my back to Colby for a long moment as I examine the crystalline flakes clinging to the hairs on the gray, blood-less flesh. I almost feel bad about Mason. It's not as though he met all my criteria, but I did what I had to so I could keep Jack under my control. That said, Mason wasn't squeaky clean either, judging by his porn interests in underage girls that I found when I went through his laptop to wipe his evidence.

I sigh, flicking the frozen skin of Mason's calf. "Have you ever heard of the Silent Slayer, Mr. Candyman?"

Colby is silent for a moment as he puts the pieces together. "I... I n-never killed anyone."

"I know that," I snarl, turning to face him with the severed leg in my gloved hand. Colby's gasp becomes a wretch. He turns away and vomits, bile spattering against the lower edge of the glass. "Christsakes. The toilet is only a few steps away, Colby. I'm not cleaning up after you."

I watch for a moment with my lip curled in disgust. I'm used to this now, men puking. Pissing themselves. Even shitting their pants. I imagine I might get the unholy trilogy from Colby the Candyman.

"I'm going to go out on a limb here," I say, waggling the leg around before dropping it onto the gurney with a thunk. "I think you've heard of the Silent Slayer. But I bet you never heard there was one person who survived his killing spree. They kept that out of the press, for once. Though I think you might be able to guess who that sole survivor was."

I spare only a brief glance toward Colby as I move to the table of implements and select a scalpel and a pair of tweezers to take back to the severed leg. My focus turns to the toenail of the first phalanx as I grip it with the tweezers, working the sharp edge of the scalpel into the membrane that adheres the frozen keratin to the flesh until it begins to loosen.

"He wasn't all that different from you," I say, freeing the toenail from the skin and dropping it onto the edge of the gurney before I proceed to the next phalanx to lift another toenail free. "I was young. Seventeen. I didn't know there was a serial killer hunting girls like me. People like the Silent Slayer were nightmares who didn't touch lives like mine. He was just a dark phantom. Until he was real. Until he had drugged me, until he entered my home. Until he sunk his blade between my bones as my parents lay dying right before my eyes."

"Please, *please*," Colby whines when he finally stops heaving the contents of his stomach across inappropriate surfaces. "I just want to go home, I'm begging you."

"How many girls have said the same thing to you? How many have begged you to take them home?" I ask as I drop the second toenail onto the table. I spare Colby a quick glance over my shoulder before returning to my work. "You're a predator. You've gotten away with preying on women for so long that you probably don't even worry about getting caught anymore. You thought that you could slide through life unscathed. But you know what? You're not at the top of the food chain. You're what we call in biology a *tertiary consumer*. Like a snake. Or a coyote." I swallow a sudden burn in my throat as I pull the third nail free. "There are wolves out there, Mr. Candyman. And they can't wait to gobble you up."

"I c-can't...I'm not...I'm not a bad guy—"

"You know, everyone fears the wolf. But do you know what the wolf fears in the kingdom of the wild?" I ask as I lift another toenail free and drop it to the table with a tick. "The lynx." Colby blubbers behind me with quiet sobs. "I know, right? Most people wouldn't guess a lynx. They look so snuggly, all plush fur and snowshoe feet and those adorable little black tufts on their ears. Super cute." I pry the fourth nail from the frozen toe with a faint, wicked grin. "But a lynx will sneak into a wolf's den. It will kill their pups. Their pregnant females. Even the full-grown males, when they get them alone. A lynx will flip a wolf on its back and gouge its stomach or neck, and then leave it to die. A single lynx will never challenge a wolf pack. No...it will bide its time. And when you least expect it," I say as I lift the final toenail free and set it down among the others, "that's when they emerge from the snow and the shadows. That's when they kill."

I grasp the leg by the ankle and return it to the freezer before gathering the toenails into a small Ziplock that I slip into the interior pocket of my jacket, tossing my gloves in the trash next to the table of implements. My gaze rests on the wall of photos and notes and I pull a picture down, the scene so familiar that the physical image is hardly needed, its details burned into memory. I slide it into my pocket next to the bag of souvenirs as I turn to face my captive with a grin. When I saunter toward the glass, Colby backs away, those delicious tears dampening his thick lashes and sliding across his skin.

"Jack is the wolf who hunts you. But guess what I am?" I press my hands to the glass and give Colby a shrug to go with my devious smile. "If the wolf never stood a chance against the lynx, what good do you think your begging will do?"

We regard one another for a long moment before I turn and stride toward the fortified steel door. "Clean up your vomit, Mr. Cameron. There are towels in the rubber container under your bed. I've got my own messes to attend to."

I leave my little den to the melody of Colby's pleas and protests, the first door slamming shut behind me with a thud that echoes up the concrete stairs. When I arrive at the second door, I pick up my rifle from where it leans against the wall and key the code into the pad to open the lock, entering the hidden cellar of my off-grid hunting cabin.

My dog Cornetto raises his head from his place where

he lays guarding the threshold to the cabin as I enter the main floor, joining me to sit at my side on the worn sofa as I lay the Savage 110 across my thighs. I take the photo from the pocket where the toenails lay hidden. It's one I took myself with a long-distance lens, a picture of Jack the year before I came to West Paine University. He's in profile, his hands buried deep in his pockets as a bitter wind lifts his short dark hair from his brow. Jack is looking across the single acre of land that the university had managed to provide for his research with a threadbare grant. That was before I came along. Before I secured an additional forty-eight acres of field research space. Before I rallied for funding to build new labs and teaching facilities. It was from the days when every step I took closer to my quarry still felt like a wonderful challenge, a tactical move across a chessboard.

My father's words come back to me. *"There's a saying you need to remember, Peanut,"* he would tell me every season, no matter the prey we tracked. *"Hunting is not a sport. In a sport, both sides should know they're in the game."*

This is not a hunt, not anymore. Even if Jack finally understands he's in the game, it's not a sport.

It's a reckoning.

I trace a finger across Jack's face, an ache flaring beneath the thin, cracked crust of rage that's built up over the years since this moment was captured. It never really bothered me much that he didn't remember me the first time we officially met. There was disappointment, sure, but it wasn't a strike deep enough to wound my heart. But everything since is different. Each of his hits has felt purposeful. Each venomous bite has burned hotter in my veins.

And it's not just that I didn't deserve the kiss of his poison.

It's what he meant to me, despite each strike.

Jack was the person I emulated. Someone who could crush the breath from an enemy while still navigating a successful life in society, his dark secrets hidden from view. I wanted to be like him. In control. Impervious to the cruelty of time. *Powerful.* And I wanted to give Jack what he had given to me; a way to thrive in the absence of light.

So, I threw myself into my studies. I crushed each degree in as little time as possible, studying endlessly until I was top of my class. I signed up for every field school, seized every opportunity. I turned my hunting skills on those men who deserved it, cleansing Ashgrove and then Westview from the detritus of civilization one mediocre soul at a time.

And when I finally got to West Paine to create a safe haven for both of us, Jack rejected me at every turn.

I need to find a way to make him suffer. It's the only way I'll finally let go. Maybe then I can rebuild the oasis I've created at West Paine and embrace its sun and shadows on my own.

I take Jack's trophy lighter from my pocket and flick the lid open, striking the flint wheel to bring the flame to life. It feels wrong to set the edge of the photo to the fire, but I do it anyway. I let it consume the paper until it scorches my fingertips, and only then do I let it go, dropping the burning photograph to the worn planks at my feet. My boot grinds the fire and ash into the floor and then I leave my cabin to drop Cornetto safely at home before I drive to the Bass Research Fields.

I text Dr. Cannon when I'm parked to let him know I've arrived, and he responds right away, though I know he won't come around to check on me. The search party had nearly finished a sweep of the grounds when they alerted Dr. Cannon to an animal behaving strangely within the farmlands adjacent to the research grounds. It was an empty-handed search anyway, of course, and most people seem to have left. There are a few cars in the parking lot but I don't see anyone as I remove the rifle and my pack from the back of my Land Rover. I don't enter the building, I don't look at the windows of the labs. I just walk toward the fields with my head down, searching for signs of my quarry.

The fifty acre plot of the Bass River Research Fields isn't a huge space to roam, but it is full of wooded patches and creeks and fields, surrounded by a mix of farmland and sparse forest. Plenty of space for creatures to hide and roam, to build dens and raise young. With the abundance of easy food for scavengers, many of those creatures stay close and aren't hard to find if you know where to look. And it doesn't take me more than twenty minutes to spot what I'm looking for.

I set my blanket down on the crisp, frosted grass, still within view of the research labs at my back. I lay down on my belly and adjust my scope, but I don't take the shot. I just watch for a while, letting the cold and the quiet wash over me, allowing the knot of regret to twist tighter around my throat as I follow the solitary beast in my crosshairs.

"You shouldn't be out here, Dr. Roth."

I huff a breath of a laugh, but I don't look up from the view through my scope.

"You think I would take the risk without permission? In broad daylight? With a fucking rifle? You must still think so little of me, Dr. Sorensen."

I hear the smile in Jack's voice when he speaks, as faint as that grin might be. "I meant there's a probable killer on the loose. You shouldn't be out here alone. For appearances."

"Rifle, Jack."

Jack stops next to me, his worn Blundstones halting in my periphery at the edge of my waterproof blanket. For a long moment there's silence between us, just the sounds of birds and the rustle of grasses to fill the gaps in my patience. I'm sure Jack is weighing the potential benefit of kicking me in the head against the possibility of being shot in the balls. But, surprisingly, he doesn't move to take the risk.

"You weren't with the search party," Jack says instead.

"Nope."

"Why would that be?"

I shrug, not taking my eye from the scope. "I had more important shit to do."

There's a quiet moment where I think he's going to admonish me for not making an appearance at the search, but the silence stretches on with no cutting remark from Jack. "You're not in camouflage," he observes instead.

"No. I won't need it today," I reply, my voice low and smooth and quiet, like a solemn prayer in an empty church. "And hopefully I'll scare away anything sane enough to notice."

I glance up at Jack. His eyes are caught on the horizon where my scope is aimed, his gaze is roaming across the landscape as he searches for my quarry. When I follow the line of my scope I can see her in the distance. Head down. Tawny fur. A broken stride.

"CBF-14," I say, shimmying to the left on the blanket. I open my palms around the rifle, looking up to meet the question in Jack's eyes. "Take a look."

Jack doesn't step closer, nor does he remove his hands from his jacket pockets. He just turns his head to give me an assessing, doubtful look from the corner of his eye. "You want to give me your weapon, Dr. Roth?"

"Shooting me in the head on the campus grounds is

hardly your style. If you wanted to kill me, which I'm sure you do, you'd prefer something far more private and...intimate...than that." I fold my bottom lip between my teeth when Jack's gaze falls to my seductive, knowing grin. A dark giggle bubbles in my throat as his eyes narrow, his pupils devouring his silver irises until only a thin band of color remains. My smile turns a shade more wicked in reply. "Why do you think I wear my hair up with that plum-colored shirt with the bow collar on the days when I want to annoy you the most, hmm? You know, the one with the decorative little frilly bit right here?" I ask as I turn my head to expose my throat to the cold autumn air, twinkling my fingers along my skin.

"I loathe that shirt."

"I know. It's the built-in ligature. So close to strangulation, and yet so far. Such a tease." I force my brief laugh to sound more sardonic than it feels as I shuffle an inch or two further to the left and offer the rifle once more. "Come on. I won't bite...this time."

A crease flickers between Jack's brows. For a moment, I think he'll just walk away, leaving some cold and cutting words in his wake. But he steps closer instead, his eyes not leaving mine as he kneels next to me, their cool, metallic glimmer burrowing into my soul until the moment the rifle is firmly in his grip. My smile fades away as the scent of vetiver rises above the smell of crushed, cool grass and damp earth. Jack lays on his stomach next to me, propped on his elbows, looking just as natural with a rifle in his hands as he does with a champagne flute and a pristine black suit at a gala event.

"Where do I look?" Jack asks, his attention falling to my lips for the span of a fleeting breath before he nestles the rifle to his shoulder and focuses on the horizon.

"On the rise, to the right of the pines," I reply, gathering the frayed ends of my scattering thoughts. A swirl of regret is all that's left when I follow the barrel of the gun. "A coyote."

Jack nods, his right eye trained on the scope, his left squeezed shut. "I've got it."

"*Her*, not *it*," I correct, but gently. "What do you see?"

"A coyote."

I roll my eyes. "You obstinate fuck. What do you—"

"She seems disoriented." I almost choke on my saliva at the hint of amusement in Jack's voice. I look over in time to catch a vanishing grin, but he doesn't pull his gaze from the scope. That smile fades into something more serious as he watches the animal struggling in the distance. "She just stumbled. She's injured...no, she's sick."

"You sound sure. Why?" I ask, though I already know he's correct.

"Her body language. Her head and ears are down. She seems like she's...reacting to something. Not us? Not our scent?"

"No. The wind is favorable to our position. Even if it carried to her, I doubt she'd run."

Jack shifts his attention away from the coyote. His piercing intellect lands on me with the weight of a blade. I try to push a wall up between us, but I feel his scrutiny in every cell of my body. Jack doesn't just look at me, he looks *into* me.

"Did you come from a hunting family?" he asks as he surveys the details of my face.

"Yes. My dad. He started taking me with him when I was ten." An ember burns in my chest, the lick of flame coating old scars in heat. Jack looks at me as though I'll elaborate, as though a simple question or two will cause me to just spill all the details he hasn't earned. Even still, the past feels like it's crawling up my throat, begging to be let out. "My dad took me hunting because I wanted to go. I didn't have a shitty childhood, if that's what you're digging for," I say, tearing my gaze away, though I can still feel him watching me. "It was picture perfect."

My whisper seems to hang in the air before the wind carries it away. The coyote in the distance tilts her head as though listening, but I know she can't hear us. She shakes her head and bares her teeth at a phantom foe.

"What's her name?" Jack asks.

I want to say CBF-14, but I know he'll call bullshit. "Sunny Bunny."

I can almost feel Jack gathering his limited self-restraint, and I think for a moment that he might throw the gun across the field. "Sunny...Bunny...?"

"Yep. Just Bunny for short, of course. Or Buns. But I knew you'd hate her full name even more."

"I don't know, Buns is pretty bad."

A weak smile flickers across my lips at the distaste I see in Jack's expression when I dart a glance his way. It's deeply satisfying to catch the way he crinkles his nose as though he's swallowed something bitter. He passes the rifle back and I find Bunny through the scope, settling into the comforting weight of the weapon, the trigger cold in the autumn air.

He never rested his finger on it.

I glance in Jack's direction to find him watching me with more interest than I expected. "The first time I saw her was on a bright summer day. She caught a young hare," I say as I turn my attention back to the canid in the distance. I shrug. "It wasn't just the weather, or the prey. The longer I watched, the more I realized she had a spark about her. A kind of goofy disposition. Hence, Sunny Bunny."

"I thought wildlife biologists were supposed to remain dispassionate about their research subjects."

I roll my eyes and sigh. "Of course you would. It's okay for the illustrious Dr. Jack Sorensen to be passionate about a bunch of cold bones but God forbid anyone else feel something remotely fervid about their work," I grumble.

I'm quiet for a long moment as Bunny turns a wobbling circle, and I realize that there's nothing I recognize of her anymore, nothing remaining of the soul that's left only fur and flesh and marrow behind. A sting burns deep in my chest, in my eyes. I blink, keeping my gaze honed on the coyote. "No. I've studied Bunny for three years. I am not apathetic to her at all, Jack."

We fall into silence as Bunny looks down at the grasses waving in the wind like tiny banners. She trots a few steps before stumbling to a stop and shaking her head, her jaw hanging open and her tongue working in her open mouth as she tries to swallow. Jack's head tilts as he watches. Bunny's behavior is notably strange, even from this distance and without the benefit of the scope. "Rabies?" he asks.

My finger caresses the curve of the trigger as my heart seems to drop in my chest, its weight too heavy against my bones. "Yes. I was informed about an aggressive coyote that was killed on Mitchell street a few weeks ago. It was tested and came back positive for rabies. I put vaccine bait in the fields, but I guess I was too late. Maybe I didn't put enough down. I should have done another round, but I let myself become caught up with other...priorities," I admit, resisting the sudden urge to glance at Jack.

The quiet threads around us, pulling tight, knotting in my throat. Silence never bothers me when I'm alone in the field observing the behavior of wildlife. But when I'm with other people, the quiet often gnaws at me, scraping at my mind, an itch across my thoughts. It's like an entity, like a living hole that begs to be filled before my imagination can drag me somewhere I don't want to go.

"No cutting remarks, Jack?" I ask, feeding the void when it starts to consume me. But truthfully, I'm also surprised he hasn't taken the opportunity to slice me down for my self-admitted mistake. "I've watched Bunny for almost as long as I've been here at West Paine. Of all the lives here, hers is my favorite, and I just told you that her suffering is my fault. Nothing to add?"

Silence. Bunny stumbles in the distance.

I swallow as my finger flinches on the trigger.

"Come on," I whisper around the knot that constricts my vocal cords. "You know nothing would make you happier than to twist another knife."

Jack's silence crystallizes beneath my skin, burning my flesh like the touch of ice. My eye stays on Bunny as her tongue lolls in her open jaws.

"Fucking hell, Jack, just cut me down already—"

"Kyrie—"

My shot stops him short, the power of the blast echoing against the creek embankments. Bunny falls into the grass and doesn't stir.

"Good enough," I whisper.

I sling my backpack over one shoulder and my rifle over the other as I rise, not looking back as I stride away to recover another soul.

One I never wanted to take.

EIGHT
PAINT IT RED
JACK

Three days.

And in that time, I've found pieces of Mason in my daily lunches. Toenails in my yogurt. Testes buried in my tofu salad. Entrails in my travel mug of egg drop soup.

When I approached Kyrie to inquire about her antics, her response was: "You said to dispose of the body... Digestion is a fantastic form of disposal, Jack."

I've since decided it's time to cremate the bodily evidence she's gifted to me with my half of Mason. All evidence to be incinerated and ashes to fertilize my Himalayan poppies.

All except the femur.

I'll keep that in a safe place. When it comes to Kyrie and her volatile temperament, it's wise to have at least one piece of evidence in reserve.

As the fall breeze scatters orange and red leaves across Main Street, I seat myself on a sidewalk bench and flip through my sketchbook. The drawings of Colby are all I've seen of my prey in as many days, also.

Colby has gone missing.

I wouldn't be surprised if he starts turning up in my salads next.

Flipping to a fresh sheet, I lightly trace my pencil over the Bristol page, the sound of graphite scratching the surface deeply satisfying. My preference is typically a rougher, heavier tooth charcoal paper. I like the texture, the finely broken lines in each stroke. But for this particular sketch, a softer surface is required in order to capture all the delicate nuances of the features.

I glance up at my subject, pencil paused over the page, before I begin shading the high cheekbones.

By the time I have the color of the irises matched to a near perfect shade of pale, crystalline blue, I see the subject of my drawing emerge from the table through the picture window of the bar. She effortlessly mingles with a group of rowdy college kids as they exit, making sure she's hidden among them as they head down the sidewalk.

I smile to myself at just how clever she is. Hiding in plain sight. Not easy for a beautiful woman who captures attention easily. I wonder if her overly expressive person-ality is a part of her method; making sure everyone knows how outspoken, outgoing, and delightful she is, so that when she's on the prowl, no one will remember the quiet, docile woman who blended into a crowd.

"That wasn't the first time we met."

I find it difficult to believe I'd simply forget someone as memorable as Kyrie. And using the rivalry to buy time and figure it out has only resulted in Agent Hayes lingering far too long.

The truth is, the more I dig into Dr. Kyrie Roth, the less I uncover. For such a remarkable woman, her life before West Paine seems rather unremarkable, if not very well orchestrated. I can't seem to find anything messy or unique about Kyrie Leigh Roth. Except for, that is, her *type*.

I know the kind of victim that captures her eye.

After I've packed away my supplies in my satchel, I pop the ballcap on my head and cross the street.

I borrowed some clothes from Brad's closet, and took the ballcap he likes to wear after work from his office desk. Before I enter the bar, I lower the bill over my eyes and push through the door. An obnoxious blast of pop music greets me first.

I find the table near the back corner where Kyrie sat for the past half hour. From this viewpoint, I spot her target right away, drunkenly and aggressively flirting with a twenty-something young woman across the dimly lit room.

She likes her victims to be of the womanizing variety.

When a waitress approaches, I order a Scotch and put it on Brad's credit card. It only takes twenty minutes before I catch Kyrie's target slipping a crushed pill into the girl's beer.

The adrenaline for the hunt stirs in my veins.

As the target guides the impaired girl out into the chilly night air, I follow not too far behind, making sure the camera mounted at the top of the display shelves catches Brad's ballcap on my way out.

The plan fell into place naturally. Brad admitted to Agent Hayes in the initial meeting that Mason brought his concerns directly to him.

Then Mason went missing.

Now, I'm practically handing Agent Hayes a prime suspect with evidence on a silver serving platter.

Although I'd like to claim this is all for Thunderdome, the wild heat sizzling my blood states otherwise. I've been denying myself too long, urges building. And the gratification of the kill is only partially what's making my heart drum inside my chest.

Like me, the target is too eager, and his impulsive nature has his victim lured into an alley only a few blocks from the bar.

I hang back around the corner and prep the syringe. When I hear the telltale sound of a lowering zipper, I attack.

Anchoring my arm around his shoulders, I pull him off the drugged girl and drive the needle into his neck. I have the plunger depressed before he has a chance to fight back. As he sags against my chest, I deposit him on the asphalt, then make quick work of checking the girl's vitals and moving her out of the alleyway.

From her phone, I send an SOS text to her most recent contacts, but ultimately leave her to chance. I'm already playing a game of risk by hunting with a fed in the vicinity. I can't chance self-preservation to make sure one girl is safe.

"If I'm going down by the feds," I say, dragging Kyrie's victim to the end of the alley by his ankle, "I might as well go out in a bloody blaze of glory."

I chuckle, feeling a rare euphoria. Or maybe she's just driven me completely out of my mind. I'm being brought down by a girl with poppy blue eyes and bubbly smile. *The sheer weakness of it.*

I close the trunk of my car with a rewarding *click*, sealing the victim inside.

DEFLESHING METHODS CAN VARY. Known more accurately as excarnation among my peers, the removal of soft tissue and organs from the skeleton, wherein not to affect or damage the bones, is a delicate process that takes time and patience.

And a lot of bleach.

This is a process I take great pride and pleasure in. The subject is typically deceased when performing the defleshing...but they don't have to be.

I might not have the time necessary to be as thorough and delicate as required to preserve the bones—but there is a certain appreciation for the more antiquated method.

I look at the naked victim on the steel table as I run the blade of my fillet knife over the sharpening stone. He's on my slab to serve a purpose. However, that doesn't mean I can't take pleasure in my work.

A tube feeds the near-empty contents of a Banana Bag into his arm via an IV drip. The mineral and saline solution will help sober him from the sedative much quicker.

To test the blade's sharpness, I set the stone aside and lay my gloved hand to his shin, right below the kneecap. His skin is cool to the touch, my personal cold room in my home set five degrees lower than the room at the university.

Positioning the blade at a sixty degree angle, I slice into his flesh, making a clean incision.

Blood pools around the cut and drips bright-red onto the steel surface. My heart rate—which almost always never accelerates above resting—spikes as adrenaline floods my adrenals.

I feel the loss of the moment when he starts to rouse. Groggy, Kyrie's victim blinks several times as he becomes conscious and attempts to clear his vision. He immediately tries to move his arm, realizing slowly in his inebriated state that he's strapped down.

Then his gaze locks on me.

"There's still a good amount of sedative in your system,"

I say to him. I wipe the blood off the blade with a clean towelette. "You'll appreciate that here in a moment."

As I reach under the slab for my garrote, he stammers the usual tired questions: *Who are you. Where am I. What are you going to do to me.* Followed by the useless screams and pleas and tears, then finally, threats.

"Good," I say, stretching the wire out above him. "It's good to end on a strong note."

While he continues to threaten my life, I grip the wooden toggles and lower the garrote, resting the wire ligature below the notch of his Adam's apple on the larynx.

Fighting, he shakes his head back and forth, and I stay right here to savor the moment. The rush, the anticipation. The closest there is to bliss—driving right through the Teflon layer that shrouds me from those elusive feelings.

My gaze settles on the vase of flowers across the steel room. The Himalayan blue poppies frozen in time, the color of the petals preserved at the exact beautiful shade of her eyes.

I imagine her just as she was in the Bass Fields. Mere inches from me, her proximity a heated current against my skin as she rested her finger alongside the trigger. Her reluctant hunter's gaze homed in on the sick animal.

She loved that coyote.

A fucking coyote, with the inability to reciprocate her feelings, who'd likely maul her face off if she tried to pet it.

And she named it fucking *Sunny Bunny*.

Since the second she entered my department, I've been trying to figure this woman out. Knowing now that we're kindred should explain the fixation I've had on her; that I sensed a killer.

But there's still something elusive keeping me from wrapping my ligature around her neck.

Her confession burns through my muscles. The pain in her eyes when she pulled the trigger spears beneath my rib cage, her kill felt with every emotion her body couldn't contain.

The whimper below hauls me out of the memory and, in a fraught effort to regain control, I wrap the ligature around her victim's neck and pull tight, throttling his scream. The garbled chokes and wheezes for air caress my skin.

When the chorus of sounds die away, I give the wire some slack, allowing him just enough air to do our dance all over again.

I pull the wire taut until my muscles burn. Until the mental image of Kyrie's smiling face morphs into one of anguish. Her mouth parted, lips pale and trembling. The way she looked at me as I choked her neck in the cold room.

"Dammit..." I release the wire, and the victim gasps. His broken coughs and desperate pleas blend with the sound of Kyrie in my head.

"Get the fuck out—" I snap the wire tight, and his skin splits beneath the ligature. His eyes bulge. Capillaries burst, and a plume of red fills the white.

As I stare into his eyes—my favorite part—waiting to feel the moment his body stops fighting death, her eyes invade my dark soul.

And all I see is her.

Her fucking hard nipples in the freezing cold room... and imagine what noise she'd make as I bit one.

"Christ." I drop the handles and back away from the table.

Furiously driving a hand through my hair, I bite out another curse. My blood roars inside my ears. I come around the table and grab the knife.

The guy on the slab panics. "Holy shit... Please! Oh fuck, don't do this—"

With a groan, I hook the blade under a restraint and slice the strap. I cut the rest of the straps away before I flip the steel table over and send it and the victim crashing to the floor.

Chest heaving, I watch as he scrambles to his feet. Using the IV pole for support, he gains balance, first looking at me, then the door.

"Do it," I dare him.

This isn't how I operate.

Clean. Precise. Meticulous.

But when she invaded my turf, she fucked up more than just my routine.

As the guy weighs his options, he lifts the shiny silver pole to utilize as a weapon. Keeping my predator gaze on him, I roll my head along my shoulders, feeling every tense muscle lock around my vertebrae.

Blood drips down his shin, and hunger ignites.

He makes a move toward the door.

Like a feral beast scenting blood, I dart forward. He gets a few wobbly steps before he trips over the tube. I allow him to right himself and face me. He thrusts the pole, jabbing it into my stomach.

The pain hits the mark. Teeth gritted, I grind out, "Again."

He's shaking now, adrenaline and fear pouring off his slick body, but he comes at me like a man who wants to live. He repeatedly slams the pole against me. Striking my ribs, arms, shoulders. I take the beating. I take each blow as punishment for my failure. The pain webs my body like a fine mesh to coat the numbness.

But I still see her—feel her.

Want her.

When he goes for my face, a roar tears from the base of my chest and I latch on to him. I rip the pole from his hand and thrust his back against the wall. Shoulder braced across his chest, I stare down into his face as I drive the blade into his sternum.

Eyes flared wide, he releases a silent wail, the horror of his doom trapped in a scream that will never be free.

I lose myself to the lust. I stick the knife in his stomach and drive the tip of the blade up beneath his ribs. I stab him again. Over and over, I sink the blade deep, mutilating his core until I taste the coppery tang of his blood as it mists my face.

His gaze has long lost the flicker of life. Breaths sawing my lungs, I remove my arm and let him drop to the floor. He sprawls over the clear tarp, and I step back and watch the blood pool around his lifeless form.

All I can think about is wrapping my hand around Kyrie's throat and shoving her to the bloody floor. My grip loosens around the hilt of the knife, and I drop to my knees as it clatters next to me.

My damn cock is rock-hard and strains painfully against my jeans. I drag the zipper down and free the thick girth from the confines of my briefs. Wrapping a blood-stained hand around the base, I hiss through clenched teeth at the erotic feel of my wet, warm palm.

I'm staring at the morbid display of death and destruction on my cold room floor, but the imagery in my head takes me to her—to where her nails dig into my hand as I choke up on her throat, her lips as pale-blue as her eyes, her tits perfect and begging me to fuck them.

"Ah...fuck." I rub my cock, the titanium studs cool against my palm as I pass over them with each stroke.

Then Kyrie is fading, losing consciousness. Her heart rate slows, breathing shallows, until she's completely subdued and helpless beneath me. I release her neck and move down her lax body and toe her skirt and panties past her ankles. Slipping between her thighs, I anxiously surround my mouth over her sweet pussy.

My strokes speed as I imagine lapping at her silky lips, scraping my teeth over her clit, hearing her breathy moans and feeling her undulate as her body begs for release. I'm a glutton as I tear into her tender flesh and push inside her first with my tongue, then finger, as I die to have her perfect cunt wrapped around my cock.

The throb builds in intensity until I slap the tarped concrete with my free hand, palm bracing my body as my hips thrust. Her shuttered lids twitch, and I know when I sink inside her, her eyes will open, and those soulful fucking orbs will be on me...

"Oh...goddamn. *Fuck.*" The orgasm takes hold, threading my spine with pinpricks of electricity as my cock pulses, and a thick ribbon of ejaculate spills free.

I pump my cock harder as the blaze engulfs my bones. I'm shaking with the release. Panting through the pleasurable shockwaves that roll through me.

It's not enough.

I want more.

Getting to my feet, I tuck my dick into my pants and take in the demolished state of my cold room. Blood, cum, and chaos.

A fucking wreck. Just like my mind.

BEFORE I LEAVE the little ranch house, I set the ballcap on the entryway table, then splash the threshold with gasoline.

I close the door and walk out into the backyard, letting the contents of the gas can spill behind me. Getting Kyrie's victim into the basement was the easy part. Once Brad left for karaoke night, I knew I had enough time to stage the scene. Making sure authorities show up before all the evidence is destroyed is the more difficult challenge.

But I play for keeps.

In one methodical move, I slide my knight into position in anticipation for the checkmate—a daring move to remove both Brad and Agent Hayes from the board.

Then I'll claim West Paine as mine.

The queen, however, is still in possession of a very sentimental trophy. Missing the feel of my lighter in my hand, I strike the match and drop it to the trail of gasoline.

Then I watch Brad's house go up in flames.

As I leave the scene, I send a text to Kyrie: ♟💀. *Your move.*

NINE

SHATTERED

KYRIE

"We're at the Drunken Duck. Come for karaoke. Brad is just finishing I Kissed A Girl," Joy says. She must be just outside the doors of the pub, because I can hear Brad belting out the lyrics without his booming, off-key enthusiasm overwhelming Joy's voice.

"Christ, that means he's only a few Tequilas away from Bohemian Rhapsody," I reply.

"Exactly. And you love his rendition of Bohemian Rhapsody."

"Only because I relish the secondhand embarrassment."

"I'm not sure if that makes you a sadist or a masochist."

"Probably both," I say, and Joy laughs on the other end. "But in all seriousness, I can't leave yet."

"Aww come on, what's so important that you have to be at the lab at eight on a Thursday night?"

"Turds."

Silence.

"Animal turds."

"Kyrie—"

"No really," I say with a laugh. "I'm just about done

writing up the findings on a fecal matter analysis I spent all morning completing and if I finish now then I can take tomorrow off. I have no classes."

"Bummer. Get it?"

I snort a laugh and Joy cackles as Brad's song ends in the background to an uproarious cheer.

"Are you there on your own?" Joy asks.

I rise from my office chair and make my way to the shelves where my photos and accolades rest, glinting in the dim light from my desk. "No, Sorensen is here." I pick up the Brentwood award as I glance in the direction of his lab. He's bent over a set of skeletal remains, his back facing me. "If I wind up murdered you know where to look."

"Oh please. As if. You should put all that dramatic diva energy to work on the stage to some Céline Dion," Joy says as I huff a laugh. It would never cross her mind that the words I've just spoken could be possible, let alone likely.

"Listen, I'll come down if I finish quickly enough. Text me when Bradley is getting close to Queen."

"Will do, sunshine."

I smile as I lower my phone and scroll through text messages from friends and colleagues, opening the message from Jack as I contemplate sending a question mark reply to the chess and skull emojis he sent shortly before he arrived, only to close his text once more. My attention is on my device as I move to replace the Brentwood award in its position next to the grainy photo of my mom.

Except I miss the shelf.

My heart plummets faster than the heavy teardrop of glass. I fumble to catch it but it slips from my fingers, and all I can do is watch as it hits the cold tile floor and shatters into a thousand glittering shards.

The blackness of my impending flashback is immediate.

It eats the periphery of my vision, consuming the present, hurtling me toward the past.

I place a palm on the wall. My heart riots. My blood heats. I try to turn away from the broken glass littered at my feet to keep myself here but I already know it won't work. And worst of all, I'm not alone. I'm about to be at my most vulnerable with a wolf in the shadows of the room across the hall.

The last thing I see as my vision narrows to a pinprick of light is Jack straightening, his head turning, his deadly gray eyes meeting mine.

The next voice I hear is the demon who haunts me.

The Silent Slayer.

"*Shh, shh.* Quiet now, baby."

The sharp tip of a blade rests against my skin, its point steady between my ribs. I'm lying on the cream carpet in the living room of my childhood home. My body quakes as I press my lips shut between my teeth until they bruise and bleed. I know what's coming. My lung already rumbles in protest of every breath, the first blade lodged deep in its spongy cavern. It shudders with each blood-filled inhalation. "You know what happens if you make a sound," the man whispers.

He pushes my head to the side, my cheek tear-streaked and burning as he presses it to the carpet. I meet my mother's lifeless eyes. Her blood still slips from her parted lips, her severed tongue a dark horror in the shadows of her mouth.

My stomach roils. I choke down a sob, swallowing bile and fear and despair. When I press my eyes closed, the image is still there. Mom's unseeing eyes. Terror etched deep into her flesh as though it clings to her bones like a phantom, lurking beneath her slack features.

I open my eyes as the man's hot palm slides across the sweat coating my skin. He presses my cheeks between his fingertips until they ache against my teeth.

He turns my face to the other side.

My dad struggles where he lays on his stomach next to me, his hands bound behind his back and to his ankles, the gag in his mouth wet with exertion and distress. There's fury in his eyes. Panic. He tries to worm closer to my side but the man who holds me in his grip kicks my dad away.

"Now, now," the man says, letting go of my face to pull an ancient camcorder from his jacket pocket. "Don't make a sound or you know how much worse his punishment will be."

The red light of the camcorder blinks on, its soulless glass eye indifferent to my suffering as it curates every expression on my bruised and swollen face. My breathing quickens. My heart thunders. I try to focus on those three little letters beneath the flashing red glow. I pour every drop of my consciousness into them. *Rec. Rec. Rec.*

The knife slips between my ribs.

I don't make a sound. Not as the blade slices through every filament of muscle and flesh. Not as it pierces my lung. Not as this man slides it in a slow procession to bury the steel to the hilt. I swallow every desperate urge to scream and beg, to plead for the pain to stop. I will not let Daddy down like I just did Mom.

But my dad, he can't stop himself from fighting for me.

For every scream I swallow, my dad begs around his gag. He thrashes against his bonds. His muffled words are a desperate chant. *Please, not my girl.* Over and over, his pleas repeat like flashes that echo the blinking red light of the camcorder. And when the second blade is sunk into my chest and the man sits back against his heels to record the handle quivering next to its twin, I look at my dad, his tears so much worse than my own.

The red light blinks out.

The scent of blood and cheap drugstore body spray floods the hot air between us as the man leans close to my ear. I struggle to trap my silence in the heat filling my throat. "You did so well, baby," he whispers, his breath and his words a sticky film that layers over my muddled senses. "Such a brave girl to stay so quiet." Stubble scrapes the angle of my jaw as the man drags his lips across my skin to press a kiss to my cheek.

The man's weight lifts from my body. I shake my head violently, my only sound the rumbling breath in my injured lung as I beg him with nothing more than a desperate, pleading look.

He smiles.

"Daddy though...he was not such a good boy," he whispers as he straddles my father's back. My dad struggles to buck him off and manages to unseat our assailant for just a moment. But that moment is nothing more than a breath of time, no longer than the beat of a heart.

The man whips a hammer free from a frayed leather loop on his belt.

It's this exact moment when I learn an important lesson, that time is so very cruel.

Time will slow at will, forcing you to remember every detail of something you would give anything to forget, like the worn patch of wood on the handle of a hammer, or the desperate cry of your father, or the shine of the tears in his eyes. It forces you to witness the flash of the living room lights on the burnished metal of the hammer's blunt head. You might not be able to remember the last time you told your parents you loved them, but time will be there to make sure you recall the sound of the sickening thud as the hammer strikes your father's temple, or the color of the blood that sprays across the cream carpet.

Time slows to ensure you never forget how powerless you truly are.

And I am utterly powerless. Powerless to do anything but to absorb every detail of the vicious assault until my mind finally starts to shut down.

The images and sounds blur and distort until a wave of cold air coats the sweat and blood on my skin. When my vision clears, it lands on the vacant expression on my father's dying face. There's a wet, rhythmic gurgling as my father's last breaths spasm in his chest, his severed tongue discarded on the carpet between us. But there's another sound, one on the other side of me, a choking, gasping plea beneath a menacing whisper.

"You are sloppy. An amateur. *Unworthy*. And this is *my* domain."

It takes a monumental effort, but I turn my head toward the sound.

My assailant is on his knees between my mother's body and mine. He struggles to pull a wire away from his neck. Another man is behind him, dressed in black, leather gloves tight against his knuckles as he pulls the wooden handles of a garrote back toward his chest.

He's beautiful. So beautiful. Older than me but still young, maybe mid-twenties. Dark hair, high cheekbones, a subtle smile on full lips as he watches his prey struggle in his grip. He's a fierce angel. Focused and determined. A savior, delivering the justice I can't.

He tightens the garrote further and whispers again to the man in his grip.

"Your bones will be nothing more than a substandard trophy on my wall, but I will take them all the same."

My assailant fights back harder at those words. The angel moves with him, a fluid grace inhabiting every mirrored motion. His sole attention is on the throat trapped in his unrelenting grip. He doesn't even seem to register my existence. It's like he doesn't hear my labored breathing or feel the weight of my watchful gaze.

He doesn't notice the tiny piece of paper that escapes from his pocket.

He doesn't see my bound hands creeping across the bloodied carpet to grab the fallen receipt.

He doesn't watch me read it, doesn't see me close my eyes to remember every detail. He doesn't know I drag it down to my side to put it in my pocket.

Arley's Campus Restaurant & Bar. Revery Hall University. Cash paid. Pellegrino. Chicken Caesar Salad. Cappuccino.

I close my eyes for what feels like only a moment, reciting those details over and over in my mind until they're burned into my brain.

When I open my eyes, my angel is gone. My assailant is gone. My father's severed tongue, the camcorder, the hammer, all gone. All that's left are the knives in my chest and my parents' cooling bodies on the floor. We've been discarded, left to chill in the draft from an open door or window somewhere in the house. But that kiss of cold air spurs me on, laying across my wounds like a whisper that tells me to keep going. Despite the pain and weakness and fear and despair, it pushes me to my hands and knees, demanding that I crawl across the broken glass to find my mother's phone. I drip a bloody trail from my mouth and wheeze past the pain of a collapsed lung and still the cold draft clings to me, imploring me to keep going.

"Kyrie."

That word is familiar enough to be real, and unfamiliar enough to drive a wedge between the past and the present.

I blink. My breath comes in rapid pants. A phantom pain sears my lung. I see the glass on the floor beneath my hands. One moment, my palms are on the carpet of my childhood home, the soft pile a caress between the sharp bite of pointed shards. But when I blink again, my palms are on the shining gray tile of my office. The only tether between the two worlds is the sound of my distressed exhalations and the shimmer of shattered glass.

"Kyrie...You can let it go."

A hand wraps around my shoulder. The skin beneath my damp shirt relishes the cool touch. I'm sweat-soaked and shaking as though fevered. My head throbs with a steady hum as the past peels away and the present claws itself free of its suffocating grip.

"It's just a memory," Jack says, his voice quiet as his other hand curls around my wrist. His fingers rest over my hammering pulse. When I pry my gaze from the glass and look up, Jack's eyes shift from his watch to meet mine, his lips set in a grim line. "It's not real anymore."

I want to tell him he's wrong, that every memory leaves behind something real in its wake. Real scars. Real repercussions. But I don't have the energy to battle him right now.

I drop my focus to the glass on the floor, to the blood that seeps from beneath my right palm where it's pressed into the shards. When I close my eyes, Jack only leaves me a few shaky breaths before he lifts my wrist from beneath me and grips my bicep with his other hand, pulling me to my feet. Glass crunches beneath our shoes as he guides me to my desk, his touch a steady anchor that never lets me go, not even when he prompts me to lower into the chair.

When I'm settled, Jack kneels in front of me as he takes my bloody hand and turns it over to examine a jagged, deep cut on the pulp of my thumb. A crease appears between his brows in a flicker of movement that's gone by the time he's reaching for the box of tissues on my desk.

"This needs stitches," he says as he presses tissues to the wound. The muscle in his jaw tics when I shake my head. "It wasn't a question. It's a statement of fact."

"I can't go in," I reply in a whisper. Jack's eyes narrow when I shake my head for a second time. "It will happen again if I go to the hospital now. I can't."

Jack glances toward my office door, a thoughtful frown ghosting across his face before he lifts the soaked tissue to look at the cut. The frown deepens as though he's just confirmed his own assertion about the stitches and is dissatisfied with the result.

"Hold this and don't move," Jack says. His grip tightens around my injured hand until I press the tissue down on my own. He backs away as he rises, every movement a choreography of restraint, his assessing gaze penetrating my skin. When he's straightened to his full, commanding height a few feet away, he turns and leaves the room.

The silence that bears down on me in the buzzing aftermath of my flashback isn't frightening this time like it often is. I can't even hear Jack, wherever he's gone. But knowing he's nearby is surprisingly comforting. And if I had more willpower right now, I'd be punishing myself for feeling that way. I know I should be slinking off to find another way to close this cut up on my own, without Jack's unsolicited help.

I'm sure there are supplies in Brad's lab that I could use. Superglue maybe. He's always breaking his shit and trying to fix it.

But I don't move from my chair.

It's a few minutes before Jack enters my office from the shadows of the corridor, and even though he was just here, seeing him stride in with a bottle of iodine in one hand and medical supplies in the other ignites a long-forgotten ache in the core of my heart. It's not just the spray of dark stubble on the perfect angle of his jaw, or his full lips that often curve in the faintest smirk like a practiced mask. It's not the black suit that's tailored to fit his athletic frame, the top buttons of his black shirt open to reveal a glimpse of skin that I want to taste. It's knowing what he is, what he's capable of. What I know he's done, because I've seen it. It's the mystery of why he makes the choices he does. Why did he leave me alive the first time we met? Simply because he thought I would suffer and die anyway? Why does he seem to want to help me now, is it only because of the threats that I've made?

I've been watching Jack Sorensen since I was seventeen and as he slows to a halt and drops to a knee to take my injured hand, I feel like I don't know this man any better than I did when I started.

There are no words shared between us as Jack gathers more tissues and holds them beneath my bloody hand. He nudges my fingers away from where they press the wound closed and then he douses the cut with iodine. Jack glances up to watch my reaction to the sting of the undiluted brown liquid, but I deny him any whisper of pain in my expression. To my surprise, something about the way the tension lifts from his brow makes me think he's relieved.

"Are you sure you'd rather not go in to see a doctor?"

Jack asks as he shifts his attention back to my wound, his eyes a slash of dark silver in the dim light before they leave mine.

"I'm sure."

"Aren't you afraid I'll sew it in my initials?"

I pause a beat. "I am *now*."

Jack huffs a laugh. An actual, real, breath of a laugh. One that lights his skin with a flash of a vibrant smile, that crinkles the corners of his eyes. I've never made him laugh before, not in a way that was genuine at least.

He doesn't look up at me but I wish he would. I want to capture the nuances of his expression and study them, right down to every microscopic detail.

There are snips of comments I want to make that seem to catch on my tongue. *You wouldn't want to mark me as yours*, I think. I definitely should not want that either, despite the vibration in my chest that says otherwise. I swallow to dislodge it, and Jack glances up from where he's about to start the stitches, perhaps misreading my tension as nerves in anticipation of pain. "I'm surprised you would do this," I whisper instead of unleashing my darker thoughts, smothering a wince as the curved needle pierces my skin near the raw edge of the wound. "You could just leave me to my own devices."

"You did say your well-being was in my very best interests," Jack replies without looking up. "Perhaps I also take solace in the fact that mending living tissue is not really my specialty and I don't have any freezing to provide, so I know this will hurt."

"I guess that makes sense."

I swipe the mascara from beneath my eyes with the clean edge of the tissue crumpled in my free hand as Jack guides the needle through the other side of the wound and pulls the thread taut. His short, dark hair is swept away from his forehead but somehow looks more disheveled than usual. A faint crease lingers between his brows as he focuses on tying the knots of the first stitch. When he glances up from where he kneels before me, something darkens in his gaze. He looks across the desk and nods toward my bottle of water.

"Drink," Jack commands, and though my expression sours a little, I realize at that moment how thirsty I really am and I do as he says. He waits for me to finish a long sip before he pierces my skin for the second stitch, his interest flickering between the needle and my reaction. When he receives only defiant silence in reply, his brow furrows, and I can't tell if he's relieved or annoyed.

"Where did you learn to do this? Stitching wounds isn't really in the practical labs for forensic anthropologists," I ask as Jack pulls the thread through the raw edge of the cut and pierces the other side with the curved needle. He could be rough with it, or sloppy. But he's not. He's precise. He's quick, but in a way that lessens the pain, not exacerbates it.

"No, I didn't learn it in labs," Jack replies as he keeps his focus down on my hand. "Let's just say I didn't have your childhood. I picked up some necessary skills along the way."

Oh, I know all about his childhood. Or at least, I know enough to understand how he became the killer he is now. I think about that in silence as he ties the knots of the stitch, looping the black thread around the needle puller and closing the severed skin tight. He takes a fresh tissue and wipes the blood away with gentle strokes.

"Dreams?" Jack asks when the silence seems to stretch too long, even for him. His voice is deep and quiet. It's like shadows in a pine forest, somewhere safe to hide beneath the boughs. I tilt my head as I watch him, though I already know he won't meet my eyes. "Nightmares?" he adds when I don't respond.

Jack starts the third stitch in a mangled section of my wound. Pain slides down my throat as I swallow my surprise at his unexpected interest in me. I try to hold on to all the things he's done over the past three years to make me feel inferior. Unwanted. But when he holds my sticky, stained hand in his cool, steady one and he stitches me back together, I find it hard to recall all but the very worst moments with him. And I find I don't want to.

"Glass breaking," I say, my voice little more than a whisper. Jack says nothing, just continues drawing the thread through the tiny hole he's made in my flesh. "Red blinking lights. The smell of a hospital. Hammers. I really hate hammers. Cream-colored carpet. That one is inconvenient. It seems like such a simple thing. It's so common you'd think I'd become desensitized, but it's one of the worst...for me..."

The motion of Jack's hand slows to a stop and he meets my eyes. It feels like the whole world could crumble away and we would still be stitched together with an invisible thread, one hewn from secrets shared, from vulnerability, from the things we fear will weaken us unless we hold on, until the moment we let them go. And I know Jack could take these secrets of mine and forge them into the deadliest blade to cut me down. But the way he leans back just a little, the way his gaze drifts over my features with a crease between his brows, I know he won't.

"The lives you've taken, do they ever bother you?" he finally asks, his eyes latching on to mine.

"You mean, in this way? Where the past infiltrates the present?" Jack gives a single nod and I shake my head.

"Never. I guess because the power is in my grasp. The control is mine. And the things that happened to me, maybe I'll keep them from happening to someone else. I feel... I feel many things about the lives I take. But never regret. You?"

"No," he says, and it's a long moment before he drops his attention back to my wound. "I can't feel regret, Kyrie."

We say nothing more to one another as Jack finishes my stitches, twelve in total, dousing the cut with another splash of iodine before he bandages my hand. When he's done, he leans back, his attention shifting to my shirt. I look down and notice for the first time a smear of blood across the champagne silk right above where my scars lay hidden.

"I guess this one is destined for the trash," I say with a sigh as I take in the speckled dots and long slashes of blood and marks of drying sweat. When I look up, Jack's focus is on the window of my office that looks toward the labs. A muscle tics in his jaw as he frowns at Brad's workspace. We both know Brad keeps a few changes of clothes there for the days when he cycles into work.

"Wait here," Jack says, and I watch him rise and walk away.

But the lights don't turn on in Brad's lab. No lights turn on at all, in fact. It's just the dim emergency signs in the hallway, casting dark shadows beyond my door. And a few silent minutes later, Jack emerges from their depths, a bag of ice in one hand, a folded black shirt held aloft on his other palm. One of *his* shirts.

"Try not to shred it, would you? I like that one," Jack says as he nods to the shirt he lays on my desk. He bends to kneel before me once more, checking the bandage one final time before he places the ice against my hand.

"I won't shred it. No promises I won't bury someone in

it though. If you'd like to leave your business card in the front pocket, that would be most convenient."

I give Jack a faint smile that he meets with a dark look, but he's not fast enough to hide his grin when he glances away toward the door. When he finally meets my eyes, the levity in both our faces fades away, until we're simply watching another.

Jack reaches forward. His thumb brushes my cheek in a caress as light as a whisper across my skin. Those slate gray eyes follow the movement of his hand as it passes toward my lips before it drifts away.

And time is yet again so cruel, because Jack's touch is gone before I can sear it into memory, before I can be sure it was even real.

I watch as Jack strides away. But I call to him before he reaches the door.

"Jack."

He stops, his head bent. It angles toward the sound of my voice, but he doesn't turn around.

"Thank you."

He nods once, but he doesn't move, as though he's torn with the direction he should take. One of his hands folds into a fist and squeezes. It feels like it chokes my heart in its grip. And I know there's one thing I can give him in return, a repayment. Something I know he would want.

"Thunderdome. This doesn't change anything. As soon as you leave my office, it's back on."

The tension leaves Jack's fist. I can almost see it loosening from his shoulders, spiriting away like gas.

Jack nods once more, and then he's gone.

I leave him enough time to disappear from the building, and then I clean up the mess of glass and blood before I go home.

When I arrive at my office on Monday morning, a replacement for my broken Brentwood award waits on my desk.

There's no card, no note.

But this one is made of brass.

TEN

COLD KISS

H ad I known how pleasant the department would be without Brad, I'd have gotten rid of him a while ago.

Gossip floats through the air Thursday morning, the rumor mill still churning with news of an arrested coworker. Not only could Brad be implicated in several disappearances around the trinity college towns, but also murder. Arson might be tacked on to his charges too, since investigating authorities are speculating that Brad set fire to his home in order to destroy evidence of bodily remains.

He's since hired a pricy lawyer and gotten released on bail, on account of his pristine reputation, but the university thought it was better if he took an extended leave of absence until the debacle is settled and his name cleared.

I roll up my sleeves and power through a pile of tedious paperwork, feeling more at ease since I fed the urges. I'm not completely satisfied...but the recent kill was enough to suppress my more animalistic desires that have recently surfaced.

The only thing disturbing my inner peace right this minute is the FBI agent still lurking around. Eric Hayes should be focused on Brad and the pile of evidence I supplied in his house. Yet he's here, skulking the hallways, seemingly more invested asking around about Kyrie than Brad.

As if my thoughts conjure her, Kyrie walks past my office door. She doesn't stop to peek inside and annoy me like she typically does. She hasn't left me anymore presents in my lunches, either. Which raises more than a few red flags.

After the other night, when she broke her award and I stitched her wound, I've tried hard to enforce the same level of contempt for the woman who invaded my turf and threatened my carefully-secured world. But, whether it's the haze of a fresh kill or satisfaction over Brad, I find myself recalling the soft feel of her hand in mine, the way her intense, liquid blue eyes held my gaze, completely trusting, as I pierced her flesh with a needle.

She never flinched.

I push away from my desk and slide my sleeves up farther as I follow after her.

I stalk her until she reaches the cold room, then I grip her elbow and tow her inside, shutting the door behind us.

She says nothing for a solid three seconds as she simply stares at me, mouth pursed. Then she says, "You have a real disturbing thing for cold rooms."

I cross my arms. Mostly to keep from touching her. "The games are done. There's something else going on here," I say. "Something serious, and it has to do with you."

One of her eyebrows hikes in amusement. "I didn't tell you to set Brad's house on fire. Did you not think that would draw just a bit too much attention?"

Beneath her sharp sarcasm is a tremble of fear. She

brushes a loose strand of hair behind her ear, then glances around the room.

"Hayes isn't here for Brad." I narrow my gaze on her, move an inch closer. "He's not even working with the local authorities on the case. He was never here for any missing person case on Mason."

Kyrie exhales heavily. "Then what is it, Jack? Can you hurry up and tell me so I can get the hell out of here and get warm?" She rubs her arms.

I remain silent, the cold not bothering me.

She swipes at the unruly strand of hair again, and mutters a curse when the stitches on her hand snag in her hair. "Dammit," she says, bringing her palm up to inspect.

"Let me see." I reach for her hand, but she pulls back.

"I'm fine." The look in her wide gaze says otherwise.

Something is digging in deep beneath her typically unshakable surface.

She's rattled.

I grab her wrist and haul her toward me, then bring her hand up slowly so I can see the stitches. "Why don't you have cream on this?"

She shrugs. "I was in a hurry today."

I nod. "Hmm." I keep hold of her, reluctant to let her go as I press my fingers against the pulse point in her wrist, feeling her heart speed twice as fast as mine.

A wicked curve tips her lips as she gazes up at me through thick lashes. "So, Jack. Speaking of framing your good friend Brad for murder, did you have fun with Ryan?" She teases me with her sultry smirk. "He was kind of special to me, you know. I had plans for him."

A faint wisp of fire curls beneath my skin. I know what she's doing, trying to avoid the topic of Hayes by poking the monster to get a rise.

My cock answers the baiting call as she conjures images of the night I painted my cold room red with her victim's blood.

"How did you do it?" she probes, pushing in closer, her fingers lacing around mine. The feel of her abrasive stitches against my skin shreds a layer of my control. "Did you drug him first. Strap him to your table. Did you strangle him before you flayed the skin from his bones. Or did you—"

My fingers dig into the back of her hand in warning. "Stop, Kyrie."

Her face winces in pain, the sight stirs my blood. "I just want the visual," she says, breathy as I grip her tighter. Her lips tremble from the cold, and my cock throbs at the sight. "Least you can offer me after you stole my toy."

The red pool of blood stains my vision, and all I see is her, there, covered in sticky red, her eyes snapping open...

My jaw tightens. "You're playing with fire."

"Oh, I highly doubt that. Jack Sorensen could never get *hot*." Her leg slips between mine, her thigh grazes my cock. Her breath catches at the feel of my rock-hard erection. "You're too fucking cold—"

I trap her throat in a brutal clutch and force her back against the body locker. A sharp breath escapes her lips as I capture her mouth with mine.

One second of shock where her body goes rigid, then as I bite into the kiss with violent urgency, she moans and dissolves under the crazed demand. She kisses me back with an angry, desperate need to rival my own.

My hand locks tighter around her throat, savoring every sweep of her tongue over mine, the way the column of her throat strains enticingly against my palm.

I release her hand to greedily grip her blouse and yank the hem free of her tight pencil skirt. My hand plunders beneath her shirt as I take her mouth, kissing her deeper and reveling at the trace of blood that bleeds into the kiss.

I roam up her rib cage, fingers tracing the sexy curve of each of her bones, her skin soft and smooth. Bearing harder against her pelvis, I practically impale her with my cock, the fucker so goddamn raging to sink into her and discover how fucking tight her cunt can grip me.

As I sweep higher and skim my thumb over her nipple peaked against the thin material of her bra, she moans more urgently, the vibration along my palm heightening my need to hear her scream.

I break away to kiss her neck, teeth scraping her skin before I bite into her tender flesh. But it's not her sudden, restrained cry that freezes my blood and my hand. The rough, beveled feel of scar tissue beneath my fingers has my spine locking to pull me up straight.

I tower over her and stare down into her beautifully flushed face. "Who did this to you?" I demand.

Chest heaving, she blinks rapidly, then shakes her head against the body locker. "It was...an accident," she says, her voice breathy, clipped. "I was young."

I don't believe her. "An accident that causes you to spiral at the sight of broken glass?"

Her glare cuts through me. I've examined just about every injury and cause of death on the planet, and as I continue to probe the twin scars on her chest, I make out the distinct evidence of severe injuries caused by a very sharp object.

"Jack...?"

The tremble in her voice triggers a flash of memory, and suddenly I see Dr. Kyrie Roth in a whole new, illuminating light.

I remove my hand from her scars and blouse, then with

a hard swallow, I place a kiss to her forehead. So completely out of character, her gaze widens with worry.

"We should get out of here," I say, reaching down to situate the member of my body not yet receiving the message.

"All right. Sure." She nods and tucks her blouse into her skirt, then fixes her hair.

She turns to go, and I grab her wrist. "Leave for the day," I tell her.

"Is that an order, Jack?"

I nod once. "Stay away from Hayes."

Some unreadable expression flits across her face before she forces a bright smile. "I'm a big girl. I'll be fine."

She escapes then, and I'm left with the rioting thrum of my heart and the sweet taste of her mouth on mine. After enough time has passed, I exit the body cooler and head to my office, where I collect my satchel and suit jacket.

The need to fit the last piece of the puzzle in place is a compulsive force propelling me forward. I walk toward Kyrie's office, not sure how I feel about leaving her here with Hayes, but if I'm right...then I'll know exactly why he's here.

Kyrie doesn't look at me as I hover at her office door, and I know she's shaken. But not from the kiss. From the secret she's kept from me for far too long.

I drive straight home and go to my office. Behind a false bookshelf panel is the biometrically sealed door that leads to my personal cold room and study—my trophy room. I pass by the glass-encased bones, not stopping until I reach the storage shelving where I stuffed a box of items from ten years ago.

I dig out the near ancient camcorder, then retrieve a power adapter.

My leg bounces as I'm seated on the sofa and impatiently wait for the 8mm tape to rewind.

When the girl's face appears on the static-filled screen, I hit Pause on the device.

There, on the grainy screen, are the pale-blue eyes I've been obsessed with for the past three years. They're open and wide and there's no mistaking the terror held in their depths.

I press Play, and the sound of Kyrie's grated scream cracks through the small speakers.

The footage plays back the earlier events of a night where a serial killer stabbed a teenage girl during a family massacre.

And as I stare at the screen, I witness her die all over again.

Because that girl was dead. I watched her *die*.

I drag a hand down my face. "*Jeg forlod hende.*"

Setting the camcorder down, I bound up and head to the glass case. I unlock the door and select the fragile bone displayed in the middle of my other trophies.

The Silent Slayer's hyoid.

I run my finger over the smooth bone—a bone that doesn't need the connection of any other bone to exist within the skeletal framework. The innermost part of the bone contains a hollow cavity, where blood vessels course through every layer, carrying nutrients and oxygen.

Even though I've studied this particular bone the entirety of my career, I feel as if I'm seeing it for the first time.

No, the lone hyoid needs no other structure to exist. Yet it's reliant on the life-sustaining marrow for survival.

That night ten years ago, when I set out to extinguish another killer in my territory, I strangled that killer to death right next to his last victim—a girl with haunting pale-blue eyes; eyes I never once looked into until the moment she showed up at my university.

This entire time, she wasn't dead. She's not the dead one at all. She's been what's sustained me here.

She's the marrow.

She's *my* marrow.

Kyrie didn't start as a killer—she was made.

And I helped make her.

ELEVEN

WINTERS

KYRIE

By the time eight o'clock rolls around, my eyes feel like they're ready to melt out of my head. I've spent the morning in lectures, the afternoon grading essays, and the evening reviewing trail camera footage from two months ago of creatures big and small as they slowly dismantled one of the bodies in a wooded section of the Bass Research Fields. Sunny Bunny even makes an appearance, trotting off with an ulna to lay beneath the cover of a chokeberry bush, the bone gripped between her forepaws and her jaws crunching the curved trochlear notch. I smile as I rewind it and watch again. Many other animals would have gone for the femur to gnaw on the bulbous head, or the ribs which are easy to crack. But not Bunny.

"Of course you'd pick something a little bit awkward," I say to the screen. "I bet you just did it to be cute."

When the sting of her loss starts to burn in my chest, I shut my laptop, stretching before I rise to pack everything up. The only other person here tonight is Jack, his profile facing me as he studies something on the computer monitors in his lab. His focus is so consumed by whatever he's analyzing that I could probably just slip away unnoticed. In fact, I'm sure he'd be happier if I left without saying a word. It's not like he's ever appreciated any attempts at simple civility before. What he would likely hate the most is if I interrupted him with a cheery "goodnight".

I sling my bag over my shoulder, paste on my most saccharine, blinding smile and march my ass to the lab to deliver what will surely be the most bubbly goodbye that Jack Sorensen has ever received.

"I'm heading out, Jack. Have a super fantastic—"

"Dr. Roth," he interjects, his voice warm and almost... anxious. It's as though a quiet note of trepidation hangs in those three syllables. "Come in, please."

My smile crumbles. I don't move an inch.

I think I hear a quiet chuckle over the sound of quiet classical music playing from a speaker on his desk, but I'm not sure if I only imagined it. "I won't bite...this time..." Jack says, the barest hint of a smile ghosting across his lips as he recites my words back to me. I hesitate a heartbeat longer before taking a step across the threshold. Jack's gaze drops to my injury as he stands and slides his hands into his pockets. "Healing okay?"

I nod, taking a few steps further into the dimly lit lab. "I had a pretty good doctor. He didn't even sew his initials into it."

"He sounds very professional. And devastatingly handsome."

"He sure likes to think so."

Silence descends between us like a heavy curtain falling in the cool air. Maybe Jack is as weirded out as I am that he's talking, maybe even...was he just...*flirting?*...like a normal person.

"Tchaikovsky?" I ask as I nod toward the speaker.

There might be a flash of surprise in Jack's eyes, or maybe even embarrassment. It's not really the type of thing most ridiculously beautiful, thirty-four-year-old men typically listen to, but then...it's Jack.

"It helps me think."

"It's great," I say with a faint smile, lifting one shoulder as I take a tentative step closer. "I know it. The Spell, *Pas D'action*. From Sleeping Beauty." Jack's head tilts with an unvoiced question. "It became apparent by five years old that I would never be a ballerina, despite my mother's initial attempts. But we enjoyed going to watch together. Sleeping Beauty was our favorite ballet."

A crease appears between his brows as his eyes fall from mine, dipping down to my side before landing at my feet.

Jack clears his throat, slipping a hand down his tie. "I have something for you," he says, turning away to silence the music before sliding open a drawer in his desk. I bite down on the questions rattling around on my tongue and simply watch as he faces me with a small, decorative wooden box in his hand. His frown deepens for an instant, like maybe he's weighing whether or not to actually pass it to me, but his expression clears just as quickly and he extends his gift.

I set my bag down on a stainless-steel exam table and take the box, holding Jack's eyes for a moment before I release the brass clasp. When I lift the lid, it reveals a hyoid bone in a nest of black silk, meticulously cleaned and preserved, a fracture splitting the delicate left wing.

"Is the name Trevor Winters familiar to you?" Jack asks.

I shake my head, a surge of adrenaline blanketing my heart. The names of every man I've killed run through my head, but there was definitely no Trevor Winters.

I fucked up somehow.

Strangulation isn't my thing, so the fractured hyoid doesn't make sense. But maybe I've made a mistake, and of course Jack would dig until he found it, and he's about to shove his victory in my face.

"No," I reply, and I nearly snap the box shut and chuck it back to him when I glance up and really *look* at Jack. There's no smug, gloating grin, no triumphant gleam in his eyes. His expressions are often so subtle, and I've spent years observing them, but this is something I've never seen on his face. It looks like he's...worried. "No," I say again, softer this time. "That name doesn't ring any bells."

Jack nods as though he's not surprised, but that subtle anxiety still lingers in his eyes as they shift between mine. "Winters was a wanderer. He rarely stayed anywhere longer than a year. He thought highly of his intellect but never settled on anything long enough to prove it. He did a lot of odd jobs. Worked with his hands to make ends meet."

I look back down at the bone, shaking my head again as I try and fail to make these broken puzzle pieces fit together.

"You might have seen him in your neighborhood, nailing roof tiles. Painting a garage. Fixing a fence. You might never have noticed him. But he noticed you."

A chill sweeps through the backs of my arms and cascades down my spine. My lips part on a gasp as everything starts to click into place.

"Winters liked to frequent a downtown bar that was popular with college kids," Jack says. "The Scotsman. I was there, waiting, but I didn't see him. When I decided to give up for the night, I saw his truck drive by. He had a passenger but I couldn't see who. It was too dark. But it was you, wasn't it."

I nod, though I can't recall that part of the night. I remember sneaking into a bar with my friends just down the road from The Scotsman with a fake ID. Winters must have been there and slipped something into my drink, because I remember nothing of the journey home or entering my house.

I try to blink the sudden tears away. They refuse to evaporate. "My dad...he had a man fix the fence at the back by the alley... Dad would have recognized him when he brought me home. He must have let Winters in."

"Probably, yes."

The sound that escapes my control might be quiet, but it holds every facet of despair in its haunting notes.

But it's not just despair.

It's the rage of betrayal revealed.

I transfer the box to my left hand, curling my right in on itself, pressing my nails across my stitches to summon pain as I close my eyes. I remember the hospital, a place I hate, loathing even the faintest memories of the clinical walls and the IVs and the burn of my injuries and the crushing, consuming loss of every waking moment. But I go back. I go back to one simple moment, one little remark.

One from Agent Hayes to a police officer standing outside my room.

"...Just make sure you know who you're getting," he'd said to the officer who was talking about the new roof he was planning to have installed. "Don't trust any guy off the street, you know what I mean? No drifters—you never know who you could be letting into your house."

The cop wouldn't have known what Hayes really meant. I didn't either, not until this moment.

Hayes knew. He fucking *knew* what kind of man that they were looking for. I'm willing to bet Trevor Winters was even on his fucking radar. And whether it was incompetence, or laziness, or plain stupidity, he cost me my family. My *life*.

"No, Kyrie," Jack says, pulling me from my thoughts. I blink and look down as he uncurls my shaking hand where my nails have pressed crescents into my flesh. His voice is soft as he lays my fingers back on the side of the box. "You'll open your wound."

A chair materializes against the backs of my legs. Cool, steady fingers curl around my elbow and then I'm sitting down, the bone inside the box vibrating with the tremor in my hands. "This is him? The Silent Slayer?" I ask, sensing Jack descend to kneel in front of me through a watery haze, but I can't look at him.

"It is."

My lashes are damp, my lips trembling. This moment is nothing like I expected it to be. It's full of the kind of relief that feels cloaked by anxiety, because I don't know what's supposed to happen next. It's full of grief and loss that won't stay buried, no matter what I pile on top of the grave I try to keep them in. And it's full of the darkest shade of rage, the kind that churns like a molten core, an incendiary begging to burn the world to ash.

"I hadn't been able to pin down his residence," Jack continues. "He was shifting constantly between motels or boarding houses. But I knew there were a few neighborhoods where he was doing some work, so when I saw him drive by and knew I couldn't catch up with him, I went looking. Eventually, I found his truck parked in the alley at the back of your house."

We both know what happened after that.

And now, Jack finally understands. The night he hunted and killed the Silent Slayer was the pivotal moment when our lives became stitched together, two halves of a raw wound that might never heal.

My fingers trace the curved, delicate bone. Part of me wants to bend it until a satisfying snap cuts through the chill in the air. But that's why this gift is so precious to me. It's another little piece of power clawed back from that demon still clinging to my memories, forever embedded in my darkest shadows. I could snap it in half, if I wanted to. Or maybe it's enough just knowing that its fate from this moment on belongs only to me.

"Isobel Clark. That's your real name," Jack says, stealing me from the memories this tiny bone has unlocked.

"It was. Isobel Kyrie Clark. But that girl doesn't exist anymore."

The weight of Jack's gaze feels so heavy on my skin, but I'm still riveted to the box in my hands, even when Jack reaches forward and gently closes the lid. "Why didn't you tell me?" he asks, and I cackle an unexpected laugh at his earnest question.

"*Tell you?* Tell you how, exactly?" I look up from the box when Jack's only reply is silence, a muscle jumping in his jaw as I raise a brow in challenge. A kernel of rage bubbles through the thin crust of my other emotions, rising from a place where it never dims or dies. "No really, Jack... how would I say that? *'Oh hello, Mr. Important Serial Killer Man, I've been stalking you for literally years and you've never noticed, but you saved me from the Silent Slayer and by the way, I also enjoy killing people, pleased to meet you. We have so much in common, want to hang out?'* Is that how it would go? How many seconds do you think it would have taken for you to kill me had I said that?"

"Zero, Kyrie. I—"

"Agreed. *Exactly zero seconds*, because you despised me from the first moment we met in your shitty old lab."

"That's not—"

"You sent Hugh a detailed process by which he should remove me from the department and suggested multiple alternative candidates he should replace me with. You used the word 'furthermore' *six times* in that lengthy email, Jack. 'Furthermore, Kyrie Roth has not accrued sufficient years of field experience to assume a position of this magnitude.'"

"How did you—"

"Or what about the time you claimed I incorrectly recalibrated the settings on the CRYO freezer and you lost all your tissue samples? You asked Hugh why he would hire someone who couldn't program something as simple as a freezer and asked to see my university transcripts. *For all three of my degrees.*"

"I didn't—"

"It wasn't even my fucking fault, of course. It never is. You know why? Because I fucking *idolized* you and I never would have jeopardized your work. It shocked literally *no one* when it turned out to be Madeleine's fault. And even after she told you, you still never apologized to *me*."

"Kyrie—"

"You *hate* me, Jack. And I've been bitten enough times by you now that I'm not very fond of you anymore either, so just because you finally put it all together, it doesn't change anything. You're only being nice to me now because you figure you can fucking dickmatize me into winning Thunderdome and then you'll finally be rid of me, just like you always wanted. Well, let me tell you something, Dr. Sorensen—"

Jack's cool palm is fixed to my mouth before I can ever finish my sentence.

"Stop. Talking," he says, and though I give him my most lethal glare, it only lands on the top of his head where it's bent over my lap, his forehead nearly resting on my knees as his free hand brackets my forearm. The unexpected intimacy of this sudden contact is the only thing that keeps me shocked enough to not wrestle my mouth free. "Jesus Christ," Jack whispers, looking like he's just run a race and lost miserably, his shoulders slumped and each breath noticeable. He gives a little shake of his head. "You are the most mercurial person I have ever met. One moment you're in tears and the next you're running two hundred miles an hour in the opposite direction without a map or a fucking clue. I don't even know where to start."

I growl unintelligible insults that are lost to the palm clamped against my mouth.

"No. Not a fucking chance," he says, shaking his head in denial with more certainty and determination than a moment ago. He meets my eyes with a darkened, haunted gaze. "First of all, I didn't save you. I *left* you." I growl again and try to pull Jack's hand free of my lips to tell him that's not up for him to decide, but I don't manage to dislodge him. His grip on my forearm tightens as he presses it to the armrest. "You were barely breathing. You had two knives buried in your chest. Your face was a swollen, bloody mess. You didn't wake up, you didn't look at me. If you had opened your eyes just once that first time, I would have recognized you the moment you walked into the lab."

I roll my eyes in my best *"As if, we both know you would have murdered me to protect yourself if you'd caught me watching"* look before turning my glare to a darkened corner of the room.

"Also, it's *zero seconds* because I would not have killed you if you'd told me who you were."

I bark an incredulous laugh against his palm.

"Third, I did believe you needed more field experience. I didn't realize you had taken every summer to do exactly that during your entire student career, which is what Hugh responded with. And yes, I'm aware that the CRYO freezer incident was an asshole move. One among many."

"*Still not an apology,*" I shoot back with nothing more than a muffled mumble and a cutting glare.

"I'm also not trying to *dickmatize* you out of your evidence. I'd think that would be obvious, as I'm giving you a bone from someone I killed," he says with a pointed glance to the box resting in my lap.

I huff.

And then we fall into the kind of silence that lurks in shadows, trapping secrets that just need a little hint of light to catch fire and burn.

I watch Jack and he watches me back, his palm still pressed against my lips and his hand across my forearm.

"Hayes is here for you. He knows you. He's the agent who worked on the Silent Slayer case, isn't he. And he's here to follow old threads."

I swallow, holding Jack's gaze as it darkens. I nod.

His eyes track across my face and when I tug on his wrist he finally lifts his hold from my mouth.

"If he'd done his job..." I whisper, my gaze dropping to the box in my hands. If Hayes had done his job, would I be a different person? Would I have a different life? Of course. If Hayes hadn't fucked up, I'd have my family. I wouldn't be alone. I wouldn't be struggling to let go of the one person I've tied myself to, the one who might want to kiss me in a fleeting moment of weakness and kill me in every other steady heartbeat.

"I was about to leave West Paine. I wanted to adhere to

my plans, and then you showed up," Jack says before I have a chance to speak, his voice low and dark. "I've stayed longer than I should have. But I couldn't go until you left first."

"That makes no fucking sense. I've seen your contract, you can leave whenever you—"

"I've tried to force you out. Naturally, you're not only the most mercurial person I've ever met, but the most stubborn as well. All I've managed to accomplish is to make myself suffer."

A derisive laugh passes my lips. "That admission brings me no small measure of happiness."

"But I have had enough. I'm done denying myself what I want."

I swallow the heartbeat that seems to jump into my throat. "You're bowing out and leaving West Paine?" I ask, trying to not let a sudden swell of hurt and disappointment color my words, even though I feel its warmth creep into my cheeks despite my best effort to subdue it. Jack makes no move to answer my question. He only watches me with sharpened scrutiny as I tilt my chin up. "Well... good. We're finally on the same page about something."

Jack presses in closer, enough that I notice the warmth of his chest against my legs. I could count every shade of gray in his eyes as they remain unerringly fixed to mine. "I can assure you, we are not on the same page. But we will be."

For a moment that lingers, I feel every beat of my heart. I could lean a little forward and inhale his scent. Maybe I do.

And then Jack's subtle warmth and his glacial gaze are gone, the temperature of the room plummeting as he heads toward his monitors, tossing a dark look over his shoulder as he goes. "Get some rest, Dr. Roth. You're going to need it."

It takes me a moment to move, but when I do, I leave without another word, the sound of Tchaikovsky resuming to follow me as I near the exit. The music clings to my thoughts as I drive home, a wraith that haunts the deep shadows of my bedroom.

And rest is exactly what I do not get.

I roll in my sheets, tangling my legs in their constrictive grip until I kick them off. It's not just my boiling rage at Hayes that has me fevered as I imagine every manner of death and torture I could mete out with my bare hands. It's not just revenge that keeps me up. It's desire too. A deep need that burns like flame in my chest. It's *Jack*.

Every word Jack has said these last few days replays in my mind only to unravel into endless possibilities. Conversations I wish we could have played out to a thousand conclusions. But even worse than his words is his touch. His kiss is seared deep into my marrow. He claimed my mouth like a man starved of light and hope. His touch was a reverential progression of worship across my flesh and bone. He gripped my throat only to let me go, pressing his mouth to my neck.

If I want to hurt you, I will.

But he hasn't.

At one point in the night, I slide my hand into my sleep shorts, circling my clit, hoping to alleviate some of this torsional need that fills my core and twists it in knots. But I give up after only a few short moments. I don't want *me*. I don't want my imagination. I want *him*. And the harder I try to convince myself that I shouldn't just makes me want him that much more.

I manage at least a little sleep, eventually. But it's not

enough, and I wake before dawn when the bedroom is still black with shadows. Cornetto long gave up on the bed with my restless turning and rises from his seldom-used dog mat when I pad a defeated path to the kitchen. I catch up on the news, social media, texts and emails, the usual Saturday morning activities as I savor my extra-large mug of coffee. Shortly after sunrise, I'm on the snakelike path that follows the river, Cornetto trotting by my side as we trace the meanderings of the slow, gray current. We run our usual loop that takes about an hour and a half, and we walk the last few blocks to the house in a cool-down.

When I round the corner to see Hayes's silver Honda Accord parked along the curb bordering my front lawn, my first thought is an unexpected one.

Text Jack.

I pocket my AirPods as Hayes opens the driver's side door and steps out of the vehicle, and thoughts of Jack are lost to the cacophony of Cornetto's bark. Hayes casts a nervous glance at my dog as he takes a few cautious steps from his car. I could silence Cornetto with a single word, but I don't, not even when I close the space between me and the grizzled agent to stop a few feet away.

"Hello, Isobel," he says with a faint smile.

It takes great effort not to grind my molars. "Kyrie."

"Right. Of course. Kyrie." The tension in our silence is worsened by the low growl that rumbles from Cornetto's throat. "Mind if we chat for a few minutes inside?"

"Sure," I say with a single nod. "Come in."

I give Hayes a wide berth as Cornetto strains against his leash to keep between me and the agent, nearly losing his shit when he realizes the unknown man is coming into our domain. I give him the command to break in a firm voice once we're inside, and Cornetto quiets but keeps his eyes on

Hayes as I lead us deeper into the house, motioning for Hayes to sit at the dining table while I make a pot of coffee. My phone taunts me on the granite countertop of the island as I pull two mugs out of the cupboard. I'm sure replying to Jack's pawn and skull emojis with an eye roll and a police officer would send him into a meltdown, but I have a feeling he'd be on my doorstep within minutes. Something about that is both worrisome and exhilarating.

"Nice husky," Hayes says when I bring the coffees through to the dining room. Cornetto sits within striking distance, his eyes following Hayes's hand as he reaches for the mug I pass over.

"Elkhound," I correct with a brittle smile.

"Ah. They're used for big game hunting, aren't they?"

His nonchalant tone is too forced. He already knew it was an Elkhound. With the comment about big game, he knows I still hunt. That I have guns in the house.

He's been keeping tabs on me.

"Yes. And guarding too. But you didn't come to talk dogs," I say as I lean back in my chair and drag my mug across the table, raising it to my lips to take a loud sip for no other purpose than to be a little irritating. "What can I do for you, Mr. Hayes?"

"I wanted to get your thoughts on Dr. Brad Thompson."

"What about him specifically?"

"Well, for one, he stated that he was with you on the night that Mason Dumont was last seen. Is that true?"

I narrow my eyes, keeping careful hold of every micro-expression that indicates truthfulness. "It's true that I went to his place after the Brentwood Award Gala and fell asleep before midnight. Brad was awake when I woke at seven-thirty, dressed for work and making toaster strudel for breakfast." I crinkle my nose and then shrug. "What he did between midnight and seven-thirty, and then after I left to my place at eight, I have no idea. I'm a heavy sleeper."

Hayes takes a cheap pen and his ragged notebook from his jacket, turning it to a fresh page to jot down some notes.

"Did he ever raise concerns to you about the body donation program at the Bass Fields?"

"Yes," I say, sure that he already knows.

"Did that concern you?"

I huff a derisive laugh and roll my eyes. "No. He had a handful of grad students and Madeleine working on the records. It should come as no surprise that anything she touched would be fucked up. Hasn't anyone told you about the CRYO freezer incident?"

Hayes just gives a thoughtful 'hmm' as he writes a brief line, and though I try to make out the wording, I can't manage to decipher his scribbled cursive.

"What about Dr. Sorensen?"

So this is the real reason he's here. With only three questions about Brad, there's no way that Dr. Thompson is the subject of his interest.

Even though I suspected he would get to Jack, it still takes great effort to keep my expressions neutral, my voice treading a careful line of boredom and helpfulness. "What about him?"

"You don't seem to think highly of him."

"You're mistaken. I do think highly of him. I just don't like him. Sometimes."

"Why not?"

I choose my words carefully, trying to see the world through the eyes of someone searching for the signs of a serial murderer. "He can be arrogant. Not an uncommon trait for men in academia, I'm afraid."

"Do you know anything about Dr. Sorensen's where-abouts on Thursday night when Dr. Thompson's house was set ablaze?"

"Yes, actually. He was at the lab, with me," I say. Hayes darts a skeptical glance my way before returning his attention to his notes, and I have the urge to rip his notebook from his grasp and shove it down his fucking throat. I barely manage to resist folding my hands into fists. "I dropped my Brentwood Award and cut myself. Jack stitched it for me." I turn my palm to face him, the neat stitches bracketing the jagged red line across the base of my thumb. "I...couldn't go into the hospital. It's too...much. Jack took care of it instead, then replaced my award. It was very thoughtful of him, actually. I'm sure if you asked, he would give you proof."

Hayes's lips turn down in a frown as he scribbles across the page with more concentration than before, as though his earlier notes were just for show and these are real. My heart turns over a heavy beat as adrenaline floods my veins. I raise my mug to my lips with both hands to hide the deep, slow breaths I take to combat its effects.

"What is this about, Mr. Hayes?"

Hayes regards me for a long moment, his eyes softening with a fatherly kind of affection. Maybe it's just pity. Maybe even remorse. "You can call me Eric."

I give him a nod.

"I believe the Silent Slayer is still active," he says. I try to look alarmed, then confused, then worried, my mouth popping open as I set my mug down with a manufactured tremor in my hand. "It's very uncommon for serial killers to stop hunting permanently. They may take time between killings, sometimes even years, but the urge doesn't disappear forever. It's possible that the Slayer changed his MO after your confrontation. And I think he could be in the area."

"And what...you think he might recognize me?"

Hayes lays a hand on mine, and I pour all my effort into turning my rage at his touch into a mask of distress.

"I think he might have known you're here all along."

TWELVE

TWENTY-FIFTH FLOOR

KYRIE

A cool touch trails down every ridge of my spine, as though the person behind it relishes the quality of bone beneath my skin.

My back tenses. My exposed skin pebbles. Electricity spins in my core, my heart stuttering with the charge surging through its chambers. The music of the club seems to slip beneath the veil of my pulse. I barely resist a shiver as those fingers trace to the bottom of my backless dress before gliding up again with the lightest caress.

The scent of vetiver drifts around me in a cold embrace.

"Blonde is not your color, Dr. Roth," a voice whispers close to my ear, stirring strands of my wig to tickle my neck.

"But they say we have more fun, and I'm looking for the very best of times tonight," I reply, my sly smile spreading at the tension I feel in the palm that splays between my shoulder blades. "Besides, my name is not Dr. Roth."

A familiar hand appears from over my left shoulder to top up my glass of wine from the bottle resting before me. "Well, that I already knew."

"My name is Bethany," I say, gesturing toward the empty chair across from me. "Care to sit?"

"Won't that inhibit your...fun?"

"Isn't that what you want?"

"Perhaps," Jack says as he walks around the high-top table and sinks into the chair to level me with a piercing glare as he takes a sip of his whisky. After two glasses of wine and a spilled history between us, it physically pains me to look at Jack, with all his cold, dark beauty and his black suit and those silver eyes that flay me open to hunt down every hidden weakness. I swallow another mouthful of Shiraz, hoping it will drown my feelings into lifeless indifference, though I already know it won't work. "You said your wellness is in my best interest, and in case you haven't heard, there appears to be a serial killer on the loose."

My gaze drops to the void between us, the reminder of his motivations dampening any static lingering in my veins. "Right...that's a memo I seem to miss regularly."

"Isobel—"

"Do *not*, Jack," I hiss, my free hand gripping the edge of the table as I lean forward. The unexpected burn of tears stings my eyes at the sound of that name falling from Jack's lips, pulling my scars taut. "Do not *ever*. I am not Isobel. I told you this. That girl is already dead."

Jack holds my vicious stare. I blink the glassy sheen away. Nothing about him changes in his observation of my swirling distress.

I knock back the rest of my wine and place the glass down on the tablecloth with a dull thud. "Well, congratulations are in order, Jack. You've been in my line of sight for all of thirty seconds and you've already ruined my evening. A new record," I snap, whipping my sparkling clutch from the table as I move to stand.

Jack's hand darts out and encircles my wrist in a steadying grip. He's careful not to touch the stitches embedded in my skin across the healing wound.

"I'm sorry," he says, as though he's never put those two words together and is just as surprised as I am that they could exit his mouth. "Sit."

I don't make a move.

"Please."

I lower myself onto the plush seat with a slow descent, Jack's hand unfurling from my wrist only once I'm sitting. We regard one another in tense silence until a loud group passes too close to our table for his liking judging by his cold stare, their proximity breaking the spell between us.

"How do you know Hayes hasn't followed you here?" Jack asks when he turns his scrutinous attention back to me.

"Because Hayes couldn't find his way out of a paper bag."

Jack snorts a laugh and takes a sip of his drink, and I savor the glimpse of his fleeting grin at my words. "Even so, I followed you here undetected."

"Did you though?" My grin widens as Jack flashes me a vicious glare. I lean forward and clear my throat to deliver my best stage whisper. "A black BMW XM is not really the height of ambiguity, Jack. In the game of who is the most lethal, you lose points for hubris."

"Just as easily you will lose points for underestimating an opponent. I should know," Jack says as his gaze leaves mine to sweep across the room. His jaw tics as though he's trying to hide a smile, but it quickly fades. "Hayes... he's not so easily fooled."

"So I've come to understand. He came by my house earlier."

That gets Jack's undivided attention. His gaze snaps back to mine and burns with molten fury. "When? Why?"

"Ten o'clock. He was waiting in front of my house when I got back from a run with Cornetto."

Jack's eyes narrow.

"My dog." Jack's head tilts and I roll my eyes. "You should really know the vitals of your opponent, Jack. Large, fur-covered mammal? Cornetto...? *Christ*. Points lost for critical details missed."

I swear I see a hint of a blush on Jack's cheeks. "I knew you had a dog."

"Did you know what his name was?"

"...No."

"Minus five points."

Jack lets out an exasperated sigh at my brilliant, cunning smile. "*Hayes,* Dr. Roth. What did he want."

"Bethany. Minus two more points for not sticking to my cover," I reply, managing to subvert Jack's growing irritation by diving into the information he wants before he can draw his next breath. "He wanted to have a little catch up, dredge up some old history. He told me he believes the Slayer is still active but that he's changed his process. He doesn't believe Brad is to blame for the body in his basement. He believes the fire was set by someone else. He's convinced the Silent Slayer is involved."

Jack's lips tense into a grim line. "I don't think he's as hapless as he first appears. I don't like him."

"You don't like anyone."

"That's not—"

"Well, aside from yourself. You like yourself. A lot."

I beam a bright smile when the silver in Jack's eyes slashes me with menace, though his ire doesn't last. He's too curious to let his irritation get the better of him for long.

"Who are you after tonight?" he asks as he refills my glass of wine. I rush to bury the intrusive thought that begs me to say *you*.

"Someone who exceeds my criteria," I reply, my voice thinning with distraction as I glance across the motion of bodies on the dance floor. "His name is Sebastian. He's been banned from a few local strip clubs, gotten grabby with the girls when he's drunk and high. There was an assault case against him three years ago but it was dropped."

My gaze pins to my target in the distance, a shorter man than Jack by a few inches but broad, powerful. Sebastian can pass for handsome until you look too close. He's only twenty-four but looks older with his slicked-back blonde hair and the early signs of bad decisions.

"He's probably not got anything of value to you," I mutter as I follow Sebastian's progress through the lace of laser lights blanketing the dancers. I know Jack has strict criteria for the bones he chooses to pry from his victims, and though I don't know what they are, I doubt that Sebastian would meet Jack's discerning tastes. I peel my gaze away from my prey. "To be honest, I'm surprised you'd follow me."

Jack lifts one shoulder, feigning disinterest, though his gaze is too cutting for casual curiosity. "I had a gut feeling you were up to something peculiar when you went to Parkside Place. Do you have a condo in the building?"

"I did, but I guess I'll have to sell it now. I liked that condo."

"I already know where you live."

"Sure, but I don't need you finding all my little lairs. I'm going to have to give another one up tonight since you'll be coming with me," I say as my attention shifts to the dance floor. My intended prey slides through the crowd toward the bar, swaggering through the swarm of bodies with his slick suit and his coke-fueled arrogance. I sweep my clutch from the table as I rise.

"Who says I'll be joining you?" Jack says, defiance heavy in his voice as he leans back in his chair with his whisky in hand, the round ball of ice clinking against its glass cage.

I'm the one who shrugs with feigned disinterest this time, and though I feel the bitter sting of disappointment, I've got enough practice to know it won't show on my face. When it comes to Jack Sorensen, disappointment is something I've grown accustomed to. "Suit yourself," I say, recalculating my next moves to lure in my target now that Jack is bowing out of the game. "I suppose this is a good time to tell you that Sebastian Modeo is Anna Modeo's younger brother, and she was murdered by the Silent Slayer twelve years ago. If Hayes believes the Slayer is still active, perhaps we should give him a reason to follow a dead-end trail that leads away from Westview. But don't worry, I'll tell you all about my fun evening in extensive, gory detail." I clink Jack's glass with mine as I stop at his side, downing my drink before leaving it behind. "Cheers. Have a great night, Jack."

"Bethany," he says with a single nod. Jack doesn't look up, doesn't shift his relaxed stance. But I think I catch a glimpse of his fingers tightening on his glass before I turn away.

I slip into the growing crowd as I head for the dance floor. That ember of disappointment dims a little as I near my mark, and I give Sebastian a coy smile as I pass in front of where he stands in the short line for the bar. He returns my grin with one that's much more lecherous, running a thumb over his bottom lip as he follows my path into the dancers. I keep hold of his gaze over my shoulder for a few steps, brightening my smile like an invitation to follow. I don't watch to see if he does, but I know Sebastian Modeo, even though he doesn't know me. I know all his next moves before he does.

I weave just far enough into the throng that Sebastian will easily find me, allowing myself to be absorbed by the music and shadows and bodies and shifting lights. The rhythm creeps into my chest, curling around my veins. My muscles loosen. The base of my spine unlocks. I move with the people around me and they welcome me as though I'm part of their circles, even though I'm the death in their midst. When the DJ blends one song into another and shifts the intensity to a driving beat, I raise a hand like everyone else, closing my eyes as my movement settles into the percussive hum.

When I open them, Jack is there with an expression on his face I've never seen, some kind of fury interwoven with a deep, cutting need, a desire that carves a path into my chest until it's slashing at my crumbling walls.

I try to smile in triumph, hoping to cover the turbulent swirl of emotion embedded in my heart. The way his attention drops to my lips and his eyes seem to brighten with intensity in the dim light makes me think I'm unsuccessful. "Oh good," I say, losing my breath as Jack takes a step closer and his hand curls around my waist, his fingertips cool on the bare skin of my back. "There's only one thing Sebastian likes more than a blonde with a low-backed dress."

"And what's that?" Jack asks as his fingers press harder to my skin, prompting me closer. His eyes are soldered to my lips, their silver flecks lost in the darkness that surrounds us, though I still feel the weight of his gaze.

"Watching. He's a voyeur. I was going to have to lure

him away with a lie, like a roommate looking for some group fun. If you're hoping this little display will put a stop to my clandestine activities tonight so you can catch him your-self," I say, giving a pointed look to the other hand Jack glides up my bare shoulder as it climbs toward my neck, "you would be wrong."

Jack's palm stops on my throat. It captures every beat of my quickening heart. His thumb glides across my neck, tracing the line where my hyoid lays hidden beneath my burning flesh. I think for a moment he might back away, but he doesn't.

Jack's hand at my waist slides across my dress until it lays a cooling cloak against my exposed back, pulling me closer. I place my palm on his chest, my fingers curling into the black fabric. I should be pushing away. I should fight back against this magnetic force. But it's like trying to think your way free of gravity, or to stand unmoving in the swell of a tsunami.

Vetiver. Flashing lights. The pounding beat, like I'm living in the chamber of a giant heart. My body is flush against Jack's, every cell within me an inferno. Time slows. I'm powerless. And I'm exactly where I want and fear to be.

"*Lille mejer*," Jack whispers into my ear. My eyes drift closed. My head tilts to the side as his lips graze the shell of my ear. Two little words and I don't even know what they mean, but they're like a spell, an elixir that drowns me. "I'm not here to claim anyone but you."

Jack's cheek grazes mine as he pulls away just enough to meet my eyes. A slash of light illuminates his face for an instant that sears his beauty into memory.

And then his lips are pressed to mine.

It's warm, alive. Electric. Like only the thinnest threads of restraint hold him back from taking every piece of me, until he's consumed my very soul. My lips part and his tongue enters my mouth, not exploring but claiming, just like he promised, my pulse surging in answer against the warmth of his hand. And I want it to never end. I want time to die, so I can feel the beautiful torture of this torrent forever. Anger and desire. Fear and relief. A kind of hunger that will never be sated, that will burn in my heart as an undying ember.

I want this. I want this so badly that the desire twists in my belly like a serpent of fire.

But I can't have it.

Because I can't trust Jack. I know it. He's only doing this to crush my crumbling walls so he can find a way free of the threats I'm dangling over his head. And his insatiable curiosity compels him to figure out how I could have slipped past his defenses. That has to be what this is. He wants to find my weaknesses and crush me with them.

And what better way to destroy a person than to fill their heart and then crack it in half.

I loosen my grip on Jack's shirt, trying to force myself to cling to my memories of pain. Every cruel word. Every time he told me I didn't deserve what I've earned. Every time he made me feel unworthy, or unappreciated. My mind settles on the image of Jack standing at the back of the gala, nothing more than an indifferent spectator while a pit of anger and hurt burned a hole in my guts. I remember cutting his name from my tongue as I held up my Brentwood award. I try to forget that it was once made of glass.

I let go of Jack's shirt. His hand lifts from my throat as his lips part from mine.

"Hey... Sebastian, right?" Jack says, turning his attention away from me with an easy grin as he reaches out his right hand. Sebastian is next to us, smoothing a moment of puzzlement beneath a slick veneer. "I'm Adam. We met at Velvet Lounge. Remember? Such an epic night, but I think I forgot half of it."

Effortless.

I feel like I'm still lingering in his kiss while I watch Jack lure in my victim with a handful of threads and a counterfeit smile.

That's how easily he will destroy you and leave you for dead.

Sebastian grips Jack's offered hand, his smile growing more relaxed despite his ongoing struggle to remember their first meeting. "Yeah, Adam, of course. Do you know—"

"This is my...friend...Bethany," Jack says, interrupting Sebastian's attempt to put pieces together that will never fit. There's a note hanging in this introduction, one that says I'm an easy score. That hurt I was searching for isn't too hard to find.

"Hi," I say, putting more effort into my fraudulent smile as I extend my hand. I take a step toward Sebastian, close enough that Jack could drop his hand from my back, but he doesn't. "I saw you at the bar. Have we met before?"

Sebastian's gaze drags up from my chest to linger on my lips. "I don't think so. I'd remember that face."

I beam as though his complement is a revelation. And I keep beaming, at every idiotic joke and stupid thing Sebastian says as we worm our way into his trust. It doesn't take long. A few drinks, a few songs. By the time Jack suggests a party at my condo where there will be more women and free coke and full bottles, Sebastian doesn't even stop to think about it. He knocks back his drink and leads the way toward the door.

It isn't until we step into the elevator at the condo that I sense the first crack in Jack's perfect mask.

He takes my hand as soon as I've pressed the button for the twenty-fifth floor, and with a gentle tug, he guides me to his side, shielding me from Sebastian's eager gaze. I don't pick up any tension in his words as we make small talk about liquor, but I feel it in his fingers as they stay curled around mine. He doesn't let go when the doors open, not until I pull my hand free to find my keys in my clutch.

I step inside first, the apartment as empty and quiet as a tomb. Dim lights and the view of the city from a wall of windows illuminate the modern, open space.

"Make yourselves at home," I say as I head to the kitchen, placing my belongings on the counter to pull a set of glasses from a cupboard. "Round of drinks, boys?"

"Please. Whisky on ice," Jack replies, his voice deeper than I'm used to. I catch his eye for only a moment before he heads to the Bluetooth speaker on a side table to connect his phone and start a playlist.

"Great place, but where's the party?" Sebastian asks as he heads farther into the living room. Jack joins him, looking completely at ease as he shucks off his suit jacket and takes a seat on the gray sectional, spreading his arms across its back.

"I got a text from Amanda, they're on their way." I give him an easy smile as I bring the drinks to set them down on the coffee table. Sebastian's shoulders seem to loosen between my lies and the liquor I provide, and he takes a seat on the matching armchair across from Jack.

"Doesn't mean we can't start our own fun in the meantime," Jack says with a secret smile to Sebastian, reaching out a hand in a request for me to join him on the couch. "What do you say, sweetheart?"

I swallow a moment of discomfort, not for putting on a show, but for the clash between my real feelings and this fabricated moment. But I keep it trapped beneath a sweet smile as I place my hand in Jack's and he pulls me onto his lap, straddling his thighs.

Jack's hands glide up my back as he takes in every inch of my face. "Anything you don't want to do, tell me," he says for only me to hear. "Traffic lights. Understand?"

I watch him back for a moment before I nod, a little surprised. When I lean down to kiss him, the energy between us sparks with a different kind of heated anticipation. I place my hands on Jack's face and my tongue lavishes his mouth, dragging across his in long strokes, and when I pull back I take Jack's bottom lip with me in a bite. Jack moans as my teeth scrape across the sensitive flesh. He wraps his hands around my ass to tug me closer until I can feel his hard length between us.

"Isn't she gorgeous?" Jack asks between kisses as I grind on his cock. It strains against his pants and I press harder, not just for show, but to find friction for the throbbing ache in my clit.

"I bet she tastes as sweet as she looks. Maybe you should find out," Sebastian replies, and when Jack pulls away from my neck to meet my eyes, a ravenous beast is looking back at me.

We could have murdered Sebastian five times over already, but the truth is, I want more than just the anticipation of the kill. I can keep trying to push my feelings away, but I still want him. I want Jack touching me, kissing me. Worshiping me.

Devouring me.

I raise an eyebrow in a challenge.

In my next breath, Jack has me on my back, his palms a cool brand on my thighs as they slide beneath the hem of my dress. He pushes it up over my hips and his mouth is on my pussy before he's even tugged my panties down, his frustration with the thin fabric mounting until he whips a switchblade from his pocket and cuts them off in a single, fluid slice, much to Sebastian's delight. When they're gone, Jack parts my lips and drags his tongue across my entrance and he groans, groans right into the depths of me as though he's been starving for my taste.

"So sweet," Jack whispers against my clit before worshiping it with licks. One of his hands slides up my body to pull my dress down, exposing my breast to the cool air. A gasp leaves my lips as the tape tears from my nipple, its sting replaced with Jack's fingers as he teases it into a firm peak.

I'm burning. I'm desperate. I barely hold onto the sounds building in my throat as I raise my hips when Jack sucks on my clit, chasing my pleasure with his tongue. The more I try to keep from moaning, the more I fail, and when Jack pushes one finger into my pussy and then another to curl them in deep strokes that glide across my G-spot, I stop trying altogether.

"Your sounds are *mine*," Jack hisses, and before I realize what's happening, he's pushing my damp panties into my open mouth. I look down my body at the fierce command in Jack's eyes, whimpering at the erotic taste of my own arousal. He pushes the last of the fabric past my lips and holds my jaw shut with his thumb. "They are *only mine*. Now come on my fucking tongue and keep quiet."

Jack gives me a flash of a wicked grin.

And then he descends on my flesh.

He pumps his fingers and works my clit until my muscles are spasming, pulsing around him, sucking him in. Tiny bombs of sparks explode across my vision. Pleasure winds up my back and tightens it like a bow. My heart deafens every sound and thought and I don't even know if I obey his command. My eyes are still closed when Jack pulls the fabric from my mouth and kisses me, sharing my taste onto my tongue.

When the kiss slows and Jack pulls away, he stays hovering over me with one arm braced next to my head, the other hand working his belt buckle open.

"I've had a vasectomy," Jack says, keeping hold of my eyes as though we're the only two people left in the world. I hear each tooth of his zipper as it opens, each one like a tick of time. "I've been tested and I'm clean. But you should know that condoms can be...difficult for me. Are you comfortable with that?"

"Yes," I say, and though I want to ask what he means, I don't.

"Are you sure?" he asks. I nod until his eyebrows raise and I confirm it out loud. "This might feel...different."

I finally look down between us.

"Oh my God."

I take in the sight of Jack's erection, the base gripped in his hand, my orgasm-addled brain taking a moment to process what I see. There are pairs of studs trailing the length of the underside of his cock, with a Prince Albert piercing at the head, the titanium glinting in the dim light. Sebastian echoes my thoughts with sounds of surprise and words of approval. But it's like he doesn't exist to Jack.

"Are you *sure*."

Heat floods my core, my pussy begging before I have a chance to.

"Definitely. Very sure. Very, very sure."

Jack smiles, and it's so wicked, so sexy, that I almost come again before he's even touched my clit with the titanium ball at the head of his cock. A desperate sound of desire escapes my lips and Jack's eyes narrow in warning.

"What did I just say, *lille mejer*," he whispers.

"Don't worry, my studded buddy," Sebastian chimes, his words slurring as the sound of rustling fabric drifts toward me. I hear the clink of his belt buckle opening. "I have a way to keep her quiet."

I blink once at Jack, my face saying a thousand thoughts that I can't seem to shape into sounds. All of them orbit the word *fear*.

One moment, Jack is there, gliding his piercing across my sensitive nerves in a gentle tease.

The next he's gone, and the sound of a pained and panicked cry rises above the music.

"She deserved to have a little fun at your expense." Jack's voice is a rumble of menace toward our guest. I scramble to my feet just as Sebastian falls to his knees. "But if you'll excuse the pun, I draw the line at you thinking I'd *ever* let you touch her."

Jack holds my eyes as he makes another slash across Sebastian's throat with his switchblade, sending a spray of blood pulsing across the floor and his clothes.

Sebastian slams to his chest with his waning strength, his gurgling pleas quieting into stuttering exhalations.

Jack tosses the switchblade into the shadows and turns, his pants barely clinging to his hips and his erection still hard beneath his briefs. He pulls his blood-soaked shirt off and stalks toward me, lethal, consuming. Inescapable. When Jack reaches out a hand it's like a magnet, and I take it, following with sure steps as he leads me to the growing pool of blood and pulls me down with him to the floor.

Jack folds a bloody hand around my throat as he lowers my back into the sticky warmth. He tugs his pants and briefs down and enters me with a single stroke to the sound of my shameless moan.

"What did I tell you at the club, Kyrie?" Jack says, his

voice sweet and alluring, his eyes alight with silver sparks of fury. He slides out of my pussy, inch by inch, every round titanium ball causing a tingling swirl of growing desperation to ignite in my belly. *"What did I tell you?"* he repeats, squeezing a fraction tighter around my neck.

"Well-being... Best interests..." is all I can manage between panting breaths as I try not to come so soon with the deceptively gentle glide of his studded cock.

"No. Try again."

"Claim..."

"Good girl. That's right. I said I'm not here to claim anyone but you. So that is *exactly—*" a vicious thrust has me whimpering with pleasure— "what I am going to do. And any man who even imagines touching you will be sliced into ribbons of flesh—" another pounding thrust, the impending orgasm unstoppable in my core— "and then I will fuck you in a pool of blood while their heart still drums its final beats."

I moan as Jack grabs my thigh in a bruising grip, pulling my leg across his back so he can bury his cock deeper, the titanium ball at its head caressing my G-spot with every rocking stroke. "Not a disincentive...will find more prey," I grit out between a growing cadence of punishing thrusts.

"I never intended it to be."

My back squeaks through the cooling blood. Jack lets go of my throat to pull my wig and cap off, tossing them away across the floor. He grips my hair in a tight fist and wrenches my head back to expose my neck to his bites and kisses. And he fucks me. He fucks me like this is all he's ever wanted to do. Like he's taking something forbidden.

Like he craves me.

"If this plan works..." I say in a breathless voice as I drag my hand through the blood gathered on the floor. Jack leans back to study me, the deep thrusts continuing unabated, his expression one of furious need. I grin as I paint a diagonal smear over his heart, and then another to make an 'X'. "Then I will have won Thunderdome."

Jack scoffs, slowing the glide of his cock as he grips my hair and bands his arm around my back. He lifts me so that I'm straddling him as he kneels in the crimson pool. "In case you hadn't noticed, I'm the one who killed him."

"And as usual, that wouldn't have been possible without *me*." Jack opens his mouth to argue, but I seal his lips with a bloody finger. "Oh and by the way, if another woman even imagines touching *you*, I'll cut off her fucking hands and feed them to you. And then I'll take her precious hyoid and crush it, and I'll enjoy every fucking second of forcing you to watch as I flush it down the goddamn toilet. Understand, *petal?*"

I bat my lashes with an innocent pout and grip Jack's shoulder with one hand as I impale myself on his thick erection, spreading my hips wide to take him deeply with every thrust. I want him to fucking destroy me. To tear me apart, to fucking *annihilate* me because I will keep coming back, forever the unquenchable fire that clashes with his indestructible darkness.

Jack tightens his grip on my hair and his eyes go black when I lay my bloody finger on my tongue and seal my lips around it. He tilts my head back and nips at my neck, hard enough to mark me. His lips drink in the salted mist on my skin, carving a path down my throat, down my chest until he envelops my nipple, sucking on it hard, lavishing it with his tongue before releasing it with a scrape of his teeth that has me gasp.

"Diabolical... and duly noted," he says. "But there's only one woman's screams I care to hear." Jack bites the side of my breast just hard enough to coax a squeak past my lips and he chuckles. "*Lille mejer*, you can do better than that."

Jack slams us back down on the bloody floor but protects my head with his hand, the air whooshing from my lungs with the impact, my breath claimed by his waiting lips. I lose myself to the feeling of his skin and muscle beneath my fingers as they dig into his back, to the pain and pleasure of the bites he soothes with kisses, to the vicious thrusts that fill my aching pussy. His distinctive scent of vetiver floods my senses as I kiss his neck and taste his skin. When my channel tightens around his cock, Jack twists his hand in my hair, keeping me right where he wants me as he stares down into my face.

"So fucking beautiful," he whispers, and he watches every moment of the release that spins through my core. I come apart with my back lifting from the blood, chanting a hymn of Jack's name that sounds as much like ecstasy as it does a despairing cry. I swear I can feel every caress of metal in my pussy, every drop of heat as Jack spills into me with a roar. Every beat of his heart.

And we lay on the bloody tiles for a long while, as silent as the body in our midst, three souls claimed on the twenty-fifth floor.

THIRTEEN
STRIKE OF THE WHEEL
JACK

The difficulty with body disposal when you're trying to *not* dispose of a body is location selection.

Too obvious, and you look like an amateur. Too hidden...and it could take years to uncover.

And we need Sebastian Modeo discovered and connected to the Silent Slayer within days, not years.

I toss the shovel in the back of my Beamer, hand braced on the trunk as I halt at the inclusive *we* to my thoughts. I imagine Kyrie would point it out, one of her perfectly sculpted eyebrows raised in mock astonishment. Then she'd twist the knife in with a taunting dig.

But she'd look sexy as hell while she tortured me.

A rare smile hooks the corner of my mouth and I slam the trunk closed despite the self-closing mechanism, just to silence the manic drum of my heart. Which hasn't stopped tearing through my chest wall since I claimed Kyrie in a pool of Sebastian's blood.

The real shame in this spurious venture is the perfectly good bones I'm leaving to be picked over by the vultures. Sebastian's skull would make a prized piece in my trophy case; a memento to remind me of staring into her beautiful blue eyes as I slashed his throat.

That moment was almost as orgasmic as feeling Kyrie's tight little pussy pulse around my cock as she lost her mind to pleasure.

Almost.

But fucking hell, I haven't stopped thinking about either since.

The early morning air is brittle with the pure scent of cold. My breath plumes the air as I round the car to the driver's side, the fresh cover of snow crunching beneath my boots. The tufts of white are illuminated in a pale sheen by the hunter's moon.

The same moon I was born under.

From the pits of my memory, I hear the strike of the lighter wheel. Feel the numbness blanket my body while I lay in wait beneath the soft snow. Then the silky slip of blood warms my hands, bringing feeling to my skin and the rest of my limbs, awakening a ravenous hunger that would never be satiated from that point forward.

My first kill.

The numb feeling I was already accustomed to. Shallow affect anaesthetizes emotions, psychopathy deadens empathy. While lying beneath that blanket of snow, the cold felt more like home than any four walls and the people who dwelled within. But the kill...

The moment I felt sharp steel slice through flesh and tendon, my dead zones came alive. Hearing the ragged gasps for air, staring into the blown pupils as terror infused the final seconds... That broke through every frozen, numb layer encasing me.

The first time I ever felt sheer, euphoric ecstasy.

At fourteen, the Teflon encasing me cracked just

enough to accelerate my heart rate. Adrenaline slammed my adrenals. The rush was addictive. It was the closest I could imagine to *feeling*.

And I knew I would never stop.

Unlike Kyrie, I wasn't made. I was born to take lives. Designed to kill without remorse. The lust for the hunt was coded in my DNA at conception. I've been a lone wolf my entire life, moving from one contingency plan to the next, my only companion the relentless hunger for the kill.

I slip behind the wheel and key the engine, leaving our victim and thoughts of the past buried beneath a shallow coat of snow on the side of the highway that will melt with daybreak.

All frozen things thaw in the warmth of the sun.

I've never once fathomed what it would be like to take life with a partner.

Now, suddenly, I'm having a difficult time picturing my life without her by my side doing exactly that.

I admit, Kyrie has a sound plan. If Agent Hayes needs a killer to chase, then giving him a thread from the Slayer's past will tickle his obsession.

Most killers don't change their MO—but it's not unheard of.

I never thought I'd change mine, a ruthless creature of habit.

Yet here I am, risking everything—my freedom, my life —to keep a girl safe, and thinking about how my blood blisters my veins in anticipation for our next kill.

An hour later, I'm pulling into Hope Springs Medical Institute. Since I can't be in two places at once, I have to make sure to establish an alibi, a reason for my trip across the state line.

Nurse Pam greets me at the welcome desk as I sign in.

"She's having a good day, Jack." Her smile is an adept mix of hope and pity. "Glad you came today, though it's a little unexpected."

"I'll be taking an extended trip soon," I say in way of explanation for the deviation in my routine. I don't stray from the design. Even the smallest departure from the norm attracts notice, and it's why I strive to never make this mistake.

With a practiced smile, I stick the visitor tag on my suit blazer, then I'm led to the room I visit twice a year. Today is not one of those scheduled days.

I place the potted flowers—her favorite; lilacs—on the windowsill, right next to the others from over the years. A mentally healthy person would feel a measure of guilt over using their loved one as an alibi.

"Those are lovely," Nurse Pam says. "Aren't they, Charlene?" She gives me a bright smile. "So lovely, Jack."

I nod solemnly. "I'll be in Canada for her birthday. Figured I should bring them now."

As I stand over the woman in a bed with paper-thin skin and take her hand, I gaze into the steely, vacant eyes, a reflection of my own. "Hello, mother."

Charlene Sorensen says nothing in reply. She's nonresponsive. Her eyes blink out of reflex, her hand flinches in mine, but it's not a sign of life. Her gaze doesn't latch on to me; she's not aware that I'm here, or that she's even here.

For two years, my mother was in a fully vegetative state. Then Charlene made a small recovery into a minimally conscious state, where her progress stalled. She's been in this fixed state since I was sixteen.

She knew from the very first second she looked into my cold, unfeeling eyes that I was off. Different.

Her husband knew it, too. Though she took the brunt of

the beatings for my anomaly. The more my behavior disturbed my father, the harder he hit her. Blaming her for the reason his son was a "fucking psycho". The night he caused her traumatic brain injury, the one which put her in a vegetative state for the next two years, was the night he drew his very last breath.

At the hands of his psycho son.

But that night, the hits stopped.

I wish I could feel a deeper level of remorse that it came too late to ultimately protect her. The truth is, for a mother with only one child to love, who saw through the mask I wear for the rest of the world, not being aware of the killer her son grew up to be is almost merciful.

She at least doesn't have to suffer that pain.

I lean down and kiss her cool cheek. After I adjust the thermostat in her room, I seat myself on the chair across from her bed, where she stares absently at the ceiling.

The doctors and nurses all claim talking to a person in this state is beneficial. It won't bring them back, but they say their subconscious hears our words, our voice, to make a connection to our emotions, that it helps them endure.

I've never spoken at length to my mother in this state. One, there's no inflection in my tone of voice to convey any sentiment. And two, the hobby I fill my days with isn't one I can whisper to the walls.

Today, however, I reach into the satchel at my feet and produce my sketchbook. I flip through the pages until I come to a recent one of Kyrie.

"This is the woman I'm...seeing," I say, finding it difficult to define the depth of what Kyrie means to me, to put a label on our relationship.

I flip to the next image, the one I sketched while stalking her outside a bar while she was stalking her victim. "She's a brilliant wildlife biologist," I say. "Intelligent, cunning, enchanting." I chuckle. "Very sociable. Very...demanding. The exact opposite of me, actually. She's the light to my dark." I trace the pad of my finger along the shaded curve of her cheek. "And I don't think I can do any of this without her now."

Closing the sketchbook, I look up at the woman who raised me, who did her very best despite the monster she was given in place of a son. I take her hand again to try to warm her fingers, but I have little warmth to share.

What I was able to give her was a dead husband with a life insurance policy to ensure she'd have the best care. I made sure of that by staging the aftermath of that night as a home invasion, one where the thieves stole more than meaningless objects.

For me, I became a ward of the state. In compliance to the will, I was placed in boarding school, a neglectful grandmother on my mother's side put in place as more of a fixture for legal appearances. At sixteen, I graduated early and emancipated myself. A steep inheritance provided for my college education.

I've been on my own ever since.

"I have to leave here soon," I say to her, giving her hand a reassuring squeeze. "I've been in this area too long. Too much has happened, so I may not be able to visit for a while, but I'll make sure you're taken care of. Always." I place a tender kiss to her forehead as I stand. "I just have one last decision to make first."

I've never been undecided on anything in my life. I make choices based on survival, not want or desire. By the time I make it through the front door of my house, I'm decided on at least one thing.

First thing Monday morning, as I stare down at the

cream Berber carpet, I call a local contractor. When the guy on the line says replacing my carpet can't happen due to the demanding schedule and material shortage, I let the line go deathly silent.

After I struck Jack Sorensen Senior over the head with his whisky bottle, wasting his drink and turning his rage on me, I waited in a snowbank for him, then I painted the snow red with his blood—the same blood that courses my veins.

If anyone is to blame for the genes that spawned a monster, it's the man who I was named after.

This is who I am.

"I'll pay triple your estimate," I say to the guy. "I want it done today. Key's under the mat at the front door." I give him the address, then: "Today, or I call your competitor on the list and offer him four times the amount."

There's an extended pause. "What color carpet do you want installed, sir?"

"Anything but white or cream."

I end the call and bring up my security app on my phone, making sure my secrets stay secret. My trophy room is safely hidden, but I still don't relish the thought of strangers roaming the interior of my house while I'm not here.

For reassurance, I reach into my pocket to grasp the cool steel of the Zippo, only to come up emptyhanded once again. I shake my head with a hard chuckle.

"My wicked *lille mejer*. This needs to be remedied."

I have killed for my mother. I've killed for survival, out of compulsion, to sate cravings, and even, at times, fun.

But the decisive difference is that I wouldn't just kill for Kyrie—I would give my life. Hell, I'd even let her take it.

Once the spare key is in place beneath the mat, I lock up. Then I head out on a mission to retrieve my trophy.

FOURTEEN
CARTILAGE
JACK

"Jack, do you have a minute?"

Dr. Cannon stands in the open doorway of my office. The creased skin around his dark eyes lends to his worried expression. I nod and stand, buttoning my suit jacket as he enters. He closes the door behind him to seal us in privacy.

"Is there anything wrong?" I ask, prompting him.

He swipes a hand down the lower half of his face. "I don't mean to alarm you. Especially with all that's happened lately. It's been...stressful, to say the least. With the investigation and Mason and—" he drops his head "—Dr. Thompson. Christ." He mutters a curse beneath his breath. "I still don't understand what happened with Brad."

I should offer some measure of commiseration. I am responsible for Brad, after all. And mostly everything else. Well, Kyrie's to blame for Mason. With two killers hunting in the same territory, staking their claim with a rivalry, things were bound to get a little out of hand.

The main reason it's time to leave.

"But that's why I need to speak with you," Hugh says,

his voice lowering to a serious timbre.

My hackles raise. I already don't like where this is going. Crossing my arms, I say, "Sure."

"I'm looking to replace Dr. Roth." Hugh glances through the door toward Kyrie's office.

Confusion furrows my brow. "I don't understand. You said she was doing well here."

"She is," he says, then expels a breath. "She's the best wildlife biologist this university has ever had."

I chuckle. "Then I'm really confused. What's the problem?"

A puzzled expression creases his weathered features. "Jack, you're the one who has demanded for Dr. Roth to be removed ever since she started. I'm offering you what you want."

I eye him suspiciously. "What is it that you need from me, Hugh?"

His gaze holds mine in firm resolve. "I need you to be the chair of the West Paine Future of STEM Initiative."

"No," I say with strict authority. "I'm not interested in wrangling a whole initiative program for your donors."

"*Your* donors, too." His mouth thins. "Look, Jack. You've got one foot out the door anyway with your transfer." He moves farther into my office. "The university is taking a hit with this investigation. Donations are drying up. Students and professors alike are wary, scared. West Paine needs to be shown in a good light, and a university-wide initiative to attract new talent from all over can make that happen."

I straighten my back, drawing to my full height. "That's a commitment that could take months."

"Months where you don't have to worry about another CRYO freezer incident," he says.

I clear my throat. "That was actually Madeleine's fault."

He squares his shoulders. "This is my best attempt at a compromise, Jack. You're leaving me with a mess of a department when you go. So..." He turns and braces a hand on the doorknob before he looks me directly in the eyes. "Do this, and I won't renew Dr. Roth's contract. You can have your pick of who takes her position."

Hugh is desperate. I've been so focused on Kyrie and Hayes that I haven't noticed the impact on the university. A year ago—hell, a week ago—none of this would affect me. It would simply be one more reason to disappear. The sooner, the better.

The talk about my impending transfer sets my jaw, a thought burrowing in deep. I've treated Kyrie unfairly these past few years, and I doubt there is anything that can be done to make up for that now, but I'm willing to try.

"When is Dr. Roth's contract up?" I ask, shuffling my stance.

"Three months."

Three months. It's taken three *years* for me to see her—to *truly* see her; the darkness hidden in the shadows cast by her light, the pain she's honed into a weapon, the pain I'm partly responsible for—and in just three short months, I could lose her.

That won't happen.

I slip my hand down my necktie. "So then you'll still need Dr. Roth to participate in the STEM initiative."

His sigh is weary. "Yes, that will be an uncomfortable conversation. I don't relish having to ask that of Dr. Roth when I know I'll be letting her go shortly thereafter."

I nod slowly. "I'll talk to Dr. Roth about her participation in the program."

His head notches back, shock evident in the widening of his eyes. "Thanks, Jack. That would be appreciated."

Once Hugh exits my office, I look over at Kyrie. She's on a video call. Probably with a donor by the full display of her brightly lit, sunshine smile.

With predatory focus, I watch how she smoothes her palms down her thighs, ironing out creases along her tight pencil skirt, then crosses her legs. How she throws her head back with a laugh.

And suddenly I'm marching out of my office and crossing the hallway.

I enter without knocking, earning a concerned glance from her as her pale-blue eyes seek mine.

"Absolutely," she says to the person, not removing her gaze from me. She hits Mute on the keyboard. "What's wrong?"

I say nothing as I walk to the corner and switch the film setting on the glass walls to opaque. The hazy-white partition instantly conceals her office, leaving us in a private cocoon.

A woman's voice sounds through the speakers to snag her attention, and she looks at the monitor and unmutes the line. "Oh, sorry, Mrs. Vanden. My mail was just delivered. Where were we?"

Stealthily, I approach Kyrie's desk and slip off my blazer. I drape the garment on the back of the leather chair, kicking the legs to move it out of the way. Then I proceed to roll up my shirt sleeves.

Kyrie does her best to give her undivided attention to Mrs. Vanden, but her gaze slides up to me before tracking back to the woman on the screen. I can't help the devilish smile that curls my lips as I kneel in front of her desk and crawl beneath.

"Jack—" she hisses.

"Do your job, Kyrie." I circle a hand around her ankle

and deftly uncross her legs.

"That's right," she says, a perceived tremble to her voice. "We've accomplished so much while I've been at West Paine."

As I hover over her lap, I snake my fingers underneath the tight hem of her skirt and inch the fabric up to the flare of her beautiful hips, my breath hot over her skin as I breathe in the scent of her expensive jasmine body lotion.

Her knees remain locked as she answers one of Mrs. Vanden's needless questions, and I nip the tender skin above one knee. She gifts me a breathy flinch, and I take full advantage of having Kyrie preoccupied.

With another light bite to the side of her thigh, I wedge a hand between her knees. She fights me for a useless second until the struggle gains the concern of the woman on the screen.

"Dr. Roth, is everything all right?"

"Of course. These web calls—"

I force her thighs apart.

"—have spotty reception. So very sorry." Kyrie clears her throat, covertly covering my groan of approval as I push in between her soft thighs. "As I was saying before, our Bass fields is the third largest research body farm in the country."

Hunger sears my fading restraint at the sight of her perfect pussy sheathed by the flimsy material of her thong. I'm a man possessed as I bury my face between the apex of her inner thighs and pinch the fabric between my teeth, then lick the coarse seam, tracing the outline of her sweet clit.

I'm rewarded with the feel of her soaked panties, the warmth stirring insatiable desire as her thighs clamp against my temples, which has me ravenously lavishing her clit through those fucking wet panties like a starved beast.

I'm unconcerned with the primal groans tearing free as I make it my mission to hear her throaty little moans. Kyrie relinquishes her braced hold on my head to drive the heel of her pump into my thigh.

I grunt against her soft lips, the pain a delicious tease. In response, I bracket a hand around her ass. My other secures the elastic edge of her panties and, using my teeth, I tear through the fabric.

"*Jack*—" Her hands dig into my hair, fingers curling and nails scraping my scalp.

"Jack?" the woman questions. "Oh, Dr. Sorensen. I've heard murmurings among the committee that he'll be a seat for a STEM initiative at West Paine. That would be such a great treat."

A tinkling laugh falls from Kyrie's parted mouth. "Unfortunately, I can almost assure you that Dr. Sorensen won't be heading up any initiatives."

"Well, that's too bad. His presence would mean a great deal to the committee."

Her slick pussy exposed to me, I suck her clit into my mouth.

Kyrie does her best to disguise her moan. "*Mmm-hmm.* Yes, well, Dr. Sorensen is a very solitary creature. Brilliant, absolutely. But not big on socializing."

"That's a true shame," the woman replies. "He's so charming when you're able to catch him for a chat."

"*Mmm,*" Kyrie intones, chest rising as she reaches for a stable breath.

Dipping into her wet pussy, I taste her, fucking her cunt with my tongue. My cock strains against the teeth of my zipper, and I have never wanted her more.

She expels a lengthy breath, fingers raking my scalp as she strives to control the tremor racing through her body. In an effort to slow my greedy tongue, she again stabs her heel into my leg.

I back off only long enough to slip her heels off and toss them under the desk. Then I clamp my hands around her ankles and yank her ass closer to me on the chair.

Her yelp startles Mrs. Vanden, and I bury my laugh against Kyrie's pussy, lapping the sweet juices with greedy, hedonistic pleasure.

"Oh my..." She arches her back, raising one arm in an awkward stretch that makes me smile against her. "I mean. Of course, you're right. What a great idea, Mrs. Vanden. I'll make sure to pass along your suggestion to Dr. Cannon." She yanks on my hair. "However, I really do apologize, but I'm going to have to follow up with you later on this. I'm apparently having connection issues."

"Oh... All right. Please say hello to Dr. Cannon—"

Kyrie ends the video call. "Jesus, Jack. Are you still trying to get me fired?"

I halt abruptly at her accusation, feeling the smallest twinge of uncertainty. It passes just as quickly, and I take her ass in both hands and haul her forward to the edge of the chair.

"Get your goddamn sweet ass down here and ride my fucking face, *lille mejer*." I band my forearm around her waist and pull her off the chair, bringing her down to the floor with me.

I muffle her squeal with my hand, then shift her so that her thighs straddle either side of my head. "Grind that perfect pussy on my tongue."

She anchors her hands to the edge of the desk for leverage as I bring her down on my mouth. "What does that mean?" she asks, breathless.

I smile against her. "I think you're clever enough to deduce what grinding your pussy means, Dr. Roth—"

"Jack..." She pulls my hair.

I release a groan, my gaze latching on to hers as she looks down at me. "Little reaper," I say, then thrust her hips forward, burying my tongue deep inside her.

Her hips rock in sexy little undulations that sets my blood aflame, and I nip at her clit before swirling my tongue and then sucking the nub into my mouth, loving her breathy moans she can't hold back.

Her thighs tremble as I reach up and cup her breast, finding the peaked bud of her nipple beneath her silky blouse. Then I fasten my other hand to her hip and force her down on my mouth harder, sneaking my fingers into the tight pocket of her skirt as she quakes with her silent, impending release.

Riding me harder, her orgasm taking hold, she belts out my name, and I let her bite into the web of my hand as she shatters against me. I push my tongue inside deep, greedily exploring the pulsing, swollen flesh of her channel as she grinds through the climax.

As she comes down, her chest rising and falling in seductive inhalations, her thighs quivering to hold her lax body, I grasp her waist and rise up, catching her back against my thighs.

She yelps, then situates herself on my torso. "Thanks for the warning."

With a dark smirk, I reach over and collect her shoes. I slip the pumps back onto her feet.

"Can I have my panties, too?" she asks, grabbing hold of the edge of the desk to pull herself up to stand. She drags her skirt down around her knees. "Or am I just supposed to walk around panty-less all day, Dr. Sorensen?"

I rise to my feet to stand over her, clasping the nape of her neck and tilting her face up to mine. "Yes. I want you aware of your naked pussy all day, thinking about me tasting you, and how I'm going to fuck you senseless later tonight."

I kiss her then, long and sensual, already starved at the taste of her mouth mingling with the taste of her pussy, so delectable.

When I break away, I hold her gaze and whisper, "I'm keeping these." I hold up her torn panties before I sink them back into my pocket.

"How very stalker of you," she snarks.

I wipe my hand down my mouth to conceal my smile, then shrug on my jacket before I head to the door.

"Tonight?" she questions, a hint of hesitancy detected beneath her bright tone.

I pause at the door. "You know where I live."

She cocks her head in a mocking manner. "Of course."

"How very stalker of you, Dr. Roth." I wink. "Be at my place at five."

A flash of something unsure registers on her face before she masks it with a pretty smile, then she nods. I watch while she runs her palms over her skirt to smooth it further, her hand stopping at her empty pocket.

I flick the lighter lid open and then shut. *Snap. Flick. Snap. Flick.* "Oh and, Dr. Roth, you'll be participating in the STEM initiative. The one I am in fact a chair on. You're my spotlight professor."

One of her eyebrows wings up. "This is all very out of character for the great Dr. Jack Sorensen. Should I be concerned?"

I snap my Zippo closed, pocket the lighter. With Sebastian's body taken care of, Agent Hayes soon to be far away from her, and my decision finalized where this relentless woman fits into my life—perhaps I do feel a measure of relief.

Licking my lips to taste her once more, I say, "Maybe your annoying positivity is rubbing off on me. Make sure to come tonight prepared to hand over Thunderdome. Emphasis on *come*."

Then I remove my phone from my pocket and pull up the audio file of Kyrie. Turning the phone where she can see the screen, I delete the file.

Her gaze traps mine, a question banked in the glistening pale-blue. This very moment, with Kyrie too stunned to speak, I resolve to dispose of Mason's femur. I know my nature, what I'm capable of—and I don't want anything in my possession that can ever be held over her.

I leave her standing in the center of the room, satisfied and flushed, maybe even flustered, as I exit her office.

On my way back to mine, Hugh walks past me in the hall. "Get it all settled with Dr. Roth?" he asks.

I nod curtly in confirmation. "I took care of her."

"Excellent work, Jack."

A smirk twists my mouth.

With the taste of Kyrie still lingering enticingly on my tongue, I unbutton my blazer and seat myself at my desk to wake the laptop screen. A few days ago, I hired a private investigator to do some digging into Agent Hayes. Unsure of what she'd find, I couldn't stop the obsessive thought that something about the fed seemed off. Especially when it came to his interest in Kyrie.

The email at the top of my inbox confirms that suspicion and more, dousing my short-lived relief in the light. Creatures designed like us were not meant to bask in it for long. Where we lurk, the darkness always finds us.

FIFTEEN

BLUE

I've stood on this street many times before. I've watched from its shadows. I've driven slowly down the wide, tree-lined road. I've seen it in every season, in every color, in the afternoon light and in the dark of night.

But I've never dared to walk up to the front door of Jack Sorensen's house.

I stand unmoving on the sidewalk, the cool autumn breeze flushing my cheeks and lifting my hair from my shoulders. Maybe Jack can see me already. He could be watching as I try to convince myself to call a second Uber and return home. That's what I *should* do.

But I already know I won't.

The magnetic force of his presence pulls me like a tether in my chest, commanding that I place one foot in front of the other until I'm standing at the door.

I don't think I've ever felt such trepidation about a simple block of wood. It takes me a solid thirty seconds before I finally pull my hand from the depths of my pocket and press the doorbell. If Jack has been watching from inside, he has the good grace to give it a moment before opening the door.

I've seen Jack Sorensen a thousand times, in a thousand places. But here, standing at the entrance of his home, it's like seeing him for the first time. His dark hair. His full lips. The perpetual black wardrobe, tailored to his lethal frame. My breath stalls at the intensity of those cutting eyes that catalog every detail of my face with a long sweep of his gaze. I don't exhale until he glances behind me toward the road.

"I didn't see Hayes," I say as Jack reaches forward to lay a hand on my arm and guide me past where he stands on the threshold. An electric hum shakes the blood in my veins at his touch, but I tamp it down beneath a devious smile. "Not to say he won't come to peep in your windows."

The black door closes behind me and locks. "If he does, I'll fucking flay the skin from his face and feed it to him," Jack says.

"And they claim romance is dead."

Jack glances at me with a smirk as he turns a second lock. "Don't even pretend it wouldn't make your panties soaking wet, *lille mejer*."

"I would need panties for that, but a certain professor with a thing for cold rooms and eating pussy in the office stole mine." A third and final lock slides into place to the rumble of Jack's chuckle before he steps behind me to take my coat. "Three locks? That seems a bit excessive, Dr. Sorensen. Maybe you should consider getting a guard dog to keep Hayes away. He and Cornetto are certainly not on friendly terms," I say with a nod toward the door. A breath of his laugh warms my neck as Jack unravels my scarf, letting his fingers trace my skin as he lifts it away.

"If I did, you'd only give it some ridiculous name."

"I would. I could see you with an Akita named Creamsicle."

Jack's quiet grumble is cut short as my jacket slides from my shoulders to reveal the shirt he lent me the day he stitched my hand. It's been freshly laundered, but I may have sprayed a little extra Angélique Noire perfume on the collar when I put it on. The sleeves are rolled to my elbow, the top buttons undone to allow glimpses of my black lace bra, and beneath is a simple pair of leggings.

"What's wrong?" I ask with feigned innocence as I turn a slow circle to face Jack, his eyes darkening as they rake across my body. He hangs my coat next to the door and wets his lips as he drags his gaze to mine. "You said I couldn't shred it. I didn't have anyone to bury in it, at least not yet. And since you have my panties I think this is a fair trade."

There's a slight flare of his nostrils, a deep inhale. I take a step closer and he swallows. One more and he moves back just out of reach.

"Are you running away from me, Dr. Sorensen?"

A conflicted groan sneaks past his lips. "We have something important to discuss. But if I touch you now, I won't be able to make myself stop," he admits when I try to inch closer and he takes another pace back. "I don't have that kind of restraint."

"Good thing I didn't wear the purple shirt with the bow in that case," I say with a grin. "You could have done all manner of terrible things to me with it."

"Kyrie—"

"I've been wondering, Dr. Sorensen, just what would you do with that ligature, exactly? Maybe tie my hands up and fuck my mouth? Or something...darker...perhaps."

Jack's hand darts out and captures my throat, the flesh of his palm tight beneath my jaw. He pulls me in close and looks down into my face. "Must you always test my limits, Dr. Roth?"

My smile is as bright as the sun in a desert sky. "Yes," I whisper around the tightening pressure of Jack's hand. "Always."

His silver eyes are the polished steel of a blade. Desire. Fury. I would balance on this knife edge forever if I could.

Jack doesn't loosen his grip as he draws us closer together, reeling me in until my chest is flush against his. His lips graze my cheek just next to the bridge of my nose. "Spare me, just for a little while. This is important," he says, and places the whisper of a kiss to my skin, my eyes closing as his breath stirs my lashes. "Please, Kyrie."

I nod and Jack's fingers uncurl from my neck one by one. His other hand finds mine and presses against my stitches, warming my wound without hurting it.

"Come in," Jack says as he pulls my hand forward and lets it go so that I can walk ahead of him, his touch finding the small of my back. "Make yourself at home."

I've probably heard those words a hundred times. But this is the first instance I've really felt like my presence has given life to a space lying dormant.

We rise three steps from the entryway, passing the staircase to the second story, the house spreading into a living room on the right where the skylights of the slanted, high ceilings let in the light of the setting sun. A dining room lays adjacent to it at the rear of the house, the polished black surface of the long table decorated with a simple bouquet in a ceramic vase. I recognize the blue flowers as the same species that Jack left in my office. To the left of the house is a kitchen of sleek white cupboards and spotless quartz countertops. Between the kitchen and dining room is an open door that seems to lead to a sunroom, but the entry is too narrow to see what's in the space beyond. And throughout Jack's home is the scent of something new. Not paint but plastic, maybe. Perhaps it's the furniture, much of which looks unused. With its pristine, impersonal details in shades of black and gray, the house could belong to anyone, or no-one at all. There are no family photos. There's no meaningful art. The music that flows from speakers spread throughout the house is the only thing that gives me any sense of Jack, though it doesn't really seem like his style. I know it can't be true, but it's as though the space has been lying in stasis, waiting for a breath of life. For *me*.

"You had Shiraz at the club the other night," Jack says, pulling me out of my assessment of his home, his gaze a heavy weight on my shoulders. When I turn to face him, he gestures to the couch in the living room in a request to sit. "Do you want the same again?"

"Sure, that would be lovely, thanks."

Jack gives a single nod and I take a seat on the gunmetal gray couch, turning to watch as he strides away to the kitchen. He opens a fresh bottle and pours a glass of red wine into a black metal stemless glass, then tops up his own drink with ice and Scotch before bringing them both over along with a set of papers tucked under his arm. There's a spread of charcuterie on the coffee table in front of me, laden with Castelvetrano olives and hummus and cheeses and chutneys, cut vegetables and dried fruits and folded meats. When Jack sits next to me I can't help the wide-eyed, questioning look I shoot between him and the small feast on the table.

"You haven't had dinner," he says simply, passing me my wine and then a small plate from next to the board. His gaze darts to my stitches and then my chest in the general vicinity of my scars, then me as a whole. A subtle frown flickers across his face.

My heart scrapes at my bones.

"Thank you," I say, wanting to claw a small victory from my constant battle with time. I sit motionless with my plate gripped in my hands just to relish the expression on Jack's face. It's one of concern. Maybe a bit of confusion. His irascible nature demands that life submit to his plans, and I enjoy denying him. But there's something guileless about his apparent worry for my nutritional needs that has me softening, laying the plate on my lap to reach forward and pluck olives and cheese from the board. I'm not really watching what I take, quite honestly. I'm watching Jack's face, the way he tracks the motion of my injured hand, the way he seems to archive what I choose to take, what I avoid. In reality, I don't even know half of what I grab, I just keep going until there's a spread of enough food that he seems satisfied. Only then does he fill his own plate, and he waits until I've had a few mouthfuls of food and wine before he draws the papers into his lap.

"I was doing some digging today," Jack starts, passing me a sheet of paper. Hayes's grainy photo is at the top of the page, though he looks a little younger in the picture than he does now. More hair. Fewer wrinkles. Smaller second chin. A brighter spark in his eyes, obvious despite the poor resolution. Beneath his photo are his details. His full name. His birthdate. Height. Education.

Years of service in the FBI.

And below that, his license approval as a Private Investigator.

A chill sweeps into my arms. I look from the paper to Jack, his lips set in a grim line.

"What is this, Jack?" I ask, though the pieces are already

clicking into place. Jack's reply is to hand me the next sheet of paper.

"Something about him wasn't sitting right with me. I couldn't get it out of my head," Jack replies as I start reading the next page. On the upper left margin of the page is the logo for the FBI.

"Jack...did you...did you hack into the FBI's records?"

One of his shoulders lifts in a little shrug. He tries to hide a self-satisfied smirk as he chews an olive, but he fails when it lights his eyes.

"You did. You hacked into the fucking FBI. How—"

"The more important issue is probably this," Jack says as he points to the middle of the paragraph on the sheet, which appears to be a summary of an internal personnel hearing. He's highlighted a single sentence.

The decision of the Office of Professional Responsibility committee is the termination of Eric Christopher Hayes as active agent for the Federal Bureau of Investigation.

I skim the details, my mouth dropping open as the information invades my cells like a vein of ice crystallizing in my flesh. "He was let go *five fucking years* ago?"

Jack nods, handing me the rest of the papers. "These are the details of the hearing. Essentially, he was reprimanded for the negative impact that his obsession with the Silent Slayer case was having on his work. It seems the case was still an ongoing investigation, but was deprioritized when the Slayer appeared to go dormant. But Hayes didn't fall in line. His other casework suffered. There were some outbursts, and when he was evaluated he was found to be combative, resistant to authority. Eventually, they let him go. It looks like he took a year off, and then resurfaced when he obtained his PI license. He's rogue, Kyrie. He's rogue and he's centered on *you*, the key to the case he could never solve."

My fingertips are cold as I flip through the pages, barely processing the words in the transcripts. My thoughts are spiraling into darker places than pages and ink. They're descending into revenge. Into blood and rage. Because I know what Jack doesn't. That it's not just me that Hayes is centered on. It's me as a vehicle to the man who is taking shape as his true prize.

Dr. Jack Sorensen.

My grip tightens on the edges of the pages until my knuckles bleach, my heart galloping as I struggle to subdue the urge to rush from Jack's house and hunt Hayes down myself.

"You should stay here until we can figure out how to get rid of him," Jack says, knocking me sideways from my thoughts of justice and retribution.

I blink as though that simple motion might bring me back from the alternate universe I seem to have dropped into.

"What?"

"I don't want you around Hayes."

"I...you...*what the fuck?*"

"He's volatile, Kyrie. Possibly unhinged. You're safer here."

I take the time to study Jack's face. He wears that same expression of worry that he had the other day in his lab when he gave me the Slayer's hyoid bone, as though something deep and fraught and unfamiliar has crawled to his surface and he doesn't know what to do with it.

My gaze drops from his and I look at the food on the coffee table. The glass of wine in my hand, which is not glass at all but metal. I listen to the playlist. It's a song I have on one of mine.

This is all...for me.

"I...um..." I try to swallow the sudden brick that appears in my throat and demands all my pain. The thought rises that it would be safer for Jack, too, if I stayed. If Hayes believes Jack is a killer and I'm not, maybe my presence here can protect him. It could be enough to prompt Hayes to reconsider his theory, and maybe we'll have enough time to create a false trail for him to follow.

I glance at Jack again before my gaze travels to the safety of the room.

"I have a dog."

Jack laughs. Actually *laughs*. I look over in time to catch the way it lights his face, crinkling the corners of his eyes, folding his dark lashes together. "I know," he says. "Apparently, I lose five points in the arbitrary Thunderdome points system every time I forget his name. Which is impossible to forget, by the way, because it's *awful*."

A breathy huff passes my lips as I drop my focus to the papers that have started to warp in my grip. Jack's hand folds around my wrist, but I struggle to look up as my heart hammers its rhythm into his grip.

My well-being is in your very best interests, my voice says, the creek trickling in the background. When I close my eyes, I see Jack there, standing in the sliver of moonlight, ready to kill me. Maybe he would have, if I hadn't made that threat.

I've never regretted my words more. They might have kept me safe, but they make it impossible to discern fantasy from reality.

"I'm serious, Kyrie," Jack says, and I swallow hard as I try to gather my diaphanous thoughts. "Hayes is dangerous.

He's been lying about being a federal agent. He's been walking around campus for days with a fucking fake badge. How much farther do you think he would go to get what he wants?"

I take a long sip of my wine. Then another. I'm going to need something a lot stronger than Shiraz to get me through this evening.

Jack takes a sharp breath to surely launch into his next multi-point argument about why this is a good idea when his phone rings in his pocket. He pulls it out and frowns at the screen.

"I'm sorry. I have to take this," he says with the slightest squeeze to my wrist before he lets go and rises. With a fleeting look of that subtle concern, he accepts the call with a formal greeting and heads for a dark hallway between the living and dining rooms.

"Jesus Christ," I whisper before downing the rest of my Shiraz. My stitches tug at my wound as they tangle in my hair. The discomfort barely registers.

I cast a glance at my empty glass and set it down. "Fuck the wine."

Jack's voice is quiet down the hall and I don't make out what he's saying, only the cadence of his occasional statements, the tone conveying his usual pragmatic, if not intimidating, style. I don't linger, heading instead to the kitchen to retrieve a fresh glass before I hunt through the other cupboards to find the liquor collection on my second try. There's a half-full bottle of Bowman 25 Year Scotch. Expensive, no surprise. A few bottles of red, including two of the same Rockford Flaxman Shiraz I had at the club. And tucked behind a bottle of Vodka is a black, unopened bottle of Adictivo Extra Anejo Tequila.

"Oh thank God." I rise on my tiptoes and slide the

bottle from the shelf. "You're such a good host, Dr. Sorensen. Thanks for the shots."

I head to a row of drawers beneath the microwave, assuming the first one might have a sharp knife to cut the plastic that seals the lid of the bottle. But that's not what's inside.

On the right side of the drawer are pens and a pad of blank paper.

On the left side are a few folded letters that Jack has received.

On the top is one from the Canadian government.

My gaze darts toward the corridor where Jack's voice still faintly reaches me past the thrumming beat of my heart.

I unfold the letter, dated seven days ago.

Dear Jack Victor Sorensen,

This is in reference to your application for permanent residence. A decision has been made regarding your request. We require your passport to finalize processing your application. Your passport must be received by Citizenship and Immigration Canada within 30 days from the date of this letter. Failure to do so could result in the refusal of your application.

I stop reading after that.

A sudden fracture in my heart splits wide open, gripping my throat and glassing my eyes.

My stomach churns. I feel burning hot, the start of a

thin film of sweat misting my hairline. Why is it so fucking *hot* all of a sudden? I have an overwhelming urge to rip off my shirt just to feel the air unobstructed on my skin. My heart riots to break free of its bone cage and for a moment I think I might be slipping into a flashback, so I grip the counter, the sharp edge of the quartz biting into the wound on my palm until the pain kicks in and keeps me anchored to the present.

"Get your shit together," I hiss at myself as I fold the letter and shut the drawer, trying the next one down where I find a set of small screwdrivers. With a shaking hand, I take the sharpest one and pierce the plastic covering the cap, nearly slicing my other palm in my uncoordinated desperation. The moment the cap is off, the bottle is at my lips and I take the longest swig of Tequila I've ever had in my life.

A smoky burn lights up my chest. I blink until I'm reasonably sure the tears have dissipated. A few deep, trembling breaths become steadier ones. I force a mantra upon myself: *you promised to make Jack suffer.*

I did. I did promise that. I wanted retribution for all the many times he was callous and cruel. And worse...

Exactly. He said he wanted to leave. He said it just the other day, in fact. And soon, West Paine will be yours. He'll be skulking off defeated and you'll be the winner. It's the reckoning you hoped for. Isn't that what you wanted?

I think so...

I keep telling myself these things as I leave my unused metal glass on the countertop, taking another sip from the bottle as I wander away. My heart seems to crave the outdoors, the fresh air. Something cleansing, away from this scent of newness like a barbed reminder that I'm in a temporary place, a showroom. I'm not really paying attention to where I'm going when I start toward the dining room but detour to the left. But my heart must have known, because it leads me into an enchanted, magical realm.

The conservatory.

There are tiers of white wooden shelves lining the glass walls, each one filled with pots of different shapes and sizes. Some of the shelves hold plants with no blooms. Over others are small grow lights to encourage the buds to flower. Emerald leaves and vibrant blooms cascade from baskets hanging from the peaked ceiling, the clouds beyond the slanted windows painted orange and pink with the last streaks of the setting sun. The herringbone pattern of the red brick floor leads to a small table and wicker chairs near the far end of the sunroom where a wood stove rests unlit.

And everywhere, there is blue.

I don't know all the flowers, but I know some. There are blue dahlias with conical petals whose ends deepen to indigo and violet. Blue roses, which I've never seen before, and I run my fingers across one as I bend to inhale its sweet scent. The fragrance of blue Jasmine and white Stargazer lilies with streaks of cerulean perfume the air. And most abundant of all are those blue flowers that Jack left in my office, grouped in different shades. Some light. Some dark. Some bright. Some pale. Each flower its own unique color, their pots numbered with neatly written labels.

I'm approaching one group of blooms when movement outside at the back of the garden catches my eye. For a breath, I startle. My immediate concern is that it's Hayes. I lean closer to the glass and see a man, but it's not the rogue agent. He's wearing a white jacket with writing on the back that I can't quite make out, picking something up from the ground next to an open gate in the fence beneath the canopy of spruce boughs. It's a rolled up carpet, the edge of the cut pile a creamy white. He loads it into the open back of a van. *Stamp & Morningstar Carpet Company*, the decal says across the doors when he closes them.

"Alcohol theft, Dr. Roth?"

I startle and nearly drop the bottle gripped in my hand, hissing a curse as my other palm lays above my battered heart.

"You said to make myself at home," I manage, my voice barely more than an unsteady whisper.

Jack pulls the bottle from my grip and reads the label. "I get the sense you're not onboard with the idea of staying here if your immediate response is to find the strongest alcohol in the house and drink straight from the bottle," he says. His smirk doesn't reach his eyes when his gaze meets mine. "I might have more work to do to convince you."

"Work..." I repeat, losing all my words as I look back toward the gate. It closes and the van departs. I lean closer to the glass. I had to have imagined it, this glimpse of something Jack Sorensen would never do, surely... But the scent in the rest of the house is real. That smell of new furniture... or carpet...? I smelled it just a moment ago...

I turn, nearly bumping into a tray of Jack's blue flowers. He steadies my arm as he prompts me back a step from the table.

"Careful," he says. "Those poppies are quite rare. They've taken me a few years to perfect."

I glance once more toward the gate before I meet Jack's eyes. That brick from earlier has returned to my throat, determined to choke my voice in a vise of pain. Swallowing does nothing but make it worse. "You... changed your carpet today? From... cream?" I ask, trying to control my expressions and force a nonchalant voice.

Jack sets the bottle of Tequila down on a shelf and

presses his palms to the edge of a table as he leans forward to look at the gate with a low and thoughtful *hmm*. "If I say yes, will that result in more alcohol theft, or less?"

He tosses me a brief, faint smile over his shoulder.

Even those who know him well would look at Jack and never notice the many faint traces of emotion beneath his subtle expression. Concern. Desire. Pain. Perhaps even fear. No one else could track them into his lightless depths.

No one but me.

Jack looks from me to the flowers, then back again. There's a flicker of movement at the corners of his eyes as they narrow, just a hint of motion and then it's gone before he's even turned back to the window. But it's enough of a trail for me to follow.

I stand in the shadow of his thoughts as a sliver of light sneaks in.

And that's all I need to see inside.

SIXTEEN

ELSKEDE

KYRIE

Time grinds to a halt.

It starts as a tremble in my lips. A tremor in my shoulders. A breath trapped in my lungs, begging to release with a *whoosh*, a tempting relief for the pain that swirls in whiteout drifts beneath my bones. I try to trap it in an unsteady exhalation, but Jack notices right away, his shoulders tensing. It takes him a moment to face me, as though he has to gather his resolve to watch me unravel right next to him.

"Why are the flowers all blue," I whisper, tears gathering on my lashes, one falling to carve a streak down my skin.

Jack could give me a hundred different lies.

Maybe he considers it as he takes a step closer.

He raises a hand to my face. His eyes follow the track of his thumb as it passes through another tear that follows the path laid down by the first.

"You're asking questions you already know the answers to, *lille mejer*," Jack says.

It takes an eternity for him to lift his gaze the short

distance from my cheek to my eyes. He leans down, not taking his hand from where it rests on the side of my face, his breath warming my tears. The softest kiss presses to my lashes when I close my eyes.

I could ask him why. Why would he spend years trying to match a flower to the color of my irises, yet spend the rest of his time trying to push me to leave West Paine? But if I asked, would he even know the answer? Whatever he feels is cocooned, and when his strongest emotions tear through the tomb of silken tissue, I don't know if he understands any of it.

My hand curls around his wrist. The stitches press against his pulse. The evidence of his care is right there in my skin, in the beat of his heart against the wound he helped to heal.

"This was never about gratitude, or recognition, or acknowledging that you deserved to be at West Paine, or even that I left you to die in your home, is it," Jack says when he pulls back just far enough to watch my reaction. When I remain silent, his brows hike in a silent request for an answer as he frames my face between his hands.

I swallow and shake my head. And still he waits, looking into me, burrowing under every layer until each one is torn away. When I try to drop my gaze he tilts my face up with gentle pressure, a wordless plea to not back away.

"No," I finally whisper.

"This is about me forcing you to feel alone. Unwanted."

Alone.

Unwanted.

Those words explode in the air like little bombs.

My chest aches. More tears crest my lashes but Jack draws them away with his thumbs. "Stop," I say, though I don't let go or try to break his hold.

"No," he replies. Just *no*. It's the softest thing he's ever said to me, and yet it cuts just as deep as his cruelest words. It's the slice of a scalpel. The glimpse beneath an incision to pull out what hides beneath the flesh.

"Stop. *Please*, Jack."

"*No*. I have wasted so much time. And now it feels like there's not enough."

I open my mouth to beg. Because if he scrapes this layer away, nothing remains to keep him out. There will be no thin veil of rage left to hide behind.

But Jack speaks before I can gather the words.

"I can't promise I won't hurt you again. We both know that life doesn't work that way," Jack says, his eyes soldered to mine even though I keep my focus trained on his lips. I can feel his silver gaze, boring into my mind like screws. "But look around you, *lille mejer*. You are not unwanted. You are not alone. You are *unique*." Jack bends his head until his eyes are level with mine and I have no choice but to meet their sharpened determination. "You are a bright and blinding light in the dark. Luminous. And I'm sorry I made you feel like anything less than that."

Jack keeps hold of my gaze, waiting for the words to sink beneath the wound he's made before he presses his lips to mine, sealing it closed. The kiss lasts no longer than a ragged breath, and then he pulls me into an embrace.

And that's all it takes to break open.

Just an embrace. Just thoughts turned to actions that might seem small, but they are keys to locked doors. He gives me the things he knows I need. Brass when I break glass. Stitches in a wound. The last remains of an enemy, a prized trophy. An apology, even though he might be incapable of feeling remorse. But he's trying.

And what is love if not that.

Maybe Jack will never feel it. Maybe he does and will never know.

But I can feel it. I know its shapes and colors, its camouflage. I was made what I am in one night and the days of pain that followed. I wasn't born and raised this way. I've loved and been loved, and lost it all.

When I look across his shoulder through my drying lashes, surrounded by shades of blue and the scent of flowers, sheltered in his unwavering embrace, I know I'm falling in love with Jack Sorensen.

Even if he leaves.

Even if he can never love me back the same way.

I can't stop myself. And even if I could, I don't think I want to fight it anymore. That's what I've been trying my hardest to crush and conquer, this willingness to let my wrath go. And I've failed. I might regret it when he disappears to wherever he's planning to go, but right now, it's all I ever really wanted. To not feel alone. To feel accepted the way I am, as the person I want to be. The one who embraced the darkness that tried to claim her and made it her own. Not the one who would only be loved for what I could have been. A mask.

Little by little, I relax into Jack's embrace, resting my head against his neck and shoulder. The sky darkens above us to a deep indigo as the sun sinks below a distant horizon. Jack's heart drums its steady beat against my skin, coaxing my breathing into a slower, even rhythm. He doesn't seem restless or keen to part. He just lets one hand drift through my hair in a slow, melodic cadence, stopping every time he catches a little knot from the autumn wind just to start at the beginning again.

It isn't until a timer switches the grow lamps off and the

only light to reach us crawls through the narrow door that Jack stills the motion of his hand.

"*Min elskede, bliv venligst,*" Jack whispers without breaking his embrace.

"I don't know—what is that?"

"Danish."

"I don't know Danish."

"I'm aware," he says, his arms tightening a fraction. Maybe he thinks I won't notice, but I do. "Stay."

"I have a dog."

"We established that."

"He sheds."

"I do know how to operate a vacuum, Dr. Roth."

"He barks."

"Often the purpose of a guard dog, or so I'm told. We can go back and get him now, and whatever else you need."

"He's at Joy's."

Jack lifts his shoulder. "Then we'll get him tomorrow on our way to get more of your belongings from your house."

"We?"

"That's what I said."

"Don't you think Joy will have questions?"

Jack shrugs again, nonplussed.

"Jack...even if she never says a word to anyone, people are going to notice, especially if I stay for days on end. We don't even know how long Hayes might remain. People will talk."

"Good. Let them. The more attention there is on you, the less likely Hayes will be to make a rash move," Jack says, releasing his embrace to take hold of my shoulders.

"But—"

"*Stay.* I do not give a *fuck* what they think, Kyrie. We need to limit his access to you on your own. I doubt he would try anything on the campus, but he might at your home. He's already showed up there. He's fucking *been inside*." The fury in his words cracks like a whip, his fingers tightening on my shoulders. Even in the dim light, Jack's eyes seem to flash, cutting a path through the night. "I will not let him get that close again."

Neither of us moves for a long, silent moment. My insides feel raw, my sharp edges debrided.

I've wasted so much time, Jack said.

And now it feels like there's not enough.

There's never enough time for the things that I cherish, and always too much for the things I don't want. As enticing as it is in some ways, I'm scared to be in Jack's domain night after night with no lair of my own for refuge. But I also loathe the thought of time winning another victory over me.

"You haven't shown me the whole house," I say, watching the tension ease from Jack's shoulders as my words settle in. "What if you have a collection of porcelain dolls? I hate those things."

"Luckily, I put them in the attic before you arrived."

"That's a shame, because when I said the whole house I meant the *whole house.*" I raise a brow in challenge with the heavy emphasis of my last words. If I'm going to stay here, I want to see it all. I want to peel back a layer of Jack, just like he's done to me.

Thoughts and worries and unspoken fears seem to weigh the air between us with thick, invisible threads. Jack's eyes filter between mine, maybe trying to discern my emotions from my neutral expression. After a moment, he gives a single nod and lets his hands fall from my shoulders, offering one for me to take.

"I'll give you a tour. And then you'll stay."

I place my hand in Jack's and he leads me past the

dining room, down the hallway where he took the call. There's a bathroom and laundry on the right, an office and a home gym on the left with weights and a Peloton and treadmill.

"Use it whenever you want," Jack says when I turn a slow circle in the center of the room.

"I run with Cornetto. At the river."

Jack lifts a shoulder as though this is not new information.

I sigh. He seems to enjoy my faint frown. "You'll be joining us, I suppose."

Jack's silence is all the confirmation I need, and he switches off the light before I can savor the glint of amusement in his eyes.

Next, Jack leads me back down the hall into the kitchen, depositing me there to retrieve the bottle of Tequila from the conservatory. He pours a generous shot into the metal stemless glass I left on the countertop with a pointed, admonishing look that makes me grin. When his Scotch is refilled, Jack leads the way across the house to the stairs.

On the second level is a large bathroom with dark gray tiles and an extra wide shower, another vase of blue flowers on the counter between the double sinks, lilies this time. There are two guest bedrooms which Jack barely stops at and have probably never seen visitors. And then the main bedroom with an ensuite, the room simple and tasteful, the decor nondescript.

I drift forward to one of the windows overlooking the backyard and the peaked roof of the conservatory.

When I turn to face him, Jack is standing at the entrance, the bed looming like a fortress between us. He studies me as he leans against the doorframe and takes a sip of his drink. His other hand is deep in his pockets, turning something with a methodical rhythm. *His lighter*. I miss the weight of it in my palm, the metallic flick of the lid.

"Which room is mine?" I ask, nodding toward the corridor.

"This one."

"Then which one is yours?"

"Also this one."

"I can stay in one of your guest rooms," I say, tucking a stray lock of hair behind my ear.

Jack's eyes darken. "No. You will not."

"I don't want to be an inconvenience."

"You're really going to take away my excuse to redden your ass?"

"I'm sure you'll find another."

We exchange false smiles that mask desire. I try not to look at the bed, hiding my emotions behind a long sip of Tequila. Even still, I can't resist the urge to chew my lower lip in the silence that draws out between us.

"The dolls are in the attic," Jack says. "Want to see?"

"I'll take a pass. Show me something else. Something you've never shown anyone."

The levity dissipates from Jack's eyes.

He seems to know I really won't stay unless he takes me where I want to go. And if this were a game, it would be mine to win. Jack might have torn down my defenses tonight, but he's the one who must give up something he covets. He must make a choice: risk his darkest secrets...

...or risk me.

I follow every movement Jack makes, no matter how miniscule. The way he looks down into his Scotch, his blink a fraction longer than typical. The twitch of the muscle in his jaw when he presses his molars together. The shift in the column of his neck as he swallows.

Jack takes another sip of his drink and lets go of the lighter before extending his hand.

"Come on. I'll show you what you want to see."

When I walk around the bed and lay my palm in his, he doesn't move from the door, pulling me closer instead. His gaze scours my face like crystals of ice and my smile unfurls, a defiant bloom beneath the snow.

"One day, *lille mejer*, I will stop underestimating your ability to turn anything to your favor."

I stretch on my toes, coaxing Jack closer so I can whisper a devious grin against his skin. "I certainly hope not, Dr. Sorensen. That would really inhibit my fun."

Our eyes lock, even though we're so close that Jack's features are unfocused. My lips draw across his stubble as I pull away. Not a kiss, but an enticement. A promise. Maybe a reward. I press my fingers a little tighter around his hand, and with a final, thoughtful frown, Jack leads the way downstairs.

We end up back in his office, where he stops at one of the three bookcases that line the walls. Jack bends and presses his finger beneath the lowest shelf, waiting until a quiet beep confirms his touch. The bookcase unlatches and swings back from the wall, revealing a narrow wine cellar, the diamond-shaped shelves stocked with bottles.

"Are you going to add me to your biometrics?" I ask as Jack continues to the end of the room, finding another sensor hidden beneath the frame of a cubby hole on the far wall. Another soft digital chime, another shelf swinging open to reveal a hidden door. "I feel like I should have access to the wine supply at least."

"Knowing you, you'll find your way in without my permission," Jack replies as he unlocks the iron door.

"I can't help but note that's not truly a response to my question, Dr. Sorensen."

He only casts me a brief smile before flicking on a light switch and gesturing for me to step inside.

Jack's trophy room is the first one in the house where I get a true sense of him. Even the conservatory is more like a window, one that only lets me peer into his thoughts of me. But the trophy room, that's like throwing open the door to his soul.

The room is long and narrow, an older couch lining one wall, its worn upholstery covered with throws and mismatched pillows that are somehow still harmonious. Aside from the flowers, it's the first time I've noticed any color and pattern in the house, though the tones are still dark and jeweled. Opposite the couch and the end tables that bracket it is a table and bookshelf that houses annotated texts and a row of binders. At the end of the room is a small storage shelving area and next to it a locked steel door, the cold radiant from its unforgiving surface.

And everywhere on the walls, Jack's art.

Pencil. Charcoal. Sketches of flesh peeled back from bones, the style clinical yet evocative. Some are femurs, each one a unique study of particular features. The shine of the smooth patellar surface. Tiny striations on the intertrochanteric line near the neck of the bone. Others are clavicles, or mandibles, or fibulae. But most abundant are hyoids. Beautiful and delicate, rendered at different angles. The shallow concavities on the body. The lesser horns that link the floating bone to the stylohyoid muscle. And next to the sketches are the bones themselves, preserved in locked glass cases.

I take time to look at many of them, comparing the similarities and differences between the sketches and the bones.

Sometimes, the drawings are faithful representations. In other sketches, it seems like Jack was drawing from a different model. "You draw them before you kill them, don't you. That's why they're not always alike," I say as I lean closer to examine one bone and sketch pairing that are markedly mismatched.

"Yes," Jack says as he stops by my side. He tilts his drink toward the case, the ice within clinking against the metal. "I was surprised to be so far off with that one."

"Not more surprised than the man you took it from, I'm sure," I say with a grin before turning away.

I make my way to the steel door, taking time to appreciate Jack's art and trophies with every step. I spot one sketch taped to the wall that's not like the others and recognize the setting immediately. It's my condo where we killed Sebastian. In the image, I'm asleep on the couch, which did happen after we spent time cleaning and Jack went to retrieve his vehicle from a parking garage near the club so he could drive the body across state lines. In Jack's rendering, however, I'm not wearing any clothes, though I know I had changed to sweats and a tank top before resting as I waited for him to return and pick up Sebastian. I remember waking to find Jack already back in my living room, watching me with a dark, unreadable look that I thought had more to do with the cold body on the floor between us than with me.

Maybe I was wrong.

Though I want to voice my questions about the pieces falling into place in my mind as I examine the details of the image, Jack steers me away from the sketch and toward my true prize, my desired destination.

The cold steel door.

My pulse pounds in anticipation. I don't want to just

see the meticulously preserved aftermath of his efforts. I want to see where Jack comes undone, to stand in the room where the angel of death bursts through his thin restraints.

I stand next to the locked latch handle and face Jack, my eyebrows hiking as he regards me for a long moment before approaching, withdrawing a key from his pocket. He barely looks at the latch as he unlocks it, keeping his eyes on me instead. With a deep breath of hesitation, he opens the door and holds it open for me to step into the rush of cold air.

Five concrete stairs descend into the square room, the walls lined floor-to-ceiling with white PVC panels. It's much like a medical suite, with stainless-steel shelves and counters and tables with wheels. An IV pole stands in one corner of the room. There's a row of medication vials on one shelf, a tray of syringes waiting next to them. There are scalpels and rib shears and toothed forceps laid out on one of the mobile tables. The faint scent of bleach lingers in the air. A pop of blue catches my eye, a vase of poppies resting on the counter near the deep, stainless-steel sink.

And in the center of the room, a gurney with thin black padding and restraints dangling from the swing-down side rails.

I drain my Tequila in a single shot before turning to face Jack. He stands unmoving at the bottom step, one hand gripping his glass a little too tight for his nonchalant stance, his other hand turning the lighter in his pocket.

"So," I say, my breath fogging as I set my glass down on a counter and saunter closer, running a finger over the mattress of the gurney as I slowly approach him. "This is where the magic happens."

Suspicion folds through Jack's eyes as I stop close enough to feel his body heat through my clothes. But the cold air still burrows in, and the instant a little chill shivers through my body, his gaze slices over me—lips, throat, breasts, back to lips again. It remains on my mouth as though fused there, even when I pull his drink from his hand. "Why do I get the feeling I should be fearing for my life?" he asks.

I keep hold of Jack's glass as I rest my other palm on his chest, capturing the beat of his heart before following the wall of muscle that tapers toward his clavicle. It doesn't escape my notice that his pulse is faster than its usual steady rhythm, the beat quickening as my touch flows up his jugular to rest at the back of his neck.

"You said to spare you, for just a little while," I reply as I pull him down until his lips meet mine. "It's been long enough."

I press a kiss to Jack's lips that deepens with every breath that passes between us. My tongue demands to taste the Scotch that lingers on his. A little nip to Jack's lips shreds a layer of his restraint and he pushes me back toward the center of the room. One of his hands grips my hip with bruising force while the other dives beneath the hem of my shirt to follow the lines of my ribs, his thumb tracing the underside of my breast with a slow sweep across the lace. It passes back over my peaked nipple and he groans, breaking the kiss to bite into the cold flesh of my neck.

"You put an idea into my head, Dr. Sorensen. And once it was there, I couldn't get rid of it," I say, my voice husky with desire as Jack's lips and teeth trace a path up my jugular.

"And what's that, *lille mejer*?" he whispers between urgent kisses.

My palm follows the hard length of his erection as I smile at his responding groan. A stronger bite sinks into my skin when I cup his cock through his pants with a firm grip.

The sound of scraping metal fills the cold air with a promise as I release the latch on Jack's belt buckle. "The cold room on campus. Do you remember what you said before the meeting about Mason?"

"Do you think I would forget?"

I shake my head and Jack grips my jaw, keeping me locked in place as he devours me with a desperate kiss. My desire matches his, my need for him ferocious, twisting my core with a demanding ache. But I force it down. I break away with a hand to Jack's rioting heart, and when he looks at me with a crease in his brows as though questioning if he did something wrong, I give him a wicked smile in reply.

"You know," I say, keeping my hand on Jack's chest as his breaths saw beneath my palm, "It took me far too long to put it all together." I raise one finger around the metal glass in a request for a moment's reprieve as I knock back the rest of his Scotch. The look in Jack's eyes is one of trepidation, and I torture him for a little longer than necessary before explaining my meaning. "The cold. The kiss when I baited you about getting hot. The piercings."

Jack's eyes are lethal with need.

I don't look away as I raise the cold metal to my lips and tilt my head back until a shard of ice slips onto my tongue. When I lower the glass, I make a show of pulling the ice chip through my pursed lips, holding it up between us like a prize. Then I set the glass down on a table within reach and grasp the waistband of Jack's pants and briefs, tugging him closer.

"Are you going to be sweet to me, Jack?" I ask, my wide eyes the picture of virtue as I press up against his chest, driving the hand still gripping his clothing down with agonizing slowness to free his erection. Jack grasps my

elbow and steadies me as I lower my knees to the unforgiving concrete.

"Not a fucking chance, petal."

The innocence of my expression lifts like a mask of fog,
burning away to reveal the wicked creature lying beneath.

"Thank fuck for that," I say, gripping his erection. I run
the shard of ice across one of the studs closest to the base of
his cock before skating the Prince Albert piercing across the
length of my tongue, relishing the bead of salty precum
gathered at the head. Jack's breathing grows ragged as the
ice moves across the titanium in slow circles, from one stud
to the next, cooling them down to what I hope is the edge
between pleasure and pain. He pulls off his shirt, his
expression almost agonized, like he's burning and desperate
for the embrace of cold air. But if he's suffering, I'm not here
to offer mercy. I caress the crown of his cock with gentle,
teasing licks, tracing his piercing before taking it between
my teeth with a gentle tug that has Jack hissing with desire.

"Jesus...fuck..." Jack tilts his head back as his hands
tangle into my hair, his eyes closing as he sinks into the pleasure of the warring sensations, the cold ice battling my
warm lips as I tighten them around the crown. I dance the
tip of my tongue along the Prince Albert and he groans, his
grip on my strands tightening. My motion slows until he
meets my eyes and I pull away to place the melting ice on
my tongue, holding his erection by the base as I lick each
rung of his Jacob's ladder. When Jack is shuddering and his
eyes are little more than a thin slash of silver around his
blown pupils, I crunch the shard of ice and grab another
from the glass on the table.

"I once promised myself I'd make you suffer," I whisper
as I drag the ice up one side of titanium studs and down the

other. "This wasn't what I first had in mind, but I have to admit, Dr. Sorensen, I like this much better."

I take my time with Jack, rolling the ice across the Prince Albert, sucking on the other studs, raking my nails across his balls, pressing my lips to them, drawing them into my mouth. Sometimes, he hisses my name like a curse. Others, a stream of Danish passes from his lips on an unsteady breath. *Din skide gudinde. Du dræber mig...*

When he's been well and truly tortured, I take the head of his cock past my lips and suck, closing my eyes as I moan into his flesh.

His restraint shatters in the heat of my mouth.

"Open your eyes," Jack commands, fisting my hair as he shifts closer, pushing his cock deeper.

I do as he says. But I take my time to meet the glare that awaits me, sliding my gaze up every inch of tense muscle that towers over me. When our eyes connect, it's like magnets snapping into place. I can't look away.

"I'm going to choke that pretty throat with my cock, and you're going to watch me do it. You're going to take everything I give you. You're going to swallow every rung of this fucking ladder and every drop of cum. And you will not take those beautiful blue eyes off me. Understand?"

My only response is the dark smile that lights my eyes and the swirl of my tongue across his piercings.

"Good girl."

And with that invitation, Jack Sorensen fucks my mouth.

He grips my hair, tilts my head back, opens my throat for the invasion of his length. The piercings roll across the depths of my tongue and the walls of my throat and I gag, tears streaming down my face. But I don't take my eyes from Jack's. Even though the ache in my jaw is brutal and the sensation of titanium slipping through my mouth is foreign, I still want more. I can't get enough of him. The pain across my scalp. The throbbing in my clit. The burning need for friction. I want it all.

Every thrust pushes deeper, giving me just enough time to acclimate to his length and girth before his cock is filling my throat again. I swallow and take it all, every rung until my face is nearly flush with his pelvis and the scent of sex and vetiver floods my nostrils. I run my hands up his abs and he shivers with my touch as it slides through the mist of sweat gathered on his skin, his gooseflesh rising in the chill of the air. And then I grip his waist and take him a fraction deeper still, bobbing my head with thrusts as I hum my satisfaction around his cock.

"Kyrie..." he hisses through gritted teeth. One of his hands folds tight around my throat and he thrusts long and deep and hard. I feel his muscles tightening beneath my fingertips, his hard length pulsing against my tongue. And then he roars my name, the sound cutting through the cold air, his cum a hot invasion that I swallow down with a contended moan.

I suck every inch of his cock as I slowly release him from my mouth with a wicked pop. Jack is trembling, his exhalations fogging the air. He turns to grip the edge of the gurney as though his legs might give out and I rise, wiping my mouth and cheeks with the sleeve of his borrowed shirt.

"That's not all, is it, Jack?" I ask as I turn away toward the shelves.

He doesn't answer, but I feel his question linger in the cold.

I look across the neat row of medication vials.

Succinylcholine. Epinephrine. Lovenox.

Midazolam.

I pull the vial from the shelf with a sly smile.

"The cold. It's not all you want," I say, taking a syringe from the tray next to the ampules. My teeth clutch around the pink cap on the needle and I spit it out across the stainless-steel countertop, purely for theatrics. I plunge the pointed tip into the vial of midazolam and tilt it upside down, withdrawing 2.5mg of the clear liquid.

When I place the vial back on the tray and turn to face Jack, his gaze burns through me. He might have just been spent down my throat, but the sight of the needle and everything it means has him straightening as adrenaline surely floods the caverns in his heart. It won't be long before he's ready for the next round.

"You want a sleeping beauty," I say, stopping at the edge of the gurney across from Jack as he pulls up his pants and briefs. The motion of his hands slows as his eyes dart from the syringe to me. "Somnophilia."

"Kyrie—"

"This is your chance to take me while I'm quiet," I say with a cheeky wink and a sinful smile. I keep the needle poised between my fingers as I hook my other hand into the waistband of my leggings and shimmy them over my ass and thighs to toe them off. Jack's hand runs through his hair when he takes in the sight of my bare legs beneath his shirt, my skin pebbling in the cold air. "Don't you want me silent and compliant, for once? You can do anything you want to me. Taste me. Fuck me. Manipulate me. Dominate me. Spray your cum all over me while my eyes are closed and my limbs are limp. Maybe I'll wake to your cock already thrusting balls-deep into my swollen pussy and I'll beg you to keep going. Anything you want, I'm giving you permission to take it. Don't you want that, Jack? Don't you want me?"

"Kyrie, Jesus Christ—"

"Stop fighting yourself. You said you were done standing in the way of what you wanted. I'm offering," I say as I clutch the side rail of the gurney with my free hand and haul myself onto the mattress, the PVC surface cold on my bare skin when I sit facing him. I poise the needle to the general vicinity of my jugular. "I want this too, Jack. I trust you."

The conflict in Jack's eyes is a delicious torment that I devour like a starved beast. "This is dangerous, Kyrie. You've had alcohol."

A sigh passes my lips through a petulant pout as I pull the syringe away from my neck to examine the dosage. I press the plunger until a few drops trickle through the needle before holding it to my skin once more. "There. Happy now?"

Silence stretches between us. Jack is torn in a torturous moment. One of need. One of fantasy. One of fear, a man who fears so little, who takes what he wants without regret or remorse. But he fears this, and it will make taking it that much sweeter if he just gives in.

I sink the needle into my flesh just enough for a hint of pain and a drop of blood. Jack's restraint blisters. It's a bubble nearly ready to burst.

"I don't even know if I'm in the right spot. Do you really want me to miss?" I ask, and before the question has even left my lips he's whipped the needle from my hand and plunged it into my jugular, dispensing the drug into my veins.

My triumphant smirk falls slack beneath Jack's heated gaze as I drop into a dreamless sleep.

SEVENTEEN

INERTIA

JACK

Bitter notes of angelica and sweet vanilla pervade my cold room. Kyrie's presence is as overpowering and consuming in my domain as the very perfume she wears, even in her unconscious state.

Like the angelica flower itself that hails from an arctic landscape, she's designed for me, her wilted petals waiting to be revived.

I remove the needle and lift her slack body into my arms. Gently, I lower her to the gurney and sweep the backside of my fingers along the side of her expressionless face. I smooth the russet waves away from her closed eyes, admiring the way the thick fringe of lashes lay motionless above the high ridge of her cheekbones.

Syringe gripped in my hand, I drop close to her ear and whisper, "You know how to make me fucking feral, petal."

I toss the depressed syringe on the stainless-steel tray as I head to the thermostat. The temperature is adjusted down a few degrees. Not so cold she'll freeze, but chilly enough I can make out how her warm breath fogs the air in the florescent lighting. The artificial light also washes her skin in a pale hue, her naturally plump, pink lips tinged the lightest shade of blue.

How I first saw her in the department body cooler, when she tested my restraint, pushing every one of my buttons until I was forced to either strangle her or fuck her.

My cock grows harder at the thought. Easing the confining pressure of my slacks, I lower the zipper, my ravening gaze trained on the sleeping beauty helplessly lying victim in my territory.

How many times have I envisioned her just like this. From that very first moment I heard the tinkling cadence of her laugh, and it slinked, like a fucking thief, right under my defenses. Taken off-guard, I wasn't prepared when I turned to see her, with her beaming smile, a bright ray of sunshine invading my dark haunt.

I looked into the captivating pale-blue of her eyes and I knew—in a fraction of a second—she would be my destruction.

And all the dark, depraved thoughts I fought to keep at bay as I tried to remove her from my reach—I felt powerless. She was so fucking beautiful. Her scent tormented me. Her laugh stirred a fiery heat beneath my cold skin as I tried in vain to imagine what her screams would sound like in that tinkling cadence.

She consumed me from day one.

How I craved with ruthless fury to punish her for that.

That goddamn shirt with the neck tie was damn near my breaking point, and I knew I had to remove her, or else I'd snap.

I fed the hunger by first sketching her, memorizing every slope along the contours of her face. Every tempting, sexy curve of her body I branded into my memory with each stroke of charcoal.

The only one of my subjects from whom I never removed the flesh. Only ever allowing myself to fantasize what her delicate bones would look like, far too wary to put the imagery in physical form, for fear I wouldn't be able to stop myself.

When I couldn't get her blue eyes out of my head, I bred my Himalayan blue poppies to match the exact shade of her striking irises, my entire greenhouse a shrine to her beauty.

At any point, I could have ended my torment. I could have relented and sliced her open to torturously peel back her skin until I was rewarded with the prize I knew lay beneath; that delicate hyoid I felt when my hand was choked-up on her pretty, slender throat. A true star for my trophy case. I could have reduced her to ash, a memory easily blown away from my mind, and scattered the remains in the poppy beds.

The need to surrender to the tireless craving and make her disappear was a fraught one I battled every day I walked through the university doors. Because if I didn't—if I let this obsession continue—it would result in breaking my own rules.

She tempted me to defy my nature.

She was a threat.

And right now, the provocative sight of her soft skin is too great a temptation, beckoning me to reach for the scalpel on the tray.

Reduced to savage need, I tear through the last of my feebly bound restraint as I storm toward her sedated, angelic form on the gurney and slide the razor-sharp blade of the tool beneath her shirt.

The sound of shredding fabric licks over my skin in sick satisfaction as I draw the scalpel up the center, slicing the garment I gave her and her lacy bra to expose her body to me fully. I let the shirt fall away from her breasts, admiring her hardened nipples, the even rise and fall of her chest.

I take my time, letting my gaze study every inch of her naked body, bare and vulnerable.

I know Kyrie wasn't born a killer. She has a conscience, a soul, empathy. She desires to love and be loved—and despite my limitations there, I will do my best to give her what she needs. But this...

This is all for me.

Debauched. Deviant. Corrupt.

The unholy way in which I'm about to take her would make angels repent.

With depraved hunger, I allow myself to feel the twin scars below her lower ribs. My fingers map the beveled edges, tracing the coarse indents where the blade split her skin.

A violent anger rises up from the bowels of my pitch-black soul, furious that another man dared to touch her, to harm her, to try to *destroy* her. Rage lashes my viscera, the scalpel clenched in my trembling hand as I visualize the unhinged way in which I'd first torture, then mutilate him.

The massacre I committed in this very cold room would pale in bloody comparison to what I'd subject Winters to if he stood before me now.

I killed him too quickly.

And I hone this feral lust. Fixated on the sleeping beauty spread before me on the gurney, I discard the scalpel and reach into the hollow of my slacks and grip my rock-hard cock. A tight hiss escapes between my gritted teeth as I squeeze the base, then track my cold palm up the rungs of my shaft. I stroke the length, hips thrusting in time with each pass over my raging erection, as I stare at her parted thighs, the pretty pink clit peeking between her smooth lips, and I can almost taste the wet heat.

With my free hand, I clasp one of her ankles and part her legs farther. I spread her knees until they touch the steel railing on either side, opening her up wide to me, posing her like a precious doll—one I can place in any lewd position I desire.

After I discard my slacks, I drop down over her slumbering body and breathe in her scent just to stir the hunger before I bite into the fleshy swell of the bottom of her breast. My fingers seek the warm slit of her pussy as I coax her taut nipple to pebble harder with my tongue. Sinking two fingers inside, I groan at the soft give of her flesh, no resistance. Her slick arousal coats my fingers as I plunder deeper, so inviting.

She doesn't move as I drive in and out, becoming more feral as she soaks my fingers. The need to fuck her with merciless depravity locks every muscle along my vertebrae. My teeth find purchase in the delicate junction between her neck and shoulder, where I devour the taste of her skin, my tongue trailing along her clavicle.

I withdraw my fingers from her hot little pussy and arch myself over her splayed form. A hard shiver racks my muscles as I trace the slippery pad of my finger over her colorless lips, then my gaze falls to the peaks and shadowed valleys cast by her bones.

A sick yearning to finally relent and peel back her layers grips me with fierce, untamed need, and before I can leash the desire, I've reached across the shelving unit and grasped the soft charcoal stick in hand.

Free hand braced to the chilled rail of the gurney, I rear up and position the stick to the bottom of her pelvis. I start by outlining her hips, using the span between the pubis to pinpoint the lumbar vertebrae.

At the sternum, I apply pressure and drag the soft tip up the column until I reach the thick manubrium, where I lighten the strokes. Branching out, I contour each rib along the cage. The clavicles I trace next, saving the column of her neck for last, where I tilt her head back and take my time shading around the mandible. My heart riots and my cock throbs as I outline her hyoid from the memory of my touch.

I raise up and gaze across her beautiful body, the silhouette of her skeleton only a vague overlay sketched on skin—the definition missing; the precision absent—but the depth and size accurate enough to turn me into a ravenous beast.

I brace my palm to the negative space of her belly and bury the head of my cock inside her slick entrance, captivated as I watch her sweet pussy eat each rung. I lower myself just enough to savor the delectable taste of her mouth, drawing in a deep breath between her parted lips as I inhale her into my lungs.

The sheer yearning to shred her tight walls with my studded cock is a demon clawing at my insides—to feel titanium hit cartilage and the vibration ricochet through my cock as I scrape across her bones.

This twisted love nurtured in the dark belongs only to us.

The sight of her drawn bones is a torture so divine, I'm barely restrained as I thrust into her with animalistic fury. I smear my hand across her pelvis, smudging the charcoal before I fasten my hands to her hips and rut into her with base, carnal want.

I could break her. My doll is so delicate, I could shatter her to pieces. A growl works free from the base of my throat.

"So goddamn perfect, *lille mejer*. I want to fuck you so brutally I turn you inside out."

I'm not the one in control here. She owns me. Every fiber of my being, every cell coursing through my marrow, she is the one dominating me, and I'm simply the depraved monster subservient to her commands.

Her body directs my next course, and I willingly obey, giving my little reaper exactly what she craves. I pull out of her slowly and gather her wetness, using my slick fingers to lube the puckered ring of her ass.

I glide my palm down my cock once to spread her arousal, then I push into the little pleated hole, thrusting all the way to the base of my shaft, where I feel her tight channel clench around me in reflex.

"*Goddamn.*" I fall over her, my hand sinks into her chilly hair where I thread my fingers, bowing her body beneath mine as I grip her closer. "I'm going to take your sweet, perfect ass, and you're going to feel every painful thrust until you're forced to open those beautiful eyes of yours."

I fuck her hard, with merciless need, surrendering to the fiend within that craves to consume her. With every unguarded thrust, her ass clenches around my cock, taking me right toward the fucking edge.

At the dosage delivered, the sedative has an elimination half-life of forty-five minutes, and I can already feel her muscles gathering stronger, hear her breaths panting faster. Her eyelids twitch, and the sight of her rousing from sleep shreds my goddamn sanity.

"I want your eyes on me, Kyrie," I whisper into her ear. Hips bearing down between the warm apex of her soft thighs, I rut into her ass, unhinged, wild. "Open your fucking eyes, *lille mejer*."

She gasps in a sudden breath and her eyes flutter open, the crystalline blue seizing the rampaging muscle inside my chest. A growl rips free and, as her pretty mouth parts to release a moan, I seal her lips with mine to swallow the sweet sound.

Her ass squeezes so hard around my cock, my blood blisters my veins. I reach between us and swirl the coarse pads of my fingers over her clit, savoring her uncontrollable muscle twinges of pleasure.

She takes me right over the cliff with her, shattering me as she breaks against me, our bodies braced for the impact. My release claims me entirely, her tight hole milking my cock as I fill her.

Chest on fire, I crash to my elbows so I don't crush her, her mind and body still coming out of the sedation. "Christ," I breathe out across her collar, then drop a tender kiss to the hollow notch in the center. "You turned me inside out, petal."

A small laugh escapes her, and I feel her fingers trail through my sweat-slicked hair. "Considering you're still in my ass, I feel really relaxed."

A breathless chuckle slips out, and I rise up to kiss her lips. She's groggy from the sedative, will likely be for the next several hours. I quickly clean us up and slide on my pants, the need to take care of her hurrying my actions.

Kyrie sits up on the gurney and glances over her bare skin. "You drew a skeleton on me," she says, no shock held in her tone. "I'm not even at all surprised, Jack."

I scoop her into my arms, appreciating the little yelp. "Just be glad I stopped there."

I carry her naked out of the cold room and into the main part of the house. When we reach the hallway and completely bypass the guest room, Kyrie taps her fingers against my pec. "Where are you taking me?"

"Just trust me."

"I do," she says, and I look down to meet her glassy eyes.

I swallow. She does trust me, completely. "You didn't have to prove it," I say.

She shrugs slightly in my arms. "Now you know."

We enter the bathroom of my bedroom and I lower her to the tile floor, making sure she's steady on her feet before I move toward the soaking tub in the corner.

Turning the tap to a lukewarm setting, I test the water flowing out of the faucet, then I once again scoop her up and deposit her in the shallow pool in the tub. She shivers, her teeth chattering, and I spoon water into my palm and ladle it over the gooseflesh along her back.

Having Kyrie in my domain goes against my nature. I share this life with no one. I'm built for secrecy, for solitude. It's a design for more than just my survival; it's constructed to protect any innocents from getting caught in my web.

But it's the moment she grabs the unused bottle of bubble bath to add suds to the water that I know I'll never let her go.

She tangled herself in my web, and I'll have to carve her out of me to remove her now. She's in so deep, fused to my bones.

If that day ever comes, that loss will resonate down to the core of me. I will have no desire to survive without her.

As I pan more water over her shoulders, she circles her dainty fingers around my wrist. "What is it, Jack? You're more pensively somber than usual."

A faint smile ghosts my lips. I lean in and place a kiss to her temple. "I just want to make sure you're all right."

"And..."

I release a lengthy breath. "And I'm thinking about Hayes, and other things." I shut off the tap. "It's getting complicated around here. Not sure how much longer Westview will be habitable for me."

She looks away, gathers a dollop of sudsy bubbles and spreads the soapy water over the charcoal lines along her chest. "I trust you," is all she says.

Her words stay with me, filling the dark space of my thoughts when we're lying silently in bed, waiting for sleep to claim us. They stay with me long after that.

EIGHTEEN
ABYSS
KYRIE

It's been just over a week at Jack's, and I already know that no amount of time would be enough.

I savor every moment. Meals next to one another at the dining table, a vase of blue flowers always standing as the simple centerpiece. Jack waiting at my office door so we can go home together after work. Running side-by-side along the river with Cornetto, following the winding path against the current as the gray water snakes by. Making love when we want, where we want. Some nights, I wake to whispers at my ear, Jack already sliding into me, his touch caressing my breasts, dipping down to paint my clit with the arousal gathered at my entrance, as though my body was ready before my mind was. The beautiful torture of biting down on the words I want to say, the love I feel that only deepens as these moments grow around us like vines.

I want to believe it could be like this.

That I'm happy.

But anxiety also breaks over me like a constant wave, always threatening to drown me in the swell.

I know this solution of staying at Jack's is only temporary. Though Hayes still lurks at the campus daily, he'll give up in time when we inevitably find a way to lure him away. And though Jack hasn't said anything further about his plans beyond West Paine, I still know he's intending to leave. The Canadian immigration documents that were in the kitchen drawer disappeared the day after I decided to stay.

I need to remain focused. Practical. Because I don't know the difference between fantasy and reality anymore.

So, I try not to become embedded in this life. I try to change up my routine. Wake up early one day. Late the next. Work into the evening one day. Leave early the next. Add more time in the field studying the creatures that come and go. I manage to slip away for a few hours mid-week to replenish Colby's supplies of MREs, the military Meals Ready-to-Eat rations that keep him fed, though he's lost a little weight with the stress of captivity. As usual, he begs for his release, but I feel nothing for his pleas. I know the things he's done and those he would continue to do if I let him go. Men like him don't change. Some sickness can't be cured. Some beasts need to be put down.

Other than my brief foray to the cabin, Jack's protective gaze feels like a ghostly, watchful presence, though I don't see him on campus any more than I did before. It's hard to believe, given how long I've watched him, but perhaps I'm even more attuned to him now. But his presence is not suffocating. It's actually strangely liberating. He never tries to tell me what to do or where to go, he's just *there*, like an extra barrier between me and Hayes, even though I rarely run into him when moving from one class or building to the next.

And perhaps as a result of Jack's influence, Hayes usually leaves me alone.

...usually.

As he stands in the back of my lecture hall, pressed to the shadows at the top of the stadium seating near the exit, I know that Hayes is starting to grow restless. I too am acquainted with the feeling of an obsession taking hold, how its roots grow too deep to dig out.

And his obsession isn't truly with me. I know Hayes has an affinity for me. He still sees me as the girl I once was, the one who survived a vicious attack from a prolific serial killer. He still sees my mask, and maybe he'll never get a hint of what lays beneath. But we're all just animals in the end. How long can those virtuous ideals of capturing a killer withstand his obsession if I'm the key to unlocking his prize?

I pull my gaze away from him and onto my laptop, advancing the slides displayed behind me with the remote in my hand. The image is one of a badly decomposed body in an open field with no tree cover nearby. I click once more for a closer shot of the remains, the body skeletonized but the bones still present and articulated. My gaze passes over the second-year undergraduate Scavenger Behavior and Forensic Investigation class. "What could a Forensic Investigator infer from the body in this state, given the environment pictured?"

Several students raise their hands. I point to Maisie, a quiet but smart, thoughtful student seated in the third row. "The bones are all still in place, despite the open location. Avian scavengers would've had clear access to the body, but other vertebrate scavengers would too. The skeletal remains would likely be disarticulated and distributed over a wider area if animals had access. It's possible the body was moved there after insect colonization was complete."

"Good, Maisie," I say, and she beams with the compliment. "Potential confounding factors to this theory?"

She thinks on it for a moment. "Clothing, though there doesn't appear to be any... Umm, weather?"

"How so?"

"Weather affects the behavior of scavengers, making it less likely that they would interact with the body on days of heavy rain or poor conditions."

"That's right. They don't like to get drenched any more than we do, in part because of the caloric expenditure required to stay warm. And also because it just sucks," I say, advancing the slide to one of Sunny Bunny lying curled beneath the low-hanging boughs of some pines, her fur soaked from a heavy downpour. She looks *miserable*, and I smile when the class laughs.

"In advance of class next week, I want you to read Haglund's Stages of Canid-Assisted Scavenging papers from the syllabus and be prepared to discuss what the *lack* of skeletal remains can tell us about a decomposition site and potential time of death," I say as the students start packing up their things to rush to their next classes. "And I almost hate to remind you, but final exams are in just a couple of weeks, folks, so start studying now. I'll be extending my open office hours from two to four on Tuesdays and Thursdays until then."

Students shoot me grateful smiles. A few hang back to ask probing questions about finals, but I only give them enough information to point them in the right direction. The rest is up to them and their own drive to succeed.

When the last students filter out of the lecture hall, it's just me and former agent Eric Hayes.

"Agent Hayes," I say, testing his reaction to the moniker. He gives none, which I find a little worrying. His lie comes too easily. "Enjoy learning about scavengers?"

"Please, call me Eric," he says as he lands on the final

step. His expression warms with pride. "And it was fascinating, but I enjoy seeing you thrive more."

I give him my winning smile, this one sweet and a little demure.

Smiles sell, baby!

"What can I do for you today, Eric?" I slip on my coat and pack my laptop into my bag, casting him a cursory glance as he takes a few steps closer to the podium.

"I wanted to check in, find out how you were doing. I've seen you around but we haven't had a chance to talk properly in a while. How's the hand healing?"

"Fine now, thanks," I say, glancing down at the red slash, the flesh still tender beneath the scar. Jack removed the stitches earlier in the week and I almost miss them, the way they'd tug at my skin and catch in my hair. Between their removal and Jack's reacquisition of his lighter, I feel somehow bare. *Exposed.*

"I followed up about the broken award that Dr. Sorensen replaced. That was...surprising."

I give Hayes a furrowed brow, tucking my papers into my laptop bag and zipping it closed. My fingers stay looped through the small handle to give myself camouflage for controlling my simmering rage. "How so?"

"From what I heard, there was animosity between you and Dr. Sorensen."

I tilt my head, trying on a pensive expression. "I wouldn't say animosity..."

...we only wanted to kill and potentially frame one other for murder some of the time...

Hayes gives a chuckle that sounds too much like a father trying to dig out information on his daughter's bad boy love interest. "Well, it seems to have eased now. From what I've heard, you're staying at his place...is that correct?"

"Word travels fast on campus," I reply with a shrug.

"Then perhaps you can enlighten me as to Dr. Sorensen's whereabouts the weekend before last."

My heart pumps crystals of ice through my veins. Gooseflesh prickles across my arms, the frozen kiss of alarm tingling in my skin. "What's this about, Eric?"

Hayes takes in a heavy lungful of air, pushing it through his thin, pursed lips. He wants to make it look like whatever he's about to say is unfortunate news, but I can see the truth in his eyes. He's *excited*.

"There was a body recovered last week, not far from state lines. It's officially a murder investigation," Hayes replies as he takes a step closer. "The man had a link to another victim of the Silent Slayer. But he's from Lakeport, Kyrie. That's not even an hour from here, in the Tri-City region. Disturbingly close to where the Slayer's only survivor lives, don't you think?"

I cackle an incredulous laugh, letting it die as though I'm astounded. "And your theory is what, exactly?"

"Where was Dr. Sorensen that weekend, do you know?"

There's a long pause of silence. My shoulders tense. My brow furrows. I catch the fleeting glimmer of pity in Hayes's eyes. "You think...you think Jack has something to do with it? Fucking *Jack Sorensen*, who has spent his entire renowned career improving techniques for catching criminals?"

My act is effortless. So convincing that I almost buy it.

And though Hayes might buy it too, it's only endearing him to *me*, not to Jack. He looks at me as though I've been fucked out of my senses.

"Do you know where he was, Kyrie?" Hayes asks, his voice soft as he steps closer. I have to dig my nails into the red slash on my palm around the handle of the laptop bag to keep from strangling him with the strap.

"Do you know where Brad Thompson was?" I counter. "Since you're so curious about my colleagues, perhaps you should start with the one who was recently arrested."

"Dr. Thompson has an alibi for that weekend. I want to know about Dr. Sorensen's whereabouts."

"He was with me," I reply, struggling not to infuse my words with venom. "We were both in the lab late on Friday. You came by my place Saturday morning. I was with him again Saturday evening, into the night. He left early in the morning to visit his mother on Sunday, and I heard from him on his way home."

"So...you weren't with him the entire time that weekend, correct? There were periods when you were alone?"

"Are you really doing this? Asking me if Dr. Sorensen is the fucking serial killer who murdered my family?"

Agent Hayes sighs, and to his credit, he does an admirable job of keeping his frustration in check. "Isobel—" I shoot him a death glare, realizing too late his use of my old name might have been a tactic to unnerve me and not a benign slip "—*Kyrie*, you need to understand there might be more to his interest in you than you think. He was in Ashgrove when you lived there. I know he came to West Paine before you, but Dr. Cannon said that Dr. Sorensen had plans to move at the time when you arrived. He wasn't going to renew his contract with the university. And then you showed up, and that very same week he decided to change course and stay."

"Surely you had a profile of the killer you were looking for," I say, using every ounce of self-control to sound genuine and not sarcastic. "Does Jack have anything to do with that profile whatsoever?"

"Profiles are not built and set in stone, Kyrie. They are refined with the evidence that comes to light as the case evolves."

"I can't help but notice that you didn't actually answer my question, Mr. Hayes. Since we're not beyond making assumptions, it seems, I'll assume that Jack does not in fact fit the parameters of your profile for the Silent Slayer. Instead, you're inferring Jack's viability as a suspect on the fact that we lived in the same city and that he happened to visit a chronically ill relative in the same state as a murder victim."

Hayes leans forward, just a little, as though he's imploring me to see something that I'm blind to. "You could be in significant danger. You said in your police reports that the Slayer was wearing a mask when he attacked," he presses, not knowing I lied so easily to authorities to protect my angel of vengeance. "Can you be sure it's not Dr. Sorensen?"

"Yes, I can be sure. It's not the same man."

"You suffered an extremely traumatic event that has negatively impacted your mental health, and he could be using that to his advantage. Is it possible you're being manipulated?"

I'm seething. *Burning.* I want to tear his trachea from his throat, but I can't eliminate the only leverage I have. The one where Hayes believes I could only ever be a victim.

Hayes takes one step closer. There's a steely determination in his eyes that wasn't there before. A predatory gaze.

I take a step back.

"What you went through back in Ashgrove was exceptionally difficult, Kyrie. It must have had a significant and lasting impact on your psychological well-being."

"You would know, wouldn't you. You've read the evaluations I was forced to undergo until I aged out of state care."

"Of course I did. It was my job."

Was.

I catch my tongue between my molars to keep from spilling my thoughts. Blood threads across my tastebuds.

"You can tell me, Kyrie."

"Mr. Hayes, this is a dangerous leap of spurious claims—"

"You must feel very alone and confused," he says, inching closer. "If you just tell me the truth, I can find a way to help you. We can—"

"Good afternoon, Agent Hayes," a voice says from the doors, the timbre deep and smooth.

It's pure menace disguised beneath a thin veil of civility.

Hayes and I both look toward the back of the room where Jack emerges from the shadows, his hands buried deep in his pockets as he slowly descends the first few steps of the aisle between the tiered seating. "I certainly hope you're not cornering my girlfriend alone in a lecture hall," he says.

Jack gives me a devastating grin, and my heart tumbles through my chest.

He's as beautiful as sin. As lethal as a sword.

And sometimes, his timing is complete shit.

I can tell by the way Jack's gaze slides between me and Hayes that he only caught part of the conversation, the part where it sounds like Hayes is trying to get me to confess to murder. He looks ready to eviscerate Hayes and smear his entrails across the lecture hall.

Hayes clears his throat and straightens, lifting the pressure of his encroaching presence. "Dr. Sorensen. Good to see you again. I would never do anything to make Kyrie feel threatened in such a manner."

"Really..." Jack keeps glancing at me as though asking a question, but it's not for confirmation of Hayes's assertion.

It's as though he's asking me permission to kill.

And I know in that instant, with absolute certainty, that he would do it.

He would revel in it. He would never take his eyes from mine as he sliced through flesh and spilled blood across the floor. He would fuck me in the sticky warmth. He wouldn't stop until I was screaming his name.

The power to command one of the most lethal predators on the planet rests in my scarred palm. And the temptation is *intoxicating.*

I press my nails harder into my skin and give Jack a nearly imperceptible shake of my head.

Jack's eyes narrow as they sharpen on Hayes and remain there. "Did you ask Kyrie if that's how she felt? Or did you just assume she was comfortable being alone with an unfamiliar man in a soundproofed room?"

Hayes glances at me as I slide my laptop bag off the table and take another step back. "In case you need a reminder, Dr. Sorensen, I am a law enforcement agent. I was doing my job, asking her details related to a recent murder investigation," Hayes replies, avoiding the question of my comfort altogether. As Jack descends the last steps and rounds the podium to stop beside me, Hayes puts his hands on his hips, pushing back the hem of his brown suit jacket in a purposeful display of the gun holstered at his side. "She tells me she was with you the weekend before last, is that correct?"

"Yes. It is."

"The whole weekend?"

"Nearly."

"Except for when you crossed state lines on Sunday morning."

"Correct."

"What reason would you have to do that, exactly?"

"To visit my mother at Hope Springs Medical Institute."

"And Kyrie didn't go with you?"

"No." Jack's eyes darken for a flash but he knows better than to lie, even if he hates this truth. "I called her on my way home. She'd just gotten in from a run with her dog."

Actually, I'd just gotten home from taking Cornetto to check on Colby at the cabin, but I'm not about to correct him.

There's a moment of taut silence, stretched thin until I'm desperate to fill it, a void where there should be voices. I know better than to give a man like Hayes more answers than he's asked for, but the silence still claws and burrows into my brain like vermin.

"I will endeavor to take Kyrie with me next time, if that appeases you," Jack says in his cool, confident tone, as though he knows I can't stand the quiet much longer. I resist the urge to groan at how Hayes might take his words.

The former agent advances a step and I slide my hand into Jack's, the motion snagging Hayes's attention. "If you'll excuse us, we have a budget meeting in the Bass research building in ten minutes," I say as Jack pulls my bag from my grasp, his other hand tensing around mine. "Have a good day, Mr. Hayes."

Hayes gives a tight nod but says nothing further as we stride away.

I don't look back, but I know he's watching.

Jack and I remain silent as we exit the building, our

hands still clasped, even when we're outside and the blast of icy air hits our exposed skin. All pretense could be swept away by the wind. But I hold on, at least until I can coil my newly forming plans around myself, the wisps and threads of spinning thoughts as fine and strong as spider silk.

I look up at Jack as we walk, staring long enough for him to meet my gaze. His eyes narrow at my beaming smile. "I'm your girlfriend?"

His eyes sharpen further. "Really? *That* is what you take away from that conversation?"

I shrug as my smile blooms brighter. "It's the only unexpected thing from it, really. I'd hoped the Sebastian idea would work, but it was a gamble." I focus on the path ahead before Jack can delve too deeply into the details of my expression. "Not an ideal result, but not our last resort."

"*Not ideal*...Your ability to see on the positive side of certain situations is...distressing." Jack lets go of my hand, but only long enough to drape his arm across my shoulders and pull me into his side. "He thinks you're unhinged," he says against the shell of my ear, keeping his voice low as we pass a group of unfamiliar students.

I snort a laugh. "He's not wrong."

"He obviously has concerns about both of us if he's asking about my trip."

"And you did such a good job making yourself look like the picture of innocence by saying you'd take me along next time. That didn't sound threatening at all."

"I need his attention off you, *elskede*."

I look up and meet Jack's eyes. The moment I do is the one that confirms that I need to act *now*, while I have the advantage with Hayes. Because fury isn't the only fire to brighten the mercury surrounding Jack's dilated pupils.

Excitement. A thirst that burns. For our kind, killing is

not just a desire, but a need, and once it takes hold it will not let go.

Jack is going to hunt him. And my instinct tells me that Hayes will be ready if he does.

Jack's jaw tics as his gaze rakes across my face. He manages to subdue his predatory craving, but not fast enough. "We need to get Hayes out of the picture soon, before he stumbles on something viable to follow. The longer he remains, the greater the risk."

He's right, of course. Hayes is not all that different to us. Feral. Unpredictable. Hayes is beholden to no process, to no master but his obsession.

I give Jack a sparkling smile, letting it touch my eyes before I turn my attention to the building in the distance.

"Don't worry, petal," I reply, patting Jack's hand. "I've got a plan."

There's a lengthy pause as we continue down the winding path.

"Care to share?"

"Not yet, no."

Jack grumbles something in Danish but doesn't let go, not even as we fall into silence, nor as we pass a trio of forensic students who greet us with grins that are ready for gossip. It's only once we're in the research lab that any space grows between us, and for the first time, the distance is a relief.

A breath of air before the plunge into an abyss.

NINETEEN

LUMINOUS

J ack and I share only a few glances as the budget meeting drags on for nearly two hours, and we leave campus as soon as it's done. We go straight to Jack's house, and though I don't feel like it, I prattle on about random shit on the short drive, keeping my happy little mask in place even though my mind is churning to the point of exhaustion. By the time we walk through the door to the sound of Cornetto's excited wooing and the new robot vacuum's whirling motor, I feel ready to down the rest of the Tequila bottle I didn't finish the other night, no glass required.

But I don't inhale the Tequila. I have to keep my head clear, even though I'm desperate to anesthetize this relentless, growing unease that crawls across my skull.

At the end of the day, I stand in front of the mirror in the bathroom, just watching my eyes, their color so like my dad's, their shape so like my mom's. Everything behind them is different from what my parents would have expected me to be. What they would have wanted. Maybe I should feel guilty for that. I'm their living legacy, after all. Yet I don't.

All I feel is need.

A need to slide my knife into Haye's throat. A need to feel his last breath tremble in my hand.

A need to protect Jack.

I'm clutching the edge of the square basin with a white-knuckled grip when he stops at the door as though my thoughts have conjured him.

"Thinking about Hayes?" he asks as he leans against the door frame, folding his arms across his bare chest, a pair of low-slung sweats clinging to his hips. I tear my gaze from the delicious display of muscle, a sudden ache protesting in my core as I drop my attention to my bleached skin stretched thin across the curves of bone.

"Maybe a little."

"You're worried."

"Sure. I guess."

"This plan of yours, are you going to share it with me?"

I meet Jack's eyes through the reflection in the mirror. Though I smile, it has little energy left to shine very bright. "After I take care of a few things first, yes. Of course."

"And how long will these things take?"

My shoulders rise and fall with a noncommittal shrug. "A couple of days at most."

I let go of the sink and turn to face Jack. This is one lie I wish I didn't have to tell. Regret unfurls in my chest like a blossom reaching for a distant light. I wonder if I've forgotten how to feel it. It's raw and unfamiliar.

Jack doesn't move, doesn't press for more. If he knows I'm lying, he doesn't call me out. Maybe he just thinks I'm rattled by Hayes, which is true. I am. He simply raises his brows, the question so clear in his subtle expression.

What do you need?

I come closer, each step slow and measured, and when I'm within reach, Jack unfolds his arms and straightens. My fingers trace his ribs as I slide my arms around him, mapping the ridges of muscle and bone in his back, his skin soft and smooth beneath my light touch. My eyes drift close as I press my cheek to the steady beat of Jack's heart and sigh. It takes a breath, as though some gentle moments still take getting used to, but then his arms enfold me and keep me pressed close.

I relish the steady thrum of breaths and heartbeats for a long moment before I take a step back into the bathroom, pulling Jack along with me. Then another, and another, until we stop at the edge of the shower and I let go.

No words pass between us as I pull my t-shirt over my head, tossing it to the floor, discarding my sleep shorts next. When I straighten, I step into the shower and turn it on, not breaking the connection of our fused gaze. The cold water pelts my skin, drawing out a shiver when it prickles my scalp and falls over my shoulders, tightening my nipples to painful buds as it cascades down my pebbled skin. But I don't turn the temperature up. I hold my hand out to Jack instead.

He doesn't take it. Not yet.

The touch of his gaze starts from the tips of my toes and the water that slides down my ankles. It flows against the current of every rivulet that snakes down my shins, passing over ancient dents, marks of accidents long forgotten. His eyes heat a path up my thighs, lingering on my pussy and the narrow patch of hair that shines with cold water. When a long moment passes, he ascends through the spray of gooseflesh on my stomach, the skin paling as blood pulls to my core to keep my vital organs warm. Jack's gaze slows again on my twin scars and darkens. From the moment we first met, our history was stitched in my skin, some threads ending where new ones intertwine.

Jack swallows before dragging his focus up higher, first to one breast and then the other, watching the rise and fall of their fullness with each breath. He pauses where my heart and its quickening beat lays hidden in darkness. His eyes follow the stream of water that flows between my clavicles, passing up my neck, lingering on my lips, pausing on my cheek where he sometimes likes to lay a gentle kiss to tickle my lashes. When he finally meets my eyes, I feel worshiped. Precious and unique.

Luminous.

Jack slides his pants off, kicking them back toward the door. The titanium at the crown of his erection shines the shade of dark gunmetal gray in the soft lights banked in smoked glass sconces. He takes my hand, not breaking his gaze away until the moment his lips touch mine.

It's a slow sweep of tongues. A reverential progression of touch. A savoring of shared breath and heat in the cold spray of water. Perfume and vetiver, toothpaste, the last faint wisp of the red wine Jack had with dinner. All of it is washed away.

I'm lost in every press of Jack's lips and caress of his hands across my skin. He kisses me like there could be a million moments like this laid out at our feet, ready to be plucked from the cold stream like delicate flowers.

Jack breaks our kiss to press his lips to my jaw, shifting my soaked hair back from my shoulder to follow the line of my pulse. He braces me close with one arm across my lower back, sweeping his other hand down to pass his thumb over my pebbled nipple. My fingers trace every inch of flesh they can consume, from the soft skin in the hollow of his neck to the broad plains of muscle spanning his shoulders, from the ridges of his spine to the firm rise of his ass.

Jack shudders when I fold my hand around his cock, letting my fingers map the bars and their round ball ends and the curved Prince Albert at the head.

When I shiver in the cold, he pulls back to meet my eyes.

"Are you going to be sweet to me, Jack?" I whisper.

Jack's palm lays on my cheek and he looks through every torn layer of my soul.

"*Jeg vil være alt for dig, elskede,*" he says, and then presses his lips to mine.

When I hook one leg across his back, Jack cradles my thigh in his palm, his thumb stroking my skin. He pushes me up to the wall and my back slips across the cold tile as he lifts me. I fold my other leg behind him as I grip his shoulder with one hand and center his erection to my entrance with the other.

Our kiss breaks. But our locked gaze doesn't.

"*Min lysende stjerne,*" he says as he slowly lowers me onto his length, his eyes never leaving mine. I feel every slip of metal as he glides into me. He watches me as though archiving the nuances of my growing need with his silver eyes. "*Min elskede.*"

"Tell me something I can understand."

A faint smile tips up one corner of Jack's lips. "You do understand."

"Tell me something anyway. Something real."

"You are mine."

That is real.

The rhythm builds slowly, every glide of Jack's cock a smooth stroke of pleasure. I wrap my arms around his neck, press my forehead to his. I stare into his eyes. Warm breath and heated skin and icy droplets clash between us. And I would change *nothing*.

I break our locked gaze, wrapping my arms across the back of Jack's neck, relishing the warmth of his chest against my cold skin. He slides his hands farther up my legs until he grips my ass, guiding the rhythm of every deep stroke. I shiver as the metal balls and bars that follow the length of Jack's erection glide across my flesh, igniting my nerves. He pushes my back harder to the tiles and kisses the line of my shoulder. When he lifts me a little higher and cants the angle of my hips to drive deeper into me, I moan his name. I trail my fingers through his damp hair. My walls grip his cock as he grinds through every thrust.

The pleasure builds to a breaking point. But I can feel him holding back. When I lay a hand to his cool cheek and coax him into view, I can see it in his eyes as his blown pupils filter between mine.

I know many of his fears are the same as mine. But I also know so many of his secrets. And I don't think I can ask whether it's fears or secrets I see in his eyes. Because I need to stick to my plan, and if he lets me in too close now, I might not be able to force myself through with it.

"Come with me," I whisper against his lips before I press my trembling flesh to his. Jack moans into my mouth and my back squeaks on the tiles as he thrusts harder until the air rushes from my lungs with every pounding stroke.

I don't feel the cold water anymore. Only the pleasure that consumes me, spinning through my nerves as it devours my senses, leaving me numb to everything beyond the release that crashes in waves beneath my skin. I feel made of light, drowning in it, my head thundering with heart-beats, sparks flaring across my vision as I press my eyes closed. A tight cry escapes my lips when Jack pulls away to bite into the tender flesh at the junction between my neck and shoulder. He grinds into me with a growl as he releases, his cock pulsing as he spills into me.

We stay clutched in our embrace until our breathing starts to slow. Jack seems just as reluctant to let go as I am. My mind would be content to stay here forever, but my body protests the cold far too soon, and when my teeth start to chatter, Jack lowers me with a flash of a smile before he sets me on unsteady feet. He turns the water temperature up, the first hit of hot spray a welcome prick of needles in my skin.

"Bed?" is his only question. I nod and he lays a kiss on my lashes before he steps out of the shower to dry himself off and brush his teeth, casting a brief smile over his shoulder before departing to the bedroom.

Once he's gone, I sit in the shower with my knees tucked into my chest until the water scalds my flesh to red blotches.

When I dry my hair and climb beneath the covers, Jack is nearly asleep, waking only long enough to drape an arm over my waist.

But I don't sleep.

I wait.

Jack's breathing deepens. The twitches of dreams pass. If there are nightmares, they don't wake him. When he's slipped beyond the realm of dreams, I rise and leave the bed, motioning for Cornetto to follow.

We head downstairs in silence and shadow. I don't turn on a light until I'm in Jack's office, going first to the closet to retrieve the bag I stashed behind a box of academic journals. I change into the clothes within. A black t-shirt. An old camo sweater my dad bought me before our last hunting trip together. My favorite green hiking pants. Even my hiking boots are laced, my jacket zipped to my chin. By the time I sit at Jack's desk, everything is ready to go.

Except me.

I pull a pen from the caddy on the desk and open one of the drawers to retrieve some paper. A leather sketchbook lays on the thick stack of unblemished sheets of Jack's personal stationery, and I place it on the desk before me. My fingers hover over the cover for a long moment as I try to convince myself that this is too private an item to open, but in the end my curiosity wins and I flip through the thick, creamy sheafs of paper.

Some sketches are studies of hands. Delicate but strong. Expressive and elegant. Others are silhouettes, their features feminine but vague. Sitting as though deep in thought, or gesturing to someone not shown on the page. Looking out the window toward a shadowy landscape in rough strokes of charcoal.

I flip another page and my breath catches in my throat.

It's a woman resting her chin in her hand, her expression pensive as she watches something in the distance. The details are rendered with meticulous precision in different strengths of graphite pencil.

But her eyes are vivid blue.

The next page, another study of her face, this one much closer up. The same style, the shading so fine that the pencil strokes are barely visible. Blue eyes with a dark center that pales toward the deep ring around the iris, variegated shades streaking away from the pupil. The color is exact, precise.

I flip more pages. Different poses. Different emotions. The same woman with blue eyes.

Me.

I slap the cover shut and force the air to move in my

lungs past the fist that seems lodged in my throat. Only three breaths. That's the longest I'll let myself delay.

When the third breath has passed, I take a piece of fresh paper from the pad in the desk and write my letter, folding it before placing it in my pocket.

On the second sheet, I write only three words:

Frozen solder distraction.

I keep the second note in my hand before I turn to Cornetto, who sits at my side, his russet brown eyes tracking my expressions. He lets out a soft whine and I caress his silver fur, resting my head to his.

"You can't come this time," I whisper, and he whines again. Somehow, he always knows when I go hunting without him. "You have to look after Jack. Go back to bed, Corndog."

With a final whimper, Cornetto turns and trots away to head back upstairs.

I turn off the light, and for a long moment, I simply sit in the comforting dark.

When I'm finally ready to go, I place the second note on the kitchen counter. Then I leave Jack Sorensen's house and stride away into the star-riddled night.

TWENTY
ARROWS
KYRIE

"You came," I say as Jack approaches from the narrow path, the brittle leaves of beech trees scraping one another as he moves low-hanging branches out of his way. There's no controlling the smile I beam at him as he enters the small clearing and draws to a halt to take in the log cabin behind me.

"You scared the fucking shit out of me, Kyrie," Jack says, pinning me with a glare. "I nearly missed the note."

"But you didn't," I say, trying not to let his concern burrow too deep into memory. My smile brightens and I spread my arms wide. "And here we are."

Jack's glare finally softens a little when he looks toward the cabin. I turn on my heel to follow his gaze, admiring the dark lines of wood and the weathered porch, original features paired with my own modifications of solar panels and hidden cameras. When I face him once more, Jack is watching me, a gleam in his eyes as though he's seeing me for the first time.

"You built this?" he asks, nodding toward the cabin.

"No," I say with a little laugh. "No, this belonged to my grandfather. But I've made some changes over the years."

Jack nods as his gaze lands on one of the more visible cameras bolted beneath the overhang of the roof. When his attention returns to me he takes a careful step forward, and then another. Maybe he thinks this is some kind of trap. Maybe there's something in the excitement I can barely contain that's a little too feral, a little too suspicious. So when Jack stops in front of me, his hands still buried deep in his pockets, I'm the one who closes the distance between us, rising on my tiptoes to fold my hand across his nape and draw him into a kiss. I grip the edge of his open jacket with my free hand, the metal teeth of the zipper digging into my palm as I pull him closer. My tongue runs across the seam of his lips, demanding entry to lavish his mouth with a taste of the desire that coats my chest in flame.

He can't resist me.

I already know he doesn't want to, even if he's tried for so long to stand in his own way. Jack's hands lay on my face, bringing warmth to my cold skin as he traces the chill in my cheekbones with his fingertips until the tingle of his touch starts coursing through my body. I have to force myself to do it, but I'm the one who breaks the kiss. It's my enthusiasm for my surprise that pulls me back, and the fear too, if I'm being honest. There's an exhilaration in following my instincts, but an awareness that I could be wrong, though that carries its own intoxicating desire that pulls me away like a tide.

"What are we doing here?" he asks, moving to take a step toward the cabin. I tighten my grip on his jacket to keep him from getting closer.

"I have a little present for you," I reply, my grin unstoppable as I turn away to the expedition pack lying at the edge of the clearing. The wary look he shoots me proves he recognizes this backpack, but instead of some grad student's severed limb, I take out a tablet, turning it on to select a thumbnail view that I enlarge before I hand it to Jack. His eyes hold mine for a long moment before he looks at the screen, his lips parting as he takes in the live image. "Do you like it?"

"Colby Cameron," Jack whispers, his voice a reverential prayer. I give him time, staying quiet until he's ready to look up from the screen. "You have him here."

I nod before I return to my belongings, drawing a rusted metal chain from the backpack. "He's in the basement. But you can't go in. It will ruin our fun."

I wink as I pass by with the chain looped over my shoulder. It's what dangles at my back that catches Jack's eye, and he follows every movement of the metal contraption as I head to the mouth of the path he just emerged from. I drop to a knee and lay the foothold trap on the narrow, worn track, opening the jaws and setting the spring levers before I cover the area with fallen leaves. It's not perfect, but I know Colby will be too desperate to take much notice of anything on the ground.

"Don't go wandering. There are more like it surrounding the property, and these traps are both ancient and unforgiving," I warn as I return to my pack and the camo print case that lays beneath it. I toss the expedition pack to Jack and he catches it, his brow furrowing when his gaze collides with mine. "There's a garrote in there. Some knives too. Hopefully something you'll like. I'm just here as a contingency plan."

I flash Jack a grin and drop my gaze to the case I've unzipped, unfolding it to reveal a compound bow and twelve arrows. I'm pulling out the first arrow and double-checking the fletchings when the backpack lands next to me.

"You do it," Jack says. When I look up, his gunmetal eyes are hooded, the shadows burning with an unnamed fire, igniting my veins like fuses.

"But he was yours," I reply, leaning back on my haunches to study him.

"We're even then, since I took one of your targeted victims."

"Right," I say with a breath of a laugh. "Ryan Young. I was looking forward to that one. And you never even gave me any details of how that all went down. What prompted you to go for him, anyway?"

Jack's shoulders tense as though he's bracing for the unknown. "I was irritated. A certain colleague was worming her way beneath my bones. I needed to let off some steam."

I huff a laugh. "What a shocker. You find me irritating. How romantic," I quip with a broad smile that only spreads as the crease between Jack's brows appears. My attention returns to the arrows as I pull another from the case.

"No, Kyrie. I was irritated I couldn't shake free of you, no matter how hard I tried." Jack takes a step closer, drawing my gaze from the work of my hands. He approaches with slow and methodical progress, a hunter hoping not to provoke an attack from an unpredictable animal. When he's within reach, he squats to study me, balancing on the balls of his feet. "I was irritated that I couldn't carve you out of my thoughts, and the harder I tried, the more impossible it became. You're the one person I couldn't stop. The only person I couldn't overcome." Jack reaches out and curls a stray lock of hair behind my ear, resting his palm on the side of my face. "I was frustrated because I didn't think I could have you, the one thing I truly wanted."

I lay my hand on Jack's and press my cheek into his cool palm. I wish I had the bravery to say it out loud, to tell him how I really feel. That I love him. I wonder if he's ever heard it before. If he has, did the person really mean it? Or was it a deception? Would Jack know that my words are true? Would it scare him away if he did?

"You have me, Jack," I say. And though I can't give him more words than that, I can show him. I pull him closer until his lips are only the width of a thread from mine. "I'm yours, always. And you're mine."

Jack's breath warms my skin, a slow exhalation. Energy courses between us like unsteady waves beneath a sudden breeze. And it's Jack who inches closer, who presses his lips to mine, whose hand threads through my hair to grip the back of my neck as he deepens the kiss, sweeping his tongue across mine. His free hand finds my waist to hold my balance steady as he presses closer, demanding more of my touch, more of my thoughts, until the outside world is gone. The arrows fall from my hand and I grip his jacket, kissing him back with the urgency of every emotion I can't yet voice, but every one he needs to know.

I'm nearly ready to tear his clothes off when Jack slows the kiss to a breaking point, pressing his forehead to mine as though the separation is as painful for him as it is for me. "I want to watch you," he whispers, his gaze soldered to my lips. My eyes drift closed as he lays a lingering kiss to my cheek, grazing my lashes. Jack loosens my hand from his jacket and lays the dropped arrows in my palm. His kiss leaves my skin only to press once more to my forehead, and then his touch is gone, my heart swelling against my bones until it aches.

Jack watches in silence as I ready my bow, removing a few more arrows and clipping them to the quiver. I move the backpack and the case against the side of the cabin where they'll be out of sight, and then I motion him over as I bring up the tablet. We crouch against the logs at the corner of the cottage where we can see through the railings of the porch toward the narrow path. I hand the tablet to Jack as I navigate through the menus to bring up the door locks and controls.

"Did you install all this?" Jack asks as I hover over the command to open all doors, including the one to the glass cage where Colby sits on his bed, his head in his hands.

"Of course. It's not really like I could bring in someone to do it for me. Might raise some questions, don't you think?" I press the confirmation button and we watch the screen as the glass door unlocks and swings open, Colby startling and rising to his feet as he considers his potential freedom with warranted suspicion.

"This is truly impressive, Kyrie."

I snort a laugh at the admiration in Jack's low voice. "Now you know why I was so pissed when you blamed me for the CRYO freezer incident."

We grow quiet as we watch Colby take his chance to escape. He exits the glass cage and turns in the room, looking for a weapon, pulling a large knife from a row of blades on the wall. His pace quickens as he opens the door at the bottom of the stairs and takes them by twos, pausing as he reaches the second door that enters the basement. When he finds the exit to the main floor, I nock my arrow and slide a glance and a devious smile to Jack before rising to peek around the edge of the cabin.

Colby tries to keep his steps light across the floorboards, but I still hear every footfall of his bare feet as he crosses the living room, the front door already opened enough for him to slip through. I lean back out of sight as he pauses for a heartbeat when he reaches the porch.

A breath later, he's running like a hunted stag.

I ready my arrow as I watch Colby dart across the planks, wild and unfocused, not even touching the porch steps as he launches himself off the deck and lands on the grass, breaking toward the path. He gathers speed across the small clearing. He's sprinting for his life.

Colby's foot hits the trap full force, the metal jaws snapping against his bones to the sound of his scream.

The cries filling the clearing are pained and desperate as Colby tries to process what's just happened and to work through his pain. I watch through the bow sight as he grabs the jaws and pulls, wailing when they won't give up his leg. The pointed iron teeth will be digging in deep, likely scraping his bone, and excitement skitters up my spine when I imagine the moment I'll be able to see the damage up close. When Colby seems to realize his efforts are futile, he rises on his good foot and limps a step forward, his weapon forgotten among the crisp, fallen leaves.

I release my fingers and let my arrow fly.

Colby drops to his knees with a desolate scream. I turn to Jack with my hand over my mouth, trying and failing to muffle a laugh.

"I think I shot him in the asshole," I whisper as Colby continues to shriek at the edge of the clearing. We peer around the corner of the cabin to watch him crawl in agony. His arm flails across his back as he tries to work out what to do with the arrow jutting from between his buttocks.

"That's definitely in there," Jack says. Colby gives up on the arrow and refocuses on the path, crying out with every arduous movement of his futile efforts to escape. "Impressive shot."

"Thanks. I think it's even better than the time I skewered Mike Connors in the dick and balls in one shot," I reply, passing my bow to Jack. "I guess I should put him out of his misery."

Colby hasn't gotten far, not even out of sight of the clearing as he drags himself along the path. He doesn't hear me approach, doesn't realize I'm right behind him until I grab the chain of the trap and tug. He screams when I bear my weight against his, clutching the rusted links over my shoulder as I turn toward the cottage and drag him back into the clearing. Jack steps in front of the porch to watch our progress, his hands leaving his pockets to form tense fists and his gaze turning lethal when Colby manages to kick my legs with his free foot. The string of insults and obscenities Colby screams at me only darken the aura of the other killer in our midst. Jack is nearly vibrating with rage as he stalks a few strides closer, but he lurches to a halt when I throw up a hand and toss him an untroubled smile.

"You really are a slow learner, aren't you, Mr. Candyman," I say when I drop the chain and withdraw the hunting knife strapped to my belt. I turn toward Colby as he tries to kick me away, dragging himself backwards on his hip, howling with agony when the arrow catches on the ground. Tears carve hot paths down his skin. A string of pleas and swears and desperate prayers tumble from his trembling lips. "There is no escaping me."

I lunge forward. Colby kicks out exactly the way I knew he would.

My blade meets his inner thigh. I drive it in deep, severing the femoral artery. When I withdraw my knife, the blood gushes in pumping spurts, soaking his thin pants.

I waste no time in dropping to my knees as Colby clutches his thigh in an attempt to staunch the bleeding. "No woman will ever have to beg you for mercy again," I whisper as I push my knife into Colby's larynx, silencing his screams. His failed attempts to breathe and swallow vibrate in my hand. In a moment that feels too short, those struggles fade away, and Colby goes slack around my blade.

When Colby is still, I pull my knife from his throat in a rush of blood, wiping the sharpened steel against his sleeve before I lay it next to me on the ground, recovering my breath. Euphoria washes through my veins with every beat of my heart. Adrenaline. Domination. There's relief in the afterglow, like a thorn pulled from flesh. But the moment Jack's arms fold around me, I realize how much better this is with him here. There's more that I want, and only he can give it to me.

"*Lille mejer...*" he whispers as he presses his lips along the column of my neck. My breath catches as his palm glides down my jacket, slowing over my breast, my nipples tightening to points against the layers of clothing that suddenly seem too hot. Jack's hand keeps traveling down until it cups my pussy. I lean against his touch, desperate for friction. For *more*. "I wonder... If I slid my fingers into your panties, would I find your cunt wet and desperate to be filled?"

A whimper leaves my lips as Jack's touch withdraws, a sound that turns to one of need when I hear his belt buckle open and his zipper lower. "Why don't you find out?"

Jack traces my hip and releases my belt and the button of my hiking pants, and then he's pulling them down with rough and impatient tugs. In another heartbeat, the stud on the head of his cock is pressed to my entrance and he enters me with a single, brutal thrust. "Just as I suspected. Fucking soaked."

"Only because you were watching," I whisper as he withdraws to the crown and slams to the hilt, his arm catching around my waist as he pitches me forward onto my hands. My fingers dig into the damp earth and Jack grips the flesh of my hips and thrusts, one pounding hit after the next, every stroke a long glide of his cock so that I feel each rung of the ladder of studs trailing the underside of his erection. The curved bar at the head of his cock ignites every nerve and deep need and dark fantasy. Jack's fingers circle my clit and tease, pressing and withdrawing to a touch that's feather-light, drawing out every moan. But it's his words that truly push me to the edge.

"Look at what you've done," he says as he leans forward to graze his lips against my ear, his powerful body covering mine. The cadence of his strokes is unbroken. "A bear trap around his leg. An arrow in his ass. Blood everywhere. What do you feel about the life you just took?"

"Satisfaction..." I grit out through the rapture of every punishing thrust. "I feel... satisfaction."

"What else? You're holding back, Kyrie."

Jack's hand wraps around my throat and I swallow. My heart drums against his palm. For the first time, I realize the danger I'm in. Every scrap of evidence I have on Jack is right here in this cabin. There's half a body in my freezer. I've just killed a man. And now all Jack has to do is squeeze, and I would be powerless to stop him from ending everything and walking away.

It's *exhilarating*.

My impending release starts unraveling in my core, my deepest muscles tensing, my nerves lighting like exploding stars. "I feel indomitable... Immortal. Like a person who deserves to be feared."

Jack hums his approval against my ear. His strokes slow to long, smooth glides of his cock. He's keeping me on the edge of an orgasm that's ready to burst through every cell of my body. "I've never seen anything more beautiful than your smile when you hauled Colby back from the path. And I've never wanted to kill anyone so desperately as when I thought he might hurt you when he fought back. But you are right, *lille mejer*. You are indomitable. You are both the warmth of the sun and the destruction of its consuming fire," he says, releasing my throat as he buries his cock as deep into my pussy as he can, until I'm not sure where he ends and I begin. Jack presses to my clit and I moan his name like a prayer. "And it's my touch that makes you tremble. My mouth on your pussy that makes you beg. My cock buried in your cunt that makes you moan. My cum that will be dripping down your legs. Tell me I'm the only one you want. The only one who can stand in your flame as you burn down the world."

Jack's words settle in my chest like falling snow. I feel their crystalline touch as they cool the darkness of my deepest fears.

"It will only ever be you, Jack," I whisper. "No matter where you go or what you do. You're the only one I want."

There's a moment of stillness. I can hear every rustle of the breeze through the curled leaves that cling to the branches reaching above us. I could count every beat of my cracking heart.

When the moment passes, the rhythm of Jack's thrusts resumes. It's a cadence that feels desperate, filled with need, like all the things we can't say to one another push us to the edge of an abyss. His fingers swirl over my clit, his touch slick with my arousal, his other hand gripping to my shoulder for leverage as he fucks me with brutal strength.

"You shred every ounce of my control," Jack grits out behind me, easing off on my clit when he feels my channel tighten around the girth of his erection. "I want to fuck you until you're begging me to stop making you come."

Unsteady breaths burn in my chest as he thrusts without mercy, just the way I want him to. "I...don't think...I ever would," I say, lifting one hand from the earth just long enough to grasp Jack's forearm in a wordless plea for friction. He presses my clit in sweeping circles and I moan, steadying myself once more as the world seems to spin around me. My pussy tightens around every deep thrust and I come, release washing over me as I cry out Jack's name.

Jack slows only for a moment, his touch lightening as he guides me through every second of ecstasy. When I'm ready to collapse in a boneless heap of flesh on the cold ground, the long, rocking strokes resume, a cadence building.

"You don't think you ever would beg me to stop making you come, *hmm?*" Jack whispers close to my ear, his voice a dark and seductive weapon all of its own. "Were you issuing a challenge, Dr. Roth? It almost sounded like it..."

Oh my God.

I'm trying to put together some kind of coherent response, but words don't want to form sentences on my tongue, especially not when Jack's rough palm glides across my ass cheek in a warm caress.

"I asked you a question, Dr. Roth. But if you're not going to answer," he says as his palm leaves my skin, "I'll happily redden your perfect ass until you do."

A hard slap smacks my skin and I lurch forward with a

yelp that dissolves into a quiet moan. Jack's hand smooths the burn in my flesh as he glides within me.

"Still no answer?"

I bite my lip, my nails digging into the earth as I shake my head.

Another slap hits my ass and I cry out as my pussy tightens around Jack's thrusting cock. An ache builds deep in my core. More. I want *more*. More and more until I can't even *think* about begging, until I'm mindless and the only thing that exists is me and Jack. Until the whole world disappears.

Jack leans back, his rhythm steady as he grips my waist with one hand.

"I have been so looking forward to seeing your skin such a pretty shade of red."

There are more slaps, their sting eased by Jack's caress, the pain indistinguishable from the pleasure of his deep strokes. Whatever the question was, it's long forgotten as he fucks me, filling me with his length. My pussy is swollen with aching need, my flesh burning beneath his palm. Jack keeps me on the very edge of coming apart, sometimes breaking from the impact to swirl a gentle touch across my clit before returning to deliver another slap to my ass.

At some point my moans form a single word: *please*.

For a heartbeat, Jack's strokes slow as he glides his palm over my stinging skin.

"I don't think I've ever heard anything as sweet as your begging, petal. Do it again."

I give Jack exactly what he wants.

As a string of pleas tumble from my lips. I beg for him to take me to the edge and push me over. I beg for him to tear me apart. For him to fill me until I'm dripping with his cum.

A feral growl fills the clearing as Jack rails me with

punishing strokes. My fingers clutch the clumps of grass. Stars shatter across my vision. My head fills with heartbeats. Jack comes a moment later, his thick and studded length pushed as deep as he can manage, his cock pulsing as he spills into me.

The world is deafened by pressure and heartbeats and ragged breaths. And Jack stays there for a long time as we catch our breath, not slipping away until a sudden chill makes me shudder. When he's pulled his briefs and pants up, Jack hauls me to my feet.

"I'm a bit of a mess," I say, looking at the mud and grass stains on my palms, dirt caked beneath my nails.

"I like you this way," Jack replies as he kneels before me to pull my panties up. He stalls as our cum drips down my inner thighs. His touch is reverential when it slips through the glistening arousal, smearing it across my skin. He takes some onto his finger and pushes it back into my pussy. "I like it a lot."

"You are filthy, Dr. Sorensen," I say with a grin.

"And you love it."

My heart drums heavy beats and I turn my gaze away from Jack as he rights my panties over my ass and hips, then my pants. My thoughts are caught on the cabin, on the box in the basement. My mind is so consumed by the swell of fears I've been pushing down into my darkest corners that I don't notice Jack watching me until he rises to his feet.

"Kyrie...? What is it?"

"Nothing," I say with a flash of a smile. Jack doesn't seem convinced by my first attempt, so I try a little harder with a wider smile that lingers. "Nothing, really. I just got a text from Dr. Cannon before you arrived. I was supposed to meet with him this afternoon but he needs to move it to this morning. He said it's urgent," I say as I check my watch, my weak grin dissipating. "I won't have time to go change. If I don't leave within the next few minutes, I'm not sure I'll make it in time."

Jack frowns. "He can't wait?" When I shake my head and shrug, Jack's frown deepens. "Text me as soon as you get to your office. I don't like the thought of Hayes lurking without me around. I can take care of this," Jack offers, nodding toward the body. A wicked grin shatters the worry that darkened his expression only a moment ago. "There are some souvenirs I'd like to take."

"That would be great, actually. If you wouldn't mind packing up my bow and putting it in the basement when you do, I'll set off the traps."

Jack nods and I turn away before he can read anything more from my eyes. No words flow between us as we work, Jack cleaning my arrow and knife as I spring the traps hidden around the perimeter of the clearing. When we're done, we stand facing one another next to Colby's body, his unseeing eyes pointed to the sky.

"There's equipment in the basement if you need," I say, my heart pounding so hard against my sternum that I'm sure it will etch my fears into bone. A crease flickers between Jack's brows, his gaze dropping to the flush heating my cheeks.

"Are you sure—"

"There's some other stuff there. In the basement. For you," I say. Jack's head tilts, his eyes narrowing. I thrust the tablet in his direction and he takes it with a tentative hand. When he looks up, my waiting smile is lopsided and sly. "It's not a trap, I promise. I can't lock you in if you have this."

Jack's gaze falls back to the tablet and before he can ask,

I close the distance between us, rising on my toes to press my lips to his.

And for once, time slows at the perfect moment.

I feel every breath. I relish every millimeter of skin my touch consumes as I fold one hand across the back of Jack's neck. I take in the scent of vetiver, warm and comforting. The taste of his lips, the smooth caress of his tongue. The chill in his fingertips as they trace my cheek to thread into my hair. The way his arm folds across my back to hold me close. Like I'm cherished. Like this could be a world where he doesn't let go.

But he does, and time rights itself, refusing to die.

"Bye, Jack," I say, letting my touch fall away with the brightest smile I can manage. Jack must be putting pieces together, because he doesn't give voice to his questions. He doesn't say anything at all, in fact. He just looks toward the cabin for a long moment before returning his gaze to me.

I take a deep breath.

And then I walk away.

I try not to turn around, but when I reach the mouth of the path, I can't help it. I stop and look over my shoulder to find Jack watching me, his expression unreadable. He's just as I would always want to imagine him. Beautiful and fierce. My angel of vengeance, with my cabin lying behind him, all its secrets in the basement, my kill lying at his feet.

"Thank you, Jack," I say. There's softness in my smile. In my eyes. I can feel it, just like I can feel the burn of tears climbing my throat.

With a look just long enough to remember forever, I leave Jack behind.

When I'm out of view, I run.

It's nearly a half mile on the winding, root-laden path back to the small clearing where both our vehicles are parked just off the logging road. My Land Rover eats the gravel road as fast as I dare to push it, and in just a few minutes I'm on the highway, heading back to Westview.

Within twenty minutes, I'm at Jack's house.

Cornetto follows close on my heels as I head upstairs, trying to keep my body language relaxed even though my guts are twisting tighter with every second that passes. I enter the spare bedroom that has a desk and set up my work laptop, logging into the university VPN. Then I open my personal laptop, and set it next to my work computer where I know my body will function as a barrier to the camera hidden in the corner of the room.

I keep my motions minimal as I hack into Jack's security system and record myself and the other rooms of the house. Then I set a few work emails up to release at random times over the next few hours before I set my mouse on a mouse jiggler. When everything is set, I take over the camera feed and set my video to play on a loop. It's not the most perfect alibi, but it will have to do.

I turn to Cornetto, whose tail swishes against the duvet on the guest bed. "Wish me luck, Corndog."

With a final pat and a kiss on the head, I leave Cornetto to guard the house alone.

I drive on the side streets back to my house, knowing there are no cameras on the route. When I get home, I park in the garage at the back, then head through the yard to the patio doors. The house is silent and still, its details both welcoming and foreign to me now. Where Jack's house feels monochromatic, mine is bursting with color and pattern. Bright paintings and enlarged photos of wildlife mix with souvenirs I've acquired during my summers conducting field research. But somehow, it feels like a museum now.

Even a few days of another life have made my days of solitude here seem like a memory.

"Better get reacquainted with it now," I say to myself.

I stop in front of a photo in my living room. It's one from
a tag and release program I worked on while supporting a
professor's research on lynx behavior. We sedated the cats
and fit them with radio collars to map their territories and
interactions. The photo is one of me smiling at the camera,
my hand resting on the plush fur of a sleeping male. The
collar was set to break away after five years. Somewhere, if
he's still alive, that lynx is free of us now, hunting and
fighting and living without our watchful gaze.

If I'm successful, the same will be true of Jack. He'll be
able to go wherever he wants without the threat of Hayes or
my mountain of evidence keeping him from his plans. And
this time, I won't haunt his tracks.

I check my watch as I run through the next steps. *Get
the pistol from the gun safe. Text Jack. Send a message to
Hayes.*

I'm about to turn for the basement when something hits
me in the back.

I drop to the floor, stunned. It feels like wasps are
crawling beneath my skin, stinging my brain. My teeth grit
together as my body trembles. The pain stops just as
suddenly as it started, but I'm too shocked to move.

Even if I could, it's too late.

A wet rag clamps across my nose and mouth. I try to
hold my breath and struggle, but it's inevitable. One inhale
of the sweet scent of citrus and acetone and my mind spins.

"It will be all right, Isobel," a man's voice says over the
protest of my weak moan.

"Just go to sleep."

TWENTY-ONE
VESSELS
JACK

The cabin is quiet. The surrounding forest whispers in hushed tones. The twitter of wood thrushes that are late to migrate. The rustle of squirrels in the dense underbrush. I pack the arrows and compound bow away in the case, appreciating Kyrie's taste in weapons.

When I look to the opening of the trail, the demanding urge to follow after her wars within me, the image of her walking away a fresh brand, and I drop a heated glare to the dead body at my feet.

This is the first time body disposal has become an inconvenience.

I place the tablet on Colby's lifeless chest and check the time on my phone, setting an alarm to alert me in twenty minutes, the time needed for Kyrie to reach the university for her meeting.

Pocketing my phone, I glance around the wooded scenery, and I see why she loves it out here. The seclusion, the privacy. The wildlife to study. The sentimental attachment to the cabin with her father and family.

It will be difficult for her to give this up.

After I lasso a rope around Colby's ankles and secure the knot, I place the bow case next to the tablet on his chest and tow him to the front of the cabin, where the hauling of severed body parts will be less of a hike.

Once I get all of him to the basement, I can start the defleshing process. Which I admit, it's been too long, and my blood jolts through my veins in anticipation.

I head down there now to locate a hacksaw, making sure I take the tablet. Not that I don't trust my beautiful little reaper, but one should always be prepared for a surprise in a basement. Especially when my vixen has been known to leave random parts of bodies in my lunch.

As I pull the door open, my eyes fall on the glass enclosure taking up half the space.

How the fuck did she get a glass cage down here?

The sheer ingenuity of the structure is remarkable, breathtaking in its horror.

And I realize, this is Kyrie's kill room.

The chest freezer in the corner calls my attention, and I bypass the numerous gleaming tools along the wall as I stride toward it and the handwritten letter I spy atop the unit. I take the letter in hand, recognizing my stationery.

DEAR JACK,

EVERYTHING HERE IS ALL I HAVE OF YOU.

I THOUGHT IT WOULD HURT TO GIVE THESE THINGS AWAY. FROM THE MOMENT WE FIRST MET IN MY HOME, I'VE CLUNG TO EVERY PIECE OF YOU I COULD FIND. I KNOW YOU DON'T THINK YOU SAVED ME THAT DAY. MAYBE YOU'RE RIGHT, BUT

NOT IN THE WAY THAT YOU THINK. YOU GAVE ME THE CHANCE TO SAVE MYSELF. WHETHER YOU KNEW IT OR NOT, JACK, YOU BECAME THE SCAFFOLDING I REBUILT MY LIFE ON.

MAYBE THAT'S WHY IT DOESN'T HURT TO GIVE THESE PIECES OF YOU BACK. BECAUSE I CAN STAND ON MY OWN NOW. WHEN I TAKE THE SCAFFOLDING DOWN, I LIKE THE LIFE I'VE BUILT. IT MIGHT NOT BE EVERYBODY'S LIFE, BUT IT'S MINE AND I AM THE WAY I WANT TO BE. AND I WANT TO SHARE MY LIFE WITH YOU. THE REAL YOU, NOT THE MAN I THOUGHT I KNEW FROM THESE PIECES YOU LEFT BEHIND AND THE MOMENTS I STOLE.

SO, I GIVE YOU THESE THINGS WITH A LIGHTER HEART. I'M NOT SO NAÏVE TO THINK YOU WON'T JUST TAKE THEM AND DISAPPEAR. I KNOW YOU INTEND TO LEAVE WEST PAINE, JACK. I PROMISE THAT I WON'T FOLLOW THIS TIME. I CAN ONLY HOPE THAT WHAT WE'VE SHARED FELT AS REAL FOR YOU AS IT FEELS TO ME.

I BUILT UP AN IMAGE OF AN ANGEL OF VENGEANCE WHO SWEPT INTO MY LIFE ON A COLD WIND IN MY DARKEST HOUR. I WANTED TO DESTROY THE MAN I MET AFTER YEARS OF WATCHING FROM THE SHADOWS. AND I LOVE THE MAN I'VE COME TO KNOW IN THE PROCESS OF TRYING TO BURN YOU DOWN.

I LOVE YOU, JACK SORENSEN. YOU'RE THE ONLY MAN I'VE EVER LOVED. THE ONLY MAN I EVER WILL.

FOREVER YOURS,
LILLE MEJER

I fold the letter slow and deliberate, lining up the corners to meet exactly before absently running my finger over the crease. A burn forms in the pit of my stomach as my gaze pans over the items she spread out next to the freezer.

I flip open a manila folder. Within are torn pages from magazine articles. Photocopied images from journal publications I've authored. A number of press releases are included, but there are also little tokens, like receipts, sticky notes, even a pen—one I faintly recognize as I grasp the familiar soft-touch barrel.

One of my syllabi are among the objects, from a class I taught while finishing out my PhD at Revery Hall University in Ashgrove.

But the lone scrap of paper is what claims my attention. Kept in pristine condition and laminated, I pick up the receipt from Arley's Campus Restaurant & Bar. Revery Hall University. Cash paid. Pellegrino. Chicken Caesar Salad. Cappuccino.

Dated for the day I killed Winters.

I brace the heels of my hands on the edge of the freezer and mutter a curse.

My little stalker.

Kyrie trailed me for years, watching me, collecting souvenirs. All without my notice.

Curious, I lift the freezer lid to find half a body. Regardless of being sealed in plastic wrap, I know it's the other half of Mason Dumont. Like one of those friendship hearts broken in two, our heart is a dead body, and she's giving me her severed half.

She just sacrificed her leverage.

Unease prickles beneath my flesh. I check my phone,

waiting for a text from Kyrie to flash on the screen. My thumb hovers over the onscreen keyboard, ready to type out a text...

I stall.

Kyrie asked me to come to her cabin. She wanted me here. Alone. Where I could read her letter in privacy. She's giving me time to process and analyze, but more so, she's allowing me the solitude to make a decision.

She didn't want to say these words aloud; she felt there'd be a chance I'd reject her offer, reject *her*.

Most days, I can mimic the emotions necessary to blend in with society, to even charm people. I've perfected the manipulation to stay hidden beneath a mask.

With Kyrie, there is no mask. She sees the ruthless killer, the unfeeling monster. Hell, she's watched me for years. She sees all of me—so can't she see what she means to me?

I unfold the letter and read it over once more, trying to decipher the full meaning.

I know you intend to leave West Paine, Jack.

She's been made aware of my transfer. Is she asking me to stay? Is she saying goodbye? Can she let us end that easily?

"Fuck." I slam my closed fist against the freezer, frustration climbing my nerves.

Imitation is simple. It's the nuances of human emotion and sentiment that confound me, and Kyrie is the most goddamn confounding of all.

Scraping my fingers through my disheveled hair, I decide that this is what Kyrie wants. She wants me here, ruminating over us and our future, and the only way I know how to fucking think clearly is while I'm defleshing a body.

She probably fucking knows that, too.

I search the basement until I find a vinyl coverup and gloves, then spend the next fifteen minutes methodically and expressly dismembering Colby in preparation. When the alarm sounds on my phone, a small morsel of anger burrows under my skin.

I yank off a glove and grab my phone to send her a text: *Call me.*

After half a minute, when she fails to reply, I decide I've given Kyrie long enough. I gave her an explicit instruction to text me when she got to the university. I don't need her to give me any more time.

I'm going straight to her.

For now, I use Kyrie's plastic wrap to seal Colby's limbs and torso, then store the pieces in the freezer with the half of Mason. I make quick cleanup work, planning to return to do a more thorough job.

Even with the tollbooths, it takes me less than twenty minutes to arrive in the West Paine parking lot. It takes me exactly two minutes to reach her empty office.

I stand at the doorway, absorbing every detail that states Kyrie has not been inside this room once today. A desperate fire stokes to life in my chest as I march to Dr. Cannon's office.

"Where is she?" I demand.

Hugh looks up from his computer screen, a deep furrow notched between his eyebrows. "I'm sorry, Jack, but who are you referring—?"

"Kyrie—" I grit my teeth. "Dr. Roth. She said she had an important meeting with you today."

Standing, he buttons his suit blazer, the concern etched in his deep complexion thoughtful. "We did. However, Dr.

Roth said she needed to reschedule, that she wasn't feeling well. She's working from home today on a few things." He lowers his gaze to the screen and clicks the mouse. "I received an email from her just a few minutes ago..."

His voice drifts out as I take off down the hallway.

Her home *is* my home.

And I would have received a security alert if she'd gone there.

I pull out my phone and check the logs. There's one recorded entry from about twenty-five minutes ago. The system was accessed using my login information. Adrenaline rushes the chambers of my heart as I tap on the cameras to view the rooms.

My feet come to an abrupt halt when I glimpse her sitting at a desk in one of the guest rooms.

Everything about this is off. Why is she in a different room? Why did she lie about the meeting? My questions die when I notice her hand hovering over the mouse on the desk, then blink out.

"Son of a fucking—" I hurl the phone at the wall, watching with satisfaction as it cracks and skitters to the floor. I plant my hands to the cool cinder block, eyes sealed shut while I try to think past the furious pounding of my heart.

"Jack...?"

Lifting my head, I glance over to see Joy nervously clutching a purse to her chest. The silence of the department filters through my senses, and I turn to take in the wide and concerned gazes cast my way. Dr. Cannon stands at his office door, watching me intently.

I push off the wall and step toward Joy. "Give me your phone."

She blinks. "I don't understand. Jack, this isn't like you. What's wrong?"

Patience shorn thin, I feel a layer of my fabricated mask slip away, and Joy registers this transition. Fear crests her shiny dark eyes.

"Your phone, Joy," I say around my clenched jaw. "It's for Kyrie."

She plunders in her bag and holds out her phone, her wide gaze never leaving my face. "Oh... Is she all right?"

"I'm going to make damn sure of it." I take the device and light the screen. "Passcode?"

Her mouth parts. "Uh... One-two-three-four-five-six."

I punch the code in to verify, then frown at her. "Tell Dr. Cannon my afternoon class is canceled."

"Sure, Jack..."

Without any further explanation, I leave Joy and my other colleagues staring after me with concerned expressions. I exit through the emergency door to reach the parking lot faster and, once I'm seated behind the wheel of my car, I breathe in a stable breath, then use Joy's phone to call Kyrie.

The call goes straight to voicemail.

Clutching the device in an iron grip, I mentally comb her letter, looking for any clues I missed. Despite Kyrie's tendency to be emotionally volatile at times, this doesn't feel like the way she'd leave things between us.

She's not leaving. She's not running away from me.

Setting up a loop on my security feed... Establishing an alibi with Cannon... Keeping me busy defleshing a body...

She's buying time.

I key the engine and crank the car. "Goddammit. She's going after Hayes on her own."

Why the *fuck* would she do this without me.

She's being impulsive, putting herself in danger. Hayes may not be the ultimate villain to fear, but he's unhinged enough we can't discount him. I wipe a hand down my face, not knowing whether I want to strangle her or kiss her when I find her.

Panic rises up from the bowels of some dormant part of my soul to torment me.

I will *find her*.

Bypassing the road to my house, I drive straight to Hayes's last known location. He's been holed up in a cheap motel since he arrived in Westview. According to the PI I hired to dig into the ex-agent, Hayes is staying in room 212 of the Homestead Inn.

Hayes's Honda isn't in the parking lot. Outside the room, I first scope out the window, noting the lowered blinds, listening closely for any signs of movement inside.

Then I stand back and kick the door. It groans but doesn't budge. Muttering a curse, I ram my shoulder into the weakened door, falling into the room as the frame cracks and the latch gives.

Righting myself, I glance around for any signs of a struggle. But then there wouldn't be, would there. Kyrie would be prepared. She'd lure him under false pretenses. She'd hunt him like one of her victims, then drug him, subduing him in a remote location under her control.

Where would she take him? Not to her cabin, to her kill room where she wanted me kept out of the way.

I rifle through the nightstand drawers, comb through the sparse contents of the closet. No gun. She would make him leave his weapon.

Spotting the laptop on the foot of the bed, I open the device and scour the files. Obsession takes on a whole new disturbed meaning as I open file after file of images of Kyrie through the years. Soon, however, his unhealthy fixation on her transfers to me, where he's been digging into my past to connect me to the Silent Slayer murders.

And I realize in a singular moment of clarity that Kyrie thought she was protecting me from Hayes. In the event she didn't succeed, she was saying her goodbye. One last kill together. One last heated moment. Handing over her amassed collection on me...and the bodily evidence of Mason Dumont.

She was setting me free.

I yank the alarm clock off the nightstand and smash it against the wall. Chest heaving, I stare down at the destroyed appliance.

Apparently, I'm only capable of two ranges. Shallow affect and full-blown rage.

Collecting myself, I turn the laptop around and dig deeper into Hayes's archives of Kyrie and uncover the purchase documentation for Kyrie's childhood home.

How the hell did the PI miss this?

I slam the lid closed on the laptop and, before I'm tempted to smash it against the wall too, I curb the violent tendency and tuck it under my arm, taking it with me as I storm from the room.

A game board needs to be set. Pieces placed. Rules have to be followed.

As I drive away from the Homestead Inn, I make a call to the local police department to report Dr. Kyrie Roth as a missing person. I'm not depending on authorities to act; it's a counter-measure.

We're going to need a few of those.

If Kyrie discovered that Hayes owns her family home,

she'd want to tear out his still-beating heart. When I find them, I'm going to make damn certain she does.

So that's where I go. With no gun. No knife. No ligature. No physical weapons.

We won't need them.

We *are* the weapons.

My neck aches, the muscles and tendons stretched for too long with the weight of my tipped-forward head. Nausea churns in my stomach and I groan.

I open my eyes but press them closed the instant my drug-addled brain processes my surroundings.

"No," I whisper. Bile climbs my throat, but I manage to keep it down. "*No.*"

"*It's just a memory,*" Jack had once said. "*It's not real anymore.*"

I take a few deep breaths, letting them out in a thin stream of air between pursed lips.

He's right. It's just a memory.

I open my eyes again.

"It's real," I say.

My eyes brim with tears as they sweep across the empty living room of my childhood home.

I summon my wrists and ankles to strain against the zip ties binding me to a wooden chair near the center of the room, but it's as though they're on a delay, weakened by the chloroform. Deep breaths flood my chest as I try to clear the drug from my body. I whimper as I turn my gaze to the ceiling, away from the cream carpet that replaced the one that once absorbed blood and broken glass. It looks just the same as I remember it.

A buzzing pain thrums in my ears as my heart kicks into gear past the residual cloud of sedation.

"*Let me fucking go,*" I yell to the seemingly empty house, rattling the chair. My tongue feels too thick in my mouth, slurring the hard edges of my words. The plastic bruises my wrists as I pour all my dampened strength into twisting my arms in a futile attempt to free myself.

"I'm sorry about this, Isobel."

Hayes enters the room from the kitchen. He looks apologetic. But also resolved. Whatever plan he's put into motion, he's determined to see it through.

"You fucking tased me. And *drugged* me. You aren't nearly sorry enough."

Breaths saw in my chest as Hayes slowly closes the distance between us, a bottle of water in his hand. He makes a point of cracking the sealed lid to show he hasn't tampered with it. I loathe the thought of him holding it to my lips like a father would for a child, but I'm desperately thirsty. I down half the bottle, glaring at him the entire time.

"I know this seems excessive," Hayes says as he wipes rogue droplets from my chin. "But trust me when I say that it's for your own safety, and that of many others."

"I do not feel safe at all right now, Mr. Hayes," I seethe, pulling at my bonds until my skin burns. "You need to let me go."

His gaze passes over my face with a patronizing look of sympathy. I can almost read his thoughts through his slate blue eyes. *Poor girl, she doesn't even know which way is up.*

Hayes's thick thumb sweeps across my cheek and I flinch away. "I'm afraid I can't do that, Isobel. This is the only way to flush him out."

Blackness eats the edges of my vision and I close my eyes, trying to slow my breathing.

Focus. Stay right here.

When I open my eyes, I pin them to Hayes, the only thing here that might be able to keep me from slipping into the past. The darkness clears, but its presence hovers like the threat of a distant storm. "Flush *who* out, Mr. Hayes? The Silent Slayer? Good luck."

"Jack is not the Silent Slayer," Hayes says as he replaces the cap on the water bottle and turns away.

"No shit. I've been telling you that all along."

"Jack is the Tri-City Phantom."

There's a beat of silence, and then my incredulous laugh fills the room. "This is madness, Mr. Hayes. What the fuck is the Tri-City Phantom? *Jesus Christ.* You just kidnapped a woman to catch a ghost?"

Hayes sets the bottle down on the floor and grabs a folding chair that leans against the wall, setting it up to sit in front of me. His attention snags on something on the floor beyond my left shoulder. I turn as much as I can and follow his gaze to a wide monitor and black box on the carpet, the screen displaying the feeds from nine different cameras, including the room we're in.

When Hayes looks back to me, he rests his forearms on his knees and laces his fingers. "I realized what we got wrong when I reviewed the footage from one of the bars in downtown Ashgrove. The Scotsman. We'd been tracking a few potential suspects, all in the construction business. One was a handyman who frequented the downtown bars, and The Scotsman was his favorite."

I swallow, the haze of chloroform lifting with every pulse of adrenaline that flows through the chambers of my heart. "So, what you're saying is that you knew who you were after, and where he went, and you didn't catch him. And then he killed my family, and nearly me in the process. And, shocker, none of that has anything to do with Jack. Is that correct?"

"Isobel—"

"*Kyrie*, for Christsakes—"

"You know nothing is that simple when it comes to the FBI, Kyrie. There are procedures to follow, potential alternative suspects to rule out. The profilers knew we were looking for a drifter, the type to not even stay in the same residence for more than a few days at a time. Someone paranoid about keeping a minimal footprint. But I was sure I knew who it was. Trevor Winters," Hayes says, shaking his head as his gaze turns away across the living room, to the place where my parents' bodies once lay lifeless on the floor. He seems lost in memory, his voice thin when he says, "Winters was the primary suspect. We received intel that a man fitting his description was booked to stay at the Treasure Motel. The FBI were going to raid it. I had convinced my boss that I had an alternative plan, to set a trap in his most likely hunting ground. He'd been seen at The Scotsman where the college students liked to go for cheap drinks, and I had the staff set up a trivia night there that evening with cheap drinks to attract the local kids. But Winters didn't go to The Scotsman that night, and the team raided the hotel anyway."

When Hayes focuses on me once more, there's both remorse and conviction in his eyes. "I was positive the raid had scared him off," he says. "It seemed obvious that we'd run the Silent Slayer out of town, that he'd changed his methods to remain hidden. I kept looking for a sign of him, *anything* that would tell me where he was. But it wasn't until I came here that I understood what had eluded me all those years. The devil was in the details. Dr. Sorensen."

Hayes pulls several black and white photos from his jacket inseam. It's a grainy image of a man in line at the bar, a still shot taken from a video feed. Even with the poor resolution and the lack of color, I recognize Jack right away.

"September seventh, the same year that you were attacked," Hayes says. He shows me another. Then another. Another. Jack is present in each one. "September thirteenth. September fourteenth. October fifth."

Hayes presents me with the final photo. In this one, I see another familiar face in profile in the foreground, with Jack sitting a few tables away.

Trevor Winters. The Silent Slayer.

Don't react. He's watching. He wants confirmation that his theories are true.

Sweat mists my brow and the back of my neck. I curl and release my toes in my boots. I dig my nails into the worn wooden armrests.

These things you can touch are real. That man in the photo is dead. Jack gave you proof. His last remains are a treasure in your cabin.

The steel edge in my voice surprises even me when I say, "Get to the fucking point, Mr. Hayes."

"After you aged out of foster care and changed your name, I kept tabs on you, just to make sure you were okay. But when disappearances started mounting up in the Tri-City college region, all of them men with seemingly little or no connection, their bodies never found, and all in a wide radius around *you*, I started believing that the elusive Slayer had surfaced. When I heard about the disappearance at the university, it was too close. I started looking into everyone connected to you. Imagine my surprise when I went back through every scrap of evidence I'd collected on the Slayer and found Jack Sorensen in the videos from The Scotsman."

"What exactly is that supposed to prove? That Jack lived in the same city as I did and had a social life? I already knew that. It proves *nothing*. Besides, Jack was at West Paine University before I was."

Hayes settles back in his chair as he shuffles the photos into the inner pocket of his jacket. "I thought at first that perhaps we'd been looking at a false profile for the Slayer all along. It made sense. Jack is a brilliant man. He could have been covering his tracks by splitting his MOs in Ashgrove—one to lure us away, maybe even placing the blame on a drifter, and one for the victims he really wanted to take. But the real explanation is far simpler, isn't it. There were two serial killers."

"I don't understand," I say.

"Jack killed Winters, the Silent Slayer. Once the threat to his territory was taken care of, he moved on. Perhaps he didn't even realize you'd survived at first. But when you showed up at West Paine all those years later, it was an opportunity he couldn't walk away from. And all the while, he's been killing in the Tri-City area, keeping himself entertained until he gets whatever he wants from you."

"That is a theory for which you have *no proof*. And now you've fucking abducted me and brought me *here* of all fucking places," I say, shifting a wild glance over my surroundings before fixing my glare to Hayes. "What are you going to do with me when he doesn't show up, hmm? Kill me in my childhood home?"

"I know this is hard for you right now, but Jack won't be

able to resist the symmetry. And there are no unnecessary hurdles this time. There's no red tape. No one to doubt the evidence right in front of us. This time, my plan will not fail."

My brows feel tight and pinched as I drop my head and press my eyes closed. I know the parts of my story with Jack that Hayes has gotten right. But I also know those he's gotten wrong.

Jack doesn't want to stay. To him, I'm not a piece of symmetry he can't resist. I'm not a prize.

He said it himself: I'm an inconvenience.

Jack has cared as much as he's able to, but only because I *forced* him. And that's probably uncomfortable, even confusing for him. I've pushed Jack far beyond his boundaries. The only reason he's truly stayed is because of the threats I made the night I killed Mason. And now, by giving him the evidence I held onto for so long, I've given Jack every reason to leave. *Immediately.*

I can only hope that he's already seized his chance.

None of it changes the way I feel. I know I love Jack Sorensen. As much as it crushes my heart to admit it, I also know Jack will be better off if he takes the chance and runs.

And he's smart enough to know it too.

"Jack will not come, Mr. Hayes," I say, shaking my head. A tear slips down my cheek. "He won't. He has no reason to anymore."

"He will. You've studied predator behavior, Kyrie. You know better than anyone that humans are inherently not that different from beasts. Jack believes he's at the top of the food chain, and to a man like him, you're the prized prey in his territory. He will come to force me out of his domain and take back what he feels belongs to him, just like he did the Silent Slayer."

"*No.*"

"He's probably even told you as much, right? That you belong to him? You're his?"

I can only shake my head, my lips trembling as I press them tight.

I'm not here to claim anyone but you, lille mejer.

My chin falls to my chest. Tears drop straight down from my open eyes as I blink at my lap. My heart is burning my bones with its furious beats.

"But he's never told you he loves you, has he. Because he *can't.* Jack is a master manipulator and he wants to keep you in his grip."

"*Stop,*" I whisper. Even though I already know what he's saying is true, it still hits my chest like a fiery arrow to hear it from the outside, not just in my own mind. It's that easy for someone who barely knows me to see what I've grappled with for these last weeks. The evidence is that obvious.

Hayes's hand lays on my shoulder, a hot brand that soaks through my shirt and into my skin. I try to shrug him off, but he doesn't budge. "Let me go."

"You're the Slayer's only survivor. Do you know how precious that makes you as a prize for someone like Jack?" Hayes leans down, trying to force me to meet his eyes. His hot breath spills over my face, flooding me with the scent of coffee and stale sandwiches. I want to vomit in my lap. "But you have to understand: you are nothing more than a trophy to Jack. He is extremely dangerous, Kyrie. We have to break you away and get you somewhere safe. And we can stop Jack together before he kills anyone else."

My head lifts only far enough to pin Hayes with my furious, feral glare. "He's not. Fucking. *Coming.*"

I twist my arms until they're rubbed raw and bleeding,

the plastic cutting into my wrists as I scream with rage, hoping *someone* will hear me. I scream until that cloud of darkness descends with a thunderous clap.

"Hush now, don't scream, baby," the Slayer whispers in my ear, his cheap cologne wafting through the room, *"or I'll cut out your mama's tongue."*

I thrash in my chair, nearly toppling it over until Hayes steadies it in his grip. I'm vaguely aware of his presence, as though it's behind a curtain upon which my worst nightmares are projected.

"Shh, shh. Quiet now, baby."

I'm still writhing, still screaming, phantom pain tugging at the edges of my scars when a foreign sound slices through the images and cuts the room into abrupt silence.

Beep.

Beep.

Beep.

"He's here," Hayes says.

Something cold presses to my temple. I blink to clear the black haze, glancing up at Hayes where he stands to my left, the barrel of his Glock pistol trained on my head. The Taser is clutched in his other hand. My chest heaves with every breath as I follow the aim of the Taser toward the hallway leading to the lower-level rooms.

"Stop where you are. I have a gun aimed at her head and I will take the shot if I have to," Hayes says to the dark hallway. There's no sound, no motion. But I know Hayes must see Jack on the monitor.

Silence.

I glance up but he doesn't look at me. Hayes hasn't released the safety on his gun.

"Toss your weapons into the room," Hayes orders.

"I'm unarmed. Let Dr. Roth go," Jack replies from the dark. "She's done nothing wrong."

"Not good enough."

"What do you want, I'll give it to you."

I shake my head as my breath catches in my throat. "No—"

"Quiet," Hayes hisses, pressing the muzzle tight against my temple. He directs his voice to the hallway when he says, "A confession."

There's another moment of silence, and then Jack appears at the mouth of the corridor, his hands raised.

Jack glances between us. One look that explodes through my heart like shrapnel. The flash of a furrowed brow. The tic in his jaw as his molars press together. A tormented slash of silver in his eyes. He's desperate.

"Let her go and I'll show you."

"*No*, Jack—"

"It's all right, *elskede*," he says, turning his gaze in my direction with a resigned smile that does nothing to reassure me. When he looks at Hayes, it's with cold, polished determination in his eyes. "There's a room. It has everything you want."

"Where?"

"Let her go and I'll tell you."

A huff of a laugh puffs from Hayes's chest. "Dr. Sorensen, the trouble with your kind—"

Hayes pulls the trigger on the Taser. The leads strike Jack in the chest, and he falls to the sound of crackling electricity and my desolate cry.

"—is that you think you hold all the cards, even when you're empty-handed."

Hayes approaches Jack and kills the power for the device. He holsters his Glock to withdraw cable ties from his suit jacket. He starts with Jack's hands first, then his ankles before checking for weapons, pocketing his phone. Jack is still stunned from the shock when Hayes pulls the two leads from his chest and hauls him to a sitting position against the wall, but his eyes find mine like iron shards to a magnet.

"You were right," I say as Hayes adjusts his Taser and holsters it at his belt. "You were right about Jack all along."

Hayes glances over his shoulder at my tear-streaked face before shifting his attention to checking Jack's cable ties.

My gaze slides to Jack's when Hayes's back is turned.

I drop my attention to my lap before Hayes faces me and let my shaking shoulders fall, defeated. "How did I not see it? How could I not know?"

Tears hit my thighs. Measured, steady footsteps approach until a pair of black boots stops in my peripheral vision. A heavy hand lays on my shoulder, and then Hayes crouches into view.

"It's not your fault, Kyrie."

I shake my head, pressing my eyes closed. "I've tried to be someone new, and I'm still the same girl, trapped in the same nightmare. I'm still Isobel." When I raise my eyes to Hayes, my look is pleading. "I'm sorry. I didn't understand."

Hayes's smile is sorrowful. Pitying. He squeezes my shoulder before lifting his hand away, retrieving a knife from his belt. "It's okay. We'll get you the help that you need."

I nod and sniffle.

Hayes slips the blade beneath the cable tie on my right ankle and cuts it free.

"Daddy used to have a saying," I whisper as Hayes shuffles to my other ankle, slicing through the second plastic tie.

My legs remain still. "He said that hunting isn't a sport, because in a sport, both players should know they're in the game."

Hayes gives me a melancholy smile before shifting his attention to my left arm. The binds at my wrists are tight, the skin beneath raw and bleeding. I whimper and grip the armrests when he draws close with the blade.

"It's okay. I'll be as quick as I can."

Hayes shimmies the blade between the hard plastic and my bloodied skin, snipping the third cable tie. When it's gone, he starts to shuffle in front of me to release the final bond.

"Mr. Hayes?" I ask, my voice frail and small.

He pauses and meets my eyes with a questioning look.

And then I crack my forehead against his nose with all the force I can manage.

Blood sprays from Hayes's nostrils. He leans back with the impact of my blow, giving me enough space to raise my legs.

"You don't know you're in the game."

I kick Hayes in the chest with both feet. The blade drops from his hand.

The chair is still strapped to my right arm as I dart to my feet. I grab the back of it with my free hand and wield it as a club, crashing it down on Hayes's bloody, tear-streaked face as he instinctively grabs for his holstered gun.

Hayes is stunned just long enough for me to straddle his hips and pull the Glock free of the holster with my left hand, but the weight of a weapon is only a brief comfort in my palm.

He strikes my hand with his forearm. The momentum swings my arm outward, the gun flying from my grip to hit the wall several feet from Jack. I hit Hayes back with the section of the broken chair still attached to my hand and then I'm scrambling to my feet, running for the gun.

A searing jolt hits my back and I fall to the floor.

My nerves are on fire. Needling pain courses through my muscles. I vaguely register a sound behind me and the agony stops, but its echo hums beneath my skin like swarming insects.

I open my eyes and look across the fibers pressed to my face, the distance of the room blurry in the haze of pain. There's commotion behind me. I reach to my back and pull one cord and then the other with a weak hand, freeing the Taser's probes that are hooked into my skin.

Blackness pulses at the edges of my vision as I turn over.

"You are sloppy. An amateur. Unworthy."

A phantom fire burns in my chest. Blood lands on my tongue with the rumble of every exhalation. Crimson stains and my father's dark hair stick to the silver head of a hammer lying on the floor. My assailant struggles against the wire cutting into his throat as my angel of vengeance smiles next to his ear.

"This is my domain."

"Kyrie—"

Jack's voice is a line into the black depths of memory. The one thing I can grab onto.

"Get up, Kyrie. *Run*—"

The gritty sounds of a struggle greet me when I surface in the present.

The flame in my chest, the blood, the wire are all gone. There is no hammer, just a piece of broken, polished wood from the rungs of the chair lying next to my hand. What truly remains is Jack, his ankles and wrists still bound as he wrestles to keep his restricted grip on Hayes, the gun just beyond the agent's reaching fingers.

A choking gasp passes Jack's lips as Hayes nails him in the neck with his elbow. Jack's hold on the agent slips, and Hayes seizes his chance to grab the gun on the floor.

I take up the splintered piece of wood as I rush for Hayes. But he already has the gun.

A click.

Jack kicks out at Hayes's wrist as the agent swings the gun in an arc to aim it at his face. Time stops long enough to sear that image of Hayes into my mind. His gritted teeth. His bloodied skin. The wrath in his eyes.

A bang.

The gun wheels from Hayes's hand as I lunge for him, taking us both to the floor.

And then I sink my jagged spear into the meat of his throat.

I loom above his face, my hair falling in a curtain around us as I stare down into his wide eyes. All that fear, that pain. Confusion. *Epiphany.*

"*Shh* now, Mr. Hayes," I whisper, sinking my weight into the wood. The vibrations of his gurgling breaths travel into my palm, absorbing into every crease. "You let Trevor Winters take my family. You will not take my angel too."

Pain radiates through my body as I rise to my unsteady feet. Hayes's legs and arms slowly drag across the carpet, some last hope still clinging to nerves and muscles before it ebbs away. He stares up at me with a pleading look. It might be salvation he wants, or mercy.

I don't give it another thought as I drive all my weight into my foot, smashing it down on the end of the pike.

My spear hits bone and slips between the vertebrae. Hayes's limbs twitch as the wood splinters through his spinal cord, his eyes going dim and unseeing. He dies beneath the unrelenting pressure of my boot.

When I'm sure the last breath is gone, I lift my foot away and stand as straight as my battered body will allow. Ragged exhalations fill the silence like aftershocks of adrenaline in the quiet room. Jack is sitting on the floor, his forearms resting on his knees as breaths saw from his chest. His gaze seems trapped on Hayes as though he fears the dead man might attack once more. When he finally meets my eyes, Jack smiles, its essence so faint but so beautiful in its fleeting moment of relief.

I kick a switchblade toward him from where it's fallen from Hayes's pocket. He opens it and starts cutting away his bonds. "Congratulations, Jack, you've just won Thunderdome," I say, trying to keep my voice light and teasing as I look down at him across my shoulder, resisting the urge to clamp my hand across my abdomen.

"You're the one who killed him, I think the title is yours."

Maybe, I want to say.

But only for a moment.

I turn away, taking a few steps into the living room. My childhood home. It feels like a shell now. I don't try to imagine it as it once was when I stop in the middle of the room.

My fingertips are cold and numb. I know what it means.

Strained inhalations become pants. I try to breathe with my diaphragm to keep my shoulders from moving too much. I know Jack will see if they do. But the pain is starting to twist like fire in my flesh, demanding attention.

My hand presses to the hole in my shirt. It refuses to be hidden much longer.

I start listing to the side. The room sways. The edges warp and blur.

"Kyrie...?"

The note of concern and suspicion in that one word is a heavy weight in my heart, dragging it down like an anchor to the bottom of a lightless sea.

I swallow the ache, denying the tears that burn as they beg to be released. My gaze falls to the hand I press against my wound.

Dark blood seeps through my fingers.

"I didn't know for sure that it was real. Not until I saw you. My angel of vengeance, come to save me for a second time," I say, casting a smile over my shoulder, trying to hold onto every moment of gratitude I feel. Knowing what we had is real brings me joy. The tragedy is what it will mean for Jack.

This wasn't what I hoped for when I vowed to make Jack suffer.

"Thank you, Jack. For giving me everything you could. Time just isn't on our side," I say as I turn to face him, my palm still clutched to my stomach. I can't feel my fingers anymore. Jack's eyes dart down to my hand and meet mine once more. I see panic and sorrow. Horror and grief.

My heart splinters into shards. It pounds as though trying to cut its way free to him.

"No, Kyrie—"

"I love you, always."

Jack scrambles forward but can't reach me before I fall.

The last thing I feel isn't pain. It's not the press of the cream carpet against my face. It's not the despair in my heart or the deafening rush of pressure in my head.

It's the touch of Jack's cool hand on my cheek.

And then the world goes black, and I feel nothing at all.

TWENTY-THREE
MARROW

JACK

B lood coats my hand. The warmth of Kyrie's diminishing body heat creeps up through the slats of my fingers. I apply direct pressure to her stomach, trying to staunch the rapid flow of blood.

She's lost too much.

She's lost consciousness.

But I can still feel the faint pulse of her heart.

"Kyrie...please. Goddammit. Don't do this to me." I curl my arm around her shoulder and lift her against my chest. "Don't fucking give that worthless, piece-of-shit Hayes the final word. You can't. It's damn impossible for you *not* to have the last word, petal."

She doesn't respond. Her pulse weakens further. And a wild rage tears through my chest wall, the world searing at the edges of my vision.

I remove my hand just long enough to strip my dress shirt and use it as a suture to wrap her injury, securing it around her abdomen. Desperation leaks into my trembling limbs as I retrieve the phone from the inseam of Hayes's jacket.

With a shaky thumb, I punch in *9-1-1*. At the operator's calm inquiry, I say, "Dr. Kyrie Roth has been severely injured. She needs urgent medical assistance." I rattle off the address, then inhale an unsteady breath as I kneel beside Kyrie, sensing her drift further away. "Get them here right the fuck *now*."

I hang up on the dispatcher's useless questions that will do nothing to help me save her. The phone slips from my blood-slicked hand. I let it drop to the cream carpet with a quiet *thud*. I collect it quickly and then brace Kyrie closer, sweeping the tangled length of her dark hair away from her eyes—those perfect blue embers I'm desperate to see flare to life.

"Open your eyes," I whisper against the shell of her ear. "Come on, *lille mejer*. You deliver death, little reaper. You're a force. You crashed into my world and shook me to my fucking core...and this isn't how it ends between us."

Her blood dampens the carpet, soaking into the very fibers she loathes, and I'm drawn into a wormhole through time. Where I watched, emotionless, cold and callous, as the dying girl stained the cream carpet with her blood as death tried to claim her.

All while she silently fought to live.

"I need you to fight now, Kyrie, *elskede*."

It's my fault. I'm the one to blame. There was another predator in my midst, and I failed to see him. If I had, if I had recognized Hayes for what he was all those years ago, my ego not so fixated on stalking and eliminating the competition in my hunting ground, I could have eradicated the threat of Hayes long ago.

Or when Agent Eric Hayes showed his face in that conference room, and I noticed Kyrie's reaction to him... I should have followed him out of the building and wrapped a ligature around his thick fucking neck.

I should have protected her.

Now, that power has been stripped away, and all I'm able to do is seal my hand over her wound, begging my soulmate not to take her sunshine and leave me in the cold.

As her pulse grows fainter, a fierce growl crawls from the abyss of my black soul, and I climb to my feet with her in my arms. I take Kyrie outside and lay her on the ground.

Then I turn to face the house.

With fury blazing the numb cavities of my heart, I gather the items from my trunk and deposit them in the same room as Hayes's lifeless body.

A quick sweep of the kitchen proves Hayes kept it stocked with the essentials. Sugar, flour, cooking oil. The perfect ingredients to bake a cake—or burn down a house.

I unload the ingredients around the dead man in the center of the room, stopping when I reach the Glock, where I kneel beside him.

"I have no doubt I'll meet you in hell, Hayes," I say. "But if she dies... I'm coming for you sooner."

I only wish we could kill him twice.

After I twist a towel around my hand to block GSR residue, I pick up the Glock. I notch the muzzle under his chin and squeeze the trigger, sending a bullet up through the base of his skull and blowing out the top of his head.

I lay the gun in his open hand, toss the towel aside, then remove the shard of wood Kyrie used to stab his jugular. I stand over him and douse his body with oil, then remove the silver Zippo from my pocket.

With a final strike of the flint wheel, I light the wick, stare into the heat of the orange flame.

Then let the lighter fall to his chest.

I walk away with the heat at my back as his body catches fire.

Stepping into the cool air, I go to Kyrie and scoop her near lifeless body into my arms, my chest dangerously close to caving as I struggle to feel her pulse. I walk us to the front of her old yard, where the wail of sirens cracks the silence. The strobing flash of lights bloom in the near distance as the ambulance comes into sight.

As the paramedics throw open the doors of the emergency vehicle, one of them asks me a question. I don't respond while I place her on the gurney, my sole attention on her and the man searching for her heartbeat.

"Sir, is there anyone else in the house?" The paramedic next to me asks again.

I look him in his light eyes, mine hard as stone. "No. She's your only concern."

"Are you injured, sir?" He forces another question.

Meeting his gaze again briefly, I consider the fact that he may question whether I'm Kyrie's attacker, and I say, "I'm not sure."

That's enough for the paramedic to sequester me inside the ambulance where I'm seated at the front. Hands clenched into fists, I watch them cut away Kyrie's shirt and the one I secured around her. They place electrodes on her chest and forearms and a Mylar blanket over the lower half of her body. I stare, unblinking, as her weak vitals appear on the screen of the cardiac monitor.

The *whoop* of police sirens compete with the blare of a firetruck horn as the overcast afternoon outside the ambulance descends into a bright swirl of colors and chaos.

The ambulance door slams shut on the sight of flashing lights and a blazing inferno trapped inside Kyrie's childhood house.

I tear my hands down my face, the powerless feeling at not being able to save her strangling my control. I reach for her hand, only to have one of the paramedics halt my movement, and the only thing that prevents him from losing his life is my need for him to save hers.

As the slow but steady beep begins to emit from the monitor, some foreign emotion grips me whole—something akin to hope. My entire being clings to this sensation as the paramedics place an O2 mask over her face and run an IV line to administer isotonic fluids.

One of the medics draws near and drapes a blanket over my bare shoulders as the other continues assessing Kyrie, then attempts to check me over for injuries. I stare directly in his eyes. "Not me," I tell the guy, controlling the lethal quake in my tone. "Her. Focus on *her*."

Breath bated, I watch the paramedics work with frantic but organized effort to stabilize Kyrie while slowing the blood loss, applying hemostatic gauze and direct pressure. One paramedic pulls a unit of whole blood from a cooler next to me and places it in a portable warmer as the other man readies the line for an emergency transfusion. *They can put back what she's lost,* I try to tell myself as I watch the blood travel down the tubing and into Kyrie's body. *She can make it.*

One moment, hope is an unfurling blue poppy with the promise of her open eyes...the next it's snuffed out.

The monitor blares a grating alarm.

"She's crashing. PEA rhythm. Start CPR," the senior paramedic says.

My entire world fractures.

I'm on my feet and standing over her motionless body, staring down at her pale face as the paramedics begin chest compressions and bag-mask ventilation as Kyrie's lungs spasm with the reflex of her dying inhalations.

I stop breathing. I want to tear my lungs out to kill the ache.

Every moment of CPR burns like a year in hell. It's endless. Torturous. And it feels like the ambulance is hardly moving.

"ETA," one of the paramedics shouts to the driver over the sirens and monitors and the aggressive honking of our ambulance.

"Ten minutes," the driver replies. I hear his fist slam down on the wheel, another blare of the horn. "Congestion on the bridge. There's just been an accident ahead. We're down to one lane."

"Can we turn back? Take another route?"

"No," the driver says, his voice low. "We're trapped."

I catch the strained, dismayed glance between the paramedics as they continue CPR, checking the monitor for any signs of change. I hear the driver talking to dispatch, asking for police to help clear our path. And as I watch, helpless, fucking useless, I can feel her slipping away.

The ECG alarm changes. A steady beep sounds from the machine.

The line flattens across the screen.

The paramedics exchange another glance. One looks to the bag of blood before he shifts his gaze to the monitor. I know he must be weighing Kyrie's chances for survival.

"ETA," he barks again to the driver. We've barely moved.

"Police are on the way to open us up, but no change."

The flat line races on, the extended beep of Kyrie's absent pulse growing louder in my ears.

The rhythmic pumping of the bagged ventilation slows

and stops. The chest compressions halt as the senior para-medic blows out a breath and hangs his head—and fury churns in my viscera.

I will not lose her.

No one dares to approach me as I lean over Kyrie, lowering myself close as the paramedic pulls the mask away from her face. I place a kiss to her cold lips. "It's time to wake and come back to me, sleeping beauty," I whisper.

My breath stalls in my lungs. The ache builds until all I crave is the fire of her touch.

I fold my hands over her sternum and start chest compressions.

"Sir... You can't do that. *Sir—*"

He must see something deadly in the steely resolve of my gaze, because he physically recoils.

I stare down at her, desperate to see the vibrant blue of her beautiful eyes, her chest bowing beneath the force of my desire to bring her back to me. I hardly notice the ambulance gather momentum and weave through the opening traffic, my sole focus on Kyrie's pale face.

There's a crack beneath my palm, a rib or her sternum fracturing under pressure. Some kind of anguished sound fills the ambulance and it takes me a moment to realize it just passed from my lips.

I do not stop. I can't.

Another snap of bone carves an indelible memory into my hand.

She's so delicate. I'm breaking her. But I will do what-ever it takes.

"I will shatter you to pieces if that's what brings you back to me," I grit out past the raw ache in my throat. "So you'd better fight me, *elskede*."

The blaring beep stretches on. A fucking lifetime of agonizing torture. Until hope slowly unfurls once again.

An alarm blares from the machine.

"We've got a V-tach rhythm," the senior paramedic says, unable to subdue the surprise in his voice. He moves to the defibrillator mounted on the interior wall and preps the paddles, the other paramedic scrambling to fit the mask over Kyrie's face to start forcing air into her lungs. "She's shockable."

He moves me away with an elbow and presses the paddles to her chest. And then: "Clear."

Kyrie's body jerks with the shock. All eyes turn to the monitor.

The steady beat of her heart appears on the screen.

And mine beats for the very first fucking time.

The two paramedics take over, and in moments that feel as long as eternity, we pull into the hospital and lurch to a halt. The ambulance doors swing open and Kyrie is wheeled toward the emergency entrance as doctors and nurses rush to take over.

As I follow her into the cacophony of the emergency ward, it wasn't just Kyrie who came back to life only moments ago. Watching the steady pulse of her heart across the screen, I feel the echo of each beat in my cells.

TWENTY-FOUR
OATH
JACK

"The remains of Eric Hayes were recovered from the house," Officer Chandler says. He flips a page on his report. "At least, from what could be recovered after the fire, the medical examiner listed cause of death as suicide. I would've preferred to get your expert opinion on the cause of death—" he peeks up from his desk "—but considering the circumstance, that would be..."

"Unethical," I supply.

He offers a commiserating smile. "I was going to say uncomfortable, considering your relationship with the victim."

I nod slowly. "I appreciate that."

"Of course." He closes the report. "I'm sorry that I had to drag you down here at all, Jack."

"It's no problem," I assure the officer. "The worst is behind us."

The local police department has a close relationship with the body farm program. I've given tours, trained a number of law enforcement on recognizing signs of a crime amid decomp, sex and age identification, and many other necessary aspects for the department.

"Your cooperation to give your account of events will help put this case to bed. Oh, and this." He nods to the laptop on the desk, the one I confiscated from Hayes's motel room—and uploaded the digital contents of a USB drive. "I'm sure the feds are eager to do a deep dive."

The device has been bagged as evidence, and holds a plethora of incriminating evidence within to tie Hayes to the murders of Ryan Young and Sebastian Modeo, along with Hayes's plan to pin the murders on Dr. Brad Thompson. There's speculation around the two missing students, Mason Dumont and Colby Cameron, as two more potential victims. No bodily evidence has been discovered on them yet, however.

Once I return to Kyrie's cabin, I'll dispose of their remains properly to make sure no evidence is ever found.

There's also plenty of proof of Hayes's obsession with Dr. Kyrie Roth, highlighting his fixation on the sole survivor of the Silent Slayer.

"I don't ever want to think one of our own could be capable of something so heinous," the officer says. "Dammit, he was FBI. Unbelievable."

I nod again, schooling my features into a somber expression.

The provided evidence tells a story of an obsessed special agent who suddenly snapped when he was terminated from the agency and became unhinged enough to start emulating the very serial killer he had been obsessively hunting, one he himself dubbed the Tri-City Phantom.

My account of events is rather straightforward. Kyrie had expressed her growing concern for Agent Hayes and her safety to me days before her abduction. Which is why she was staying at my home, and why when no one within the university department could get ahold of her by phone —after Kyrie had rescheduled a work meeting due to feeling poorly—my extreme concern prompted me to check on her, where I found the laptop, leading me to believe Hayes had been at my house.

I called the police, where I was told Dr. Roth could only be reported as a missing person after twenty-four hours. I then took it upon myself to search the files in Hayes's computer that led me to his purchase of Kyrie's family home.

I arrived at the house to find Kyrie injured outside of the house, where it appeared she'd just escaped the fire before collapsing. I then made the call to 9-1-1.

The suspicious set-up in the guest room of my home was a part of Hayes's scheme to abduct Kyrie, as the police report details, after a warrant was issued to search my residence. Authorities theorize that this was an attempt to give the ex-agent adequate time before Kyrie was reported missing.

Timestamps of calls are logged. The evidence supports my account of events. As Eric Hayes is no longer alive, having first attempted to murder Dr. Roth before setting the house on fire and then turning his own firearm on himself, the only person to either corroborate or dispute the events is currently recovering in the hospital ICU.

Officer Chandler sighs. "I'm just relieved Dr. Roth is all right. How is she doing after everything?"

I clear my throat, situate my tie. "Things have been... difficult for her. She's making a full recovery health wise, but it will likely take some time for the psychological part."

"Makes complete sense. With what happened to her family, I can only imagine." He shakes his head. "To be a victim all those years ago at the hands of one killer, only to have to face another. She's one strong person to survive not one but two attacks."

I nod and rise to my feet, buttoning my suit jacket. "Dr. Roth is exceptional. I have no doubt she'll come out of this ordeal even stronger."

Officer Chandler stands and extends his hand in offer across his desk. "Thank you again for coming down, Jack."

I accept his handshake. "Just let me know if there's anything else I can do to help."

I exit the police building, making one stop to West Paine before I head to the hospital.

In the week that has passed, I've spent majority of the time working out details, so I'd be prepared for this moment right now.

I find Kyrie asleep when I enter the step-down recovery room. Knowing how she struggles with hospitals, I decide not to wake her, and instead seat myself on the chair beside her bed and wait. I remove my leather glove and reach out to clutch her hand. I rub her wrist, feeling the burn on her skin from the cable ties as I try to ignore the tubes in her arms and stomach.

After the trauma surgery to repair the damage caused by a single bullet, Kyrie was monitored closely in ICU, then moved to a step-down unit where she's been in recovery. I had a semi-altercation with the trauma surgeon who wanted to keep her on a ventilator. I demanded for it to be removed, insistent that Kyrie was strong enough to breathe on her own, and in fact needed that fight.

Lying here, letting a machine breathe for her... Not only could that lead to infection, giving her body one more obstacle to overcome, but she'd wither inside this place. Her fragile mental state would work the opposite to hinder her recovery. She's strong—she's always been strong. She needs to fight.

"No flowers?"

Her raspy voice breaks into my thoughts, and I gently squeeze her wrist. A smile ghosts across my face as I look into the pale-blue of her eyes, the color of her irises becoming more vibrant every hour as she recovers.

"I figured that'd be too cliché," I say.

Her smile is wan. "You figured right."

I glance at the PCA pump that distributes patient-controlled pain medicine. The remote to the pump rests beside her waist. With my free hand, I reach over to press the button.

"I'm okay right now," Kyrie says, stopping me. "It makes me too sleepy."

"You need the sleep," I insist. I can tell she's trying to mask her pain level, and I don't want her in pain.

"I just need to get out of here," she says, then changes the topic. "So..." She shifts her head to glance at the envelope I placed next to me on the tray. "What did you bring me?"

I hold her hand a moment longer, stroking my thumb over the abraded skin of her wrist before I release her to grab the envelope. "A reply to the letter you left me at your cabin."

She blinks, her soft gaze holding my stern one as I open the seal flap. I remove the folded leaf of paper.

"With all that's happened—" I unfold the page "—with how you took risks and put yourself in danger—"

"Jack—"

"I wasn't given a chance to respond, Kyrie. So let me talk." My tone turns as coarse as the raw ache in my throat. I lower my voice a decibel. "You went after Hayes without me, without even including me in your plan."

She expels a shaky breath, and I'm trying to feel some measure of guilt, but it's not part of my chemical makeup. She has to know what she nearly cost us—cost *me*.

"If this thing is going to work between us, then never again," I say adamantly. "There is only ever you and me. Us. Together. A duo. A real partnership."

She swallows hard. "I don't... What are you saying?"

My jaw tightens. "In reference to your letter, where you clearly snooped and uncovered documentation of my upcoming transfer to Canada..." I meet her eyes. "Yes. I had planned to leave West Paine. That was always the plan. People like me, like you, can't stay in the same place for long, and I've been here far too long, Kyrie."

She nods sagely. "I know, Jack. That's why I wrote what I did—"

"But, while I was in the process of setting up a new location, I had also been meticulously arranging a career opportunity for you at the University of Alberta's Forensic Anthropology department." I stare directly into her shimmering eyes. "Where I'd be."

I place the letter in her outstretched hand, and she grips the edge, her gaze lowering to the first line of the letter of intent, outlining a scheduled interview with the director of the University of Alberta's forensic department.

"Of course, with my nature, I was far too tempted to just tie you up and steal you. I thought about that," I admit, "many times. I even went to great lengths to start the expedited approval process for your Canadian work visa before the date, putting everything in place."

Her lips tremble as she asks, "So then, what's stopping you from taking me, Jack?"

"I've just come from a meeting with Dr. Cannon," I say. "Where I showed him this letter. He's offered you an increase in salary for you to stay on and renew your contract at West Paine."

Confusion draws her dark eyebrows together. "I really don't understand."

I take her hand, closing the gap between us as I move nearer to her. "I can't scold you, or even be angry with you—though, as soon as you're out of this hospital gurney, you'll be right back on mine to receive a punishment." A dark thrill spikes my blood at the thought. "But I can't do that to you when I'm just as guilty for thinking and acting solitarily. I've done so my whole life. So I do understand what you did, that you were trying in your own way to protect me. But all that ends now."

Fear crests amid her eyes, and I barrel forward. "In the end, I can't steal you. I can't force you to go with me. Because I can't take your choice away, Kyrie. You've already had too many things taken from you, and I can't be responsible for taking any more.

"Everything *here* is all I have of you." I squeeze her hand tighter, reciting the first line of her letter back to her. "But I can't give you away. I refuse to. You're a part of me, soldered to my very fucking bones. So I wish you would follow me. Follow me forever. I want that more than I've ever wanted anything, and I swear, I'll do everything within my power to show you the depth of how much you mean to me, Kyrie." I bring her chilly hand to my lips briefly. "But if you're happy here at West Paine, then I'll stay here with you. We'll find a way to make it work."

Tears brim her eyes, and she inhales a labored breath. The beep of the monitor increases with her rising heart rate. She uses her free hand to swipe at an escaping tear. "I've heard Alberta could use a body farm research initiative." Her smile is shaky, but the light in her eyes shines so brightly, a piece of my black heart cracks. "This might come as a surprise, but not too long ago I was trying to burn you right out of my life with the greatest amount of your suffering as possible."

"I'm shocked. Truly."

Kyrie's smile grows a little brighter, a little steadier. "But it was partly because I wanted to find my own way, my own path. So yes, I want to go with you, Jack. I want a new opportunity for me as much as I want one for you and for us."

I place a lingering kiss to her knuckles. Then I gift her a dark smile full of hunger and promise. "Alberta has no idea what's coming for it, my little reaper."

Creatures designed like us were not meant to bask in the light for long. Where we lurk, the darkness always finds us. This is the design. Yet, with Kyrie, there are exceptions to the rule. She is my exception. She is my light.

And I will forever protect her light against the darkness.

EPILOGUE

THAW

~Three Years Later~

"Where are you going?"

"To get champagne," Jack says simply as he stands and straightens his black blazer, running a hand down his tie. I look over my shoulder at the bar where a small lineup snakes toward three overworked bartenders and then to my phone, tilting it to check the time.

"Jack—"

"Don't worry, *lille mejer*." His breath warms my temple as he leans down to place a kiss on my cheek. "I'll be back in time. Champagne, Sydney?"

"Sure, thanks."

Sydney and I turn to watch Jack stride away in the direction of the bar before I take a long sip from my half-full glass in a futile attempt to drown a tiny flare of irritation.

"You two are gross," Sydney says.

"Thanks."

"Too hot. Too smart. Way too much in love. It's disgusting."

"That's the reaction we hope for."

"And I'm still single, having to put up with your blatant disregard for my relationship status on a near-daily basis. It's torture."

"I'm a fan of torture, so...go me." I scan the room as I tug on the ends of the high ponytail that skims my shoulder. "What about the guy standing by the pillars back there? Silver fox. He's hot."

Sydney follows my gaze to a man with short salt-and-pepper hair and a neatly trimmed beard. He smiles broadly at something a companion says and shifts his weight with an air of confidence and ease.

"Yeah, he's pretty hot," Sydney says, her voice falling distant as she watches him. The chime sounds for the end of the brief awards intermission and the man's eyes pan in our direction. I dart my attention away, but Sydney is not so quick and gives him a shy smile and half-wave that seems to disintegrate before dropping her gaze to the tablecloth. "Fuck, why am I so *awkward*."

"You're not awkward, you're endearing." I turn away and crane my neck, trying to spot Jack's tall frame among the throng of people returning from the bar. He's nowhere to be seen. "What's *awkward* is me publicly murdering my fucking husband for his goddamn disappearing act. What the hell is with him and these fucking things."

"Jack's not at the bar?"

I rise halfway to standing, weaving my gaze through the crowd to see if he became snagged in conversation, but I don't find him anywhere. A molten core of wrath sparks to life deep in my chest. "Evidently not."

He's not one of the few patrons waiting for their drinks at the bar. He's not taken a random seat at a table of strangers. He's not standing by the doors, watching from the shadows.

Jack is *gone*.

"What in the ever-loving fuck—"

"Thank you all for returning to your seats," the retired newscaster host says from center stage, blanketing the audience with her warm, rich voice. "The Silent Auction is now closed, and winning bids will be announced at the end of the ceremony. Thank you all for your generous donations."

A round of polite applause filters through the decorated reception hall, but I'm too busy tapping out a short message to Jack on my phone to clap. It says simply:

GET YOUR ASS BACK HERE OR I WILL STRIP YOUR BONES FROM YOUR FLESH AND FEED THEM TO CORNETTO.

I set my phone down with a thud and give Sydney a strained smile in reply to her questioning glance.

"And now, with the annual Educator of the Year Award, we recognize the contributions of one educator who makes an extraordinary effort to uplift and encourage students, creating an environment of excellence in learning."

I cast a final glance around the room and check my phone for a reply. Naturally, there's no sign of Jack. My fingers twist in my lap until they crack in protest as I school my features into something that hopefully looks decorous and not murderous.

The host smiles across the audience as photos of the campus and me with students light the screen behind her. "In addition to her teaching and research responsibilities, this year's recipient has worked tirelessly to expand the University of Alberta's Forensic Anthropology department by implementing the new Central Parkland Body Farm field research initiative, and for the last three years has chaired the Northern Lights Girls Mentorship Program to inspire the next generation of Canadian women in science. Presenting the award tonight to Dr. Kyrie Roth is her husband, Dr. Jack Sorensen."

"*What the fuck,*" I hiss, Sydney cackling next to me above the sound of applause as I stare at the tall figure striding across the polished stage with all the confidence of a wolf sauntering through a field of lambs.

"Your *face*. That was great."

"You knew about this?"

Sydney grins as I shoot a quick glance in her direction. "Of course I did. I was sworn to secrecy."

"But you're shit at keeping secrets," I whisper with a doubtful flash of a glare.

"Not when there's a bottle of Moët on the line," she replies as she clinks her glass to mine. I give her an incredulous look as she elbows me and nods to the stage.

When I look up, Jack's gunmetal eyes are fixed to mine.

"Hello, petal," Jack says, leaning toward the microphone. His sly grin annihilates my rage and I huff a laugh, the audience chuckling. "I got your text asking where I'd disappeared to, but I don't think you should feed my bones to the dog just yet. Maybe let's see how the introduction goes first, shall we?"

I laugh along with the audience, dropping my forehead into my hand while a crimson flush ignites my cheeks.

When I look up to the stage once more, Jack is waiting, his gaze fusing to mine as the rest of the room seems to melt away.

"I should say a quick word of thanks to the awards committee for allowing me to present this recognition to my wife, but truthfully, I didn't really give them much of a choice." Jack looks down at the black and gold plaque in his hands. There's a long and thoughtful pause as his faint smile fades before he returns his attention to me. "A little over three years ago, I was due to present Kyrie with the Allistair Brentwood Philanthropy Award, but I was late to the ceremony. Though it set off a chain of events that would finally bind us together, I nonetheless failed to recognize Kyrie's achievements on a night that meant so much to her. I'm grateful for the opportunity to do it properly this time."

My heart aches as though it's grown too big for my chest. I don't break my gaze from Jack as he looks across the audience.

"Those who know Kyrie well know that her many facets were cut from the sharpest edges of life. But with each one, she has not only survived. She has found her own way to thrive, on her terms. She carries her hard-earned qualities into every aspect of her work. As an educator, Kyrie models leadership, and empathy, and passion. But she is also fierce, formidable, and fearless. And having the privilege of knowing her better than anyone, I can confidently say that her most central quality, woven into everything she does, is her resilience.

"I've been fortunate to work with my wife for six years. The first three were...not my shining moments. At least not when it came to her. But, as Kyrie does, she lured me in, despite my best efforts to remain frozen. Even when she claimed to have given up on me, she didn't. She persevered. And slowly, I began to see life through her eyes. It was like looking through a keyhole. The more I watched, the more she unlocked a secret world. Sometimes, there is violence and loss. Sometimes, there is beauty and joy. Sometimes I see grief, others elation. Despite it all, as though standing in the eye of the storm as resilient and unblemished as a polished, precious stone, is Kyrie Roth. And isn't that what our best teachers do. They unveil hidden worlds, sometimes those that were right before our unseeing eyes. They ignite our curiosity. They make us question what else is waiting to be discovered, if only we let ourselves thaw."

Jack looks to me once more, and I see in his eyes what belongs only to me. What he never shows to anyone else. "I didn't know what life could be like until you shone your light into the dark. You are as indomitable as the sun. As integral to me as the lattice of marrow within my bones. And I love you, *lille mejer*."

I'm up from my seat and weaving through the tables before Jack has even asked me to come on stage, the path to him hazed by a watery film.

But I will always find my way to Jack.

The applause is like rain behind a veil. Jack's heart thumps a steady beat beneath my ear as I grip him in my embrace, and it's the only sound I care to hear.

"You're supposed to take this thing," Jack whispers against my ear, nudging the corner of the plaque into my arm as his other hand holds steady to my exposed back. I nod, but it takes him pulling away before I let go. The heel of my hand grazes my damp lashes as Jack turns my shoulders toward the audience.

"I...um... I don't think I can feed his bones to the dog," I say in a tremulous voice as the audience laughs. "That was pretty great, Jack. Made up for the Brentwood thing. I'm not really sorry about the punishment that followed but maybe that's a story for another time."

The audience laughs again and I gather momentum as I rely on the details I memorized before tonight. I thank the faculty for the nomination. I thank my friends and colleagues, my students. My parents might be in my past, but I thank them too, for giving me the tools to cut my own path.

And finally, I glance over at Jack.

"Dr. Sorensen doesn't know this, but I sat in the back of his class once. It was long before we became colleagues, back when he was a PhD student. He was teaching an osteology class." I glance down at the plaque in my hands. A wistful smile ghosts across my face as I recall the thrill of being able to sit and watch from the shadows, to just listen to his voice, this man who had given me the chance to keep going, even though I wasn't yet sure how to pick up the broken pieces. "It was a time of loss and uncertainty in my life. Watching him guide and excite this group of students with his extensive knowledge and passion for his work inspired me. He mentioned something about scavenger bite marks on bone, and that started the questions in my mind about the animals that left them and their behavior, questions that would eventually lead me here. But that one moment was a lightning strike. It ignited the hope that I too could be something more than what I had lost." When I turn to him, Jack's gaze seems trapped on the floor for a moment with a furrowed brow, but I'm waiting to catch it with a smile when he looks up. "So thank you, Jack. You showed me that the sun could still shine, even on the coldest days."

A moment of time suspends in the flash of a camera. One I'll remember forever. Jack's expression, his smile a reflection of my own. The audience, the lights that bathe us in warmth. But it's not just what I see that becomes branded into memory. It's the way I feel. Loved not just for my light but for the darkness too, not in spite of it. Grateful, not only for this moment, but for surviving the difficult ones that have gotten me here. Cherished. *Luminous.*

The moment might pass as the flash falls to shadow, but the feeling still lingers on like a flare in the night.

A few more photos are captured before Jack offers an arm. I lay my palm into the crook of his elbow, his other hand resting over mine, cool and steady on my network of bones. We descend from the stage where he slips back to the table, leaving me to mingle with donors and well-wishers as the next award is announced. And when I return to my seat next to Jack, we only exchange a brief smile before I join his conversation with our colleagues, our fingers laced beneath the table.

We stay only long enough to charm some donors and influential locals, and then we leave for home, a chalet-style log cabin overlooking the North Saskatchewan River on a remote parcel of rugged land. After a full day of work and an evening of socializing, we both slide into bed exhausted, and I fall asleep quickly with the steady drum of Jack's heart beneath my ear.

And when I wake the next morning, it's to an empty bed and the scent of coffee.

I stretch, my hand tracking over Jack's side of the mattress. The sheets are cold.

Cornetto snuffles at the foot of the bed, his tail wisping across the duvet as he rubs his face on the covers and slides up toward me.

"That's right, Corndog," I say, patting Jack's pillow where Cornetto flops to his back for a morning belly rub. "Get your fluff on Jack's side."

When Cornetto is satisfied with our morning ritual and hops off the bed to tip-tap downstairs, I roll over, shifting my weight to an elbow to grab the steaming coffee on my nightstand.

Next to it is a small box wrapped in gold paper, the creases clean and precise.

No note. No card. Just a bow in a familiar shade of blue.

I pull the box onto the bed next to me, smiling at the precise wrapping execution before I tear the paper free.

Inside is a worn zippo lighter.

I look at it closely, knowing it's not the same as the prized trophy Jack sacrificed when he set fire to my old house. The initials *S.B.* are engraved over a faded flower design. My brow furrows with the mystery as I turn the lighter over in my hand to admire it next to the scar on my thumb before I flick open the lid.

Snap. Flick, snap.

It's a comforting possession, and I smile with the weight of it in my palm as I fold my fingers around the cold steel. "Thank you, Jack."

My heart tinkles like chimes behind my bones as I get dressed and slide the lighter into the pocket of my hiking pants to head downstairs with my coffee. There's no packed lunch waiting, which is my usual clue that Jack is making it a mission for me to find him. As soon as my coffee is done, I'm heading out into the bright March sun, its rays a promise of spring as it reflects on the lingering snow.

Cornetto leads me down the path that winds toward a rocky ridge on the property, weaving a few feet in front of me with his nose to the ground. I pick up Jack's trail immediately in the melting snow and the frost-heaved gravel, the prints of his Blundstones still fresh enough to see the tread. When we near the ridge and pass the pines, Jack comes into view, standing in the small clearing near the edge of the rocky outcrop with his hands in his pockets. I smile as a fleeting memory of his photo ignites in my thoughts, the one I took of him at West Paine just before I joined the faculty. The moment passes before I think too much about setting it aflame, and I appreciate the view I have now instead. The one where my husband greets our dog before he lifts his silver eyes to mine with a smile.

"You didn't make it much of a challenge to find you today. That was probably a record. What are you up to, Dr. Sorensen?" I ask, grasping his coat as I rise on my tiptoes to place a kiss on his lips.

Jack steals a stray lock of my hair from the wind, tucking it behind my ear. "I think you're smart enough to figure out it's a surprise, Dr. Roth."

I huff a laugh and Jack takes my hand, leading the way up the remaining distance of the path. We climb the rise of the hill where the familiar terrain stretches below. Bright morning sun bathes the pristine snow in light, glittering on the tributaries of meltwater across the plain that slopes to the wide river. I can just make out the sound of the current in the distance when Jack draws us to a halt in front of a large wrapped box on a waterproof blanket, the paper and ribbon and bow all in gold.

I look toward Jack, a dark hunger flashing in his eyes before they leave mine and he nods to the box. "Go ahead," he says.

Cornetto joins by my side as I kneel on the blanket and tear the paper and ribbon free from a black case. I release the two latches and open it to reveal a beautiful compound bow, the bow riser and limbs painted in shades of blue with arrows to match. "It's stunning, Jack," I say, letting my fingertips run across the curve of the riser. "Thank you so much. What's the occasion?"

He shrugs, trying to look nonchalant, but I catch a familiar gleam in his eyes that he can't keep from me. "You told me once I should grovel. You didn't say when I should stop."

I cackle a laugh and he smiles. "Yeah...that won't be happening." My grin turns wistful as I slide my touch across the hand-painted details, the variegated streaks of blue shining in the sun.

"Take it out," Jack says. "If the size and spec aren't right, we can change it."

I toss him a brief smile and then lift the bow from the case, examining the details, getting accustomed to the weight. Jack bends next to me and studies an arrow before passing it to me and we rise, the arrow already nocked by the time I straighten to look through the bow sight toward the horizon.

"I think it will be perfect, Jack."

"Best to be sure."

My gaze falls on Jack next to me as he navigates something on his phone with a devilish smile. He glances my way before jerking his head toward the flats. A moment later, a middle-aged, powerfully-built man stumbles onto the plain from our hidden kill room built into the rockface below us, raising his hand to his eyes as he scans the terrain ahead. Panic rolls through the crisp air on a string of quiet swears as he takes a step forward, his bare feet sinking into the melting snow.

"Sean Bailey. Former owner of your new lighter. Trust me when I say he meets all your criteria, petal."

"Oh, I trust you, my love."

I raise my bow as the man starts running toward the river.

"Maybe you shouldn't trust me *too* much," Jack says, his voice as rich as melted honey as he steps behind me, careful not to obstruct my hold on the weapon. His touch glides across my hip, his cool fingertips sliding beneath my shirt to caress my skin. His breath warms the shell of my ear as he whispers, "Tell me, *lille mejer*, would your panties be soaking wet right now?"

"Only one way to find out."

I grin.

And then I let my arrow fly.

THANK you so very much for spending your time with Jack and Kyrie! We hope you fell as deeply in love with them as we did. To read a bonus spicy chapter, head to Marrow "Threads" and join our mailing lists!

Keep turning the pages for an excerpt of *Lovely Bad Things* by Trisha Wolfe and *Black Sheep* by Brynne Weaver & Alexa Harlowe.

LOVELY BAD THINGS - by Trisha Wolfe
He's the devil. And she's his wicked game.

"Hello, Halen." The gravelly rasp of my voice curls around the syllables of her name. The first tremor of excitement rolls under my skin.

"Professor Locke," she replies formally. "I'd prefer if you addressed me in kind as Dr. St. James."

"This is the first time I've lain eyes on you in months, and here you sit, making demands. Impressive. Once you stepped out of those shadows, it seems you never returned." My gaze skims her composed features, probing for the crack in her armor. I thought I found it once, but I was *un*pleasantly surprised to stand corrected. Amid twelve jurors, no less.

"Am I being recorded?" I ask, not curbing the hard edge in my tone of voice.

"No. This conversation if strictly between us—"

"I thought the last one was."

She tips her chin higher and presents her phone, proving there are no recording apps, before she slips the device back into her bag. "But I'd like it if our conversation remains formal."

"Oh, come now," I say, "we can toss out nominal letters and propriety bullshit. We're both on equal ground."

She arches a fine eyebrow. "Does it rub you raw I won't refer to you as Dr. Locke? Because, given the doctorate in philosophy is the most common in academia, I only presumed you'd find it insulting. Although, I could always tack on the post-nominal lettering if it helps your ego, Professor Locke, *PhD*."

She's been a busy little bee investigating me to learn how I tick.

Ryder—who I suppose one may consider my closest friend—relayed how she'd been interrogating professional associates and what few friends I have left after this debacle. I may have used him to feed her some interesting morsels.

What tangled webs...

I lick my lips slowly, savoring the burn of her arousing

scent as it stokes my senses. A mouthwatering combination of lily of the valley and ylang-ylang, a unique scent well-suited for her.

Poisonous. Toxic, but only if ingested. With a hint of aphrodisiac.

She could market the scent with her own brand: *Lure and kill.*

"Rubbing me raw, little Halen, has all the promise with no follow through." I spin the silver ring around my thumb.

She visibly shifts in her seat, refusing to be baited.

Scratch, scratch, scratch.

"What a waste of your doctorate," I press on, expelling a lengthy breath. "You should be working in academia yourself, fielding your own research. Instead, you're still traipsing around crime scenes, playing chase."

"Keeping tabs on me?"

I smile. "I have loads of time to kill."

Her mouth parts, as if I've said something to confirm a suspicion.

Daringly, I let my hand settle past the midway point on the table. There are no plastic dividers. No metal grates. I could reach out and touch her if I wanted—but I'm not yet ready to tear in and claw that itch.

Her gaze drops to my hand, to the faded inked celestial rose on the back of my hand and sigils that mark my fingers below my knuckles.

"I'm surprised you didn't request I be shackled." I drum my fingers on the surface of the hard plastic tabletop.

When she raises her gaze to meet mine, her resolve is firmly in place. "Should I have? Do you plan to hurt me?"

The vision attacks so suddenly and with startling fierceness—my hands collared around her slender neck; her breathy gasps for oxygen—I have to blink hard and push farther away from the table to escape her scent.

"Anger is an acid that can do more harm to the vessel," I say.

"That didn't answer my question."

"Mark Twain answered it, if you can surmise his meaning. Brilliant writer, horrible businessman."

With a clipped, sardonic laugh, she stands. "I don't know why I'm here. This was a bad idea. Apparently, you really are insane."

On impulse, I reach out and grab her wrist.

A charged pulse ignites a fire beneath my palm. The air, volatile and tense, suspends time for a mere blink, allowing my body to ravenously absorb the feel of her where I've only permitted my eyes to touch.

Our gazes collide on impact of that touch, and I see the conflict in her fearful eyes. I'm not the only one affected.

Her chest rises with uneven breaths as she twists her arm to break my hold, and despite the intense desire to keep her in my grasp, I let her.

My fingertips memorize the erratic beat of her pulse as she slips away. *Bah-dah-bump. Bah-dah-bah-dah-bump.* I want to carve it in my skin.

She crosses her arms, anxiously waiting for my rebound. I flex my hand as my gaze lingers on the visible imprint I left on her wrist. "It must have been difficult for you to come here," I say, sifting her from my thoughts to collect myself. "You should at least tell me why you came before you run away."

"I'm not running." Her strained swallow drags enticingly along the column of her throat to challenge her assertion. Then: "I need a philosophy expert."

"And how convenient you know right where to find one."

She recoils from my insult. I study her soft yet distressed features. I've never witnessed a more emotional creature. Even in her attempt to shield her grief, as she walked the grounds of the university, I could sense her pain. It tasted like the sweetest melancholy, like honeysuckle and cloves, leaving a lingering ache in the back of my throat.

And touching her is like touching the hottest part of the flame, and being unable to escape.

Buy Lovely Bad Things on Amazon.

BLACK SHEEP - **by Brynne Weaver and Alexa Harlowe**

She's not your meek little lamb.

The handle twists and the door opens, letting the moonlight slide down the hall as it frames the tall and familiar figure on the threshold.

"Duke?" Kaplan says with a worried, wary tone, closing the door behind him. He's used to the dog bounding down the corridor as soon as he gets home. He can't see us here in the shadows with his eyes not yet adjusted to the interior darkness.

He flicks on the hallway light and I smile.

"Good evening, Dr. Kaplan."

He startles. But it takes only an instant before the surprise turns into a heated longing as his gaze trails down my body. A purple lace bodysuit hugs my skin, closing high on my neck but with a wide keyhole at the top of my breasts and stomach, leaving swaths of exposed skin while covering my back. I make a show of uncrossing and recrossing my legs so he can see the two ribbons at the bottom of the bodysuit with no fabric obstructing his view of my pussy. I can almost hear Kaplan's heart pulsing in his chest, sending blood to the growing bulge in his jeans.

Kaplan slides his satchel down his arm and I watch with predatory interest as he sets the bag on the floor next to the door. Duke's tail swishes furiously across the hardwood and his muscles tense with the desire to race down the hall toward his master. "*Zustan*, Duke," I say, and the dog flattens to the floor.

"Did you teach my dog Czech?" Kaplan asks. My smile blooms. Kaplan's eyes darken, but not with anger. "Let me guess, skills I don't even know about, right?"

I lift a shoulder. "*Pust.*" The dog gets up and rushes to Kaplan's side. He gives Duke some scratches but keeps his eyes on me, as though I might either launch an attack or disappear. I think it's the latter he fears most. "You should get him better treats. The ones you buy are little more than flavored cardboard."

Kaplan swallows as he straightens. "Duly noted."

We watch one another for a long moment. To his credit, Kaplan doesn't ask why I'm here or how I got in. I think both are pretty fucking obvious. He takes off his motorcycle jacket and sets it on a small table next to the door. Then he unbuttons one sleeve of his black shirt, rolling it over the tanned skin of his tense forearm. He stops at his elbow and does the same to the other, his eyes never leaving mine.

"What game are we playing, sweetheart?"

My heart rams against its bone cage. I bite my lip and the iron tang of blood threads across my tongue. "Hide and seek."

He chuckles. "In my own home?"

"Indeed. If I stay hidden for more than five minutes, I win. If you find me before my alarm goes off, you win."

"What do I get if I do?"

"Anything you desire for the whole night. You can take what you want when you want it. If I'm asleep, you can wake me. You can tie me up a thousand ways. You can fuck me any way you want to, but on two conditions. No impact play unless I say so. And my little ensemble here stays on unless I take it off," I say, pointing my gaze down my body before locking it to Kaplan's once more.

His energy is another dimension at the end of the hall. It's like an aura that vibrates. An essence. The beast surfaces in his eyes and it can't wait to consume me. "And if you win?"

My eyes dart to where his leather bag lies in a heap on the floor. "Do you have a sentimental attachment to that ugly bag of yours?"

"Only inasmuch as I know you despise it."

A wicked smile crosses both of our lips. "If I win, I get the same prize. I can do what I want with you for the entire night. Only difference is, I get to cut the strap from that repulsive satchel and tie you with it." I stand, my motion slow and careful as my muscles brace with anticipation. "Do we have a deal, Dr. Kaplan?"

"As long as you know that when I win, I'm going to tear you apart. I will not be gentle, Bria. I will not be kind. Unless you tap out, I am going to make you suffer in every moment of your pleasure. You'll beg, Bria. I promise you."

Kaplan's eyes are that of a killer. A tiger in the shadows. A wolf in the woods. A falcon, plummeting from the sky.

I hope he can keep his promise.

Buy Black Sheep on Amazon.

ACKNOWLEDGMENTS

Trisha's Acknowledgements

Thank you to:

My co-author, Brynne Weaver, who came to me with this epic idea of rival serial killers. Of course, the temptation was just too fierce. Rival serial killers...? Oh, abso-fucking-lutely. I fell in love with Brynne's stellar, insanely talented writing in Black Sheep, and I knew right away if there was ever another writer I could work with to bring stories to life, this woman already had my creative heart in her hands.

To the readers—the dark little souls who hunger for stories to set fire to their dark little hearts. You are the reason I breathe. Thank you from the bottom of my black heart for reading my words so I can lose myself in my love of storytelling. I hope to always bring you some escapism.

And to everyone else who—to be honest, there are so many after all these years; you know who you are—thank you for always being there for me, and for enduring my crazy.

Brynne's Acknowledgements

First and foremost - a huge thank you to Trisha for wanting to embark on this crazy journey together. I couldn't believe my luck when Trisha was into this idea of coauthoring a dark romance, and then she actually wanted to *continue* writing it when she realized I'm an obsessed, demanding weirdo with a questionable sense of depraved humor and absolutely no chill. We had a motto that started early on in the course of this project: "no pain, no gain, or some dumb shit like that UGH" – and we really stuck to it (I made sure of it HAHA). Trisha, thank you for sharing your knowledge and experience and talent and time with me, it's been a JOY and I'm both honored and humbled that you'd want to take this adventure together. I had a BLAST with you.

Najla at Qamber Designs for the kick-ass cover, it's everything I could have hoped for and then some – thank you so much!

To my amazing readers and supporters, I wish you knew how much you keep my creative fire alive on the dimmest of days. Your enthusiasm and energy bring me true joy. I never thought I'd say this, but there are too many of you to mention by name for fear of leaving someone out by accident. Just know that I am so grateful for your kindness and your willingness to spend your time reading my work, that blows me away. And I love hearing from you, so don't be afraid to hit me up with your questions or comments!

And of course, last but certainly not least, my wonderful friends and incredibly patient family, who have been enthusiastic cheerleaders and supporters during every step of this crazy author journey. I could not do any of this without your love and guidance. Thank you, thank you, thank you, and I love you.

ABOUT THE AUTHORS

Trisha Wolfe

From an early age, Trisha Wolfe dreamed up fictional worlds and characters and was accused of talking to herself. Today, she lives in South Carolina with her family and writes full time, using her fictional worlds as an excuse to continue talking to herself. Get updates on future releases at TrishaWolfe.com

Connect with Trisha Wolfe on social media on these platforms:

Instagram: @trisha_wolfe

Facebook: join Trisha's private readers group, Trisha's Lil Monsters

TikTok: @triswolfe

Brynne Weaver

Brynne is a fan of velociraptors, the Alien movies (well, most of them), red wine, and wild adventures. When not busy at her day job or writing, Brynne can be found working with her husband and their son on their family farm in Nova Scotia, Canada, or enjoying her other passions which include riding horses & motorcycles, reading, and spending time with family and friends around a raclette and a bottle of wine.

Get updates for future releases at brynneweaverbooks.com

Connect with Brynne Weaver on social media on these platforms:

Instagram: @brynne_weaver

Facebook: join Brynne's private readers group, the Dark Romantics

TikTok: @brynneweaverbooks

Printed in Great Britain
by Amazon